D0271080

A Fine and

ALSO BY CHRISTOBEL KENT
FROM CLIPPER LARGE PRINT

A Time of Mourning

A Fine and Private Place

Christobel Kent

W F HOWES LTD

This large print edition published in 2010 by
W F Howes Ltd
Unit 4, Rearsby Business Park, Gaddesby Lane,
Rearsby, Leicester LE7 4YH

1 3 5 7 9 10 8 6 4 2

First published in the United Kingdom in 2010
by Atlantic Books

Copyright © Christobel Kent, 2006

The right of Christobel Kent to be identified as
the author of this work has been asserted by her
in accordance with the Copyright, Designs and
Patents Act, 1988.

All rights reserved

A CIP catalogue record for this book is available
from the British Library

ISBN 978 1 40744 578 6

Typeset by Palimpsest Book Production Limited,
Falkirk, Stirlingshire
Printed and bound in Great Britain
by MPG Books Ltd, Bodmin, Cornwall

Libraries NI	
C900155966	
W.F.HOWES	25/2/2011
	£18.95
NTSOMA	

For Ilsa

The grave's a fine and private place,
but none, I think, do there embrace.

Andrew Marvell, 'To His Coy Mistress'

They crested the hill to see the winter sun hovering on the far horizon, a wide vista of pale grey hills and leafless woodlands ahead and the dark ribbon of a river threading the valley floor below. The driver braked abruptly on the rise and a cloud of dust rose behind them, enveloping the big brute of a car. He turned towards his passenger and with a sweeping gesture bestowed upon him all that they surveyed.

'Here,' he said, in English so heavily accented that even that single syllable was barely recognizable. 'Castello Orfeo. Welcome.' And he smiled, a flat smile that didn't reach his eyes, a glint of gold far back in his mouth.

Beside him the traveller looked down an avenue of dusty black cypresses that dipped and rose straight ahead of them, bisecting the landscape and ending in dark woods from which rose the grey stone flanks of a handsome fifteenth-century castle: steep, solid and unadorned. Not strictly speaking a fortress but a keep, even in the last rosy tint of a fading winter afternoon, the Castello Orfeo, uncompromising as it had always been, made no attempt to endear itself to its newest guest.

She was waiting for them, the massive fortified doorway in which she stood emphasizing the daintiness of her figure, her girl's shoulders, her tiny ankles. The huge, luminous blue eyes gazing at him; the cloud of red-gold hair. She held out her delicate painter's hands towards him, and the flicker of a satisfied smile settled on her lips.

'Mr Fairhead,' she said for the benefit of a small, impromptu reception committee. A tall girl in an apron stood at the back; she had long, black, centre-parted hair, and her face was the perfect, pale, melancholy oval of a country Madonna. And with her were the other guests, whose company Alec Fairhead completed: two men besides him, and two women. All present and correct. 'We are so very honoured.'

Anyone looking at Alec Fairhead in the rapidly growing dusk might have been forgiven for thinking that all he wanted to do was to turn and climb back into the car and tell the driver with his gold tooth to get him out of there. But as everyone waited on the new arrival's response to the Director's greeting, darkness had fallen behind him across the wide, dusty landscape and it was too late.

CHAPTER 1

At the wheel of his dark and silent car half an hour before a February dawn, Sandro Cellini sat up a side street in a southern suburb of Florence, thinking about his wife. Luisa.

He should have been thinking about the job, but then not wanting to think about the job was part of the problem.

For three days Sandro Cellini had been paid to follow a seventeen-year-old girl to her upmarket school in the city, and then home again. Her parents thought she had got into drugs, and they wanted to know who was leading her astray. Carlotta Bellagamba was an only child – a 'precious' child, as the euphemism went; conceived through medical intervention.

So far: nothing. Friday night was often, according to her parents, the night Carlotta stayed out till the early hours, and today was indeed Friday, but Sandro had no great hopes. Not in life, nor of making any significant discovery that would help Carlotta and her parents understand one another better.

It was the modern world: parents so busy or so

nervous they paid a private detective to watch their kid, rather than tackle their own flesh and blood head-on. Children too precious to be allowed a wild moment or two, but that wasn't Sandro's decision to make; he was just the hired hand. As Sandro's part-time assistant Giuli Sarto had put it succinctly, what else was the precious child to do but go off the rails? An open and shut case.

Children. Having none of his own, Sandro was all too well aware he was not in a position to judge. What kind of a parent would he have made, anyway? Taciturn, like his own father, anguished, like his mother, worn down with work and worry? He couldn't really even begin to think about how much they would have loved a child, he and Luisa. The fine detail of it: the first day at school, seeing a child learn to ride a bicycle or play football. Rebellious teenagers, thinking they know it all, a girl like Carlotta making a face at her stupid old dad.

The girl's home was up a leafy side-turning; a handsome two-storey villa – three if you counted the garage and cellar beneath the raised ground floor. It was perhaps twenty years old, with a terrace, a verandah, five olive trees in the front garden, a fronded palm to the rear and two shiny cars in a garage. The job was not a complicated one; it was nursemaiding, pure and simple. The problem was that Sandro didn't want to be a nursemaid. For thirty years a police officer, with all the dirt and boredom that entailed, at least he'd been a man.

'It's bound to start slowly,' his ex-partner Pietro had warned, the man with whom he'd shared a squad car for fifteen years. The life of the private investigator would be like that of any other free-lance; he'd just have to adjust.

Only it hadn't started slowly, not at all. More than a year before, his first case had flung him in at the deep end with the search for a wayward English girl whose parents didn't seem even to give much of a damn that she might be dead, and a grieving wife pleading with him to make sense of the suicide of her husband. Flailing about in the worst weather the city had seen in forty years, Sandro had found himself fighting from the outset – with his old colleagues in the Polizia di Stato, with the disbelieving arrogance of the rival force, the Carabinieri, with the expectations of the bereaved and, most of all, with himself. With his own new status: private investigator. Lowest of the low, without a badge or comrades, doffing his cap to people he despised, holding his tongue when he wanted to shout the place down.

It wasn't as if there was anyone else he could blame for his dismissal from the Polizia. Some might have called it no more than an indiscretion, a mis-demeanour, even a good deed, passing information to a murder victim's father. But he'd broken the rules. Other men might have fought it, clung on to their job for the pension and a warm office in which to sit out the last five years of their working life. Not Sandro.

He had found the English girl, alive, just about. He'd nailed her abductor. He'd unpicked the terrible truth behind the architect Claudio Gentileschi walking into the river and leaving his wife to go on alone, and he'd gone to his doubters and he'd proved to them that he knew what he was doing. Proving it to himself was still a way off.

And then it had all gone quiet. The floodwaters had receded, winter set in. Christmas came and went and Sandro sat in his quiet office in San Frediano, watching the thin sunlight move from one side of the room to the next and wondering if the phone would ever ring again.

In January, after a month of twiddling his thumbs, he'd forced himself to sign up for a computer course; the rudiments. How to retrieve data, how to tell if a machine has been wiped. It had taught him how little he knew, mostly.

There had been two weeks' work in March, following an elderly baker's young Chilean wife to find out if she was having an affair or not. Not, as it turned out, though she did have a daughter she was keeping secret from him. She'd thought the baker wouldn't marry her if she had a child. Would it all end well? Sandro had no way of knowing; stepfathers, in his professional experience, were not reliably kind to their charges. But that was not his business, once the case was closed.

In April, some protection work for the owner of a small chain of garages in the suburbs, a month of accompanying the man – a crude, arrogant piece of work – around the city collecting earnings, while his regular guard was recuperating from a gunshot wound. Sandro hadn't told Luisa about the gunshot wound.

In June, after a month of twitchy idleness in the crowded city, an Italian-American Trust running a castle in the Maremma had been put on to him by some ancient contact in the British Council. The Trust – an artistic community of some kind – had asked him to do a decidedly pointless bit of background checking on an employee; practically a handout. Was this, he wanted to ask Pietro, as they sat shoulder to shoulder in the friendly, work-manlike bustle of the bar they'd used to go to as working police officers, Pietro's blue cap between them on the table, was this how it was going to be? Fag-ends and vanity work, waiting for those scraps to fall from the rich man's table?

As the engine ticked down in the dark, frosty air, the interior of the car grew cold; Sandro opened the flask he had filled with hot tea. On the top floor of the Bellagamba house a light came on behind the frosted glass of a bathroom window: someone was up.

Another light went on downstairs. Did the mother get up first? Did she pad into the warm kitchen in her dressing-gown to make her husband some coffee? And all over again Sandro was not thinking about the job but about Luisa. His wife, with whom he had not shared breakfast for more than a month. What with one thing and another.

7

When they'd said goodbye outside the bar, Pietro had taken hold of his shoulders in a quick, fierce hug: not like him at all.

He'd said, 'It's good if you find you've got time on your hands, Sandro. Luisa needs you now.'

Luisa had needed him, when she got ill. Now he wasn't so sure.

People had rallied round. If you'd asked Sandro before Luisa got her diagnosis, he'd have said they had a handful of friends, no more. But when word got around Luisa had been in hospital, men, women and children would be stopping him in the street to ask if they were OK, if they needed anything. Even the taciturn newspaper seller was searching out freebies for them from the back of his kiosk; restaurant guides, maps of Sicily, dog-eared postcards. Luisa had got tired of it quite quickly; she'd just wanted to get back to work, and anything that smelled of charity made her irritable.

After the operation in November fifteen months earlier, Luisa had taken a month off, December, for the chemo, and though they'd continued the course through January and February, by then she'd had enough of sitting at home twiddling her thumbs. She only took the Friday and Saturday off each week: Friday to have the drugs, Saturday to lie down in a darkened room while he fed her dry biscuits and camomile tea because just lifting her head off the pillow made her throw up. And Sunday to snap at Sandro all morning, although by the evening she'd have softened and become tearful; he wasn't sure which was more difficult to handle.

And Monday she'd be back at work, reliable solid Luisa on the shop floor at Frollini, in the shadow of the Palazzo Vecchio, selling 500-euro shoes to pretty, spoilt women from across the world; unfailingly polite, occasionally generous with her discount, irreducibly proud of her wares. Not so solid as she used to be; the chemo had shaved a few kilos off her, and the surgery had taken one of her breasts and left a foam-rubber prosthesis in its place. They'd talked about reconstruction at the hospital, but Luisa's face had turned blank and stubborn at the mention of more surgery, any more time spent in the hospital than was strictly necessary to save her life; the prosthesis would do fine.

There'd been a check-up in late March, an unseasonably hot day out at Careggi, the two of them waiting for an hour and a half in a Portakabin that was serving as a temporary clinic. Sandro had tried to hold his wife's hand but she'd been impatient with him; it was too hot, she'd said. When they'd finally got into the consulting room there'd been a rash close to the scar line that might have been a cause for concern, but it had turned out to be the heat; nothing to worry about. Another check-up in September had been clear; we'll leave it nine months till the next one, they'd said.

Next to that piece of news, of course – the outcome so covertly longed for he still hardly dared believe it – work didn't matter. Shouldn't matter. But Sandro hated not being able to provide; he didn't want Luisa having to worry about money.

In the quiet suburban street – quiet but for that ceaseless hum of drones on their way in to the city – the light was grey still. The sun was no more than a lemon-yellow glow behind the eastern hills, but the sky was clear, only a couple of wispy scraps of cloud to the east, tinged with pink. It was very cold.

Sandro took a slug of his cooling, sugary tea, pulled on his gloves, and rubbed his upper arms vigorously. He felt as though he was in a kind of no man's land, in this anonymous street where it was neither day nor night. The invisible man. A useful quality in a private detective, perhaps, if not in life.

'Take her away for a break,' Pietro had said.

All year, since the chemo finished, he'd been asking her: fancy a trip up to the Cinque Terre, for Easter? Maybe we could go down to Puglia again, for summer?

'Let's wait till after the next check-up,' it had been to start with, then, 'Not now.' Frollini had stayed open all August, and she wasn't going anywhere. Her boss, smooth old Frollini himself, older than Sandro but in better nick, had told Luisa she was the jewel in his crown.

'We can't afford it,' had been Luisa's weary trump card.

Because you're not earning, are you? Not really. That was what she had not said.

10

Before this job had got him out of the house by six, Sandro had lain awake every morning thinking what he'd say to her, if he was brave enough.

I don't want you seeing more of your boss than you do of me, he'd say. I want my coffee at home, at the kitchen table with you in your big white dressing-gown fussing about at the stove.

I want it to be like it used to be.

But now it was too late, wasn't it? Sandro always seemed to be one step behind; while he was still working out how to talk to his own wife, things had taken a new turn at Frollini. Luisa was going places, and he was going to be left behind.

And suddenly there was action. Up ahead the girl banged out of her front door, shouting something over her shoulder into the dark house. In a tight plaid bomber jacket, tighter jeans, sheepskin boots and fingerless gloves, she hauled a bright pink Vespa out from under the verandah's overhang, dropped the satchel into a top-box, reached down for a helmet, wheeled the vehicle at a run out into the road and was off.

Sandro's day had begun.

CHAPTER 2

It only came into view at the last minute, shielded from her by the mass of willows that grew up beside the river; Caterina Giottone only saw it in time to do a little swerve and wobble on the *motorino*, and she was safely past. The high, white flank of a truck, lifting equipment on its flatbed, the flicker of red and white tape; intent on getting to work, she didn't look back, so that was all she saw. Then she hit the patch of ice and it was just as well she hadn't been craning her neck to look behind her or she'd have been on the tarmac with a broken bone or two.

The scooter steadied when she changed down a gear. Hunched over the handlebars, Caterina – Cate to her friends – crept up the hill. It was cold; oh, Jesus God, it was cold.

It was so cold that even through her layers of fleece and wool and leather, Cate could no longer feel her toes. The defined ridges of her cheekbones, exposed to the breathtaking, knife-sharp chill, felt as though they had been flayed. As her *motorino* sputtered to the crest of the hill, Orfeo finally came into view and Cate reflected, as she

12

did on her way to her place of work most mornings, that it was nothing like home.

It was partly the geography. Cate had grown up in the wide, flat Val di Chiana, where you could see for miles and everywhere you looked there was habitation: the great grazing plains of the Chianina cattle punctuated by square, turreted farmsteads, hay-barns and, increasingly, by *capannoni*, the low grey hangars of light industry. The closest hills to Cate's home village were soft and round and topped with towns and bell-towers, their slopes clustered with restaurants and bars and crowds of teenagers.

This place was a different matter, the Etruscan Maremma; two hours to the south, yet the hills were rocky, barren, inhospitable and wild, surmounted by the occasional bleached and silent village. To a town girl like Cate it seemed so empty, dusty and brown and bare and wild in the depths of winter, the leafless trees and desiccated brambles clinging like cobwebs to their slopes. Cate had been renting a room in the closest town to the castle, a flyblown place on the edge of the plains called Pozzo Basso, and on her eight-kilometre *motorino* ride in to work, she passed only the occasional farmhouse as she wound through the silent hills.

Some of them had become ruins, overrun with wild vines, re-absorbed by the landscape. They gave Cate a chill, the half-discernible mounds beneath ivy, the scattered stones, like half-buried bodies. They made her think, how quickly a human being would disappear.

13

They called the castle quite simply Orfeo, though what remained of the Orfeo family themselves were holed up in Florence in their luxurious villa, the castle being too uncomfortable, too draughty, too expensive to heat. Most of the staff, unlike Cate, were locals, their families associated with the place for generations, and the Trust meant nothing to them; the prodigal son who had crossed the Atlantic in the thirties, made his money in steel during the war and then returned, in awe of the American way, to set up an English-speaking artists' retreat. They tolerated the Trust, run from offices in Baltimore, but fifty years didn't count for much in this landscape, pitted with Etruscan caves, where even the Romans were relative newcomers.

Ginevra the cook had once expressed surprise that Cate didn't commute from home, if she didn't want to live in; she was of a generation for which it would be entirely natural for a twenty-nine-year-old unmarried woman to live with her parents – or, in her case, mother and stepfather – even if it meant a long drive to work. But Cate, who had spent most of her teenage years arguing with the stubborn, old-fashioned man her worn-out mother had married when Cate's father left them, had not lived at home now for more than ten years. She had worked on the cruise ships off the Florida coast, restaurants on the Côte d'Azur, even a coffee bar in Bath, England, but this place – the Castello Orfeo, two hours' drive from where she'd been born – sometimes seemed the most foreign of them all.

And this morning more than most, Cate was wondering whether the fact was, she simply didn't belong here. Had this been coming a long time? Perhaps; the winter season was certainly harder going than the summer; the guests wondering what they were doing in the middle of nowhere, in the cold and the rain; this wasn't the Italy they'd signed up for. But yesterday had been a tough one; yesterday everything had seemed to turn sour. Yesterday, nothing had gone right.

On a sharp, wooded bend the convex mirror that discreetly marked the rear entrance to the castle came into view. Cate turned across the bend between the trees and revved to get the little Vespa over the stones and rubble of the rear access road. Visitors and guests were not encouraged to use this route, though it represented a considerable shortcut: there was no view, no avenue of trees, no framing of the castle's lovely, forbidding profile, and the terrain was rough. This way, one approached through a gloomy thicket of overgrown holm-oak trees, and the flank of the castle loomed up quite suddenly overhead.

There was a small clearing in the trees marked by a flagpole where the staff's assorted vehicles were parked, out of sight, and Cate dismounted and pushed her moped into the space unofficially reserved for her. Down to her right was the laundry building, and the studio apartment, where the curtains were firmly drawn; it would be a while before that one was up. In her pocket, her mobile tinkled its merry little ringtone. Vincenzo.

She tugged off her helmet and set the mobile to her ear. 'V'cenz. *Caro*.'

They hadn't been together so long; five months. He'd met her in the late-night supermarket in Pozzo where he worked, buying herself some beers on the way back to the bedsit she rented over a biker bar. Vincenzo was younger, by a year or two, and he had led a quiet life. He looked at Cate and she knew he saw a girl who had travelled the world, who had earned her independence, who drank beer on her own late at night; his eyes shone when he looked at her. He was sweet, mostly.

'Yeah,' she said, in response to his question. 'Just arrived. Fine, yeah, I'm fine.'

She'd told him her troubles last night, and he was looking out for her, that was all, even if it felt oppressive. Turning to register that the gardener's pick-up was parked in its usual place, she said, 'Mauro's back.'

Vincenzo was on the early shift and she knew he'd be at the till, between customers; he wanted to know if he could see her tonight, making his case. Really what he wanted, Cate knew, was to move in with her; she let him talk, looking around her absently. If the pick-up was evidence, then the surly Mauro, factotum, handyman and gardener, had returned – to the Director's fury, he'd spent all yesterday helping a farmer haul cattle out of a stream on the other side of the valley. But something was different;

16

she didn't yet know what it was. The phone wedged under her ear as Vincenzo talked, Cate opened the shiny box on the moped's rear and pulled out the bulging canvas satchel she took to work. Her fingers felt like frozen sausages, even inside the gloves.

'OK, darling,' she said gently, 'tonight, should be great. Can I call you though? Got to get inside, I'm freezing. *Un bacio*, OK? *Un bacio*.' Grumbling, he let her go, and Cate hurried under the trees towards the castle.

Even though it was six months since she had started at Orfeo, Cate still did not quite understand its principles. Between five and ten guests arrived every ten weeks, all – or almost all – single people, and all creative people of one kind or another. You could have described them as artists, Cate supposed, but while she always thought of artists as painters or sculptors, Orfeo's guests might be poets or writers of novels or plays, or they might make tiny indistinct objects out of feathers and clay or compose operas using the sounds of underwater creatures.

Whatever they did, they were disposed around the place, accommodated in the castle's apartments and outbuildings for those ten weeks, fed and watered; they were entertained, now and again, with expeditions here and there, to galleries or churches, or by visiting speakers. Cate had always assumed they were here to work, but some of them seemed to do nothing at all, and certainly

17

no proof of achievement was ever demanded of them. Put frankly, Cate knew nothing about art. And this lot – well. They were an alien species to her. But then again – a couple of Americans, an English novelist, a Norwegian poet – Cate reflected, as she headed round the walls for the castle kitchen, that wasn't so surprising. They *were* foreign.

There were often a couple of Italians too – although this time only one, and as he was from Venice he was exotic enough to a girl from the landlocked plains of the Val di Chiana – but even they were supposed to conduct every conversation in English, the castle's official language. The Norwegian and the young American woman, who both wanted to improve their language skills, occasionally tried to engage the staff and the Italian guests in their own language, but it was frowned upon. Cate couldn't find fault with the house language rule, because it was the reason she, an outsider, had been brought in. Her English, and her calm, quiet way with funny foreigners, learned on the cruise ships. But this rule, like so many others, was weird; it made the place like a strange kind of island state among the lonely hills. In fact, what Orfeo seemed most like to Cate sometimes, with its prohibitions and punishments, its smiling, implacable headmistress, was a boarding school, or a prison.

The kitchen and dining room were housed in the old stable block that clung to the rear of the castle, its blind side, and there was a staff entrance in the wall that enclosed the complex, then a small stretch of close-cropped lawn. The vents from the room that housed the castle's heating system were billowing steam, and the grass was crunchy with frost under her heavy boots. The door to the kitchen was ajar. Cate heard the voices and she stopped, her bag slung over her shoulder, her breath clouding in front of her, and listened.

There were too many voices, and they were raised too high. The Director didn't like racket, particularly not Italian racket. Cate had been brought in after a kitchen girl – waitress was too modern a word, it seemed, for the castle's image, everything had to have the mediaeval touch – had muttered something rude in Italian to an American woman. Not even a guest, but a guest's wife, visiting for the evening. The girl had been dismissed; apparently she'd shouted across her shoulder all the way out, her rough, defiant Tuscan accent resounding around the courtyard.

So it was unusual to hear this kind of clamour of heedlessly raised voices; even if there was a row – and there were plenty – it would without fail be conducted in a kind of hissing, spitting, under-the-breath mode. So: something had happened.

Cate liked to know what she was walking into, so she stayed still on the crisp frosted grass, thinking. From the other side of the hill, from the little huddle of farm buildings where the others lived, the dogs bayed, the sound bouncing across the slopes. That first sight of Orfeo from the crest of the hill had been different somehow this morning. In her mind's eye Cate checked off the detail of what she'd registered: trees, the dark, crenellated silhouette, the windows too mean and narrow for the facade, and the great gate into the courtyard standing open. Was that the cause of the commotion?

Still out of view of the kitchen door, Cate backed away, retracing her steps quietly to the small gate that would lead her back outside the walls. They were kind enough to her in there, but she was an outsider still. She needed to be prepared. She looked at her watch; it was barely eight o'clock and she was still early for work. Standing there another minute, she looked back where she'd come from, took in the trees, her *motorino*, Mauro's pick-up and Ginevra's Punto, the granary, the flagpole. The flag had been lowered; she'd never seen it like that before: that was one thing, certainly, even if she couldn't see the significance of it. And she registered that the castle's big 4x4 was nowhere to be seen. The Monster, they called it, *Il Mostro*.

Well, thought Cate, puzzled, *nothing much then*. An open gate; *Il Mostro* out on some jaunt. Had the *Dottoressa* been going somewhere last night, after dinner, in the car she seemed to treat as her personal property? Or this morning, even? But it was too early for her to be up and about, and anyway Cate glimpsed something now, in the gap

20

in the trees a hundred metres away where the main drive led to the great gate.

A low blue shape. A police car.

And she ran across the frosty grass to the door, bursting into the kitchen as though she'd just arrived, and they all fell silent.

CHAPTER 3

As Sandro drove along the Via Senese in the grey dawn light, keeping the pink Vespa in his sights, he was on autopilot. After three days he could have done it blindfold: Sandro had always had a knack for navigation. If not for negotiation.

Last night he and Luisa had talked about the job, which had surprised Sandro. Delighted him, to start with.

She had already been home when he walked in, at 7.30.

He'd followed the girl to school, where she had remained all day; he'd followed her home again. He'd followed her to a bar in Galluzzo where she'd had hot chocolate with three girlfriends, then she'd gone back to the house.

Luisa had been cooking *polpettone*, and the mingling smells of veal and pork and herbs and wine issuing from the oven had lifted his spirits higher than they'd been for weeks. He had put his arms around her gratefully at the stove, and she'd turned and pecked him quickly on the cheek before returning to her pans.

Sandro had sat at the table, and poured himself a glass of the Morellino di Scansano he'd picked up from the wine shop in Via dei Serragli on the way home, as a celebratory gesture; a job was a job. The owner, a tall, husky blonde he occasionally wondered about – her voice too deep, her Adam's apple too prominent – had recommended it; she, or he, had excellent taste.

Luisa had opened the window to pull the shutters to, and he'd seen her shiver in the icy air. Something about the chemo had returned her to the menopause, and she was still prone to tearing off cardigans in a sweat.

'You'll catch your death,' he'd said, in exasperation.

'I'm all right,' she'd said impatiently, then seemed to relent. She'd pulled on a sweater that was draped across the back of a chair; Sandro didn't remember having seen it before. Cinnamon-coloured, fine merino. Expensive looking. If Luisa had felt his eyes on her, she hadn't acknowledged it.

'Nice sweater,' he'd said mildly.

'Isn't it?' she'd said, offhand. 'Old stock, hardly cost anything.'

He should have been glad she was taking pride in her appearance. 'You look beautiful,' Sandro had said awkwardly. 'My beautiful wife. Come and have a glass with me.'

'In a minute,' she'd said, her back to him again and stirring something in a pan.

'What are you making now?' he'd asked.

'Just some ragu. For the freezer. Thought I might as well, while I was at it. Bought twice the quantities at the market.'

Something about this cooking marathon had begun to unsettle Sandro. But before he'd been able to formulate his unease Luisa had pulled off the apron and was in the chair beside him. Her skin bright against the fine brown wool of the new sweater, she'd raised the glass Sandro had poured her.

They'd talked about Carlotta, and Sandro had felt the wine and the warmth of Luisa's attention mellow him. Lull him.

'Sounds like a normal teenager to me,' Luisa had said.

'We never took drugs,' Sandro had replied. He'd been twenty or so when he met Luisa; close enough to Carlotta's age.

'Things were different then,' Luisa had said, the ghost of a smile on her lips. 'We had no money.'

She'd taken a tiny sip of her wine; Sandro knew she'd read somewhere that more than a glass a day increased your chances of breast cancer. She'd never been a drinker, never; he'd wanted to say, there's no reason to it, *cara*. Don't look for a reason.

'There's that,' he'd said. 'True, we had no money.' *Not that we've got much more now.* 'But there were no drugs, either, not like there are these days.'

Luisa had given him a sharp look. 'Not so many,' she'd said. 'But they were around.'

'How would you know?' Sandro had been taken

aback. His wife shrugged, and it came to him that her shoulders were as slender now as they had been when they'd first been courting. She raised an eyebrow, gave him a sly smile.

'When I first started work – there were girls who took – certain pills. Drugs that kept them slim. The American students brought plenty over, amphetamines, I suppose. They called them speed. Don't you remember the jazz club behind the station?' Her eyes dancing, with mischief, or nostalgia.

And Sandro had remembered it, though he hadn't thought about the place in thirty years; not that he'd ever been inside it when it was open. It had been closed down in the late sixties, boarded up and derelict until it reopened as a discount shoe store a couple of decades later. The *Gatto Nero*.

'Did you ever go there?' he'd asked her curiously. 'To the *Gatto?*' Thirty years, and still there were things he didn't know about Luisa.

'Once or twice. The photographer took me there.'

The photographer had predated Sandro; he'd been twenty years older than Luisa and a friend, not a boyfriend. Sandro had been bitterly jealous of the man all the same; it had only occurred to him when he was in his fifties himself that the photographer, now long dead, had almost certainly been gay. Luisa had adored the man; that was all Sandro knew.

It was an age since they'd talked like this. Their marital speciality had been peace and quiet. And not since long before the cancer had they gone over old, old, times. Sandro had known he should go with the flow, enjoy it, but he could not, quite. What did it mean?

'An only child,' Luisa had said, shaking her head. 'They're all only children these days. A recipe for disaster.'

'Don't know about that,' Sandro had said ruminatively. He hadn't told her how the child had been conceived; the precious child. Would they have had a child of their own, he and Luisa, if they'd ever overcome their shame and consulted the experts? They'd never know.

'I suppose they're only doing the right thing, nip it in the bud if she is into drugs,' he'd continued. He'd thought of the girl giggling with her friends over hot chocolate. 'Though so far she hasn't put a foot wrong. End of the week generally, though, that's when she goes out, Thursday, Friday: last night she stayed in.' He had shot Luisa a glance. 'So I guess I'll be late back tomorrow.'

Luisa had nodded, looked suddenly anxious.

'She's a nice kid,' Sandro had said, touched. 'She'll be all right.'

'Good,' Luisa had said, giving him a little pat, getting back to her feet. On the table her glass had been barely touched.

'So what's this all about?' Sandro had inquired as he bent to check on the progress of the *polpettone*.

'What?' Luisa had said over her shoulder.

'This cooking frenzy,' he'd said, smiling. 'Not that I'm complaining.'

He hadn't really thought there would be a reason. But there was.

'Lay the table,' she'd said, 'and I'll tell you.'

He'd known he wouldn't like it.

Just outside the city walls the pink Vespa went across a big junction on amber, and Sandro jumped the red after her, because suddenly he just didn't care. A delivery van blared his horn, cutting behind him, and Sandro didn't even look round.

The sun was just up, topping the hills of the Casentino to the east, shining down the silver length of the Arno as he wound under the huge umbrella pines that lined the Viale Michelangelo. They were almost there; ahead of him Carlotta Bellagamba slowed, the little Vespa swaying, as if she too was taking in the view. As if she too was brought up short by it, their staggering city. The low, flat sun gleamed off the golden ball that topped the vast red dome of Santa Maria del Fiore, and beyond it to the south-west the distant Appennines were dusted with snow.

The pink Vespa darted to the left at the last minute; an old man in a hat and overcoat hopped angrily out of the way. Sandro took the turn in leisurely pursuit.

The school – the Liceo Classico Marzocco – was the best, naturally enough. The high plastered walls that lined the street – no more than a country lane, it might seem to the outsider, with overhanging wisteria and magnolia – concealed some of the most exclusive properties in the city. Ahead of Sandro his target was slotting her Vespa into a long row of mopeds in front of a pristine façade, as she'd done every day he'd been watching her.

Sandro drove on at a sedate pace, and once out of sight he pulled up in someone's drive and hopped out.

The pavement outside the school was crowded now with students smoking and chatting, stamping their feet in the cold and laughing before going inside. They were leaving it to the last moment; it was gone eight now. Sandro walked slowly so as to give himself time to pick Carlotta out. He had to step off the pavement, it was so crowded, and then a shiny, powerful new Audi forced him back into the crowd, coming to a halt right in front of the school gates. A handsome, moustachioed older man in an impeccable suit – a bit of a Frollini, thought Sandro, 1,000-euro suit, nice tan, and disliked him on sight – climbed out and began to lecture the lanky, long-haired boy who climbed sulkily out of the passenger seat. Son, or grandson? Son, Sandro decided; this man was clearly wealthy enough, and smooth enough, to have picked up a woman of childbearing years later in life. He seemed entirely indifferent to any obstruction his wide, low car might represent. Eventually the boy sloped off and, after standing an arrogant, leisurely minute to watch him go, the man climbed back in to the Audi and left.

Impatiently Sandro waited for the big car to move off, half an eye on the tall boy, moving through the crowd. To his mild surprise it was at Carlotta that the lanky boy stopped, Carlotta, in her violet knitted hat, and stooped to greet her. He was casual, but Carlotta's body language told Sandro that if the kid wasn't her boyfriend, she wished he was. This was the first time Sandro had seen him, which would imply that he didn't observe the school timetable very scrupulously. His long hair was smooth and shiny, and he was carrying an ex-army backpack. Carlotta put her hand through his arm; he didn't object. They went inside.

Sandro waited, leaning against the wall of the school as he had done every day, in case she came back out. There were young people practised in the techniques of truancy; they knew enough not to just go missing, they knew how to sign themselves in then slip away. But there was also this: the street was so lovely in the sharp blue light, so suddenly peaceful now that the students had disappeared inside, that he felt he might stand there all day. So as not to have to think.

The school stood opposite a low stone wall behind which the ground fell away and down into a little valley filled with olive trees and an immaculate villa before rising again to meet his beautiful city's imposing mediaeval wall, slanting across the hill. It was possibly the most perfect view Sandro had ever seen: the silver-green of the trees, the golden stucco of the villa, the rough grey stone of the city's fortifications and the distant, stately outline of the great cathedral beyond them.

Woodsmoke was drifting up from somewhere on the slopes below, the light was rosy with the early hour, the sky was an almost impossibly clean, clear blue.

Luisa.

It turned out that standing here was not the way to avoid thinking, after all. Sandro stamped his feet in inarticulate frustration, and the sound grated on the quiet air. He should be hand-in-hand with Luisa walking through these narrow lanes and gazing on the city; they should be enjoying their retirement.

Smoothing things over had never been Sandro's strong point in the marriage – he preferred to sit out a disagreement in silence – but he had tried last night; in fact, he thought he'd succeeded. Luisa had genuinely thought he was delighted for her; it wasn't like her to deceive herself but perhaps, on this occasion, she had just heard what she had wanted to hear.

'Darling,' she'd said, tapping the wooden spoon on the side of the pan, replacing the lid, untying the apron, 'there's something I need to tell you.'

Six months earlier the words would have raised the hairs on the back of his neck. But that terror had eased; now Sandro had the luxury of a lower-grade anxiety, the nagging, guilty, self-pitying kind that said, what about me?

'Well, not so much tell you,' she'd reconsidered, 'as ask you.' Her eyes had danced. And she'd held his gaze. How was it, he'd found himself wondering, that after all the poison they put in her system, her skin still had that soft, luminous look? They'd said something about not going in the sun, about some effect or other the chemo could have, but it couldn't be just chemical: she'd looked glorious, transcendent in the steam from her pans.

'Go on,' Sandro had found himself smiling into her eyes. How bad could it be? He was worrying over nothing; she had good news of some kind, that much was clear.

'They're promoting me,' she'd said, a smile twitching at her lips. She'd tucked a stray hair behind her ear and Sandro had seen that she was wearing a little make-up. 'Well, sort of, anyway.'

'Uh-huh,' Sandro had managed to say. '*Cara*, that's great.' Then he'd considered. 'But you're the manageress. How can they promote you when you're already in charge?' He was still smiling but he could hear himself sounding querulous, questioning her news. Grudging her the triumph.

'Ah, well, Frollini –' and she'd flushed, barely perceptibly, 'he wants me to play more of an active role. In buying, you know.'

Frollini. And there he was again, between them, with his tan, his fine moustache, a beautiful villa not far from where Sandro stood, and a shiny sports car. He'd always been very good to Luisa; whenever he met Sandro, perhaps a couple of times a year, he would seize Sandro's hand between his and shake it vigorously. 'You're a lucky man, Cellini,' he'd say, before clapping him too hard on the shoulder.

31

On the frosty hillside Sandro made an involuntary, throat-clearing sound of exasperation at the thought of Frollini, at the memory of his own deceitful responses to Luisa last night, and at the pay-off. Served him right.

'Well,' he'd said earnestly, 'that's fantastic.' He didn't know what idea he'd had of what buying meant; Luisa looking through slides, or brochures, perhaps, or surfing to websites? Going to the Florentine shows, Pitti Uomo and the like, and picking out whatever took her fancy for the new season; harmless enough.

Well, up to a point, it had turned out.

'When do you start?' he'd said.

'Well, that's the thing,' Luisa had replied. 'He wants me to start going with him to the shows. Frollini does.'

Sandro had felt his smile turn rigid at the thought of the handsome old man in his cashmere suits, holding his car door open for Luisa to climb in. He had a wife, up in the villa; they'd been married forever, their children grown up and working abroad. There'd always been rumours about Frollini and his mistresses, but he was discreet all right. And it came to Sandro that Luisa had always defended her boss against any such charges. 'He's not like that,' she'd always say. 'He's not sleazy like that. No.'

But then you'd expect her to say that; loyalty was Luisa's middle name.

'Right,' he'd said, nodding vigorously to cover

32

up the fixity of his expression. 'Shows. So, when? And where?' He'd shrugged, with pretend nonchalance. 'Milan?'

Next to him on the narrow sunlit street someone emerged through the arched side door to the school: the janitor. Sandro had already introduced himself. He'd had to; middle-aged man hanging around outside a school. Grudgingly the man had given him the benefit of the doubt; turned out he was an ex-cop himself.

Sandro nodded; the man nodded back.

Last night, Luisa hadn't been able to look him in the eye. 'Actually,' she had said, and the flush deepened, 'New York. The next shows are in New York.'

Sandro had nodded, dazed, not even asking the next question because the whole edifice he had constructed – the world in which Luisa would return to her old self and they would spend the weekends and evenings together on sedate meals out, picnics and drives in the country – was crashing down around him with such calamitous inevitability that he knew there would be no need to help it on its way. She was going to tell him.

'Next week,' she'd said, looking up from her hands. 'Flying out Monday morning early. Back Wednesday.' Her expression had been half defiant, half guilty. 'Late, Wednesday.'

He'd been dumbfounded. She was leaving in two days? So it was already arranged. So there was nothing he could do, anyway; feeling anger stir and

33

knot inside him, childishly – ask me? She's not *asking* me – Sandro had made a supreme effort.

'How exciting,' he'd said numbly. *'Mamma mia.'*

She'd leaned across and put her arms around him then, having heard his assent; Sandro could feel her softness against him, could smell her sweet familiar scent mingled with the richer smells of cooking and wanted to rage like a thwarted child. He'd said no more; he'd eaten the *polpettone*, which had smelt so delicious and tasted like nothing but sawdust in his mouth; he'd washed it down with too much Morellino and become too falsely jovial. He hadn't slept well.

But this was where they were.

The sun was higher in the sky and the wall was warming despite the fine dusting of frost still visible in the valley below; beside Sandro the janitor was taking advantage of it, standing in satisfied contemplation. His bunch of keys dangling from the gate's lock, he held a lighter in cupped hands around a cigarette, leaned back and let out the blue smoke with deep fulfilment.

It was 8.30 and Carlotta was inside, at school, where she should be.

The janitor turned to Sandro. 'So,' he said, 'how's it going?' He nodded at the open gate, and the keys dangling. 'The surveillance operation?'

The whole scene was so absurdly peaceful, the sharp blue winter light, the dazzle of white stucco, the picturesque, winding lane and the city spread

34

out below them, that the question for a split second made no sense; for that second Sandro had even forgotten why he was there. Then the faint sardonic edge to the question hit him.

'I saw her with a boy this morning,' he said roughly. He wouldn't have this man patronize him.

The janitor took a small circular tin out of his pocket, opened the lid and stubbed out his cigarette in it before shutting it up again with the butt inside. 'Otherwise I only have to clean it up myself,' he explained. 'Tall, skinny boy? Long hair?'

'That's the one,' said Sandro. 'Is he bad news?'

'Alberto? Depends how you look at it.' Tight-lipped. 'I wouldn't want my daughter going out with him.' Then he seemed to take pity on Sandro. 'Though *her* parents might not object to him.' His tone was sarcastic; Sandro looked at him blankly.

'Very rich,' said the janitor patiently. 'One of the old families, but they've consolidated; they own half the warehousing in Prato. They've got a castle somewhere in the country, keep a yacht in Porto Ercole, mother spends half the year in India somewhere. Goa? She's there now.'

He looked at Sandro expectantly, waiting for him to ask more. Sandro was damned if he would; he wasn't interested. Leave it to airheads to buy the celebrity magazines. Goa, though: mostly what he knew about Goa was that there were plenty of drugs there. Or was she one of those religious nuts, yoga and Zen stuff? Either way, this wasn't the kind of family he liked. As if responding to

35

his expression the janitor laughed sourly. 'Open house when the old man's away visiting one of his girlfriends, that's what I hear. And she's – she's a good kid, don't get me wrong – but she's not in his league.'

'Ah,' said Sandro. 'I wonder if she's told them about it. The parents.'

The janitor shrugged, already turning away. 'Maybe there's nothing to tell them, anyway,' he said. 'He's just stringing her along.'

Hands in his pockets, Sandro nodded. He was cold.

'Come back at one,' said the janitor. 'School's out at one today. Get yourself a coffee, you look frozen.' And he was gone.

Just inside the Porta San Miniato, a little bar was spilling its customers out into the cold air where they were smoking with gloved hands; inside it was warm and bright and bustling with local oddballs and artistic types, and a fat, theatrical, bearded barman served him an excellent coffee and a pastry. Sandro settled himself down, and dialled Giuli.

At one he headed back up the hill to the Liceo Classico Marzocco. Carlotta Bellagamba was gone. He had lost her.

CHAPTER 4

They called a meeting at eleven in the dining room, for all the staff. Luca Gallo, obviously, was in charge; he ran the place, after all, not her, even if she was called the Director. Dottoressa Loni might host the dinners and greet the guests and talk painting or books with them, but Gallo, who ate at his desk most nights, did everything else. Everything; his crowded office, above the kitchen, was like a general's bunker; he even had a map of the world on his wall, with pins in it. Each pin represented a guest, past or present; Venezuela, Finland, Mexico, Germany, America, wherever.

Sitting quiet at the furthest end of the row of kitchen staff as Gallo talked to them in his soft, patient voice, Cate Giottone was still stunned.

For a moment or two after she had walked into the kitchen and slung her bag on the table and everyone suddenly stopped talking, Cate knew, they were really thinking whether they should tell her anything at all. Ginevra – the cook, sixty-five, rough-voiced, tight-lipped and rarely, grudgingly, kind – had exchanged a glance with the next most senior member of staff, Mauro, his face like thunder.

'Well?' Cate had demanded. 'I just saw a police car.'

And then, of course, they had all started talking at once, Ginevra and Mauro, the other kitchen girl, Ginevra's niece Nicoletta – Nicki – each with their own version of what had happened, although, it turned out, none of them had actually talked to a policeman. What was certain was that it concerned Dottoressa Meadows, and the missing car. Ginevra had put a stop to it eventually; there was coffee to lay out in the library for the guests, and lunches to be prepared. They had to keep going as normal; they'd find out at eleven.

As she had filled the labelled wicker lunchboxes each guest was issued with on arrival, Cate had tried not to think about it; wait until you know, she'd told herself. But in the pit of her stomach she'd felt a kind of dread she didn't quite understand. In each linen-lined basket she'd laid the small packages in their waxed paper – *frittata*, grilled peppers, a slab of bread and a couple of tomatoes – and then buckled the lid. Mauro or Nicki would deliver the lunchboxes to the castle's apartments by one o'clock.

The American women were in the outbuildings; the artist, Tina, because she needed the studio housed in the *villino*, Michelle the poet in the bungalow behind the laundry, with huge windows looking into the woods behind the castle.

The others were in the keep itself; Tiziano the Venetian in the ground-floor suite on the corner, the Englishman on the top floor, with the Norwegian next door; they usually put guests of the same sex up there. Just in case, she supposed, though they all seemed to her to have their minds on anything but enjoyment; if Cate had learned anything since she got there about the artistic process, it was that it wasn't much fun. The *Dottoressa* on the *piano nobile* below them, a corner of it turned into an apartment for the intern, but the *Dottoressa* had the lion's share, great long windows looking down the cypress drive.

'You do the coffee,' Ginevra had said, preoccupied.

She had come to rely on Cate for anything even slightly complicated. It had to be done in three relays; silver trays with insulated flasks of coffee – American style – hot and cold milk, cups, saucers, silver spoons, three kinds of sugar, biscuits and pastries. There were thirteen steps up to the old library: Ginevra couldn't manage steps and was terrified of the small ancient, creaky lift; Nicki might be family but her English was non-existent so she had to be largely kept to kitchen tasks and besides, she was clumsy. So Cate did it, just as she served every night at dinner, seven days a week, before heading home in the dark on her *motorino*.

Last night she'd thought she might get home early, hadn't she? Last night the guests had dispersed from the dining room nice and promptly, for once; sometimes they sat for hours guzzling the liqueurs while in the kitchen Ginevra and Cate snapped at each other, getting wearier and wearier. Waiting for them to leave. Last night the dining room had been empty by ten, and if it had been the three of them, it would have taken no more than half an hour to clear up. Only Ginevra had said Mauro wasn't well, she had to get back, and when Ginevra went, so did Nicki, because Ginevra was too much of a nervous nelly to walk home in the dark alone.

So Cate had to finish up on her own, and it had taken her an hour. She'd thought about that little settlement over the hill as she rinsed and stacked, Ginevra and Mauro in the run-down tied farm; Nicki in the two-room cottage adjoining it, with her widowed mother. No wonder Nicki looked unhappy most of the time.

The money was good. But Cate really earned it.

The library was Cate's least favourite room of the castle, although the truth was there weren't many rooms she did like. Her mother had been in awe, looking at the brochures she'd come home with after her interview, and Vincenzo very impressed at the thought that she'd be swishing around the place from ballroom to *salotto* like some kind of princess. But it quickly seemed to Cate that mediaeval life must have been a pretty uncomfortable business, even for the inhabitants of castles. In the winter the castle's tall and beautiful windows rattled in their frames, letting in a gale; its passages were damp and its ancient radiators silted up; Orfeo was freezing and dark at the best of times and the library was its cold and gloomy centre.

The room was immensely high-ceilinged, accommodating a gallery about six metres up lined with books, and a huge fireplace, almost never lit, with a great chimney flue that seemed to suck any tract of warmth from the building. From the coffered beams hung the only light source apart from the four long windows, a vast wooden chandelier with half its bulbs blown. Mauro should have replaced them, but the list of things Mauro had to do was long.

The Englishman had already been there as she'd entered by the wide double doors that led to the landing. He was walking up and down in front of the windows, through which a thin winter light fell; the room faced north-west and the sun barely arrived here at this time of year. Alec Fairhead was always the first, always pacing out the space in which he found himself, made twitchy by the confinement. And shy, she thought, or was it just being English? His eyes would slide over her and away when they talked; she'd noticed the other women had the same effect on him.

In an attempt to improve her English, Cate had borrowed a first edition of his novel from the library – if the guests were writers, their work was always added to the bookshelves. She'd been under the impression it was a kind of love story. But if it was, it wasn't the kind she recognized, and she'd pretty much given up on it. She didn't like dark books, books about betrayal and death; Cate sometimes thought people's lives were too easy, if

41

they wanted to make themselves unhappy reading about other's people's misery.

'Ha,' he'd said abruptly, 'Caterina. You are an angel.'

Despite the circumstances, she'd smiled; he was awkward, stiff, wary, but she couldn't help liking the man. Like her, he seemed an outsider, but he was always polite, always thanked her for any service. He never complained, not even of the dark and cold, unlike the others, but then Cate imagined that the English were probably more used to it.

Fairhead had poured himself a cup of the weak, black coffee. It had been explained to Caterina by a wearily disbelieving Ginevra that *caffè americano* had been settled on as it suited the widest range of tastes; outside Italy it seemed that a good *espresso* set the unaccustomed heart racing dangerously, and there was the possibility of lawsuits. Cate, used to the bizarre eating habits of foreigners, had merely smiled sadly. Fairhead had set his hands around the wide white cup to warm them; from outside the double doors had come the sound of the lift as it clanked into motion.

'Cate,' Fairhead had said, 'have you any idea what's going on? The police?'

Her eyes accustomed to the dim light now, Cate had seen that he looked pale. He was, she had guessed, in his fifties; about the same age as Dottoressa Meadows. Not old; but old enough. Someone had told her he hadn't written another novel since the one he'd read from at his presentation, the same book she'd tried to read before putting it back on the shelves, defeated. Fairhead himself had told her, during one of their over-polite bouts of small talk, that he did bits and pieces. *Just hack work*, was what he said reluctantly; helpfully Luca Gallo had told her that meant journalism. Travel stuff that kept him on the move, apparently.

The guests mostly seemed to be like that, migratory. Cate had listened in as she served dinner one night, early on in the current group's stay, about where they would be going next. Visiting fellowship in Beijing, concert tour in California, creative writing course in Spain. It came as a revelation to Cate that people could exist in this permanent state of transit; it made her feel less of an oddity in fact. But even she assumed – hoped, if the truth be told – that one day the travelling would stop. Some day, surely, they would all arrive.

She'd heard the lift doors open; Tiziano. And slowly she'd shaken her head. 'I'm not sure. Signore Gallo has called us to a meeting, eleven o'clock. The *Dottoressa* – the Director – she is – she isn't here.'

'Not here,' Fairhead had said wonderingly. As though it might be something miraculous: and it did seem to Cate that Loni Meadows was everywhere in this castle, as a rule, even when she was away from it.

The wheelchair had glided through the doors, and Cate had felt her heart lift. Tiziano – from

Venice, like his namesake, although not a painter but a pianist – was the only one who ever used the lift, which was commonly considered, not only by Ginevra, to be an antiquated deathtrap. By contrast Tiziano's wheelchair was state of the art, like nothing she'd ever seen before he arrived in the castle some six weeks earlier. It was streamlined and bright, with tilted wheels, gleaming chrome and black rubber, and he could move like lightning in it when he wanted to.

Cate had fallen in love with Tiziano the moment he first beamed that wide, white smile up at her from his broad, stubbled face. Not much hair, a good fifteen years older than Cate, but there was something about him. Broad-shouldered, he was always in T-shirts, never a sweater; he kept himself warm, he said, manoeuvring the wheelchair. Tiziano was always in motion, and for twenty years he had been paralysed from the waist down. An accident, in which his father had died. So fiercely private, so capable, she didn't want him to think she even considered his disability: she hadn't asked him about the accident. They had offered him a live-in helper at the castle, but he had refused.

Tiziano played the piano like a tumultuous force of nature; most evenings, Cate would come and stand at the foot of the stairs and listen when she heard him begin, until Ginevra called her back.

'*Buongiorno, bellissima,*' Tiziano had said, winking up at her. Cate couldn't stop herself smiling.

He'd known very well he should be speaking in

English, but Tiziano was as adept at disobeying rules as he was at circumventing obstacles to his wheelchair. He'd seemed exactly as cheerful as always; Cate'd supposed he had heard nothing of the police visit.

The two Americans – the women – weren't here yet. They both lived in the outbuildings of the castle, and were often late, and they were as unlike as chalk and cheese, though it didn't stop them sticking together. Tina – who made strange, graphic pots, stuck with leaves and detritus, a kind of Caribbean folk art – was from Orlando, in Florida. She was shy and slight, although some of her pots were as big as Greek oil jars and needed some manhandling.

As she knew Miami a little from the cruises, Cate had tried to talk to Tina once or twice about Florida, but it was hard going; Cate had come to the conclusion she was simply homesick. She was supposed to produce a little show, next week; there had been some talk about it from the others, but not from Tina. She was jumpy about it. She'd started slipping into the little room next to the dining room to watch the castle's only television and catch the news every night; news of the world outside.

Then there was Michelle from Queens, New York, who lived out of choice in the modern studio behind the laundry building, with her long, unkempt grey-blonde hair and air of perpetual whirlwind fury. Cate, walking past the wide windows of Michelle's apartment one day with an armful of tablecloths from the laundry, had seen her hunched bodily over the long white table and writing furiously, like a child hiding her work from the class cheat. She'd seemed to sense Cate there, and had turned on her a blinding glare.

Michelle was a poet and a librettist, which, Cate knew, was someone who wrote the words for operas. She'd read her poetry early on in her residency, stonily, challenging her audience to comment. Cate wondered about the presentations; most of the guests seemed to dread them, when it came to their turn. Michelle was childless.

Tina didn't drink coffee and half the time she didn't turn up at all; when she did, she sipped a brew of her own, made of boiled-up Chinese herbs. She inhabited the small *villino*, divided now into an apartment on the first floor and a workshop below, where Mauro had grown up, although his family had never owned it. A tied house: Mauro's father before him had been the castle's gardener and factotum, but the tied house had lapsed on his death and the creation of the Trust. The office in Baltimore, established proudly by old Orfeo, setting his faith in American reason and logic and justice, got blamed for an awful lot around here. The *villino* was only five minutes away, at the end of a stunted avenue of cypresses planted by Mauro's father and sadly neglected.

Michelle sometimes went to see Tina late at night; Cate had seen the two of them walk down between the cypresses, and some days Cate

46

suspected she stayed over there. It had a spare bed.

'I should go,' Cate had said, now feeling nervous. She knew she could leave them together. Tiziano seemed to like the Englishman so perhaps they would want to talk. In fact the Venetian was good at getting on with everyone; Cate could not claim any special friendship with him.

She'd been almost out and home free, when she'd heard it, on the stairs, a commotion. A bellowing, like a charging beast.

'It's her, isn't it? Where is she?' Coming from up above her so it could only be Per Hansen, but his voice had been hardly recognizable. 'What's happened to her?' Could he be drunk? He did drink, glass after glass some evenings and never a sign of being actually drunk. But at this time in the morning? He'd leaned over the banisters, his sandy hair sticking up, his bushy fair eyebrows even wilder than usual, and Cate had seen that he was alone. He must be talking – shouting – to himself.

She'd fled.

Five minutes later, the staff – Mauro, Anna-Maria the cleaner, Nicki, Cate and Ginevra – had all gathered in the dining room.

Luca Gallo stood at the head of the dining-room table, a piece of paper in his hands that he kept folding and unfolding.

'I'm very sorry to tell you,' he said, and for a moment he stopped as though unsure of how to proceed. He looked as though he really was sorry;

47

his twinkling eyes were dull and distracted, and his cheerful, bearded face was for once sober with shock. He started again, and this time he spoke for ten minutes, and no one said a word; they all just stared.

Dead.

'Last night – between here and Pozzo Basso. On her way to Pozzo. Some time around midnight.'

The dining room suddenly seemed to grow cold. Everyone stood very still, not sure of what to do next.

An accident. She always drove too fast; for a seasick moment on hearing the words Cate had seen the dark road as though through a windscreen, coming up to meet her.

As always, Luca took the initiative. 'We must continue our work as usual,' he said, in answer to the unspoken question. 'We must carry on: this is an unfortunate accident, a terrible accident – but we can still function.' He leaned forwards, both hands flat on the table, his ardour revived. 'The guests have another month here, and they have their work to do. We have ours.'

There was a ground murmur, a shifting around the table, the muttered sounds of relief and shock mingled as people took permission to return to real life. Mauro got to his feet first, exchanging words with Ginevra, who looked visibly shaken. Nicki seemed half excited, half frightened, watching for Ginevra to get back into gear, and as for me, thought Cate, I'm on the outside.

Answerable to everyone and no one, with the little *motorino* for a quick getaway. She sat, numb.

Per Hansen had been right: something had happened to her.

Could it be true? Dead? How could she be dead? They'd all seen her only hours earlier, only last night, fizzing with life and energy and flirtation and malice, those blue eyes bright and dangerous. Loni Meadows, *Dottoressa*, Director of the Orfeo Trust; suddenly it seemed to Cate absolutely impossible that such a person could die.

Yesterday morning, alive and well, in one of her haughty tempers at coffee because not enough of them wanted to go to the Pinacoteca in Siena next week. Walking down to the *villino* later, to see Tina's work in progress. At drinks, talking to Alec Fairhead about someone she knew at his publisher's. 'Gorgeous girl,' she'd said, giving him a sly look, 'just your type.' At dinner, telling Per she planned to go to Oslo for his premiere. Talking about art galleries in New York, putting people's backs up, her life full to the brim and now gone.

Cate had seen her at eleven, and something like an hour later, she'd been dead. Cate shook her head in disbelief.

As everyone dispersed, she saw Luca Gallo's eyes on her, and when she returned his look with a questioning glance he held up a finger to detain her.

'I'd like to see you in my office, Caterina,' he said. 'Half an hour?'

★　　★　　★

'You've what?' Giuli wasn't good at disguising her feelings; she sounded like a kid at the back of the class, crowing over a teacher's slip.

'I've lost her,' said Sandro.

Sandro's part-time receptionist, secretary and assistant, Giuli – Giulietta Sarto – did not have much of a CV. The daughter of a drug-addicted prostitute who worked the Via Senese and over-dosed before her child was fifteen, Giuli was a graduate of prison and psychiatric hospital who had come into Sandro's life when he had arrested her, four years earlier, for the murder of her one-time abuser. It had been his last case as a serving police officer, the same case that had led to his early retirement, and in its wake he and Luisa had as good as adopted Giuli.

Her rehabilitation had worked better than expected – thanks to them, some had said, though Sandro always argued it was down to the girl's sheer stubborn determination – and Giuli was on his side, for better or worse. Skinny, razor-tongued and sharp as a tack, she was as close to a daughter as Sandro and Luisa were ever going to get, and Sandro for one could not have got through the previous year without her.

Half the week Giuli worked at the Women's Centre, around the corner from the Via del Leone in the sleepy little Piazza Tasso; since close on a year earlier, more or less when Luisa started the treatment, Giuli had taken to calling in on Sandro, for a chat, or to bring him a coffee. She brought him stories from the Centre too; who'd got clean, who'd got pregnant, gossip about bent police officers and pimps and respectable women.

Then one morning she'd caught him swearing at his computer and had nudged him aside. Sitting next to him at the desk she had taught him how to organize his email address book, how to re-boot, to clean up his data and update his word-processing package, how to use internet search engines properly. And when a week or so later she'd got down on her hands and knees to pull all the drawers out of his filing cabinet to retrieve a wedge of papers that had got caught at the back, Sandro had suggested, tentatively, that she might think about formalizing the relationship, two mornings a week to start with.

Financially, of course, it made no sense at all; Sandro was hardly earning himself. But he'd always liked to find the odd twenty euros for Giuli, and this way, she was happier to take the money. And God knew, there was always something for her to do; she'd even followed the baker's wife for him, one morning when Sandro was worried the woman had started to recognize him. By the end of the year Giulietta had saved enough to pick herself up a battered brown *motorino*. It looked pre-war.

'Wouldn't you want something a bit brighter?' he'd asked, eyeing the ancient machine doubtfully, and Giuli had tapped the side of her nose. 'If I had something in metallic pink with Barbie decals,' she'd said, 'it wouldn't be so handy, would it? For surveillance.'

Sandro hadn't known if she was joking or not, and the sharp, conspiratorial nudge she'd given him with her bony shoulder had not enlightened him. He'd said nothing, mulling the idea over. He didn't want to disappoint her. But why not? Giuli was clever, and she was good at making herself invisible, a thin, watchful forty year old in market-stall clothes. She was even taking English classes, two evenings a week; she thought he didn't know that was where his money went, but Luisa had let it slip.

He'd think about it; or at least, if they ever got another proper client, he would.

In the meantime they had an arrangement: if he was on a job and she needed to talk to him, she'd text. If she rang him, she might interrupt something; she might draw attention to him precisely when he wanted to stay invisible. The faceless bystander no one ever noticed or remembered.

Sandro mumbled. 'What did you call about?' He was sitting in the car, in the cold, outside the Liceo Marzocco.

His mobile had bleeped at him as he stood on the cold pavement grinding his teeth with impotent fury. *Call in?* The message had been sent when he'd been at that signal-free zone at the foot of the Monte Alle Croci; in the nice stuffy bar, filling up on *brioche* and *caffe latte*, reading the paper and congratulating himself on how well the day was going.

He had been able to see the gap where the pink

Vespa had been as he walked up the hill. He'd planted himself on the pavement, no longer caring if he was seen, and waited for them to come out, watching for Carlotta, waiting for the long-haired boy. No show.

He'd climbed into the car to look at his phone, and dialled Giuli.

The crowd of kids had more or less dispersed now; just one or two stragglers around a lamp-post. He watched them, the phone to his ear, mouth turned down. 'So?'

Giuli wasn't going to let him off that easily. 'You're getting old, Sandro,' she crowed, 'I tell you, I know all the tricks in the book, where high-school students are concerned. *I* should be following the girl.'

And then what would I be? The redundant detective, out to grass.

'Well, if you behaved yourself,' he said mildly, 'maybe I'd let you do some tailing. But for now, just tell me what you called about.'

'Right,' said Giuli, remembering herself. 'OK. A call from a guy called something – um –' she fumbled, the sound of papers rustling took over and Sandro had to restrain a sigh. Bright, but disorganized; give her a chance.

'Here it is.' She resurfaced. 'Luca Gallo.'

Sandro leaned back into the driving seat. 'Uh huh,' he said vaguely. For a moment the name meant nothing to him, then it did. 'Right,' he said. 'The guy from the whatsit Trust.'

Across the road the kids at the lamp-post had turned to look at him; he shifted his position a bit to obscure his face from them, shoulder against the window.

'Um – Trust, yeah. Wants you to call him.'

'Orfeo,' repeated Sandro automatically, his brain re-engaging. 'The background check.' He sighed at the thought of all those other employee checks awaiting him, and the bodyguard work. Nightclub bouncer, that's where he'd end up. Employed as a charity case by one of Luisa's admirers.

'He sounded – funny,' said Giuli hesitantly.

'Funny?'

At that moment someone came out through the school's gate, and a cheer went up from the boys at the lamp-post. Sandro turned to look and saw that it was the lanky boy into whose eyes Carlotta had been gazing. Alberto the rich kid.

'Call you back,' said Sandro, stuffing the phone in his pocket.

The three overgrown boys clustered around the parked *motorini*, jostling each other, pulling on helmets. Without a moped of his own Alberto ousted one of his pals, taking control and forcing the kid to ride pillion.

Fortunately for Sandro the street was one-way, because it would have been impossible to manage a U-turn in the confined space; certainly not without drawing attention to himself. His tailing skills needed a little attention, that was for sure; a battered, nondescript *motorino* such as Giuli's mightn't be a bad idea, either. He sat with the engine running until they went past, a cigarette clamped between Alberto's lips as he talked around it, helmetless and entertaining his entourage, taking a hand off the handlebars to gesture in the air, the *motorino* swerving as he did so.

Not for the first time, Sandro felt a spasm of pity for little Carlotta Bellagamba.

At the bottom of the hill they swung through the Porta San Miniato, left past the little bar where Sandro had lost the plot, down the high-sided canyon of the Via San Niccolò, then a sharp right around the great bulk of the Palazzo dei Mozzi with its huge, studded door. They were on the Piazza Demidoff, overlooking the river, where the rich kids hang out.

The gang pulled up in front of what looked like a closed-up restaurant or club with shuttered windows, on the corner of the street; they seemed to be fishing through their pockets, looking for something. Sandro double-parked outside a bar thronging with outdoor smokers, and watched. The shuttered windows weren't completely dead; a string of red fairylights twinkled along the top of the shutters, and there was a dim light visible through a glazed section at the top of the door.

Whatever it was the boys had been looking for – and Sandro guessed it was money – they found it. They were lined up at the door now, Alberto, the tallest by a head, in the lead, pressing a bell and talking into an intercom, and then they were inside, the boy at the back shoving a little to hurry them in.

Right, thought Sandro, with gloomy satisfaction. He knew what kind of place it was; he knew they weren't in there spending their parents' money on dried-up sandwiches. He knew, too, that if he went in after them, a man in late middle age on his own, he might as well attach a flashing beacon to his head and imitate a police siren.

He got himself a slice of pizza, returned to the car, and watched.

The afternoon faded. Half a dozen times Sandro stuck the key in the ignition, ready to jack it in. He was being paid to watch Carlotta Bellagamba, not her boyfriend, and he was being alternately chilled to the bone or suffocated by the car's faulty, fume-laden heater. He thought of Giuli, wondered idly what Gallo wanted. It had been money for old rope, that job; he supposed he wouldn't mind another like it, running a few things through the system, checking credit and criminal records, following up references. He hadn't even needed to leave his office.

Sandro knew he should call the man, and should call Giuli back too for that matter, but that would require him to climb out of the car and walk to the riverbank fifty metres away where there was a mobile signal, out of the lee of the hills and the stone mass of the Palazzo Mozzi. So he sat and chewed his nails, and wished he was a policeman again and his partner Pietro was sitting next to him, talking about food. And tried not to think about what it would be like returning to a flat empty of Luisa, for three whole nights.

At close to four o'clock she appeared. Not Giuli, not Luisa, but little Carlotta Bellagamba. The pink Vespa tilted around the corner, dangerously laden, Carlotta's curls springing out from under her helmet. Two big carrier bags from a flashy chain store dangling from either handlebar, and another between her knees. She'd been shopping. Jesus wept.

Sandro killed the engine, which he'd had on to run the heater as the sun went down and the chill grew. He saw Carlotta smile as she spoke into the intercom, then she was inside. Shocked to breathlessness by the cold as he stepped out of the car, Sandro made the five, ten quick strides to the river. As he got into phone range he turned to keep the door to the club and the little Vespa in view.

'And where the hell have you been?' demanded Giuli, the instant she heard his voice.

'You know where the Zoe is?' Sandro said, and it was an answer, of a kind. 'Lock up and get over here, and put some make-up on. I want you to play my girlfriend.'

CHAPTER 5

When Cate had come for her interview at Orfeo last summer, it had been Dottoressa Meadows who'd picked her up from the station in Pozzo. The Director, coming to collect an interviewee. Cate had been surprised, and impressed, by this at the time: it had seemed to her a good omen. A sign of something democractic in the system, to be chauffeured by the boss.

But Dottoressa Meadows had barely even shaken her hand at the station, and said nothing, or close to it, as they drove, the car sweet with an expensive fragrance Cate remembered from her most sophisticated aunt's top drawer. Now, of course, Cate knew – everyone knew – that Loni Meadows regularly found reasons to nip into town; that the big offroader smelled of her perfume because it had become to all intents and purposes her personal property. Then, Cate had ended up staring through the car's high windows at the great sweeping hills, glittering in the heat haze, miles and miles without a single farmstead. On their way through the hills they'd passed at least one car wreck being examined by the police, only the car's bonnet visible, thrust out from under a dense thicket of myrtle.

Was that why Cate didn't remember the white truck she'd passed on her way to work, with its lifting gear and the police tape, until much later? Shock does weird things, they say; when someone dies, you might think about something that happened, oh, years ago, but what happened that very morning is wiped.

'Her car came off the road, some time last night,' Luca Gallo had said to their little group in the hushed dining room, his bright face solemn with shock, and still Cate didn't make the connection; at that moment she'd been thinking, for some reason, that it had happened much further away. Not in the next valley, not barely out of sight of the high grey walls of the castle. 'She sustained head injuries. With the cold –' and he had faltered then, perhaps at the sight of them all staring back at him, perhaps as the reality hit. It had been minus eight, last night; she'd have lain there alone, in the dark and the cold. Dying; dead.

An accident. Did all accidents feel like this? Frightening: the suddenness of it, the randomness? But if it had certainly been sudden, it hadn't felt quite random to Cate. She was scared.

She might have done anything in the half an hour before she had to be outside Luca's office; no doubt he intended her to complete whatever tasks Ginevra had for her and then come straight to him. Cate had got so far as retrieving a tray from the library, but when she came out into the wide hall something stopped her. A tiny gust of fragrance, no more than the memory of Loni's scent. And she set the tray down carefully and before anyone could ask her what she thought she was doing, she walked up the stairs.

Softly she took two steps to the double doors that faced her, the doors that led to the double-fronted *piano nobile* apartment that Loni Meadows had appropriated for herself. One of the doors was open, just a crack.

Cate paused. Around her the castle was silent; around her ankles suddenly the air turned cold, not quite a draught, more like a steady cold breath. She shifted, but it was still there, insistent as a presence. Cate felt the chill up to the back of her neck, raising the hairs; she was jumpy as a cat. No such thing as ghosts.

And before she could allow herself to consider what she was doing, Cate pushed, and the doors swung open.

The room was south facing and flooded with a winter sunlight that was thin but surprisingly strong. Cate had to blink and hold a hand to her eyes. Loni Meadows had not closed her shutters, had she? That was what Cate had seen from her *motorino*; the *Dottoressa* had never got to bed last night. As her eyes adjusted, Cate took in the room; the huge gilded bedhead, the plumped pillows, the smooth velvet counterpane. On it, four or five outfits, as if she'd pulled things out of the wardrobe and thrown them down, choosing what to wear. The disarray of the inlaid dressing table, the clothes dropped carelessly on the velvet bedspread. A splash of green silk on the floor, a pair of boots, one on its side, and the whole room full of her scent, sweet and musky. Cate closed her eyes, breathed it in for a second. It was only last night: I only saw her last night.

Wearing the green silk blouse at the dinner table, velvet jeans, boots. She'd come up here and changed to go out.

On the desk was Loni's tiny laptop computer, closed. Cate laid a hand on its textured white surface and suddenly she had the strangest, most horrible sensation of not being alone, as though these elements of Loni Meadows scattered around the room had brought something else to life somewhere close, and it was breathing.

Quite still, and holding her own breath – holding that sweet, cloying scent inside her – Cate listened: was the sound human? Was it just the castle's fabric, the wood and stone settling? Was it wind, on the windows? She lifted her hand from the little computer, and then it came, something weightier and more definite than breath, or even than the movement of clothing: it might be a footstep, a light, soft step, and another one. And then without thinking Cate turned and walked – ran, almost – towards the sound, towards the door to the landing, pulling it back.

There was no one there.

'Who is it?' she said, and her voice echoed in

the stairwell. Had she heard it, just as she came to the door, had she heard the tiniest sound of a sharp intake of breath from somewhere above her? Or was it her overactive imagination?

Cate took two steps to the wide stairwell across the landing and looked up, into the dark. 'Who's there?' she said again. But there was only silence, and as suddenly as she had taken fright Cate felt stupid. Hysterical. Overhead she heard the scrape of a chair from one of the rooms belonging to the men. Her imagination.

Downstairs, the library and music room were silent. Her imagination.

When she arrived at the office, Cate could hear the murmur of Luca's voice inside. He was already on the phone.

It was Luca Gallo who'd interviewed Cate, all that time ago; Dottoressa Meadows had cracked a smile when they'd arrived and Luca had come out, then she'd wafted her hand vaguely in Cate's direction before hurrying into the gallery, already dialling on her mobile phone.

Luca had been easy; Cate had liked him immediately. Impressed with her travelling, not asking her, as some had – as her mother and stepfather never failed to ask – why didn't you stick at anything? Why didn't you want to settle down?

'New Orleans,' he'd said, instead, 'wow. And Spain. And cruise ships? That must have been interesting.'

62

On the desk between them were fanned brochures giving the history of the Trust, but Cate didn't need to read them. She had already Googled the set-up before the interview, so she knew the romantic story, of how an Italian migrant called Fabio Orfeo, grandfather of the current incumbent, had made money in America and come back to set up the Trust; of how he had hoped to gain artistic credentials of some sort by establishing an anglophone community in the family's big white elephant of a crumbling castle in southern Tuscany. For 'the promotion of inter-disciplinary fraternization,' whatever that meant. To provide space, time and quiet for artists of every colour to discover of their best.

Niccolò Orfeo was the family's representative now, a handsome man in his late sixties, barrel-chested, powerful and fluently charming, with a fine moustache. He came out from his villa in Florence to give introductory speeches to the guests and to bolster the numbers at dinner from time to time as the course progressed. Sitting next to the *Dottoressa*, he would pass disparaging remarks to Loni Meadows about Ginevra's cooking, barely bothering to lower his voice.

At her interview the first thing that had struck Cate was that Luca's little office was packed to bursting; stacks of brochures, a map of the world, computers, printer, coffee-machine, train time-tables, a pinboard with photographs of Trust events. It looked like fun: a smiling group ranged on the curved stone seating of an amphitheatre, in a pavilion at the Venice Biennale, in a sculpture park. Only if you looked very hard could you find any evidence of a life outside the Trust: a tiny, passport-sized photo of another smiling, bearded face, half hidden under the computer screen.

Cate now knew this was Luca's Sicilian boyfriend Salvatore, who came up a couple of times a year. They were strict about partners at the Trust, he'd made that clear.

'The principle is, a bit like a retreat,' he'd said earnestly. 'A monastic existence, if you like, just concentration on the work. And if the guests aren't allowed their spouses, or their partners – well, it would be a bit much, wouldn't it? We – the staff – the least we can do is to make it easy for them. So we keep our private lives away from Orfeo too.'

Cate hadn't really talked about that to Vincenzo, nor about the gentle, persistent pressure for her to live in.

'Look,' Luca had said at the interview, 'it's not a condition of employment. It's your choice.'

She had just nodded, and he hadn't pressed her.

'You'll begin by doing a bit of everything,' he'd said, still cheerful. 'You've got so much experience; I mean, I'm impressed. We'll start you in the kitchen, with some cleaning work. But with your languages – Spanish and English?'

'And a bit of German,' she'd said, shy all of a sudden.

'And German.' He'd clapped his hands. 'The

languages will take you further than kitchen work. If you want to go further.'

There was something about the way Luca looked at you, so direct, so open and full of plans, so evangelical. You had to smile back.

'That would be great,' she'd said, and he'd gone on.

'I'm thinking of – well, we could call it liaison, with the guests. There are interns,' and despite himself Luca's mouth had turned down as he'd pronounced the word, 'they come from colleges in America, but they're young. They have – unreasonable expectations – they get homesick, they're not in it for the long term.'

That had certainly been true. Ten days ago the latest intern, Beth, the third since Cate's arrival six months earlier, had left. The one thing the three young American women had had in common was their apparent dislike of more or less everything Italian, and their longing to be back in the land of the free. Beth had seemed to grow smaller the longer she stayed, terrified as she was of everything: the isolation, the climate, the food, the adders and wild boar, and Mauro's temper.

'Well,' he'd finished abruptly, the mention of interns perhaps a source of disappointment to him. 'As I say. We'll see how things go.'

'Yes,' she'd said, and in that moment she'd been sure that she hadn't got the job.

Mauro had given her a lift back to the station, then a short hop on a dusty *regionale* to Arezzo,

65

and her stepfather had collected her. By the time she'd got home, Luca had already called to offer her the position, and Cate had found herself wondering why.

That hot summer evening seemed a long time ago now, as she stood once again outside Luca's office, waiting like a child to see the headmaster.

'Caterina,' he said. 'Cate, thank you.' He pulled out a chair for her. He sat, elbows on his desk, and put his close-cropped head in his hands.

'Caterina. Listen. I need your help, now.' He spoke quietly, but she knew this would not be a request, not really. It would be an instruction.

'My help?'

He held her gaze. 'There are – there is so much to do in the aftermath of – an event like this, I am sure you understand.' He passed a hand anxiously over his head again, and his face was pale. 'There is – everything. An accident and –' he mimed an explosion with his big hands. 'Suddenly everything is unknown.' He tried to smile. 'In the short term, there are people I need to contact.'

'Of course.' Did she have family? Did she have parents? It was hard to imagine.

'And then there is – there are the guests. They must be protected – they must be reassured.'

'Yes,' said Cate.

'And without an intern –'

Cate nodded, careful not to show what she was feeling. Exasperation with Beth for leaving, although

66

perhaps it was just as well. She'd tried to turn to Loni Meadows as a mother figure, and was met with short shrift; even Cate had seen that Loni didn't want to be anyone's mother, with her bright vivacity, her tense, birdlike frame always poised for flight and her high-breasted figure, too youthful for her age. Which was? Fifty some; Cate would have guessed fifty-three. With a small shock she realized all over again that the woman was dead.

'Yes,' she said. 'It's a nightmare for you, I can see that.'

'Yes,' said Luca, his voice firming. 'Well, the thing is, I'd like to offer you a kind of promotion – provisional, of course, a step up, on a trial basis. You can go on helping Ginevra a bit too, but I'd like you to – um, shift your focus, upstairs. While we wait for another intern,' he stopped, his faced clouded, 'and of course the appointment of a new Director, well. I'm going to need all the help I can get.'

Cate gazed at him, trying not to show her very mixed feelings: doubly an outsider in the kitchen, with this promotion. 'Wow,' was all she could risk saying. Then, realizing it wasn't enough, 'You're very kind.' And took a deep breath. 'I'd be honoured.'

'Of course,' said Luca, and she was in no doubt who was the boss now, 'you'll have to live in, you know, at least for now. You'll have to go and collect some things, today. Now; Mauro'll take you in the – um –' He stopped, and they stared at each other. The Monster was gone, wasn't it? Cate wondered

67

if it was a write-off, or perhaps the police would need to examine it? When, ten years earlier, a school friend had flipped his car – under the influence of not very much marijuana and a couple of cocktails – and died on a roundabout on the outskirts of Arezzo one Friday night, the police had put the Datsun Cherry in the crusher without delay or ceremony. His parents had given it to him on his eighteenth birthday three weeks earlier.

Holding Luca's friendly, trusting gaze, Cate swallowed.

'We'll be getting another car soon,' said Luca evenly. 'But in the meantime Mauro can take you in the pick-up.'

'Yes,' she said, resigned. Vincenzo, she thought, but already he was receding, his hopeful face at the checkout, beaming up at her, his eager voice on the mobile this morning. She'd think of something. It seemed as though her time was up; Luca was on his computer, checking something, frowning at the screen. She stood to go.

'Oh,' said Luca, looking up, 'listen, I know you're up to this, Caterina. I wouldn't have asked if I didn't.'

'Right,' said Cate. But there was something in his voice that told her Luca Gallo wasn't even sure if he was up to it himself. Whatever it turned out to be.

'He called again, you know,' said Giuli, as soon as they were sitting down inside.

The make-up hadn't been that great an idea, Sandro decided, although it did have the advantage of making her look marginally closer to him in age. Rough around the edges though she might be, Giuli could look fine, unadorned, now she had a bit more weight on her. There was a liveliness in her face, a crinkled-up, well-worn sort of look that Sandro had a soft spot for, only make-up turned it clownish. 'You look nice,' he'd said on the pavement, trying to be kind, but she'd just shaken her head at him. 'I know what I look like, Sandro,' she'd said. 'Let's just convince the man on the door, shall we?'

The man on the door was in fact an Indian boy, maybe twenty years old, and he didn't seem to care. 'Members?'

Giuli had taken charge, stepping into the cramped space behind the curtained door. 'Not yet,' she said. 'How much?'

At her shoulder Sandro had tried to look seedy, a middle-aged man – well, almost old – slipping off on a Friday afternoon with his bit on the side. God, he'd thought belatedly, what if Luisa hears?

'Five euro each,' the Indian boy had said without much interest, and Sandro had taken out his wallet. And that was it: they were in.

Almost immediately Sandro had wished he was back out on the street. The room they'd edged into was kitted out in a fake Moroccan style, tasselled velvet clashing horribly with wall-to-wall leopard print. A false ceiling had been fitted to squeeze in a mezzanine overhead, making the place screamingly claustrophobic, and certainly a deathtrap in any kind of emergency situation. Fire, for example. In one corner a man Sandro's age was sitting next to a sallow, bored-looking girl in a miniskirt, his hand on her thigh. He was leaning back against the leopard print, eyes half-closed. Averting his gaze, Sandro had followed Giuli up a spiral staircase in the corner.

The light was so bad, Sandro hadn't seen them at first, then he'd nearly stumbled over the boy's foot, stretched out into the cramped aisle between low Moroccan stamped-tin tables and banquettes and lampshades. There'd been a murmured exclamation, a hand raised palm out in apology, and to Sandro's relief the foot withdrawn without a glance being exchanged. Not looking back, he'd proceeded to a vantage point on the far side of the cramped, dark room where Giuli had settled herself in a corner. Behind him a girl had tittered. Carlotta. He hadn't known if she was laughing at him, at something the boys had said, or if she was just stoned.

This was what the parents wanted, wasn't it? Yes, she's taking drugs. Talk to her about it.

'He phoned again,' said Giuli then. 'Luca Gallo.'

'Oh,' said Sandro glumly. 'Sorry.'

'It's all right,' said Giuli softly. 'You were busy. But he did sound kind of – weird.'

'You said that,' said Sandro, remembering that she had. 'Really?' The softness of her voice had an odd effect on him; he felt the cushions trying to reclaim him, and stifled a yawn. It was like he'd entered a different world, where different rules applied. He thought of the man downstairs; how did he feel when he came back out, into the real world? What did he tell his wife, if he had a wife? Dangerous to come in here.

'Uh huh,' assented Giuli, 'just a little bit freaked out. Something about an accident, he said.'

'An accident,' repeated Sandro absently. Luca Gallo. He laid his head back, and thought about that job, the woman with startling blue eyes, that castle in the Maremma. With Giuli, an expert in the art of computer applications, he'd looked for it on Google Earth, zoomed in on it, in from the bright blue sea and the coastal motorway, past ugly little towns in the flatlands. A great grey prison of a place around a courtyard, an avenue of trees, a scattering of outbuildings, standing proud and isolated. The bare hills around it, the narrow, empty country roads.

'I'll call him in the morning,' said Sandro. 'Did he leave a number?'

'Yeah,' she said. 'And I gave him yours – your mobile, I mean. He said he was in and out. Keep trying, he said.'

'Right,' said Sandro.

His eyes had adjusted to the gloom by now, and he could distinguish the members of Carlotta's little group. The boy Alberto lay with his head back, trance-like, and earphones in, just a slight rhythmic shifting of his head from side to side

71

indicating that he was not asleep. Carlotta sitting up straight and eager: his heart sank, thinking that she did after all need his protection.

'What do you make of them?' His voice was a murmur. Giuli shrugged.

'They're stoned, but she isn't, not yet. She wants to be one of them; I guess if she's not doing drugs now, she will eventually.'

Sandro chewed his lip, trying to work out what he would say to the Bellagamba family.

'Saw Luisa on my way over,' said Giuli. 'Having lunch with the boss, it looked like.'

'What?' said Sandro.

Her face flicked upwards. 'Hi,' she said, not to Sandro.

Sandro looked around. A dark man in a grey leather jacket was smiling down at them without a trace of warmth. Sandro struggled to extract himself from the cushions and into a more dignified attitude, and failed.

'Ciao,' said the man in a thick accent and sat down beside Giuli, a hand immediately on her knee. He wasn't North African, but something else. Eastern European? Turkish? From somewhere where cultures met, and went to war. There was something in his other hand, something he was clicking and shifting, like worry beads: Sandro couldn't see it. Giuli kept smiling.

'New members?' They nodded.

'Where you from? You from the city? How come I never see you before?'

'Tavarnuzze,' said Giuli without missing a beat, and he winked at her, picking at his teeth with a long and dirty nail. 'Country girl,' he said, 'I know the country girls.' He flicked something to the floor.

He thought Giuli was one of the prostitutes who worked the back roads out towards Siena. Not far from the mark; Giuli's mother had done just that, though when Giuli had been a hooker she'd chosen a different pitch. It was a remark that might have made the old Giuli, the Giuli who didn't care much if she lived or died, the Giuli just out of rehab and as tender and exposed as a clam, fly at the man, hissing and spitting.

All she did was wag a finger at him, smiling.

'OK, OK,' he said. 'Peace, peace. Live and let live.' And suddenly he was on his feet and Sandro could see that the thing he was clicking and swinging in his left hand was a set of handcuffs. He saw Sandro unable to look away, and laughed again, loud, delighted. Then he was clattering down the stairs.

Sandro gave her a nod. 'You're a cool customer, Giuli.'

'You think?' She shrugged. 'You just have to tell yourself, there's no right way to go. If they want to hurt you, they'll hurt you.'

Sandro laughed shortly. He took a deep breath. 'You saw Luisa,' he said roughly. 'Having lunch.'

Giuli eyed him curiously. 'Yes,' she said. 'In that bar next to her shop, you know. The fancy one.'

OK, thought Sandro, trying to be casual. Standing at the bar, a quick bite. Fair enough.

'Looked like they were having fun,' Giuli went on. 'Nice to see Luisa having fun again. And eating.'

'Yes,' said Sandro. 'Eating a proper meal?'

'*Scaloppina* with mushrooms, it looked like to me,' said Giuli wistfully. 'Nice to have a boss who appreciates you, not just a tramezzino at the bar. Table with a tablecloth, glass of wine.'

Despite himself, Sandro let out an explosive sound. Thinking of Luisa pushing away her glass at the table last night.

'What?' said Giuli. 'What is up with you, Sandro?'

He scratched his head, blinking down at his hands. It felt as though there was a great weight on him, bearing down. Months of tension; months of waiting for it to lift, when they got the all-clear, but then there was always something else. Another test in eighteen months, then two years. Had he thought it would bind them, this fear? It hadn't.

'Sandro,' said Giuli, 'what's this all about?'

He raised his face to hers, saw the worry in her eyes and out it came.

'New York?' said Giuli, incredulously. 'Luisa, in New York? You never said.'

'I didn't know,' said Sandro, then hurriedly, 'I guess it was last-minute. Maybe – someone else dropped out.'

'Look,' said Giuli, and he could see in her eyes she knew what he was thinking. Or did she know something else? 'I can handle this. You need to go

74

home and talk to Luisa.' She stared at him, glanced over at Carlotta in the corner. 'I can handle this. You know I can. She's going Sunday night? You'd better sort this out, Sandro.'

He gazed at her, knowing when he was beaten. 'Go home.'

CHAPTER 6

She saw them coming up through the woods in the fading light; at first she didn't know who she was looking at, just the slow-moving outline of something denser than the leafless trees.

It was an unfamiliar angle, the view down the hill through the woods; Cate might have been in the little room behind the gatehouse once or twice, but she wouldn't have had time to stand at the window gazing. In the summer, the leaf canopy would have made the dense woodland impenetrable and you might come right up to the castle unnoticed. On a winter evening the effect was no less spooky, though; the screen of spindly, leafless limbs made Cate's eyes ache the longer she stared at it.

The room was smaller than she remembered it, and the woods were closer. Its smell was a layering of wood, red cotto wax and disinfectant; an anonymous smell. She'd make it her own; it wouldn't be the first time.

Mauro had taken the long and ugly route to Pozzo, using the dual carriageway. Cate only realized later, when they came the usual way, that he'd

76

been avoiding the crash site. There were plenty of things that weren't occurring to Cate today; she felt slightly stunned, on autopilot.

It hadn't taken her long to clean out her bedsit over the biker bar; half a dozen books, some clothes, a couple of pots. Her radio, which doubled as a speaker for her iPod. She shouldn't have been surprised by how little affection she felt for the place; it was so easy to say goodbye. But then that was Cate all over, her mother would say. Drifter. She knew she should speak to Vincenzo; she could have called in on him at the supermarket, only Mauro was waiting for her. That was her excuse, anyway; she'd call him – later. When she'd got back to where she'd left him and the pick-up, she'd found it empty but unlocked, and started loading alone. When Mauro had reappeared, close to ten minutes later, she'd been on her knees in the back, sorting stuff, and hadn't seen what direction he'd come from. He'd looked flushed.

'Where've you been then?' Cate had said, never one to mince her words. He might have nipped off for a quick coffee, but his general air of shame-facedness had told a different story. 'One for the road?'

He'd drawn himself up stiffly. Mauro was a countryman, through and through, and old-fashioned: he didn't like lip from girls.

'You done?' was all he'd said, roughly.

Once back with him in the stifling cab of the pick-up, though, breathing in sweat and stale cigarettes, Cate had kept quiet. She didn't want to get on the wrong side of Mauro, particularly not when he was at the wheel. She'd been driven by him on several occasions, and his style was forceful and headlong, rarely braking on roads he must have known his whole life. And now the light had been leaching out of the sky, the sun close to the horizon and the road ahead of them grey and indistinct, especially in the valleys.

They'd come past the bend, and he'd slowed, kept to the centre of the road. Cate's head had turned despite herself: the truck was gone, the car too. Just some churned mud and a flash of tape to show where they'd been. Without even looking Mauro had spoken contemptuously. 'She's not the first to take that bend too fast,' he'd said, his jaw set as he ground the gears. 'She won't be the last. That's what I said to the police.'

'They talked to you?' Cate had simultaneously tried to absorb the viciousness in his voice and to process the possibility that Mauro had been interviewed by the police. She'd doubted that they would have found the experience rewarding.

He'd grunted. 'Ginevra made them coffee in the kitchen so, of course, we had a chat. I've known Commissario Grasso since he was a boy, and the other one too.'

Very cosy. But when Cate had arrived, they'd all pretended they didn't know anything, hadn't they? All right, Cate had thought, if that's the way you want it. She'd felt that the journey might never come to an end, she might be stuck in this dirty cab with Mauro and his sweet grappa breath forever.

'The car went into the river?' she'd asked. The pick-up had slewed on the gravel as he turned on to the back drive, and Mauro had grunted an affirmative. He hadn't spoken again.

The boxes were stacked in the room behind her now: she'd carried them up herself. Mauro had other things to do; she wouldn't have asked him even if he had hung around, but Luca had come out of his office to meet her and Mauro had stomped off towards the kitchen without a backward glance, leaving them to it.

At first she'd thought it might be Mauro she saw coming up through the darkening trees, his stocky outline, hunched with temper, still in her thoughts, but quickly she saw that it could not be him. Apart from anything else, it would have been difficult for him to get around the castle to the bottom of the hill in time, even supposing he had barely paused to conduct whatever business he had in the kitchen. There were two figures, moving slowly, stopping and starting, neither with anything of Mauro's distinctive, stamping gait about them.

Two women, as physically unlike as two women could be. Tina, the pale-skinned girl from Florida with poker-straight, colourless hair, upright and slender to the point of emaciation, and Michelle the New Yorker, strong, muscular, fierce, her grey-blonde hair stuffed into a beanie. Michelle was wearing a parka with a fur hood, short leggings and trainers; this was her uniform. Tina was in the loose Japanese trousers she often wore – not warm enough, and they made her look even thinner; she had little flat oriental gym shoes on her feet, small like everything else about her. Her hands were in her pockets, shoulders tense. The two women leant into each other for support, an awkward, slow-moving arrangement, neither of them constructed for co-operation, thought Cate, and they kept stopping.

When they were less than twenty metres from the castle they stopped again, and Cate saw that it wasn't so much that Michelle was comforting Tina, as restraining her. Tina's movements were jerky; she was pulling at her hair. She was hysterical. Then Michelle put two arms up to Tina's shoulders and held her still, looking into the younger woman's face. Cate tentatively took a step closer to the window, hands up to the glass; she hadn't turned the light on in the room yet and the two women below her were illuminated by the soft yellow of a carriage lamp attached to the wall of the castle. She could hear Michelle's harsh accent as she said, *No way, baby. It's not your fault. Get a grip.* Then Tina tilted her head sideways and suddenly she was looking straight up at the window where Cate stood.

Instinctively Cate took a step back, but not before she saw that Tina's face was puffy with tears; swollen as though she'd been crying – or raging – for some time. When a moment later Cate stepped back to the window, the woods beyond the soft semicircle

80

of light were quite dark, and the two women were gone.

As she stood there in the darkened room it felt to Cate as though she was marooned, the castle her chilly, unknowable island. With something like homesickness she thought of Pozzo, its avenues of dusty trees, its run-down station, its sleepy bars; she thought of her bedsit and Vincenzo on the till at the supermarket.

Getting out her mobile, Cate gazed at the screen and its image of her and Vincenzo, little V'cenz, cheeks pressed against each other, on that outing to Rimini at the end of the summer. She knew she should phone him, but she didn't want to get into it; she didn't want to hear the little boy in his voice. With a dextrousness born of long practice her thumb darted across the keyboard and she flicked off a message to him. *Sorry,* caro, *stopping at the castle tonight, they need me here. Call later?*

Because Ginevra needed her in the kitchen – she'd made sure Cate knew it too and didn't get above her station – and dinner would be at seven. She didn't know if she'd be eating it or serving it or both, but she had to be there; she didn't have time to placate Vincenzo, nor to explain the new situation to him, to talk baby talk and tell him she loved him.

She stared at the phone, willing the message on its way: like so many things in the castle, the mobile signal was unreliable, subject to mysterious fluctuations. *Message sent,* it said.

Still in darkness, the room suddenly felt cold; Cate could feel the deep chill of the castle settling in at her back. The grand, draughty apartments, the second floor where the Englishman would be sitting and staring out across the winter fields, writing nothing, and the Norwegian would be stamping around, pulling down his big old books and leaving them scattered on the floor. Tina should be hunched intently over her work table ornamenting her pots with weird things she picked up around the grounds, hairballs and dust and pins and bottletops, only she was sobbing on Michelle's shoulder. Tina, the most private, contained person Cate had ever come across.

It came to Cate that these people, whom she had until today lumped together as customers, another set of foreigners who would be gone in a month and never seen again, were suddenly, in the aftermath of Loni Meadows's death, more real and distinct to her than her own family. She felt a sudden, urgent need to understand them.

And now they'd all be converging on the great cold library that sucked all the heat from its radiators, gathering again for the *aperitivo*, a niggardly few bottles of prosecco, ready-mixed Campari soda and perhaps some spirits. Every night as Ginevra went into the storeroom she complained of how much the guests drank; Michelle for one might be late up for coffee, but every evening she was bang on time for the *aperitivo*.

'I'll brief you properly tomorrow,' Luca had said,

meeting her out of the pick-up in the dusk, a sideways glance at Mauro. They'd never really got on, she realized; like her, Luca was an outsider, and Mauro's surly intractability didn't yield, even under the full warm glow of his attention. As he'd watched the gardener slope off through the trees towards the shed where he kept his tools and his ride-on, Luca had looked weary in the grey light, not glowing at all. Loni Meadows's death seemed to have crept into every corner of the place, clammy as fog.

'Just – keep everyone happy, for the time being,' he'd said in the quiet dusk. 'I don't know how much time I'm going to have – for all that.' And so, reluctantly closing the door on the warm safety of her new accommodation, Cate had headed for the main keep.

When she walked into the library there was no sign of Luca, but Per the Norwegian was there, muffled up in a padded corduroy jacket and a scarf, drinking whisky at the side window. He was looking out of the window; he showed no sign of being aware of Cate's arrival, and she turned to check that everything was in order for the *aperitivo*.

'They'll complain,' Luca had said beside the pick-up. She'd been surprised to hear anything but enthusiasm in his voice; a sign of strain. 'Believe me, whatever the circumstances they'll find something to complain about, the size of the olives, too much salt, not enough salt, no soda. You'd think they were paying.' Not bitterness perhaps, just disappointment.

The drinks had been laid out, presumably by Nicki, although she must have scuttled directly back to the kitchen: she believed the library to be haunted, some ancient story of a faithless Orfeo wife walled up alive. As well as the whisky there was Campari, a separate bottle of soda, a small bowl of ice, pasteurized orange juice, six bottles of prosecco and two of red wine. Ginevra had obviously been leaned on to be generous, under the circumstances.

'Where do you think it happened?' came Per's flat voice from the window, without preamble, and Cate started. Had she dreamt it, his bellowing like a calf down the stairwell? She stared at him, and he looked back; there was something dull in his eyes.

'Down by the river,' she said hesitantly, chilled all over again by the heedlessness with which she'd sped past the tow-truck. The body might have still been there, mightn't it? Behind the red and white tape, flickering in the wind, under a little tent, waiting to be taken away. 'Not far.'

Per nodded, and she smelled the whisky as he raised the glass to his lips.

Had he been drunk, this morning? She tried to remember the precise quality of that shout: wounded, belligerent? It was extraordinary. Cate had always thought of him as a comfortable, solid presence; in the evenings at dinner in the early weeks he had enjoyed the company of guests, jovial then, an attentive listener, modest and serious. It occurred to her now that gradually he had grown ever quieter. She had guessed that he missed his wife; he'd been married to a Spanish woman for twenty-five years, he once told her. Yolanda.

Perhaps he'd been bellowing about his own wife. Perhaps he'd woken from a bad dream.

He wasn't talking now, and as he turned away from her, Cate was wondering if anyone, apart from her, had been into the *Dottoressa*'s room yet. Then from the gallery came the sound of a throat being cleared. Cate jumped. Glancing up in the dim light she could just about discern the narrow face, deep-set eyes and unshaven chin of the Englishman. It was Alec Fairhead, gazing down at her, a book open in his hand. She tilted her head back to look at him; Per stared through the window and resumed his contemplation of the darkness.

'Hello,' she said. 'Mr Fairhead.' And she remembered the day he'd arrived, looking like he wanted to get straight back in the car; remembered Loni Meadows standing in front of them holding out her hand and saying, *We are honoured*, with that sarcastic edge to her voice.

'Caterina,' he said, and his voice was so low and quiet that she thought he might be in some kind of shock himself. He came down the stairs, reluctantly.

'May I get you a drink?' Cate smiled her warmest at him; she wasn't quite sure of her role yet: servant or friend?

'Yes,' he said with tired irony, 'you may.'

She poured him a glass of red wine without thinking, but she knew what he drank. She knew what all of them drank, and what they ate too, for that matter. Tina ate no fat, leaving it delicately on the edge of the plate: Michelle ate everything that was put in front of her, with a kind of desperate haste.

'You look different, Caterina,' said Fairhead. He meant she wasn't wearing the small white apron she put over her clothes for work; it was unusual for him to make any kind of personal remark, however politely. It was as though he had unwound a small fraction. 'Are you off duty?'

In the dark Cate blushed uncomfortably. 'I – have been promoted, for the time being. I'm sort of the new intern.'

'Yes,' said Fairhead sadly. 'You know, I'd hardly noticed she'd gone? And it's weeks now, isn't it? Since she left.'

'Ten days,' said Cate. 'But perhaps it's just as well, she's not here. All this –' and she gestured around to indicate what they were all feeling. Each in their own way.

'Yes, I see,' said the Englishman. 'Yes – they were close, weren't they?'

'I don't know about that,' said Cate. 'I think Beth wanted someone to be close to, but maybe the *Dottoressa* wasn't the right person.'

'No,' Fairhead said, and he looked at her with his sad eyes. 'You're very perceptive, Caterina.'

86

'And you too,' said Cate, wanting to cheer him up. 'The novelist? Always noticing?'

He laughed unhappily. 'Well, once upon a time,' he said.

And Cate remembered the shame with which he'd admitted at his presentation that he was reading from a book he'd written more than a decade ago. He'd stood in the library while the others gathered to listen, Michelle squatted against the wall to ease her back pain, Loni standing in the gallery with Orfeo, the guest of honour as he often was at these things. He'd sounded as though reading caused him pain, but he'd done it without complaint. Cate had been oddly affected, and when she had gone to the smaller library the next day to borrow the book, she had half expected that someone else would have got there before her. No one had, though: poor Alec Fairhead.

'At times like this – you try to remember,' she said, changing the subject, or so she thought. 'When someone dies? You try to bring the face up in front of you, or remember the last thing they said to you, or, or – I don't know.' She faltered, suddenly becoming aware that Per had moved closer – or had he been there all along, staying silent? – and was staring at her. Fairhead's expression had grown dark.

The Englishman shrugged eventually. 'I suppose so,' he said slowly.

Per was still staring. 'That's it,' he said, his voice oddly stilted. 'I can't remember what happened last night, you're right.' And the whisky glass in his hand shook. Alec Fairhead put a hand on his arm.

'Steady,' he said to Per, then apologetically, to Cate, 'we're all upset.'

Who was the last one to see her? Luca, maybe; she sometimes called in on him to give him instructions for the following day. Although after yesterday – perhaps not. Everyone had been on edge, Luca more than most: he'd joined them for the *antipasto* then excused himself, saying he had work to do. He'd given her a sideways look as he went too, Cate had seen it; after the bawling-out Loni had given him earlier, in full earshot, that hadn't been surprising.

And for a second, it occurred to Cate that Loni's death might not be terrible news for Luca.

She smiled at Alec absently, trying to think. Tina had left the dinner table early too, that much Cate remembered. Practically ran out of the room after something Loni had said, not even directly to Tina. What had they been talking about? Some gallery in New York, some show Loni had reviewed. Tina was like that, prone to flight. Which left who, at the table with Loni?

Cate frowned. 'It's so hard, isn't it?' she said, half to herself. 'You try and remember how they were, when you last saw them – you try to – I suppose you try to bring them back, in a way.'

She looked at Alec Fairhead but she thought she'd said the wrong thing. He seemed distinctly uncomfortable, and when he changed the subject it was a relief. 'And will Luca be joining us?'

'Well,' said Cate gently, 'Luca's very busy, with – ah – with all this, that's why I'm here.'

'It's clever of Luca,' said Fairhead. 'I'm sure you'll be a marvellous intern.' His eyes were sad but he was trying to sound bright. She did like the English, sometimes. They always seemed to think it was their duty not to bother you with their feelings.

'Thanks,' she said. She saw that he had finished his glass of wine already and she refilled it.

'What's the book?' she said, pointing at the volume he'd taken from the shelves.

He looked down as though unaware he had it in his hand. 'Oh,' he said slowly. 'A history of the family. The Orfeo. Upstarts apparently; they've only had the castle since the seventeenth century, a gift from some duke, an attempt to buy the favour of a daughter of the family.' He looked up into the cavernous recesses of the ceiling. 'Not much of a love-gift, really. More like a prison.' He clapped the book shut. 'And she turned out to be a bad lot.'

Per made a low sound that might have been a kind of agreement, and walked away from them to refill his whisky glass, leaving them as unceremoniously as he had joined them.

'A bad lot?' said Cate, valiantly trying to keep up the conversation.

Alec Fairhead smiled unhappily, 'No good,' he said. 'Unfaithful, or something,' and the small talk seemed ridiculous, suddenly.

Impulsively Cate blurted it out. 'I'm so sorry,' she said. 'It must be – awful for you, I mean, even if you don't – didn't know her very well. There was a special sort of relationship; this is a very particular place.'

She didn't know how to phrase it; she had seen Dottoressa Meadows mixing with them at the *aperitivo* hour, all graciousness, her hand resting gently on this shoulder or another. Presiding queen-like at dinner, eyes glittering, her smile charming them, each in turn, around the table. And tonight they would all have to sit there and eat, perhaps Cate too, and Loni Meadows's place would be empty.

'Yes,' said Alec Fairhead, and turning he seemed to look straight through her, in a way that made the hairs on the back of her neck rise, before he looked away. When she spoke her voice faltered. 'You didn't know her, did you? I mean, before?'

He turned back, and the look he gave her was calculating now, as though he was wondering if he could trust her or perhaps, a look she was used to after ten years and more of service, debating if she was worth talking to at all.

'Ours is a small world,' he said, his face pale. 'We pick up a – a placement here and there. You'd be surprised how many times our paths cross.' And in the slight pause before he went on, Cate reflected that this was not what she'd call a straight answer. 'Yes, I knew her,' he said. 'A long time ago, though. Ancient history.'

Cate stared at him, trying to make sense of this. How could she have missed it? She'd have sworn neither he nor Loni had ever said a thing about knowing each other before. She'd never understand the English.

He seemed to be gauging her reaction and for a moment Cate thought he was about to say something else when the creak and groan of the old lift set up. It was beyond a joke, thought Cate; it was dangerous, the mechanism must be a hundred years old.

'I hope they service that lift,' said Fairhead, and she looked at him, startled at the echo of her thoughts. He almost smiled. 'I wouldn't want to lose Tiziano.'

But before Tiziano could appear, Michelle was in the doorway, her tanned, lined face framed by the untidy grey hair. She walked to the table then stood there fidgeting before suddenly pouring herself a tall glass, draining it, then pouring another.

'Jesus,' she said, and Cate could have sworn her hands were shaking as she poured. 'This is a mess, isn't it? Isn't it.' She looked around the room. 'What happens now?' She looked at Cate. 'Poor bitch,' she said roughly and for a moment Cate thought she was talking about her, only then she realized she meant Loni Meadows. Was this how Michelle expressed grief?

91

We have to make them feel safe, Luca had said. 'It's very sad, yes,' said Cate carefully. 'But you mustn't worry. We'll continue to do our best for you.' Out of the corner of her eye she saw Alec Fairhead turning away; he stood at the window, his back to them.

Tiziano wheeled in with a flourish. 'Evening,' he said cheerfully. Cate poured him water; Tiziano didn't drink at all. He had once told her that it was horrible, being drunk in a wheelchair. 'I used to do it, at the start,' he'd said, and the sudden cold distance in his eye had unnerved her, he was always so cheerful. 'You think you can do anything, just for a bit, then you remember that you can't,' he'd said. Now, she crouched beside him. She saw Per turn to watch them.

'This is awful,' she said in a quiet voice, in Italian.

'It is,' he agreed. Then in polite English, 'But I hear it means we'll be seeing a bit more of you, Cate. Every cloud has a silver lining, a nice English phrase.'

'A nice phrase for a cloudy country,' she said. 'Did Luca tell you? About my new – position?'

'Ginevra,' he said. 'She thinks you'll get ideas.' But he smiled again, to reassure her that he was joking. Ginevra; Cate really didn't want to get on the wrong side of Ginevra.

Michelle was staring at Alec Fairhead's back, as if planning something; to harass him into conversation, or shove him out of the window. Cate guessed he'd rather go out of the window; at the best of times Michelle could be hard work. Something about the Englishman's politeness seemed to provoke her particularly, as if she suspected him of making fun of her.

'Michelle thinks she was drunk,' said Tiziano softly, looking sideways at Cate. 'Loni was driving the Monster drunk, lost control, came off the road and ended up in the river.'

'Did they say that? The police?'

He shrugged. 'The police haven't talked to us.' He looked thoughtful. 'I wonder if they will?'

Cate stared at him. He smiled. 'No. I think it's her own theory.'

Tiziano and Michelle got along fine, thick as thieves some days. She'd written a little libretto for some music of his and he'd played it back to her one evening at the grand piano next door while she sang in her cigarette-roughened voice. You could see that evening that when she was young she'd have been pretty, maybe even beautiful. Her body had thickened; Cate had seen her out running, with her face set, in an attempt to stave it off. But she had surprisingly delicate calves and ankles, and under the features coarsened by age and a bit too much booze, her eyes were very clear, her mouth soft and sensuous. Not this evening, though; this evening her eyes were small and vindictive in the pouchy face, her mouth set. Michelle was prone to rage.

'People make up stories, don't they?' Tiziano

said thoughtfully. 'When things happen. Ask your friend the novelist.'

And they were both looking at Alec Fairhead's back, still turned on the room, when Tina appeared in the door like a ghost, willowy and pale and anxious. Fairhead turned as if he'd heard her come in, only Cate couldn't imagine he had; Tina moved like a ghost too. She looked so lost and frightened that Cate got to her feet, only Fairhead was there before her, a hand tentatively on the girl's shoulder. Girl – she was close to thirty. 'Are you all right?' she heard him whisper gently. Tina looked at him with swimming eyes as if she didn't know him. Looked down at his hand.

Not wanting to spy, Cate turned away quickly, gazing down at Tiziano, and her thoughts reverted to what he'd just said. 'What do you think?' she said, 'About her being drunk?'

'She wasn't a drinker, is what I think,' said Tiziano, staring straight ahead, and he was right. 'Loni Meadows was a control freak, didn't you see her at dinner every night? She wouldn't refuse the wine, but she would only ever sip. Never refilled her glass herself, like a drinker would. No drink, no drugs, is my theory, though she'd act all tipsy if required.' He reflected. 'And snort a line to show willing, only she'd never get addicted. A charmed life – until now.' Cate frowned.

He looked up. 'Do I sound like I didn't like her?' Cate met his gaze, saying nothing. 'Well, maybe I didn't,' he said meditatively. 'She had her favourites,

94

and then there was the rest of us. I don't imagine I'm the only one.'

The gong sounded from the foot of the stairs.

No sign of Luca. It was going to be a long night.

CHAPTER 7

As Sandro let himself into the building in which Luisa and he had spent their entire married life, he fumbled with the lock, his hands stupidly clumsy. He realized that he was nervous. Once inside he pressed the illuminated button of the timed stair light and just stood there a moment, gazing around himself in search of reassurance. There was the scuffed and cracking plaster – eighteen years since it was last refurbished. There were the electricity meters, the postboxes, a bicycle. He didn't know whose bicycle it was.

He inserted a tiny key into the postbox marked Cellini T Venturelli. Not all women used their unmarried names, although most did; Luisa had proudly used his name for the first fifteen years of their marriage, then started using hers again, around the time her mother died. She said it was her last link with her parents, and Sandro had been fine with it. He knew how close Luisa had been to her mother.

The postbox was empty, but then he had expected it to be. Luisa generally collected the post these days; that was fine with him too. She had her private correspondence, he had his. They would never open each other's letters, would they? Had it been since the testing had started, the letters from the hospital with their shiny cellophane windows? She always wanted to open those on her own; sometimes she showed them to him, sometimes she didn't.

Suddenly Sandro was overcome by a desire not only to rip open those horrible letters but to take Luisa's strong pale face between his hands and hold it up close to his own and make her tell him everything. Not just the test results, not just Frollini, but did she love him? Had he been a disappointment to her? No more politeness, no more respectful silence. I love you. I want to know. Why couldn't he just say that?

Was she really going to New York on Monday morning? On the stairs he paused at the thought and leaned heavily against the cold wall. All that way, over a wide dark ocean, to a place where terrorists flew planes into tall buildings. It frightened him: Luisa so far out of sight; Luisa in a foreign hotel room, a place where he couldn't turn over at night and put his face against her shoulder.

He barely paused at the door before pushing it open; the thought that he might press his ear against it first entered his head only briefly. The hall was dark, and it was only just warm inside; he knew straight away that she wasn't there.

One thing Sandro had always known was how to be a man; how to be silent in the face of fear, how to keep going when things grew dark and uncertain. Being a man, he had to admit, was not always the right approach, but it was something, and now it appeared to have deserted him. All around him the apartment told him that he was alone, that he could no longer rely on the Luisa he had married to stand beside him.

He knew that he should put down his bag and go into the kitchen and set a pan to boil for a bowl of pasta. He could call Luisa on her mobile and ask where she was, when she'd be home; he could even ask her to come back because he needed to talk to her; that was what Giuli would say. Call her, idiot. But what remained of the man inside him, it appeared, would not allow Sandro to do that.

And so when, a good ten minutes later, Luisa's key turned in the lock he was still standing there in the hall in his coat, bag in hand, drained of any kind of volition. Was it just tiredness? He'd been up very early. That, anyway, was the face he presented to Luisa.

She was alone; there was that, at least. What had he expected? Of course she was alone.

'What are you standing there like that for?' Luisa said, frowning, hanging up her coat. She had make-up on; it looked better on her than it had on Giuli. Dark eyes, strong mouth; she'd always had good skin.

'Sorry, *cara*,' he said, fumbling with his own coat. 'Worn out; maybe I'm coming down with something. Just got back.' Luisa eyed him narrowly, and

98

he regretted the suggestion he might be under the weather. She'd think it was a bid to keep her at home. 'I was going to put on some pasta,' he said.

With a tut Luisa bustled past him, and he smelled a gust of her scent. Like a Pavlov's dog, he felt himself submit to her presence.

'I've already eaten,' she said in exasperation, turning the tap to fill a saucepan, her gloves still on. 'I thought you were coming later?'

'Yeah, well,' he said, 'Giuli – well, I got Giuli to take over.' He wasn't going to say it had been Giuli's idea; he wished it hadn't been, now. 'I'll do that, you sit down.' Gently he edged her away from the sink, set the pan on the stove. He wasn't hungry at all; he could see that this new situation required a new approach from him, and this was all he could think of.

'I wanted to see you.' He hesitated, thinking of what he really wanted to say, and not saying it. 'You're going away. It's so – so sudden.'

Luisa subsided into her chair, pulling off her gloves. 'And I'm at work all tomorrow,' she said warily. 'You know that, don't you?'

'Sure,' said Sandro, keeping his voice even. 'If you don't think it'll wear you out.' In frustration he turned away from her and took a garlic clove from a small terracotta dish, peeled it, chopped it, crushed it. Set the frying pan on with oil, pressed a fistful of spaghetti down in the boiling water. Even Sandro knew how to make *spaghetti all'olio aglio e peperoncino*; even the most old-fashioned of men had that in their repertoire along with *pasta pomodoro*.

'There's always Sunday,' she said vaguely, sounding distracted. Turning to observe her, he saw she was looking for something in her handbag, a half-smile on her face.

And before he could stop himself, Sandro found himself saying, 'Giuli saw you having lunch with Frollini.' And heard the accusation in his voice. Luisa looked up at him, startled.

'She saw me?' she said. If she hadn't been his wife he might have had a better idea of whether the confused expression she offered to him held a trace of guilt, but as it was, he had no idea.

'In Rivoire,' he said shortly, turning back to tip some chilli into the frying garlic. The room filled with the sweet, spicy scent. He turned the gas off carefully, not wanting to burn it. 'Any parsley?' he said. Luisa reached into the fridge and gave him a handful of sprigs.

'Well, yes,' she said, her face hidden again, back down into the depths of her handbag. 'It was quiet,' she said, 'and we had the trip to discuss.' She looked up at him. 'He's a busy man; we had to make time.'

Sandro didn't believe in coincidence. 'Looking for something in there?' he asked. He wanted his voice to be easy and kind, but all he could hear was petulance. He turned to the stove, took the pan, drained the pasta, tossed it sizzling into the oil and garlic and chilli, set it on the table, took out a bowl and a fork and a napkin, poured himself a glass of last night's Morellino. Touched none of the food, but drank the wine.

'Just my mobile,' said Luisa. 'I must have left it in the shop.' She settled the bag in her lap, both hands on top of it and either accidentally or deliberately shielding its contents from him, and finally she met Sandro's gaze.

'What's going on, Sandro?' she asked quietly. 'Is something the matter?'

And now his opportunity presented itself so baldly, Sandro wasn't ready.

His mobile rang in the hiatus, and he took it out, stared at the screen; Luca Gallo, it said. Damn the man; he let it ring a few times, then pressed reject.

'The Bellagamba case,' he blurted, not having the faintest idea what he was going to say next. 'It's a worry. The girl's in bad company.'

Luisa stared him down, not buying it. 'And you're the man to sort her out?'

'What do you mean by that?' said Sandro. On an empty stomach, the wine was not helping matters one bit.

'I mean,' said Luisa, hands still resting on top of her bag, 'that you're behaving like an idiot. If there's something the matter, then tell me, don't just sit there getting drunk and making snide remarks.'

'All right,' said Sandro, setting the glass down harder than he'd intended to and slopping wine on the tablecloth. 'Are you really going to New

101

York with Frollini? Are you –' he hesitated, then took the plunge. Too late. 'Is there something going on between you?'

There was a long, cold silence.

Slowly Luisa stood up, setting her bag on the table between them, brushing at her front for invisible crumbs. 'Something going on?' and the mocking note in her voice cooled his blood instantly.

'I – I –' Sandro felt the wine fumble with his tongue. Felt his own stupidity like a fog in which he was blundering. Because he didn't know, he didn't even know what he was asking. He looked at her helplessly, but she didn't take pity on him, not this time.

'Do you think I am going to deny anything?' Luisa said, holding herself quite still. 'To provide you with witnesses or proof, to show you my appointment book in New York or bring Frollini in here to explain precisely the nature of our relationship?' Pale and terrifying and handsome, she held his gaze, and the worst of it was, he was still thinking, she could be bluffing, this could be a cover.

'That would be fun, wouldn't it?'

He said nothing; she didn't want him to speak; he stared at the congealing pasta, the stained tablecloth. Her handbag sat there, inviting him to up-end it, searching for clues. He averted his eyes.

Luisa leaned down to make him look at her, and when he raised his head she spoke. 'Do you know what they say?' she said. 'That counselling they insisted I have? They said it can have unexpected side-effects, this kind of illness. The thought of your own – mortality, or something. Women up sticks and travel the world, some of them. Run off with younger men; take up painting or write novels. Of course, some of them just sit at home and wait to die. But I'm not going to die, Sandro.'

'No,' he said helplessly. 'I know you're not.' But he didn't know, not yet. Was he more afraid that she would leave him for Frollini, than that she would die?

Luisa stared at him, then swept the bag off the table and into her arms. He wished she had not done that.

'No, Sandro,' she said. 'Do you know what I think?' He bowed his head. 'I think a little time apart wouldn't do us any harm.' And she was gone, closing the bedroom door behind her.

Within ten minutes of Sandro leaving, Giuli had managed to make herself less visible. Her first worry had been that if she stayed in the corner on her own the Indian doorman or one of the waiters would have her down as a hooker and have her out on her ear, but either they didn't notice, or they didn't care. She'd ordered a Coke from a waiter and he'd just taken her money and brought her the drink on his grubby tray. And in her jeans and biker boots, it could be that these days Giuli actually looked like a normal girl, in the right light.

All the same, when a pair of English girls sat

down at the other end of the banquette, giggling stupidly on hash, she edged into their orbit, for camouflage. One of them looked at her with fleeting distaste, as if she was trying to sell them something. Not me, baby, she thought, keeping her temper.

Giuli concentrated on sipping her drink slowly, gazing into the distance as though thinking deep and stoned thoughts. What she was really thinking about, as she kept Carlotta in her sights, was what she had seen as she zipped past Rivoire on the *motorino*, wobbling as she slowed, catching a glimpse of Luisa's familiar profile.

Next door to her place of work, sitting in the window having lunch with her boss. Of course she wasn't having an affair, and Sandro would know that by now. He'll have talked it over with her, she'll have laughed him out of the kitchen. Giuli felt a kind of terror; was this what it was like, she wondered belatedly, for all those kids she'd used to envy, the kids with a house and two parents, when they hear them arguing and wonder if they're going to get divorced?

She and Frollini, they'd known each other thirty years or more, hadn't they? It occurred to Giuli that Luisa had known her boss as long as she'd known Sandro; since she was not much more than a kid. And the illness had changed her; it had slimmed her, made her eyes bigger and darker, given her a kind of restlessness she'd never had before. Had her boss looked at her and seen her

104

differently, all of a sudden? Had she looked at him? With his tan and his beautiful suits and the big gold ring on his little finger, so rich, so comfortable, so easy.

This was crazy. Giuli squeezed her eyes shut to stop her train of thought and when she opened them Carlotta was on her feet. She wove her way downstairs alone, leaving her bags and coat on her seat, and Giuli, taking hers with her, followed the girl without attracting a single glance. Ladies' room, she guessed; and not before time.

Which had turned out to be behind the tiny leopard print-hung entrance and not so much a ladies' room as a smoking room; a carpeted lobby with two gold-tiled washbasins and a lavatory cubicle off the far end, the whole set-up perfectly decent, and with Carlotta Bellagamba perched dreamily on the washbasins, and swinging her legs. Smoking a joint.

Bingo.

These kids. The thought of Luisa and Sandro nagged at Giuli, soured her stomach.

The girl smiled sleepily at Giuli from under her curls, and Giuli smiled back. And when Carlotta held the joint up to her vertically, she knew she shouldn't say anything, but she did.

'No thanks,' Giuli said, still smiling. 'It's not good for you, that stuff.'

Carlotta shrugged, and slid off the washbasin. 'Feels good, though,' she said, taking a deep drag. The carelessly rolled paper glowed bright; the girl didn't even know how to roll a joint properly. But Giuli wasn't going to point that out to her.

'Maybe,' said Giuli, then shut up. Wondered what Sandro was going to say to the parents tomorrow; whether he was going to take the money and wash his hands of the girl.

'That your boyfriend?' she said eventually, nodding upstairs. Carlotta flushed. 'Kind of,' she said. 'Gorgeous, isn't he?' Giuli shrugged.

From behind the door came the cascade of a faulty flush, and one of the English girls emerged with a blush of scarlet on her cheeks, like a doll. She brushed past them without washing her hands.

Giuli nodded towards the cubicle but Carlotta Bellagamba shook her head, holding up the joint. Giuli had no choice but to go in, locking the door behind her; after two, three giant Cokes, it was just as well. But when she came out, Carlotta wasn't there any more.

At the gold-tiled basin Giuli washed her hands with deliberate care, eyeing herself in the mirror. She didn't want just to rush back out there and blow what cover she had.

The lower room was empty when she emerged and in the entrance the Indian doorman was sitting absorbed in his cash box, counting notes into a cloth bag. It was nearly two; if Giuli went back up the spiral staircase and found Carlotta and the boys gone, she'd have wasted valuable time. She grabbed her jacket, her helmet, and slung her bag over her shoulder and edged outside.

It was bitterly cold; the bare trees of the little piazza were silvery with frost. Where were they?

'They haven't come out,' said the voice at her shoulder. It was Sandro, leaning against the wall.

'You're not warm enough,' he added, holding out a hand for her helmet, so she could get her jacket on properly. She didn't know whether to hug him for being there or give him grief for treating her like a kid.

There was movement behind them, voices in the doorway, and Sandro took her by the elbow, moving them both aside.

'Good move,' he said in a low voice, 'leaving before them. Clever girl.'

Behind her Giuli heard the guttural accent of the man in the grey leather jacket. '*Alla prossima*,' he was saying. 'Any time, baby.' Slurring, insistent.

'How long have you been out here?' hissed Giuli. 'You did go home, didn't you? You talked things over with Luisa?'

'I did,' said Sandro shortly. 'Look, I just came back to make sure you were all right. And the girl, of course.'

'I was going to follow her home,' said Giuli, keeping her voice down. 'On the *motorino*.'

'You'd die of exposure,' muttered Sandro. 'And you're worn out, look at you.' Giuli grimaced, remembering the shadows under her eyes in the cloakroom mirror. 'I'll follow her back in the car. Only –' he stopped.

'Only what?' Giuli had her shoulders hunched

against the cold and even in the lovely padded jacket Luisa had given her she couldn't stop shivering.

'Only I might want you to take this over a bit from tomorrow. I promised him – Bellagamba – promised him we'd come by and update him.'

So he was going to stick with it – or she was. She said nothing; Sandro mistook her silence for reluctance. 'I know tomorrow's Saturday,' he said apologetically. 'I'll make it up to you. I just want Bellagamba to know you're part of the deal.'

Giuli felt her face break into a smile. She could do it, she wanted to say, she could. She restrained herself, as Sandro had taught her to do. 'Why?'

'Well, for a start you've done most of the legwork,' he said, hesitating. 'And something's come up. Another job. At least, I think it has.'

'What?'

'I'm not sure yet,' said Sandro. 'I've got a garbled message from Luca Gallo on my mobile.' He was looking over her shoulder, distant. 'Says it's urgent. Says he needs to see me tomorrow.'

His gaze shifted over her shoulder, and turning her head a little Giuli saw the three boys and Carlotta on the street. From behind them came the sound of a bolt being shot across the door. 'Chucking-out time,' said Sandro. It was after two.

'You get on your bike,' Sandro said, 'I'll follow the girl home.'

They walked together as far as Giuli's *motorino*; he handed her the helmet. 'Go home and get some

108

sleep now.' And before turning towards the little car he and Luisa had used to come and visit her in rehab together, he put a hand to her cheek. Then he hunched his shoulders and went.

As she swung around the corner, heading for home, Giuli looked back and saw his silhouette as he sat solitary and motionless at the wheel, watching the kids on the pavement. *You'll be OK*, she promised silently. *Everything's going to be OK.*

The frost that glittered on the city pavements also dusted the trees and gates and fences out through the suburbs and up into the dark hills. Down in the Maremma, the icy tributaries of the rivers that criss-crossed the land were beginning to freeze at the edges, and high up where Orfeo sat under a waxing moon the clear night sky had lowered the temperature to eight degrees below zero, and hardened the rutted fields to stone.

Down in the steep-sided valley, on the sharp left-hand bend where Loni Meadows had come off the road, the deep ruts the heavy vehicle's careering descent had carved in the earth had set like rock. It had gone almost all the way down, into the river; it had taken the crew of the tow-truck hours to haul it out of there and now the chaos of crushed vegetation and churned mud was the only obvious evidence of Loni Meadows's headlong passage, in the dark, to her death.

In Orfeo itself all illumination save the security lights that twinkled deceptively softly at even intervals around the castle's massive fortified walls had been extinguished, but in her new bed, in her small, bare room, Cate could not sleep. As she half-dozed, snatches of the day's events – faces, expressions, things said and left unsaid – replayed themselves in her head, in and out of order.

At one point she started up, halfway through the fragment of a nightmare, and shouted 'No!' before lying back down. She drifted, half-awake, half-dreaming, in and out of time, seeing a rumpled bed, a green silk blouse, the big ugly car outside a hotel and finally only Dottoressa Meadows's bright, wicked face, hearing her sharp, light, mocking voice before she fell, at last, into sleep.

CHAPTER 8

'So what about the husband?'

It occurred to Cate that Ginevra, speaking these words in a gruff undertone to Mauro, might have forgotten she was there. She was standing at the work surface in the little cold pantry off the kitchen, keeping her head down and following orders. Which in this case were to make the paste for the evening's *crostini toscani*. She'd been doing it for forty minutes or so, since coming down not long after 7.30 and taking Ginevra by surprise. 'Oh my God,' the old cook had said, clasping a hand to her flushed chest at the sight of Cate in the doorway. 'You gave me a start. What are you doing here so early?'

Saturday evening was Ginevra's evening off, and the dinner was a buffet prepared in advance: Cate had thought, more fool her, that what with all the goings on her offer to help would be welcome. Last night, sitting at the silent dinner table, hopping up and down clearing the table as well as trying to make some kind of conversation with the guests, Cate had felt sorry for Ginevra and Nicki, knowing how much extra work there would

111

be behind the kitchen door. And to be frank, it had been torture trying to play the host, under the circumstances.

The bed had been comfortable, the room warm, but Cate had woken early after her troubled night. She had felt a sense of doom, of bad news awaiting. One of her dreams had featured the barking of the dogs from Ginevra's farm, and now wide awake, she could still hear them baying in the pre-dawn light. All she had wanted was a bit of human company, to make the world normal again.

To get to the kitchen Cate had to come down the quiet, dark back staircase, found herself tiptoeing in fact, so as not to wake anyone, past the closed and silent door to Luca's office and apartments, out into the castle's courtyard, grey and silent in the early light, and round the back to the kitchen door.

And it had looked like she wasn't welcome. It had seemed to Cate then that her new status – and she wished she had a clearer idea of just what that status was – wasn't the only thing annoying Ginevra; the cook was also unhappy about having Cate breathing down her neck. She'd wondered what time Ginevra got up herself; she was in here by seven every morning, and never mind the ten-minute walk from the farmhouse where she lived.

And it had been a cold one, this morning. Off to the north-west, Cate had noticed, looking out over the frosted fields in the blue-grey dawn, there was a bank of heavy cloud waiting on the horizon.

Snow moving down from the Alps, her radio had told her.

Nicki didn't get in until 8.30; Ginevra had set Cate to making the paste as an alternative to sending her back to bed; a slow, time-consuming job requiring plenty of fine chopping. Onion, carrot, celery, oregano, chicken livers, oil and wine.

When Mauro had come in she'd known it was him before he spoke from the boots being stamped on the mat, the heavy tread, the cold whiff of fields that came in with him. Cate had known without having to look that he was crossing the kitchen to the big two-litre bottle of wine that stood beside the stove; she'd heard the glug of the tumbler being filled.

They'd stood in silence for a bit, a few muttered complaints about the cold, then they'd started.

'I suppose we'll have to clear her stuff,' Ginevra had grumbled first. 'I suppose someone'll have to take it away.'

He'd grunted. Ginevra had gone on. 'What did the *Commissario* say about that? Anything?'

At the mention of the policeman Cate had paused in her careful chopping, and listened.

'Nope,' the gardener had said with satisfaction. 'I think they're done with the whole business, don't you? Foreigners are always driving into trees and killing themselves, it's a pain in the backside for them, our poor lads having to clear up the mess.'

And it was then that Ginevra said, with something malicious in her voice, 'What about the husband?'

113

For some reason the question came as more of a shock to Cate than anything she'd heard since the news of Loni Meadows's death. Husband? There was a husband. Well.

There was another grunt from Mauro. 'What about him?' he said with contempt.

'Well,' Ginevra said cautiously. 'I suppose he'll come out and collect her stuff, will he?'

'I don't suppose he's in any hurry,' said Mauro. 'I mean – it wasn't what we'd call a marriage, was it?' He laughed sourly, and for a moment Ginevra joined him.

'Do you think he knew?' said Ginevra after a bit. 'About her?'

'Probably,' said Mauro with bitterness. 'Different rules for their sort.'

They were sitting at the table now; Cate could hear the scrape of chairs, and Mauro's tumbler being set down on the wood. Refilled. Ginevra herself would be drinking peach nectar, her sickly secret vice. She ordered the stuff by the case, on the Trust's bill, but no one ever drank it but her. The glasses chinked.

'He said she didn't die straight away,' said Mauro, and Cate put a hand to her mouth in the chilly pantry.

'The *Commissario*. Said it. Said it'd have been the cold, finished her off.'

Ginevra made a grudging sound. *'Brutto,'* she said. 'Nasty.'

'She had it coming,' said Mauro, his voice slowed

up, almost thoughtful-sounding under the influence of the wine.

'Oh yes,' said Ginevra. 'She did.'

As the silence persisted, the chicken livers still between her fingers, Cate realized that sooner or later Mauro and Ginevra would work out she was there, and she had no idea what she would do then. And as if on cue her stomach, empty for close to twelve hours, rumbled loudly.

Suddenly Ginevra was in the doorway to the pantry glaring down at her. Cate got to her feet smiling, as though she'd heard nothing, and presented Ginevra with the wooden board loaded with its cargo of fresh, neat piles; glossy livers, carrot, celery, parsley.

'*Mamma mia*,' she said brightly, 'I'm starving.'

Behind Ginevra the door banged and in came Nicki, with Anna-Maria hard on her heels, overcoated and grumbling.

But Ginevra didn't turn at the sound; instead she leaned down to Cate's ear. 'Now you listen, my girl,' she said in a low, fierce voice; 'we both know what you heard. And if you breathe a word –'

Cate shook her head, mesmerized. Ginevra went on, muttering fiercely. 'She did have it coming, there's no one would disagree with that. There's not one of us – and I mean none – she hasn't accused of stealing or lying or drinking on the job, except you, and she'd have got around to it, believe me. Mauro, Gallo, Nicki – accused Nicki of stealing an earring!' Her eyes bulged with outrage.

'A single earring! And it had got caught in the bedspread all along.'

Cate's words fell over each other in an attempt to placate Ginevra. 'No – I – I wouldn't –' Then something crept into her mind, and wouldn't leave. 'I didn't think – well, it's just – he did have a row with her, didn't he? That very day.'

'What are you talking about?' said Ginevra, hands on hips, then something dawned. 'Don't be silly. Like I said, not a day passed she didn't row with someone.'

'And then he was out all day,' said Cate, half to herself. 'Hauling cows out of a stream, he said.'

Ginevra's eyes were black as currants. 'Oh, you stupid girl, of course he was. Besides, she was alive and kicking the whole day, wasn't she? He doesn't need an alibi, he wouldn't –' She looked momentarily bewildered, and when she spoke again her voice had lost some of its certainty. 'It was an accident. Well, even if he did need an alibi, yes, he was off with the cows, then he came back in time for the bitch to bawl him out all over again, for helping a friend in need, as if she'd have understood. But one thing's for certain, when she drove into the river and killed herself, he was tucked up in bed beside me, snoring his head off.' Looking her age, Ginevra took a breath.

'Look,' she hissed, 'he thinks there's something funny about it. We all do. Something not right. But it's nothing to do with us.' And her small black eyes glittered.

'Did he tell that to the *Commissario*, then?' asked Cate. Ginevra turned her back by way of answer.

At the stove Anna-Maria and Nicki were still grumbling between themselves, but looking over the old cook's shoulder Cate saw they were beginning to take notice, and Ginevra turned to glare at them.

'And what are you looking at?' she snapped.

'He's said I'm not to clean the rooms,' said Anna-Maria. 'Some story about not wanting anything thrown away by mistake? Couldn't make head nor tail of it. No one's complained about me, have they?'

There was a story, Cate had always thought it a myth, that Anna-Maria had incinerated a piece of artwork in progress that one of the guests had left out on their kitchen table; something made out of sprouting green potatoes and bleached chicken bones. Or was it congealed blood? The story varied.

Anna-Maria was still complaining. 'Well, I don't know, they'll be pigsties by the time I get back in. The girl from Florida's freaking out already. The Englishman doesn't know how to keep anything clean – but then, they never do, the English. Don't know a dishcloth when one's laid out for them.' Cate shushed her; if she was caught badmouthing the guests so loudly she'd be out on her ear. 'And that northerner – Swedish, is he?'

'Norwegian,' said Cate.

'Well, whatever he is, he hasn't let me inside his

117

door in a week anyway, just glared at me the first few days, then wouldn't answer when I knocked.' She plonked herself at the table, puffed with outrage.

Nicki was hanging up her coat. 'Mr Gallo said you can start on the library,' she soothed. 'He didn't say he was going to dock your pay, either, so come on. No harm done. Oooh,' she moved on, without a pause, eyeing the slice of *pandoro* that Cate had cut herself, 'can I have some of that?'

Nicki was greedy, for a skinny little thing. Cate cut another piece of the sweet yellow yeast-cake and pushed the plate across the table to the girl, who parked herself at a chair and began to wolf it. And what with Mauro looking like thunder at the sink, Nicki stuffing her face and babbling and Anna-Maria still padded in her layers of coats and taking up as much room as a water-buffalo at the table, the kitchen suddenly seemed very crowded. Cate stood up.

'I'll check on the dining room before I go, shall I?' she said.

'You'd better,' said Ginevra, giving her a beady look. 'I'm sure we didn't have a proper chance to clear yesterday. And before you go where?'

'Well, to check in with Lu – with Mr Gallo,' said Cate cautiously. 'If he's up and about. Anna-Maria?'

'Well, I don't know about up and about,' said the cleaner huffily. 'He just leaned out the window to shout at me, and if you ask me he was still wearing what he'd slept in.' She sniffed.

118

Poor Luca, thought Cate. What was Anna-Maria's problem? His alternative lifestyle, maybe; poor Luca, fighting this lot's prejudices all these years. He must be made of strong stuff. Cate swallowed the half-cup of lukewarm coffee Ginevra had grudgingly poured her, and left.

By the light of day the dining room looked sad; Ginevra was right, they had all wanted to get out of there in a bit too much of a hurry, last night. The table was smeared and there were crumbs on the floor, so Cate got the cleaning materials from the cupboard in the kitchen and set to.

It might look sad this morning, but last night had been something else. Once out of the library, with its dark, echoing corners, where voices seemed muffled and whispering acceptable, and into the modern wood-and-glass dining room, the guests had simply stopped talking.

Whether it was the cheerful lighting, the effort of looking – or not looking – each other in the eye around the great oval table, or the fact that Loni Meadows's absence was most unavoidable here, her place literally empty, Cate couldn't have said. The memory of the night before – the *Dottoressa* in green silk telling a dirty story about Fellini; *I knew him, you know*, she'd said, sweeping the table with her flirtatious gaze, so you couldn't tell who her look was meant for.

She had her favourites; who'd said that? Probably Tiziano. Per, Tina; they were her favourites.

Last night they hadn't even complained about

the *baccalà*, traditionally the most disliked meal of the week, Friday's fish supper, salt cod stewed in sauce. They hadn't got noisily drunk and bickered or pontificated or embarked on impromptu poetry readings, although Per had worked his way steadily and without obvious effect through two bottles of red wine and Michelle had been woozy on prosecco even before she sat down. Tina had drunk glass after glass of water, as if purging something from her system, and pushed the food around her plate.

'Did they say – did she suffer?' Cate had heard Tina say at one point, in her high, light voice, looking around with spaced eyes. The question had seemed deeply shocking; certainly no one had answered.

Anna-Maria thought there was something wrong with Tina. Her room smelled bad, said Anna-Maria; it smelled sour. Maybe she was ill. Maybe she was just unhappy.

In fact, no one had eaten much at all; when Cate had risen to help Nicki clear she had noted that most of the plates had hardly been touched. Tiziano, bless him, had cleared his, but even he had been far from his usual boisterous self. Each one of them had seemed determined to keep their thoughts to themselves. Why? The thought popped into Cate's head that they were afraid to say the wrong thing. Afraid to incriminate themselves.

Cate had set out the tray of brandy and liqueurs, and Per and Alec Fairhead had poured themselves big slugs in silence; it was only after his third, or maybe fourth, that Per had sat up and said something, his voice ragged. The first thing he'd said all through dinner. 'Where was she going? Does anyone know where she was going?'

At the door, Cate hadn't been able to see their faces in the sudden silence. Then Michelle had said, 'Jeez, Per. We all know. Don't we?' And there'd been movement then, clearing of throats and chairs moving. Their cue to go.

Under the table collecting crumbs and warm with the effort, Cate sat back on her haunches and for the first time she really thought about what Mauro and Ginevra had said.

She deserved it.

Really? Did they really think that? What could Loni Meadows have done to deserve to die? Smashed to pieces; Cate closed her eyes as she thought about that. Her face, all bruised and broken. The long, delicate fingers, the fine ankles, caught in a horrible snarl of metal and rubber. The life leaving her; how long would it have taken? Face down in the river, or face pressed against the frozen earth.

Where had she been going? On the road to Pozzo Basso. Even Cate knew Loni Meadows made regular, late-night visits to Pozzo, Thursdays, Fridays, returning at all hours. And once, early one morning a month or so back, Cate herself had seen the Monster in town, parked outside a hotel.

Tiziano had been the last to leave, as he often was; Cate supposed the wheelchair must have

121

taught him patience. She'd noticed over the weeks that he liked the others to go ahead of him out of most situations; she assumed because he didn't like feeling he was getting in the way, blocking the door, people exchanging words over his head. Though he never showed it.

She thought somehow, though, that the night of Loni's death he had not been the last to go. Had he been upset by something too? Had he been tired? She couldn't remember.

'Am I keeping you up?' he'd asked gently, there in the dining room. Cate supposed she might have yawned; certainly at that point she'd been thinking longingly of her bed.

She'd shaken her head, with a sleepy laugh. 'It's been a long day.'

'You're telling me,' Tiziano had said. 'And you're a late bird at the best of times, I know you. Always another little job to get done. It'll be even worse now you're living in, won't it? Always on duty.' He'd held out a hand, taken hers. 'Don't work yourself too hard, sweetheart.'

Cate had felt embarrassed and pleased at the same time, shaking her head. 'I'm lazy, really,' she'd said. 'You should see me when the alarm goes off.'

He'd rested his eyes on her then, the hint of a smile at the corner of his lips. 'What time did you get to bed last night?' he'd said. 'You didn't leave here till gone eleven.'

'Didn't I?' She'd looked at her toes.

Getting to her feet in the dining room, which was now pristine, even by Ginevra's exacting standards, Cate flushed at the memory.

So Tiziano kept an eye on her, did he?

She thought of the Venetian sitting at the window of the apartment that had been modified for him, on the ground floor. Sound-proofed, with a piano, ramps and a customized bathroom. Sitting at the window and watching.

She had indeed left at about eleven. The dining room had been empty, Ginevra and Nicki gone. Why did it suddenly seem important to Cate to get those things straight? Loni Meadows had died in a car accident, simple as that.

But it had been her last night on earth, and it had to matter.

And now Cate wondered if there was anyone out there asking questions about Loni Meadows's death, or if she was going to have to ask them herself.

By the time Luca Gallo phoned him back, somewhere around nine in the morning, Sandro was one coffee down, the paper open in front of him, and he already knew what the man was going to say.

If Luisa had been there, she'd have made him explain; she'd have helped him sort his thoughts.

'*What* do you know, exactly?'

She would have challenged him, looking over his shoulder at the newspaper spread out in front of them. They'd be sitting at the kitchen table together; he'd have gone out early for the paper and some pastries, Luisa would have had coffee going on the stove, ready for his return.

This is all wrong, Sandro would have said, not meaning him and Luisa because in an ideal world that conversation last night would never have happened. No, he'd have tapped the paper and said, *This is all wrong. I knew something funny was going on, back then, last summer.*

He was hungry, but he didn't feel like eating.

Luisa and he hadn't exchanged a word this morning. When Sandro had got back at nearly three in the morning from following Carlotta Bellagamba safely home to Galluzzo, let himself quietly into the apartment and come to bed, Luisa's overnight bag had been inside the bedroom door, packed and ready to go, even though she wasn't leaving for New York until Monday morning.

When Luisa left for work, close to eight, Sandro had been lying silent in the bed, feigning sleep; it seemed to him that if he didn't know what to say to her, he'd be best not saying anything at all. But he couldn't sleep, however much he needed it; as he lay there a hundred questions pressed in on him. The nagging, insinuating ones about Luisa's trip (*Why didn't she tell me before? How long has she known? Has she got a visa, is her passport up to date?*) he pushed aside, but others crowded in on him. And what most of them boiled down to was simple: was he ever going to be any good at this?

So, within minutes of the door closing behind Luisa, Sandro was out of bed, his head thumping, and by 8.30 he was in the Oltrarno. Not for him this morning the marble and glass of Rivoire, and the knowing glances of the barmen and Luisa just around the corner. He had texted Giuli to tell her he was sitting in a dingy bar called the Caffé Medici, off the Piazza Santo Spirito, not far from Giuli's rooms in the Via della Chiesa. It was a place where no one would come up to Sandro, clap him on the shoulder and ask how Luisa was. At the bar one of the square's glassy-eyed and shivering addicts gulped *caffè latte* and in his booth Sandro was reading *La Nazione*.

The story was on page three, accompanied by two photographs. Sandro read it once, twice, then a third time, moving his lips at certain words, and finally he laid the paper flat on the table.

> *The fifty-five-year-old woman found dead in the wreckage of her car in a ravine in the province of Grosseto yesterday morning has been identified as Dottoressa Leona Meadows-Mascarello, Director of the Orfeo Trust's celebrated Creative Arts Program, based for twenty-two years in the Castello Orfeo. American-born Dottoressa Meadows-Mascarello, who was apparently the car's only occupant, had been the program's director for seven months. She was married to Giuliano Mascarello, the well-known human rights lawyer based in Florence, who has been*

informed of his wife's demise. It is thought that the accident occurred in the early hours of Friday morning, and no other vehicle has so far been traced in connection with the incident.

In Sandro's head something shifted, turned, presented itself to him. An old trick his brain had learned over decades of police work, a trick of information retrieval; you think a case is dead and gone and never mattered much anyway, but when required that little drawer in the brain's filing cabinet pops open, just like that. When he first received the message yesterday morning that Gallo had called, he'd have had trouble telling anyone the name of the employee he'd been hired by the Orfeo Trust to do a background check on. Now he could have told the bored-looking barman of the Medici – at present trying to eject the *latte*-drinking junkie – the woman's birthday; he could have told him the colour of her eyes.

Leona Meadows, known as Loni, architect; sculptor in mixed media; cultural critic. Born 4 July 1952, Topeka, Kansas. Studied architecture at Columbia University and the Sorbonne, Paris, arrived Florence 1972 to study for a doctorate in Fine Art at the Accademia di Belle Arti, married Giuliano Mascarello 1979, Visiting Fellowship at the Courtauld Institute, London, 1981–2, and Fashion Institute of Technology, New York, 2000–2001. Work exhibited San Francisco, Rome, Florence, Nice, London. Excellent credit rating,

126

clean driving licence, no bankruptcy proceedings pending, no criminal record. No children.

Died 22 February 2008.

Eyes: blue.

What had he learned about her? Only what he'd been asked to learn, that her CV, that all her references, dates and qualifications checked out, all the institutions she said she'd attended had records of her attendance, all the galleries named had in fact exhibited her work when she said they had. That her eyes were indeed blue; the one superfluous judgement Sandro had made, in fact, looking at the passport-sized photograph attached to the sheaf of papers sent to him by Luca Gallo last summer, was that Loni Meadows's eyes were the most mesmerizingly blue that he'd ever seen.

The credit check and criminal records he'd put through on the sly, calling in favours among his ex-colleagues at Porta al Prato. People did it all the time.

She died perhaps thirty hours ago, mused Sandro; so Luca Gallo, the Administrator of the Orfeo Trust, had called Sandro practically the moment he found out about the *Dottoressa*'s death.

All right, Sandro said to himself, *something's going on here*.

If Luisa had been there – but she wasn't, was she? And for the first time in weeks, perhaps months, in chemical response to the challenge Sandro felt the knot in his gut unclench, just fractionally. *There's something here.*

And it was then that Luca Gallo called; they spoke for approximately five minutes: having a better idea from the newspaper article of what this would be about, Sandro felt that his questions could wait. They arranged to meet at 10.30, at an address north of Santa Croce. Sandro hung up, then immediately dialled Carlotta Bellagamba's father. It didn't take long.

'Hey, boss.' The voice was cheerful, hoarse with lack of sleep; Giuli's voice. He looked up to see her at the bar, unbuttoning her coat, ordering coffee with a nod to the barman. 'This is my local, how'd you know?'

He hadn't known. 'Bit of a change of plan, Giuli,' he said.

CHAPTER 9

Standing under the trees, Cate watched Luca Gallo leave, the car's exhaust fumes clouding in the freezing air. All around her the landscape was silent, white with frost, and overhead the sky was still a lovely pale violet-blue.

At her back stood the towering grey bulk of the castle, watching for the approach of its enemies. From the top floor, thought Cate, you might be able to see as far as the river; you might be able to see down into that dip where Loni Meadows had died. Luca's car was out of sight now.

Cate was in charge. It was a kind of joke, wasn't it? As if she could be in charge of that lot in the kitchen, whispering and bickering and falling silent when she appeared. Not to mention the guests. But she had to take it seriously, even if they didn't. Luca trusted her.

When she had finished in the dining room earlier, Cate had hesitated at the kitchen door, apron in hand; she had been able to hear raised voices.

'Where was she off to, that's what I'd like to know.' Ginevra; her hands would be on her hips, lower lip stuck out.

'Off to the fancy man in Pozzo.' Mauro.

'What fancy man?' Nicki, dozy as ever; the others had all laughed at that.

Suddenly Cate hadn't wanted to listen any more, and she certainly hadn't wanted to open the door and have them all stare. She'd stuffed the apron in a drawer of the sideboard and left by the garden door.

She had crossed the frosted grass to the terrace where in summer the guests ate under a pergola, out through the hedge and round to the pretty brick gatehouse where Luca's office and apartment were. An unfamiliar little black car with a hire company logo on the driver's door had been parked on the gravel outside it. As she'd approached, the office door had opened and Luca had come out, carrying a stack of files; Cate had been startled to see that he was wearing a suit. She'd never seen him in anything but checked shirt and combat trousers, not even yesterday, when he had stood in front of them all in the dining room and told them the Director was dead.

'Caterina,' Luca had said, and sighed. 'Yes. Just a minute.' He'd locked the door and given her the key. 'I'm sorry about yesterday, Cate. I spent the whole evening on the phone, talking to the office in Baltimore. About advertising for a new Director, about arranging a new intern.'

'Oh,' Cate had said, surprised by the fact she hadn't felt particularly disappointed.

'It's all right,' he'd said, with a faint smile. 'I told

them there's no need for the time being. I told them you were an absolute treasure, and we need to hang on to you.'

Cate had smiled back uncomfortably. He'd patted her on the shoulder. 'I've got to go to Florence. Just for the morning, I hope. There's someone I've got to see.'

'Yes?'

He'd frowned, and she'd seen he was pondering how much he needed to tell her. 'Ah, a couple of people, actually.' He'd taken a deep breath. 'I need to see Dottoressa Meadows's husband.'

'He doesn't know yet?' Cate had been horrified.

'Oh, yes,' Luca had replied grimly, 'he knows. He – well. There are things that need to be discussed.'

'I see,' Cate had said, knowing when to shut up.

'You can manage, for the morning? Perhaps until early afternoon. There was a trip to Pienza planned for today, but I have cancelled the minibus; I assume no one will expect to be going. The guests will need to be told, of course; can you do that at the coffee assembly?' He'd looked at his watch. 'In half an hour? I really must go now.'

'Of course,' Cate had said, thinking of how little she wanted to see their averted, unhappy faces, or to pretend to be in charge.

'Just a few hours,' Gallo had said, as if he'd read her thoughts. 'I'll be back by mid-afternoon, at the latest.'

And the little black car with the logo on its door had gone.

131

Cate's phone jumped in her pocket; she had it on silent these days. It seemed more professional. Without getting it out, she knew it would be Vincenzo.

The library was empty when she laid out the coffee, and Cate wondered whether the guests might not bother to come at all today.

But when she returned ten minutes later with Ginevra's hard-baked *cantucci* – there'd be lawsuits one day, Luca had warned, holding his jaw and laughing, when someone finally broke a tooth on one – Tiziano was there, his chair parked by the long window. He could just see out; the sills were low enough here. She wondered how he kept his temper, sometimes; if she was in a wheelchair she'd always be raging at what she couldn't do. She came up to him with the plate of biscuits, and looking out of the window she could see Michelle and Tina wrapped up in padded coats on the grass, each with a cup of coffee.

'Probably warmer out there,' said Tiziano ruefully, looking up at her.

'I can wheel you out, if you like,' said Cate quickly.

He shrugged. 'I could do it myself, if I wanted,' he said calmly, giving her a level look. 'I'm pretty good in this thing, you know.'

He was too, she'd seen him flying down the lanes, faster than most pedestrians. Someone said he'd been in the last Paralympics. Basketball.

132

'Oh, I didn't mean – I know –' She felt her eyes prick and grow hot.

Calm down, she thought, crying is ridiculous. This whole business was getting to her. Her mother would say with wheezy dismissal, *Of course, you're no good at responsibility, Caterina Giottone, you're just like your father. All this free spirit business, it's all very well. You need something to tether you.*

Vincenzo was trying to tether her. He'd sounded angry, though to be fair to him, he'd sounded like he was also trying to control it. 'But what exactly is going on?' he'd asked, disgruntled. She'd explained.

'It's a dangerous road,' he'd said, sobered. 'And this time of year too. *Madonna.*' There'd been a pause. 'Are you upset?'

Cate had thought about it. 'A bit,' she'd said. 'I'm OK.'

'You liked her, didn't you?'

She'd been taken aback at that. 'I suppose I did, yes,' she'd eventually replied. 'She was a bitch, actually, but yes. I did like her.'

Tiziano was looking at her. Did I really say that, she wondered? She *had* been a bitch, though; it hadn't really occurred to Cate until she'd gone; she hadn't dared say it. Did I like her, though? Admired, maybe, grudgingly respected, and when she was being funny, at the dining table, when she held everyone in the palm of her hand with some story or other – yes. Liked her.

'I just meant, if you want the company,' she now said to Tiziano, recovering herself.

'Actually, I prefer it in here, this morning,' said Tiziano meditatively, looking down at Michelle and Tina. 'Those two – well. They can get a bit much, together. A pair of Gothic witches, casting spells.'

Cate knew she shouldn't agree; she smiled in the gloom. 'Mm-hm,' she said. 'I saw Tina crying. Michelle was – I suppose she was comforting her.' She hesitated. 'Are they – um – a couple, do you think?'

Tiziano drew his head back in mock surprise, then took pity. 'No, Not a couple.' It occurred to Cate that she could ask him anything, and he would know the answer. Sitting in that wheelchair, his brain whirring, all that time to watch and learn.

'What, then?' she said. Could she trust him not to tell Luca she was asking inappropriate questions? She thought she could. Too late now, anyway.

'Well,' said Tiziano, 'I'd have said Tina is only interested in her work. Human relationships are not her thing. Not entirely healthy – but then, artists often aren't. Even the able-bodied ones.'

'But she was crying,' said Cate obstinately.

Tiziano shrugged. 'Loni was in the same field, wasn't she? A sculptor, once upon a time, before she became a critic. Maybe they bonded over it.'

Cate looked at him, not quite buying it; wondering if they all knew as much about each other's careers as Tiziano seemed to. He'd been doing his home-work. 'And Michelle?'

'Michelle's main emotion is rage, wouldn't you say?' Tiziano cocked his head up at Cate, his eyes alive with interest. 'Anger, not love. Though I don't think she's always been that way.'

Just like she'd once been beautiful too. Cate nodded, and together they looked down at the women. 'I think she must be fond of Tina, though,' she said.

'There's a bond,' said Tiziano. 'Sure. Maybe thwarted maternal love. Maybe Michelle should have taken a different path, gone out to a farmhouse in Woodstock or somewhere and had babies. What good is art, anyway? All that poring over a desk, thinking of words.' He sounded almost angry himself. 'What for? Who reads Michelle's poems? She told me her last book sold 1,000 copies, worldwide. The music lovers, the people who come to listen to me, with their smug, snobbish educated faces, do they matter? Sometimes I want to wheel the chair as fast as I can off the stage and launch myself on to the front row, just to see their faces.'

'You don't really think that,' said Cate.

He lifted his cup blithely to his lips, and gave her no clue as to whether he was joking. 'Perhaps I don't,' he said, and he smiled.

Outside on the grass Tina had set her own cup down on the wooden garden table, where in the summer the guests might sit and watch the sun go down. Her hair seemed flatter and straighter and more colourless than ever; her lips blanched. Her shoulders were hunched and her hands wringing each other in the cold. She bobbed her

135

head, and Michelle gave her a brusque nod back, and Tina hurried away towards the studio. Tiziano was right; Michelle's whole body language, as she stood there with her arms wrapped around herself and watched Tina go, was of tightly wound fury. And when she turned and looked up at the window her face was set.

'But why is she so angry?' She turned to him, took his empty cup gently from him.

'Ah, that,' said Tiziano, and he looked away. 'It's – well. You should ask her that.'

Cate laughed. 'Ask Michelle? Are you crazy?'

'Not me,' said Tiziano. He spun the chair and wheeled back to the table.

Cate persisted. 'Do you know?' From the foot of the stairs came the creak of the outside door opening. Michelle. 'Is it the children thing?' And having thought it was a bizarre suggestion of Tiziano's, suddenly she could quite imagine Michelle a mother, the angry kind, the kind prone to sudden, tender outbursts and fierce hugs.

'Not unconnected, maybe,' said Tiziano, not attempting to lower his voice. 'But not exactly. She married late, and was widowed early. She was widowed last year. Her husband was a composer; they'd applied to come here together.'

Cate stared at him, considering what he had just said. This great loss she had not known about. And then there was Michelle in the doorway, and at the sight of Tiziano her glowering face relaxed, almost into a smile. 'Hey, baby,' she said gruffly.

136

'I've told you not to call me that,' said Tiziano, winking at her.

'I think I'll take some coffee upstairs,' said Cate. And left them to it.

Luca Gallo had nominated a members' club in a narrow street near the market of San Ambrogio for their meeting, declining Sandro's offer of his own offices. Sandro had accepted the choice of venue without demur, offices being a rather grand term for two rooms in San Frediano with a view of a builders' merchants; perhaps Gallo had guessed as much.

Pondering this possibility, Sandro found himself wondering for the first time why Gallo had ever selected him for the job of checking up on Dottoressa Loni Meadows, when the job might easily have been done by one of the bigger and more anonymous agencies with a smarter address. Perhaps it was a matter of discretion – Sandro was certainly discreet – or of a preference for an old-fashioned way of doing things. Or perhaps, thought Sandro, eyeing the spiffed-up staff of the members' club with suspicion as he waited in its panelled lobby, ten minutes early as he always was for everything, perhaps he was being paranoid.

As it was, the club was not far from Sandro and Luisa's flat, even if the reason Gallo had given for suggesting the place was that it was just around the corner from the offices of Loni Meadows's husband – now widower – Giuliano Mascarello.

And they would be proceeding from the club to those offices.

It had been a crisp, cold morning when he had set out from home, not quite as luminous and blue as yesterday, but as he crossed the river, the light had fallen gold on the soft yellow of the Palazzo Corsini's façade, and Sandro had almost allowed himself to imagine spring. Only then it had come to him painfully that under normal circumstances he would have been imagining a trip up the coast with Luisa for Easter, perhaps, the azaleas blooming along the motorway's central reservation, a picnic in the boot. And now, the possibility of the new season had retreated anyway; the sky had thickened and clouded, and the wind was bitter as he headed up the narrow canyon of the Borgo Pinti, towards the Circolo Boheme.

A professionally friendly young woman in a suit had greeted him, and asked him if he would mind waiting. The decor looked as though it had been lifted from a Sherlock Holmes movie of the seventies; the lobby was wood panelled with shelves displaying wine; through a red velvet curtain that led into the main part of the club Sandro could see the gilded and leather-bound spines of books on a wall of shelves, and some low, leather button-backed chairs. It appeared to be quite empty; at least there would be no problem with eavesdroppers.

He'd told Giuli straight away that they wouldn't be going to see Carlotta Bellagamba's parents together, after all. Not today. Giuli had looked just a tiny bit crestfallen when he'd told her he wouldn't need her for his meeting with Gallo, either. Perhaps just as well, given the surroundings. Giuli would have been uncomfortable here, and more bemused than he was by the place.

'I've already spoken to Bellagamba,' he'd said briefly, to get her disappointment out of the way. 'I told him you would be quite happy to come and report to him on our progress so far with his daughter, but there was in fact little of consequence to say. He seems happier already, to be honest, just to have us – involved. We agreed, if she goes out again over the weekend, he'll be in touch. With you.'

Bellagamba, a man of few words, had indeed grunted his assent; relieved more than anything else, thought Sandro, that his daughter was safely back home in Galluzzo and getting on with her homework. Sandro had presented Giuli to him as his equal in surveillance as boldly as he could, and it seemed she had been accepted. Giuli had appeared happy enough with that, at least.

'And you,' she'd said. 'You're not really going away?'

He'd shrugged uncomfortably. 'Let's wait and see. What Gallo says; he did ask, though. If I'd be able to leave town.'

'But what about the office?' she'd persisted.

'There's the laptop,' he'd said, absurdly pleased at that moment that he had complied with Giuli's

139

pleading and invested in the blasted thing. Not to mention all kinds of accessories – expanded battery capacity, mobile broadband – he'd felt completely duped into buying at the time. 'I can take it with me.' Giuli had looked at him sceptically. 'And I'll divert calls to your mobile. It'll only be a couple of days, and anyway, tomorrow's Sunday. Bellagamba's hardly likely to ask you to follow the girl tomorrow.' A sigh. 'Really, Giuli. You said yourself, you'd be better at trailing the girl than me. And I want this job. This – this is a real job.'

And that was it; leaving town was a matter of a call or two, a single technical adjustment. If Luisa could do it, so could Sandro; up sticks, was how she'd described it, wasn't it? *Some women just up sticks.*

For some reason the image of his own mother came to him, sleeves rolled up and frowning as she knelt among her rows of beans and artichokes searching for slugs, reaching out a hand to pull him, her only child, down next to her. Rooted to the earth as Luisa was not. He had not married Luisa because she was like his mother, though, had he? Even if in some respects they were alike. He had married her for her temper, quick to anger, quick to soften, her sharp wits and the soft skin of her lovely pale neck.

'You've told Luisa?' Giuli had said, giving him a look of deep and justifiable suspicion.

Sandro had blinked. 'Well, I will do, obviously,'

140

he'd said defensively. 'Give me a break. I've only just found out myself.'

'You had an idea last night,' she'd said. 'When's she going away?'

'Monday,' he'd muttered, not wanting to think about it, 'returning late on Wednesday. I'll be back by then. Probably.'

'And if you're not? It could be almost a week before you see her again.'

Sandro really hadn't wanted to think about it. 'She said we could maybe do with some time apart.' He could hear himself, a spoilt child. Cleared his throat.

'And actually, it's the job. They want me down there. There are questions need asking. Apparently.'

Giuli had hunched her shoulders, staring down into her empty coffee cup. He'd offered her a pastry but she didn't want one; she was washed-out and withdrawn. This business with Luisa; you'd think Giuli was still an adolescent, their adolescent. They'd dealt with her rage – the fury of a forty-year-old child and the shivering bouts that had followed rehab and prison. She'd grown to depend on them. To love them? And now she was frightened they were going to leave her; Sandro had wanted to say, don't be daft. But the truth was, he didn't know. He'd felt sick.

'Don't they have police to investigate car accidents?' she'd said.

He'd grunted at that. 'Not as simple as that,' was all he'd say. And he didn't know the detail himself, that was the truth.

'You'd better talk to her,' was all Giuli had said, truculently, before she'd sloped off. Out of the bar and back to bed, was his guess. It had been a late night, hadn't it? Sandro didn't want to think about it.

He'd call her. When he had time; he just hadn't had a minute. Reluctantly he got out his phone in the club's lobby, and was staring at it when Luca Gallo arrived.

They'd not done more than exchange emails last summer, but Sandro still retained a vivid impression of efficiency, a polite but economical writing style and the voice, distinctive, soft, deep, persuasive. In person, Gallo was a solid, somewhat scruffy bearded man who looked uncomfortable in his suit. And nervous, to boot. He was carrying a briefcase and an armful of files.

The manageress reappeared behind Gallo and ushered them through the curtained door and to a corner table. The place was, as Sandro had thought, completely deserted; from an adjoining room there was the muffled clatter of tables being laid. Sandro told the man straight away that he'd read the paper.

Gallo ran his hands across a near-bald head, then sighed. 'So you know.'

'It's about her, then? Dottoressa Meadows.' Sandro spoke cautiously; he didn't want to jump the gun.

Gallo made a tent with his fingers on the polished table. 'It's about her. Yes. Her – death.'

Sandro scrutinized him. 'In the newspaper – it seems it was an accident. You've spoken to the police?'

Gallo nodded. 'They say it's straightforward, as far as they can tell. She lost control, going too fast on an icy road. They're doing the full post-mortem this morning. They say it's a dangerous road; there are warning signs but –' and he spread his hands. 'But what can you do? That's the police line. People are people, that's what they say; they don't always pay attention.'

'OK,' said Sandro.' 'Are you saying you think they're wrong?'

Gallo sighed. 'I'm not saying anything,' he said wearily. 'The police say it's an accident, as far as they're concerned. There are certain elements to it that –' He broke off. 'There are certain questions. The chief problem is – well. You will meet the problem, very shortly.' He put both hands to his face, rubbed his eyes. The man needed sleep. He dropped his hands and looked at Sandro with resignation. 'That was wrong of me. I shouldn't have called him a problem. The man's grieving. Of course he is.'

'You're talking about Loni Meadows's husband?' said Sandro.

Gallo shot a glance over his shoulder and Sandro half-turned to see the woman who'd shown them to their table approaching with a tray of coffee.

Had Sandro registered last summer, carrying out this routine employee check, that his subject was married to one of Florence's best-known *avvocati?* Of course he had. Mascarello was nothing like as high profile as he had been two decades ago, but he was a name; to be truthful, it had been one of the little troubling question marks over the job that Sandro had chosen to ignore, in the name of a quiet life and some easy money.

Why would you run a check on a woman who must already be well known in high cultural circles, that gossipy, prying mafia of artists and writers and bullshitters from whom nothing could be hidden? A woman who, in addition, was very well connected? That was a question he would have to ask. At the right time.

The smiling woman took her time setting the coffee things on the table, leaning between them. She smelled of gardenia; nice, thought Sandro, who had never in his life been tempted by a woman other than Luisa. Nice, though. He waited until she had left the room again. 'So?' he said, quietly.

'Yes,' Gallo said. 'I'm talking about Giuliano Mascarello. He thinks she was – he refuses to believe it was an accident.'

Sandro exhaled. 'Why would that be?' he asked cautiously. 'In your opinion? Grief? Denial? Or something more concrete?'

Gallo picked up the briefcase and set it on his knee. 'I have the preliminary police reports here. But you'll forgive me if I don't show them to you now. They are private, obviously. I need to be sure that – this investigation will go ahead. As for

144

Mr Mascarello – he'll give you his reasons.' Then he sighed again. 'He's used to getting his own way; perhaps there is something like guilt too.'

'Guilt?' Sandro leaned forward, picked up his cup of coffee. It was weak and tasteless – the humblest bar in the city would have served something better. Even if the girl did smell of gardenia.

'They were – estranged is not exactly the word. They had led separate lives for some years. More than a decade.' Gallo looked uncomfortable. 'Or so I understand. They were – at least, she was – quite open about it.'

'And he?'

'Perhaps him also; I have never discussed this with him. We are not – I don't know him well.' Gallo made an impatient sound. 'Anyway, this is not the point. I suppose I meant he may feel guilt because he assumed she would always be there – and now –' Again Gallo's shoulders were up, uneasy. 'We should get to the point. He wishes her death investigated.'

Sandro had stopped short a sentence earlier. *He assumed she would always be there.* It was how one had to live, wasn't it? One could not live expecting the worst.

He became aware of Gallo's eyes on him, and caught up. 'He wants her death investigated. Yes.'

Gallo held his gaze. 'He has talked of engaging a private detective. I told him you had come highly recommended and we had already used you. For routine work.'

145

'He knows you had his wife checked on?' Sandro was startled.

'Of course,' said Gallo shortly. 'It's normal, from time to time. Routine.'

Sandro began shaking his head because he was quite sure that it had not been routine at all. But he stopped; he said nothing.

There was something about Luca Gallo that bothered him; he could not get the measure of the man. Did he think Loni Meadows's death had been an accident, or not? There was something he wasn't telling Sandro. Sandro said so.

There was a long silence. Beneath the beard Gallo's round face looked pale and exhausted.

'All right,' he said. 'I suppose – well, I didn't think this was the right place.' He lifted the brief-case he'd arrived with on to his knee and peered inside. He pulled out a folder and set it on the table.

'There was an email,' he said, and slowly, reluctantly, he pulled out a sheet of paper, looked at it a long moment, set it on the table and turned it towards Sandro. 'Anonymous. Ah – unusual.'

CHAPTER 10

On the soft red stone of the the top-floor landing Cate hesitated, a tray of coffee in one hand. On one side was Alec Fairhead; on the other, Per Hansen. Both doors were firmly closed.

On the floor below, Dottoressa Meadows's door had now not only been shut, but locked. Cate had tried it. Obviously. She realized that she was becoming bolder, although the rattle the handle made in the great quiet building gave her a guilty qualm. Who was there to ask her what she thought she was doing, with Luca away? Although Ginevra, she supposed, would not think twice about it.

Cate had been up here plenty of times. She and Nicki shared the delivery of lunches and break-fast supplies; sometimes, out of the goodness of their hearts, they'd return forgotten washing to the men from the laundry room. The guests were supposed to be responsible for their own laundry, but these two – and Michelle – remembered only erratically. Tiziano and Tina were scrupulous, never left a trace of themselves, Tiziano bending supple from his wheelchair and scooping stuff off the floor into his lap. And neither Nicky nor Cate would do it for Michelle, since she screeched at them to leave her stuff alone. She didn't need her ass wiped, she wasn't a mental patient, that was what she said.

Not much you aren't, thought Cate. The woman was angry, right enough, just like Tiziano had said.

She'd been up here plenty of times, but everything was different now; the castle was not somewhere she would be leaving in a few hours, to speed down the hills on her *motorino*, to find Vincenzo waiting on her doorstep in the dark, wanting to take her to a movie and chatter about his day. On the landing, in the warm gloom scented by wax and wood, it suddenly felt very much as though she was trapped.

Alec Fairhead's door almost always used to be open; that was how she knew he spent each day sitting at his window, staring out, the screen of his computer blank. She would set the lunch hamper down in the corner of his room and he would turn and give her that faded, sad smile. This place was his last chance, Tiziano had said.

Per Hansen's door would always be closed; the further north you went in the world, Cate speculated, the more you liked to shut yourself in. He wrote plays, she knew that, but also screenplays, for films, to make money.

Were they in there, either of them? She hesitated, tray in hand, on it two cups of rapidly cooling coffee. In front of her on the landing was a beautiful old chair, like something Egyptian, a curved X-shape of polished wooden struts. She sat on it.

When would this be over, she wondered? When there was a new Director, when the *Dottoressa*'s husband had come to take her things away and the *piano nobile* had a new occupant? Perhaps they would give it to one of the guests; there had been some trouble over it going to Dottoressa Meadows, Ginevra had said. The wide, beautiful room with its two sets of windows, its old heavy furniture, the inlaid dressing table and the gilded bed – worth a bomb, Ginevra had said that too, half of it listed in the *Catalogo delle Belle Arti*, and Loni Meadows had spilled nail varnish on the dressing table.

Beth had spent a lot of time in there with her, hadn't she? Gossiping at the dressing table. Cate wondered if anyone had Beth's phone number, in America? Luca would. Would he have called her, to break the news?

From downstairs Cate heard a brief but loud cackle reverberate up the stairwell. Michelle; Tiziano would have made her laugh. She couldn't imagine what he might have said, what things he shared with Michelle.

As the silence settled back she heard other things. From behind Alec Fairhead's room a soft sound, like water running over pebbles; she listened harder. A sound she almost knew, and then it came to her; the chatter of a computer keyboard, not tentative, one finger at a time, but hurried. He was writing. She hesitated; better not to interrupt him then.

From behind Per Hansen's door, nothing. Cate got to her feet, moved closer to the door, so her cheek was almost against the wood. Silence. She knocked.

Complete silence. Cate took a cautious step back, her tray in front of her.

'Mr Hansen?' she said. And then – though she wondered if it was her imagination – after a sound like a low growl, a sound of frustration, the door was opened abruptly in front of her and there he stood, barefoot, in a sweater, red-eyed. Beyond him on a chaotically overloaded table she could see a half-full bottle of red wine. It was eleven o'clock.

For a moment they stood there, him glaring, Cate shocked into silence. He made an effort. 'Miss Giottone,' he said, looking at the tray in her hand as if he didn't know what it was.

'Caterina,' she said. 'I'm sorry. I hope I didn't disturb you?'

He laughed bitterly. 'You mean, was I working?' She shrugged, smiling. 'No, I wasn't working,' he said, and the bitterness had gone; his voice dead.

She glanced past him into the room, which looked as though a tornado had swept through it.

He followed her gaze, then said, 'You want to come in?' He stared around the wreckage of his room as if he didn't recognize any of it. 'Are you checking up on me? Caterina?'

'I brought you some coffee.' She stepped past him, still holding her tray.

There was nowhere to put it down. Every

150

centimetre of the long table's surface was covered, the half-full wine bottle and an empty one on its side, papers, books, spines split, face down, others stacked in an unstable tower; two wine glasses with tidemarks of dried red in them, circular stains on the papers. A coat lay on the floor; a chest stood with every drawer open, and clothes spilling out or stuffed in. The wardrobe, its doors yawning open, was empty save for one dark suit, hanging. The bed was not made.

This man had a wife; surely this wasn't how he lived?

Gently Cate set the tray on the floor. Handed him a cup. She looked backwards at the open door and decided that Alec Fairhead would have to do without his. She sipped at the other cup herself.

'You were – upset,' she said, thinking of the sound she'd heard him make. Looking around at the room. It was more a statement than a question.

He stared into the cup. Then nodded.

'Yes,' he said eventually. 'I was upset. I am upset.'

When Cate said nothing, just looked at him encouragingly, he went on. 'I'm not sure how I would say it even in English, let alone Italian. I was fond of her. I had – a strong feeling for her.'

A picture came into Cate's head of the dinner table at which she'd served these guests six days a week for as many weeks, of Per Hansen gazing across the table at Loni Meadows, distracted halfway through a conversation with some visitor or other.

151

'We were, all of us,' said Cate. It was what you said. Per Hansen stared back at her. 'No,' he said. 'Not all.'

Cate didn't know what to say, because of course he was right.

He was looking at her in a different way now. 'You like our Tiziano, don't you?' he said. Cate stared at him.

'Of course,' she said quietly.

He made a sad, impatient sound. 'I don't mean simply, *like*, though.' He spread his hands. 'Life is too short, that's what they say? A very good phrase in English. Too short not to say what you mean. *Fond of? Like?* Soft little words.'

'I don't know what to say,' said Cate. 'Tiziano is a very special person.'

'He is the opposite of me,' said Per abruptly. 'My life has been – quiet. Uneventful. I have had everything I wanted, but I have not been ambitious.' Cate nodded, waiting. Per took a deep breath. 'I am a little crude, perhaps, reserved, a little thoughtless? I do not know my own emotions.' He frowned and she could see he didn't require a response. 'Tiziano is open and outgoing and generous, full of energy, everything outward, I am everything inward.' He sat at the heaped desk, thrust papers aside and set his elbows on the leather. Put his head in his hands.

'You should be careful with Tiziano,' he said wearily. 'He is not everything he seems.'

'No?' said Cate reluctantly, and she felt cold

152

suddenly, in the warm room. *Don't,* she wanted to say. *Don't tell me, don't ruin it.* Set the cup, still half-full, down on the tray.

'You know how it happened?' Per looked up at her between his hands. 'The accident.' Slowly she shook her head. 'A bomb,' said Per. '*Una bomba.* It was a terrorist attack on a bus depot. Where he was waiting with his father to go to a football match.'

'His father died,' Cate whispered.

Per nodded. 'He cannot be what he seems to be,' he said. 'After that?' He shook his head. 'Can he really be so happy, so full of determination, so warm? No.'

'You don't know him,' Cate said stubbornly.

'Neither of us knows him,' said Per sadly. 'You want to believe the best of everyone, don't you, Caterina?'

She didn't answer, and after a moment Per rubbed his face and got to his feet.

'I'm sorry,' he said. 'Now I have upset you also. I only wanted to say, that all is not obvious from the outside. We don't know Tiziano. You don't know me.' He crossed to the window, looking out, and when he spoke it was with something deeper than reluctance, something more like horror. 'Over there, you said, didn't you? She died over there, just over the hill. Just out of sight.'

'Yes.'

She came to his side by the window. From here they could see down the hill, over the trees, down

153

the straight line of the road that was the front approach to the castle. You couldn't make out the river, after all. The glass was old, and swirled with uneven thickness; the frames let in a draught that made Cate shiver. The sky was a luminous white. There would be snow tonight, she thought.

'I know the place,' said Per Hansen distantly. 'Where the road bends, by the river.'

'You know it?'

But before he could answer there came the sound, far off but distinct, of an approaching vehicle. They both turned their heads at the same time: at first there was nothing. Nothing but the bare hills, the still trees, off to the left the corner of Mauro and Ginevra's roof tucked between two curves of the land. And the sound.

And then it appeared. A small red car, bright between the frosted fields. They watched as it dipped out of sight then reappeared. Whoever it was, was driving very fast.

'It's her,' said Per flatly, as if to himself.

'Who?' said Cate faintly, but he had stopped speaking, just shoved his hands in his pockets and gazed through the window. She stood another moment and when he said nothing more, did not even turn to look at her, she took her tray and left.

The library was empty when she got back downstairs; clearing the coffee cups, she could hear that something was going on outside. Voices: a woman's voice, raised, gabbling in a foreign language. Spanish,

154

a language in which Cate had said on her application form she was fluent. She hadn't spoken it in four years, not since she was on the cruises out of Miami.

Setting down the tray, Cate went to the window; the small red car they had seen approaching from the top floor was parked askew on the grass in the front of the castle: a shocking sight. It was totally forbidden to park on the grass. Mauro was running awkwardly up from the *villino*, his face purple with anger, and Ginevra in her apron was shouting at a small, dark, plump woman who had just climbed out of the car. The stranger was dishevelled, bare-legged in boots and a coat as if she'd woken in the dark and run out of the house with the first things she could lay her hands on.

By the time she reached them, Mauro and Ginevra, both glaring, had been joined by Nicki, who was goggling delightedly at the spectacle.

'She says something about the Norwegian,' said Ginevra, looking with reluctant need to Cate. 'She wants him, Hansen.'

'Wait,' said Cate in Spanish, crossing the grass to the woman, holding up both hands in an attempt to calm her down. Coming closer she saw that the woman was worn-looking but handsome, dark-eyed, and pulling some pieces of paper out of her pocket she started waving them in the air.

'Per!' she shouted in her deep, foreign voice, staring up at the castle's grey façade. 'Per!' Then she turned to Cate and rattled off some Spanish. Cate stared.

'All right,' she said, 'All right.'

'Tell her she can't do that,' Mauro butted in furiously, his anger, it seemed to Cate, close to boiling point this last twenty-four hours. 'Tell her to move the blasted thing. She can't leave it there.' He pointed at the churned grass. 'Look at my lawn. She can't leave it there.'

'What does she say?' said Ginevra with impatience.

'She says she's his wife,' said Cate slowly.

'His wife?' Ginevra looked from the woman's face up to the deep-set windows on the top floor of the castle.

Cate nodded. 'She says he wrote to her last week, asking for a divorce.'

'After twenty-five years,' said the woman in Spanish, not so different, really, from Italian. Cate put out a hand; the woman was quite still now, all the furious energy evaporated. 'After two grown children. He asks me for a divorce. Because he is in love with someone else.'

The first thing that struck Sandro about Giuliano Mascarello was how very old he was.

Perhaps because the lawyer hadn't really been visible for twenty years, perhaps because when his activities in connection with this or that peace initiative, this or that protest against infringements of civil rights, *were* still reported, an ancient photograph was used, one of the lawyer in his heyday, a streetfighter, eyes blazing, hand aloft in a revolutionary salute. The same picture had, in fact, been used next to the photograph of his dead wife in that morning's paper. But the man who sat in front of Luca Gallo and Sandro in the lofty rooms that were his offices on the Borgo degli Albizzi was shrunken, liver-spotted and bald, his wrinkled neck retracting into his collar like an old tortoise's.

The tawny, reptilian eyes that looked at his visitors were bright, though, his handshake was wiry and strong, and when he spoke it was quite clear that all Giuliano Mascarello's faculties were intact.

'You've told him about the email?' was the first thing he said, addressed peremptorily to Luca Gallo. It was clear that there was no love lost between these two, and Sandro wondered if the mutual hostility was a result of Loni Meadows's death, or had predated it. Almost certainly the latter.

Luca Gallo was polite, unsmiling. 'Of course,' he said.

So they'd shown the email to Mascarello, and presumably also to his wife.

Mascarello turned to Sandro. 'You have read it?'

Sandro had.

At first he had wondered what Luca meant by unusual. The English was stiff, formal: entirely clear, even to Sandro, but he'd had a frustrating sense of missing something. This was not his language; but he couldn't tell if it was the first language of the writer, either.

I write as a well-wisher to inform you that Doctor Loni Meadows should not be appointed to this position.

So far, so ordinary. But it had gone on, and Sandro had felt uneasy; even though he was reading a foreign language, he had had a sense of something in pain; something tormented.

Doctor Meadows is not what she seems. She is not beautiful, she is ugly. She has nothing to do with art, she cannot create, she can only destroy. Loni Meadows is evil.

Not explicit, not violent, but off-beam: woodenly repetitive in a way that became sinister, to Sandro at least. His immediate impression had been that the words were neither calculated nor calculating, but rather that they were the product of a disturbed mind.

The email address was an apparently random set of letters and numbers. 'Sent through a proxy server,' Luca had said shortly, without even needing to be asked, and Sandro had scrabbled fruitlessly through his memories of the computer course he'd been on last year in an attempt to understand what that meant. 'Completely anonymous.'

'Completely?'

Gallo had shrugged; on this subject, Sandro could see, he was confident of knowing more than Sandro. 'Apparently, there's no such thing as complete anonymity, but the computer office in Baltimore said there wasn't anything they could do to trace it.' He had paused. 'There was only the one. And the internet is full of crazies; do you know, if you ask for anonymous internet feedback on anything – on our courses, even – people will say things you could not imagine them saying out loud?'

Sandro had had to agree; the same applied in the police service.

Gallo had shaken his head in disbelief. 'And we weren't to know – were we? That it would be more than that.'

Sandro had nodded, musing. It said something, though, didn't it? That the person who sent them at least knew that such things as proxy servers existed.

'Do you think – your artists would know how to do that?' he had asked. 'Do they know about computers, these days?' He had thought of the little workshops in the back streets of the city; an electric light bulb all the techonology required, old men in brown coats bent over a piece of gilding. But then perhaps they didn't qualify as artists, only artisans.

The look Luca Gallo had given him then combined pity with curiosity. 'Actually, these days – yes, they do,' he had said. 'Or they know people who do.'

It was only Sandro who was utterly ignorant then.

Gallo had replaced the printout of the email in

the folder. 'In any case,' he had continued brusquely, 'Mascarello has now put someone of his own on that; he says, if there is any method of tracing the sender of the email, then he will do it.'

'Right,' Sandro had said at that, unable to disguise his relief that he – or Giuli – wouldn't be expected to solve an internet deception.

Luca Gallo had held up a hand. 'What Mascarello will tell you is that he suspects someone from among the castle's guests. In here,' he had said, now passing the folder to Sandro, 'are copies of each guest's file. It might perhaps impress Mascarello that we are taking him seriously.'

And are we? 'Suspects them of what?' Sandro had felt the need to be circumspect.

'Of – well, he will tell you,' Gallo had said, his face closing.

And now, under the high-coffered ceilings, the whitewashed walls and the beady-eyed portraits on Mascarello's walls, Sandro held the lawyer's gaze and said, 'Yes. I've read it.'

Mascarello regarded him carefully. 'Of course, they'd rather I – we, my wife and I – had never found out,' he said. 'Much easier for them.'

'They?' Sandro inquired mildly.

'The great Trust. They might have carried out their investigations into my wife unhindered by any objections she or I might have had.'

Sandro could hear the adrenaline in the man's voice and he understood that this was meat and drink to him. The fight. Was that why he was embarking on this crusade? For the thrill of the chase? Sandro had to admit, though, that after weeks – months – of inactivity, he could guiltily feel something of the same spark igniting in himself. He looked across at Gallo's face: it was unreadable, but pale.

'But of course, I found out,' Mascarello went on. 'Did they think I wouldn't? Did they think I wouldn't know that investigations were being carried out, behind our backs?' Sandro smiled a little, to conceal his disquiet.

'Naturally we would have informed you,' said Gallo levelly. Mascarello snorted.

'You raised objections, then?' asked Sandro. 'To my – to any investigation?'

'By then it was too late,' said Mascarello, pursing his thin lips, staring out of the window. He turned back and fixed Sandro with a prosecutor's look. 'And what did you discover about my wife, Mr Cellini?' he said with disdain.

He wouldn't ask Sandro to pursue this investigation, would he? Not in a million years; he must have any number of dubious types at his beck and call who'd make inquiries, call in favours and, no doubt, encourage betrayals of confidence. Giuliano Mascarello might be a defender of human rights and an attender of marches for peace and justice, but Sandro didn't like him much. And didn't trust him, either. He reached down and took his own slender file on Loni Meadows from his briefcase – the file he had removed from the cabinet in his office on the Via del Leone as Giuli had stood there, reproachfully watching his every move.

'I discovered that her CV was accurate and all her references genuine,' he said quietly. 'That she had no criminal record and no driving offences.' The lawyer's eyes flickered, but he said nothing on the question of how Sandro might have obtained this information. Because she was dead, perhaps; or because Sandro had not discovered anything incriminating.

The room was silent, and the thin February light fell wan and beautiful through its long windows; for the first time in months, thought Sandro, it held a trace of warmth. He turned to Luca.

'Were all of the present guests of the Castello Orfeo already selected,' he asked, 'before Dottoressa Meadows was appointed?'

Luca Gallo frowned. 'Almost all,' he said, after a while. 'One was chosen afterwards,' he looked down at the page. 'In the um – the July. Per Hansen. The Norwegian. Unfortunately one of the original selection died. He was a composer, Joseph Connor, husband of Michelle Connor, and we had to appoint another.'

Mascarello made a sound of impatience, which was perhaps why Sandro said what he did next; out of recklessness born of anger, out of a sense that it was a lost cause, anyway, a set-up of some kind, in which Sandro's lowly status as a reject from the police force was on trial, and he would be exposed and humiliated as no more than a cheap snoop and a superannuated piece of hired muscle.

'If I were investigating that email,' he said, holding up Loni Meadows's CV and looking coolly at it, 'or indeed, your wife's death, I think that this —' and he held the little passport shot of her between finger and thumb and turned it to face them, 'this would be more useful to me than anything else, don't you?'

Mascarello leaned forwards just a little over his heavy polished desk, but said nothing.

'She was a beautiful woman, much younger than her husband. And you will no doubt tell me if I am wrong, but I would say that your wife had considerable influence over men, and exercised it regularly.'

Sandro had not even known himself that he had deduced these things, until he spoke.

'Clearly,' said the lawyer in his rusty voice, 'no such information can be discovered from a photograph.'

'If you wish,' said Sandro. 'I think, however, we both know that it can.'

Mascarello sat very still; Luca Gallo looked petrified.

'I would like to know what it is that are you saying,' said Mascarello with quiet menace.

Sandro could see how the man might skewer and terrify any witness, any government minister, any criminal or indeed any innocent into confession. But he held his nerve.

'I'm saying that she was an extremely attractive woman who lived apart from her husband and had done so for some years. I am saying that it is not impossible that she may have been in another relationship, or possibly more than one, or that she used her – her femininity – to her advantage. And those things might have been the source of animosity towards her.'

Mascarello regarded him steadily, saying nothing. Sandro went on. 'If I were investigating this – accident, I should begin by speaking with those closest to your wife: those with whom she was intimate or those who wished for intimacy with her, which I suppose would include yourself. That is what I am saying.'

There was a silence.

'My wife and I were close,' said Mascarello, 'but we have not lived together for more than ten years; that kind of intimacy is – was – not what I required of her, nor did we discuss her life, in that way.' He paused, taking a careful breath. 'Put plainly, in answer to your implication I did not know who her lovers were. And put even more plainly, on the night my wife died I was in the hospital at Santa Maria Nuova, receiving – a routine treatment. Forgive me if I do not oblige you with the details. I was accompanied back to my apartment by a nurse, who remained with me that night. Would that satisfy you, as an alibi?' There was the ghost of a smile on the man's lips.

Sandro inclined his head stiffly. 'I would need to speak with the nurse,' he said. 'But yes, I think so.' He paused. 'And now I wonder if you would be kind enough to tell me what it is you suspect?'

There was a silence so long that Sandro could have sworn the light cast on the whitewashed wall had time to shift.

And then, slowly, Mascarello stood, set his splayed fingers on the desktop and faced them.

'My wife was a woman who knew exactly what she wanted. And she made sure she got it. That email was sent in the days following the announcement in the arts and educational media of Leona's appointment. It was not widely known or broadcast; we are talking about a small set of those people –' and he seemed to sneer '– who move from retreat to retreat, from reading to festival to internship, all around the world. They live on the misplaced charity of others.'

Pausing, Mascarello took a breath, apparently reconsidering this line of attack.

'My wife – Loni was not some kind of cour- tesan. She was an artist, she was active in arts administration and an influential critic, in the press and on the internet.'

She cannot create, she can only destroy. A critic.

'She wrote for a very widely read weblog. What's known as a blog.'

'A blog.' Had his tone betrayed a measure of

ignorance? Sandro thought it hadn't, but Mascarello explained anyway.

'A kind of running commentary on matters of interest,' he said impatiently. 'In this case the arts, through the medium of the internet. Often anonymous, although their writers' identities are the subject always of much speculation.'

'Was hers anonymous?'

'She wrote under the name Lonestar,' said Gallo, darting a glance at Mascarello. 'Certainly I was aware that she was the author of the blog; I imagine others were.'

'What I am saying,' Mascarello went on abruptly, leaning forward as if in pain, 'is that I believe –' and from the way he said it this was not a matter of belief but of certainty '– I believe that the email was sent by someone who had applied to be a guest at the castle, and I believe that that person, in the writing of the email, in the taking up of a fellowship that would place the person close to her, was motivated only by a desire to wreak some kind of revenge on my wife. To exercise some kind of punishment.'

He sat down again, and Sandro heard a brief whistle in his breathing. The man was old, after all. He was old and ill.

Sandro waited to be sure that he had finished. 'Revenge for what?' he said. 'So your wife did have enemies?' He watched the man disguise his frailty by taking in breath in small, silent movements of his ancient pigeon chest, refusing to gasp.

'That is for you to discover,' said Mascarello eventually, and when Sandro saw that the disdain was now gone from the lawyer's gaze, he realized that he had been given the job.

CHAPTER 11

As they emerged on to the Borgo degli Albizzi, Gallo had looked so shaken that Sandro had taken pity on the man and wordlessly steered him by the elbow into a bar, a little further down the street.

The morning was still cold, and the bar full of Saturday shoppers, teenage girls on their way back from the cheap clothes stores of the Via del Corso, and women coming back the other way, laden with carrier bags from San Ambrogio. As he and Gallo came in to the pleasant fug of coffee and baking, Sandro had to smile and apologize half a dozen times, bumping against yet another woman's load of prickly artichokes and blood oranges. Sandro thought of that castle, out in the cold, dark hills, and didn't want to leave his city, this place full of life, and women shopping, and bars with sparkling marble and brass. He thought of Luisa, less than a kilometre away, presiding over her shop floor, and knew he should go over there.

Explain the situation calmly, tell her he'd certainly be back before she left for New York. But even the thought of that place got him churning again: New

York, those steel and glass buildings, those hustling crowds, Luisa laughing and clinking glasses with Frollini thousands of kilometres away.

Damn it, he thought. Put it out of your mind, and do your job.

Without asking what he wanted to drink Sandro bought Luca Gallo a *caffè macchiato*, one for himself, and two small shots of brandy. Edged the man ahead of him into the rear of the long, narrow bar-room and located a quiet space.

'He's a hard nut to crack,' said Sandro, eyeing Gallo closely. 'Mascarello.'

Gallo downed the *macchiato*, but left the brandy alone.

'Yes, he is,' he said. He had a careful way of talking; measured, polite, even when, as now, he was rattled.

It occurred to Sandro that it must be a tricky sort of job, running the Castello Orfeo. All those foreigners, and a woman like Loni Meadows to deal with. He reached into his briefcase and got out the brochure Gallo had given him, turning the pages. Photographs of buildings, a gallery space, staff and benefactors, lists of names.

There was an aerial shot, the grey, prison-like block of the castle with its outbuildings, spread across the ridges of the hills. He'd had a bad feeling, even last night, about the place.

A picture caught his eye, a familiar face he couldn't quite put his finger on: he peered more closely. It was a small world, though. This city was a village, and this country was a bundle of villages, tangled up in each other.

'Did he come down to the castle ever?' he asked, turning the page. 'Mascarello? To see her?'

'Oh, no,' said Luca Gallo, as though the idea was rather alarming, 'Never. I met him, oh, once or twice before, at receptions in Florence. Arts gatherings, you know, at the British Council. Some of the American university campuses.' He gave the brandy a thoughtful look. 'But they didn't live together, you know, not any more, even before she came out to us, to Orfeo.'

'You were there for a long time before she arrived?'

'Oh, yes,' said Gallo, nodding. 'Eight years. She's the third Director I've worked with. Before that I was the administrator of an opera house, in Sicily.'

'And you've always had happy relationships with them? You don't mind – the division of labour?'

Gallo smiled. 'I love my job. I wouldn't want to be Director, no; behind the scenes, that's how I like it. So yes, very happy.'

'And other – longstanding staff?'

'A couple,' said Gallo, 'Mauro and Ginevra; handyman and cook. And Ginevra's niece, Nicki. Mauro's family has been there for generations: he was born at the Castello Orfeo, more or less.'

The set-up came into sharper focus for Sandro. 'That can't have been easy,' he said. 'They must have been – wary. Country people don't like incomers at the best of times.'

Luca Gallo stiffened. 'They're hard workers.

They've had to learn to adapt, with each new Director, obviously.'

'This one in particular? Any – specific problems?' Gallo looked down at the bar top, his unease palpable. 'With the staff or the guests? Any –' Sandro searched for the word, 'any history?'

'I couldn't possibly say,' said Gallo, looking alarmed, his hands fluttering in protest. 'The guests – well, there are privacy issues. Really, I don't think – I don't pry into their lives, I don't ask questions. Really, I don't gossip. This place –' and he leaned forwards, impassioned, a believer. 'The Castello Orfeo is a sanctuary for them, to produce art. A safe place.'

'All right,' said Sandro easily. 'Let's look at it from another angle. Think of yourself as a witness.' He spoke softly. 'That day. Tell me what happened. Everything you can remember.'

Gallo sighed. 'Loni and Mauro did have a – disagreement. That day. That last day. Over his leaving Orfeo to help another farmer; it was nothing. Nothing.'

Gallo's voice had descended to an anguished whisper. It was to his credit that he wanted to defend his staff as well as his guests and Sandro could picture the handyman in question, suspicious, territorial, taciturn, like all *contadini*.

'And she sounded off at him?'

Gallo nodded stiffly. 'I explained to her that it was something that was expected, in the countryside. Helping others. She didn't really understand.'

171

Sandro had the picture now. 'I see, and was there anything else – unusual?'

Gallo shrugged. 'A trip to Siena was cancelled that afternoon, because some of the guests – were busy with other projects. The *Dottoressa* was annoyed about that; the guests are generally expected to attend organized activities. Although there is some leeway, of course.'

There was silence, in which Sandro felt growing resistance: just defensiveness, perhaps.

'I suppose you get to know them well,' he asked, as casually as he could. 'Living in such close quarters. Like – I don't know – being in the army, or something. No secrets.'

Gallo might be the peacemaking, non-confrontational type, but he was no fool. 'You mean, did I know any of Loni Meadows's secrets?' The colour was back in his cheeks now; if anything, they were positively ruddy in the warm bar.

'I suppose I do,' said Sandro calmly. 'I could hardly ask her grieving widower if he knew who she was sleeping with, could I? Even if he didn't happen to be the powerful Giuliano Mascarello.'

Luca Gallo was turning the little shot glass between his fingers, on the bar. He said nothing.

'For example, where was she going, when she crashed that car, in the middle of the night? Might there have been somebody going with her?'

Gallo looked up from his contemplation of the amber liquid. 'I believe that she was having a – relationship. She – well, it was well known that on

172

certain nights she would go in the car, late, down to the town. And not return, sometimes, until the next day.'

'Certain nights?'

Gallo looked at him, head on one side, his sharp, intelligent eyes at odds with his soft, shambolic exterior. 'I believe it was generally towards the end of the week. Though I didn't make a chart.'

'And she would go alone?'

'I didn't watch her go,' Gallo said. 'It was never a part of my job to monitor the private lives of the guests, or of the Director. We do have – at the Trust there are certain principles –' and at this point he stopped, looking uncomfortable.

'Principles?' Sandro probed gently.

'Well, it's clearly not a religious order, but – we discourage partners' visits, that kind of thing. The time the guests spend with us is most productive if they are allowed to focus more intensely on their work. Without distractions.'

'I see,' said Sandro. It made sense, of a kind. If he was obliged to live without Luisa, would he focus more intensely? Perhaps he'd find out; actually he doubted it, very much. 'And did this – rule, or principle, or whatever – apply to staff as well as guests?'

'Well, not the kitchen staff, obviously,' said Gallo, 'and not formally, to anyone, but – well. It was always felt to be appropriate, for those of us who were involved on the artistic level.'

Which would explain why Loni Meadows went elsewhere for her – liaisons.

'But you don't know who he was? The man with whom she was having a relationship?'

'If it was a man,' said Gallo, smiling faintly. It occurred to Sandro that Gallo was gay. Did that make things simpler? It meant he hadn't been sleeping with Loni Meadows.

'You think it might have been a woman?'

'No,' said Gallo uncomfortably. 'I don't think so, actually. I was just – well. One can't assume.'

'No,' agreed Sandro. 'Absolutely.' And they sat in meditative silence for a brief, almost contented moment. Sandro thought of that great, forbidding castle, of those people held up there; thought of Loni Meadows speeding away from it in the dark, those blue eyes focused on a distant point, a lover, escape.

'What kind of place is it,' he said, 'this town she'd go off to?'

'Pozzo Basso?' said Gallo dismissively. 'A pretty ordinary little place, you know, a bar or two, hotel, railway station, hospital, police station.'

'So I start there?' Sandro pulled out the preliminary police report Gallo had given him; it had an address. He went on talking, almost to himself. 'I'll need half an hour to sort everything.' He shuffled the pages.

He came to a photograph, and stopped short.

'She wasn't in the car, when they found her?'

He saw it, that awful stiff pose. One shoe off, face down in the water, matted hair. A woman got up one morning, got dressed, chose those shoes, and didn't know she'd die in them.

Gallo shook his head slowly. 'She must have come to, they think. Struck her head against the door pillar, enough to kill her, came round. But all the time she was bleeding into the brain, and with the cold –' He broke off.

'It's all right,' said Sandro. 'You don't have to go through it again. I'll talk to them. With Mascarello's authorization, they should let me see – well. Everything I need to see.' He sighed. 'I'd better get going, if I'm to get any more – photographs of the scene, for example. The autopsy report; the report on the vehicle, the drugs screen, all those things. I'll have to come today. Yes?'

Luca Gallo had gone pale again. 'Yes,' he said carefully. 'Clearly, that's what you must do. I suppose I hadn't thought – you'll have to be discreet.'

Sandro held back a snort. 'I know how to be discreet,' he said.

Gallo pushed his brandy glass away from him. 'Drink it,' said Sandro. 'You might need it.'

'It had to be her,' said Ginevra. 'He was sleeping with the *Dottoressa*. Who else could it be?'

The kitchen was warm, and full once again: Anna-Maria, with her coat off by now, Nicki, Mauro glowering at the back door, keeping an eye out through the glass, for more unwanted guests, perhaps. On the stove the biggest Moka coffee machine was bubbling and five little cups and saucers sat on the table. It was close to lunchtime and the hampers still hadn't been distributed, but no one seemed to be bothered.

Per Hansen had appeared at the top of the castle's wide stone stairs as they came through the gateway. A little deputation of women, Mauro with them, had ranked behind the man's wife.

'Yolanda,' she had said. 'My name is Yolanda.' And past caring, she had burst into tears in front of them all; having delivered her furious speech, it seemed she had no anger left in her. When she had seen her husband in the big, dark, arched doorway she had run awkwardly ahead of them, and up to him. Everyone else had stayed where they were, in the courtyard, waiting for Hansen to speak.

Yolanda had reached Per but then she had stopped just short, as if there was an invisible barrier preventing her from touching him. The Norwegian had broken it, putting a hand to his wife's, saying something in tender, muttered Spanish. He had said nothing to the women or Mauro, but led his wife inside the great gloomy hallway, and closed the door.

'I think Ginevra's right,' said Cate now, and everyone looked at her. 'He used to watch her. The *Dottoressa*. I saw him, at dinners, watching her. And that time they went in the minibus to Rome, he was carrying her bags when they got back. All the way up to her room.'

She'd forgotten that; it had just jumped back into her head, when required. Per Hansen had followed Loni Meadows like a footman, carrying her two cases, she just flashing the odd smile back over her shoulder at him. She'd held the door open for him, he'd come inside her room. She'd shut the door behind him.

Did that mean she was sleeping with him? Why go all the way to Pozzo to sleep with Per Hansen in the Hotel Liberty, when she could have just slipped into his room, or he into hers? Separated by only one floor. Would people have found out? Almost certainly.

It didn't make sense to Cate: she didn't believe it.

'And besides, who else could it have been?' said Ginevra, hands on hips. The coffee bubbled up inside the aluminium pot, filling the room with its smell. Cate found herself longing for the biker bar, the friendly silence each morning as she snatched her *espresso*. Ginevra poured.

'Maybe,' she said, 'he wanted to leave his wife for the old one from New York, Mrs Angry? Or the little crazy one with her mess and her pots?'

'Well,' said Cate reluctantly, 'it could have been Beth, I suppose? The intern. Could be why she left.'

There was a silence while everyone considered that thought, and dismissed it; Beth, more timid than a small brown rabbit, and the big, taciturn Scandinavian.

'Beth was gay,' said Nicki, from the corner, and everyone stared.

'What?' said Ginevra and Anna-Maria in unison.

'She's gay,' said Nicki, folding her arms defensively across her bony chest. For the first time
Cate noticed a little tattoo of a daisy at her wrist.

'How do you know?' said Ginevra, outraged.

Nicky said nothing; she rolled her eyes. 'Come
on,' she said; 'don't tell me you didn't know?'

In the corner Mauro made a sound like a growl
in the back of his throat. Ginevra's mouth was set
in a line.

Cate laughed abruptly, and they all turned to
look at her with uniform hostility. She looked
down at her feet.

Nicki, apparently liberated from a year or more
of mute obedience, didn't seem to be able to stop
talking now.

'I think she liked it,' she said. 'The *Dottoressa*.
Lo-nee. The more gay girls the better.' There were
red spots of colour in the girl's cheeks. 'I think
she vetted everyone who came through this place
according to what she could get out of them,
whether they would fancy her or whether they
might be tempted to fancy anyone else. She had
to just be the queen bee, didn't she? Didn't want
anything in the way of competition.' She turned
to look at Cate. 'I'm surprised you slipped through
the net, though. Not old, not ugly, not married,
not gay.'

Cate stared at her, speechless.

'That's enough,' said Ginevra sharply. Mauro
yanked the door open and disappeared.

Looking around the room at the other women, at each pair of watchful, unfriendly eyes, even Nicki's, it took Cate no more than three seconds to make the decision to follow him.

Outside the sun was all but gone; there was a bitter wind and the sky was a white blanket. There was a tang in the air, borne on the breeze.

'Jesus Christ,' said Mauro, 'someone's lit a fire.' He was staring down the slope in the direction of the *villino*. The women turned to look and there it was, a thick column of smoke between the black cypresses, eddying in the wind.

'Is it the house?' said Mauro, and his face was murderous, white with emotion. 'The *villino*?' He let out a string of expletives. Belatedly Cate remembered that the *villino* was the house Mauro had grown up in; in his eyes she saw the rage of one bitterly insulted. 'Jesus, fucking idiot foreigners,' he said, talking to himself now, striding stiff-legged for the tractor. 'What in God's name are they doing lighting a bonfire?'

Cate ran after him as the tractor jolted between the cypress trees down towards the smoke. And as they approached, choking and coughing through the acrid cloud, the tractor swung out of the way and the two women came into view standing on either side of an oil drum from which the thick plume of smoke billowed and climbed. Tina and Michelle, and their faces were defiant.

Cate saw Michelle, in her leggings and an ugly, oversized cardigan, move around next to Tina, a restraining hand on the slighter woman's arm. Behind them, framed by the last yellow leaves of a pomegranate tree, the door to the downstairs studio stood open; she could see old newspapers on the floor, and a trestle covered with bits of pottery and tools.

'*Che cazzo state facendo, sceme?*' shouted Mauro. 'What the fuck do you think you're doing, you idiots?' They looked at him in mulish incomprehension and the rage still raw in his voice stopped Cate in her tracks. Mauro, of all of them, would be the one she could imagine doing violence: Mauro, for whom every imbecility of these foreigners was a reminder of betrayal. He turned away, muttering.

Cate peered into the oil drum; there was all sorts in there. She saw the curled ash of paper, orange wool, a ball of crumpled fabric, its Indian pattern of orange and green blackening and smouldering. The unmistakable smell of burning hair.

'What were you doing?' said Cate quietly to the women. She saw Tina give Michelle a pleading look, and the older woman answer.

'Listen,' she said, her harsh voice muted for once. 'The cleaner said she wouldn't do anything today. Told Tina she'd been told not to touch anything. What were we supposed to do?' She seemed weary. 'Art generates a lot of crap, sometimes. You need to get a clean sweep, if you want to move forward.'

The woman was usually so direct that on this occasion there was something about Michelle's dark, averted eyes that made Cate persist. 'Really?' she said drily. 'But actually, I think there was a reason Anna-Maria was told not to clean. The police –' And she fell silent, spreading her hands. Not saying more because actually she did not know why Luca had said what he'd said.

Tina made a convulsive movement. 'The police?' she said, wideyed, and at the almost forgotten sound of her soft, frightened voice Cate realized the girl had hardly said a word since Luca had first gathered them together in the library, to tell them Loni Meadows was dead. She was trembling: it was cold, though. Cate was beginning to feel cold herself, under the dark cypresses, the bleached sky full of snow.

Mauro appeared beside Cate with a bucket of water, grunted something and doused the smouldering detritus in the oil drum. It hissed and stank.

'Don't worry,' said Cate, forcing herself to remember that she was here to look after these women. 'The police – it'll be no more than a formality.' But Mauro and Ginevra had said the police weren't coming back: it had been an accident. So who would be coming to check through their rubbish then? Why were the rooms not to be touched?

'This will all be over soon,' she said meaninglessly. She could feel herself begin to shiver.

'You hear that?' said Michelle, looking down, surprisingly gentle, her arm around Tina's shoulders. 'Don't worry.' She looked up at Cate, and the expression in her angry black eyes seemed almost grateful. 'Over soon.' She hesitated. 'She feels guilty,' she said.

'Guilty?'

'You'd better tell them,' Mauro butted in threateningly, 'that if anything like this happens again, I'll kick them out myself.'

Cate stared at him. 'That's enough, Mauro,' she said, trying to keep her voice firm. 'I'll speak with them.' He glared a long moment, then turned on his heel, still ramrod-straight with rage.

Tina and Michelle watched him go; Michelle appeared to relax, although Tina still had her arms wrapped tight around herself. Michelle saw Cate looking at the younger woman.

'She had to clean the stuff,' she said abruptly, one eye still on Mauro's back. 'I wasn't going to tell that goddamn Neanderthal bastard. She's got this thing. OCD.' And in response to Cate's blank look. 'Obsessive compulsive.'

Slowly Cate nodded; she thought she knew what that was. But somehow it didn't explain everything. She resisted taking another look inside the oil drum. There'd been something unpleasant about the way the bundle of fabric and sticks had looked. And she'd seen that Indian patterned stuff before.

'Has anyone told Beth?' said Tina out of the blue, in that small, otherworldly, fine-china voice.

Michelle made an ugly little face. 'Why would anyone call her?' she said.

Cate looked at her, curious at her reaction. 'She

was fond of Loni,' she said. 'They –' and she tried to find a way to describe the unequal relationship between the two. 'They – talked.'

'Oh, yeah,' said Michelle. 'What would those two find to talk about? Beth was a fool.'

'Did – did something happen between them?' asked Cate. 'Is that why she left?' Michelle shrugged, and said nothing.

Cate looked at her set, obstinate face a long moment, then turned to Tina. 'What were you burning?' she said. 'Why did you feel guilty? That stuff – that Indian-patterned fabric, that was Loni's, wasn't it?'

Tina looked at Michelle beseechingly.

Michelle looked from Cate to Tina, and back again. 'Ah, shit,' she said. 'What harm can it do?'

'Harm?' said Cate.

'Let's get inside,' said Michelle, nodding towards the studio's open door. 'And we'll tell you.' Tina stood stiffly, not responding to Michelle's hand on her arm.

'We'll tell her, baby,' Michelle said soothingly, as if talking to a child. 'I mean, it's not like you really killed her, is it?'

CHAPTER 12

There was snow forecast. As Sandro drove out through the southern suburbs in Saturday traffic and on to the forest-shadowed Siena *superstrada*, the only clear patch of blue sky was dwindling behind him. He hadn't needed to turn on the TV, as he had done in the gloom of their flat in Santa Croce at midday, to know that the weather was going to turn nasty.

If it had been a Saturday afternoon any time after April, the Siena *superstrada* would have been slow and packed, but no one wanted to go down to the Maremma in winter; the beaches would be deserted, those barren hills in hibernation. Checking his mirror, with apprehension Sandro saw the red-tiled rooftops of the city recede behind him, the pale fortifications of the Certosa high against the skyline. His city. Already he was surprised by how much he missed the narrow, bustling streets, the crowded bars and Saturday-shopping housewives.

He was abandoning the quiet of the Piazza Santa Croce in winter, the pigeons fluttering up from the flagstones, the terraced gardens of the Villa Bardini, the *pietra serena* and arched windows that soothed the eye, and for what? On either side of him the unkempt forest of Chianti crowded in on the narrow, potholed road, and ahead of him clouds pressed down on the distant hills of the Maremma.

His back ached. He hadn't driven this far in a while, and he shifted painfully in his seat as he tried to ease the knotting between his shoulder blades. Mascarello and his wife: that relationship was one of the things tightening the muscles of his neck. As a policeman, of course, he'd been present at any number of domestics, screaming and yelling and tears and sweat, stab wounds and brandings and broken cheekbones. He knew the words that couldn't be taken back. Perhaps that was why, when it came to it, he would go to any lengths to avoid the first step in his own marriage: the first accusation.

He'd once been called to a handsome apartment block in the suburbs by an anonymous call, a man's voice saying someone was going to die. Sandro had seen a good-looking blonde, not even thirty, skip out of the glass doors, climb into her little Mercedes runaround with a secret smile on her face and he had just had time to think, *off to meet her lover*, before she turned the key in the ignition and the car went up. Why had the husband wanted a policeman there? A fellow male, a witness to that secret smile, an accomplice? He'd never forgotten the fraction of a second before the terrible sound of the explosion, a kind of vacuum, an intake of breath in which he knew – and the husband, stepping out from behind a truck, knew – that it was too late. Sandro had managed not to look at the bloody mess inside the car as he ran to find something to take a pulse from, but that moment of the world holding its breath and willing the terrible thing not to happen, after all – that had never left him.

He might have stopped it, if he had got there faster, if his reactions had been sharper, if he had been more intelligent. Or, as Luisa would have interjected, if you could fly or read minds. And it hadn't been him who'd planted the bomb, a surprisingly effective home-made device, had it?

The husband had been off his head afterwards, laughing in the street, blood on his trouser legs and a deep cut on his forehead from the flying metal. He'd cut his wrists in the police holding cell with a shard of biro casing. Ingenious. The human capacity for inflicting injury.

Mascarello and his wife, though, had had what some would call a happy marriage. He had tolerated whatever it was she got up to: they had an understanding. At the wheel Sandro found himself shaking his head violently at the thought and his neck stiffened even further. But Mascarello was not the one who had killed her: he had been in a hospital bed. He might, Sandro supposed, have paid someone else to do it. He had the contacts and the resources. But he was the one demanding an inquiry into her death. And he could have reined Loni Meadows in, if he'd wanted to. And how might that have felt, if you'd been her lover?

Now Sandro's eyes were aching. The light was uncertain, the trees here overhung the carriageway. Gallo had offered him a lift; Sandro had gazed at him in incomprehension. The thought of not having independent means of transport down there was inconceivable to him, but he was beginning to understand that Gallo operated on different principles to your average jaded, city-dwelling ex-policeman. He had ideals – of green living, of artistic freedom, that kind of thing.

'I'll drive myself,' Sandro had said shortly. He had turned down Gallo's offer to guide him down there in convoy, Sandro dutifully following on behind. 'I'll find the place all right,' he'd said. 'You go on ahead.'

And he needed time too, without Gallo breathing down his neck. Time to look over the police report, the photographs and the folderful of brochures and CVs Gallo had given him. Time to call the police station in Pozzo Basso, to sit down in front of Giuli in the office and brief her on what to do in his absence.

And, of course, time to talk to Luisa. A proper talk, to clear the air, to say sorry for all that hysterical nonsense about having affairs, to tell her, really, how he's feeling. Time to go quietly along to Frollini and get her out of there for ten minutes to sit down side by side in the Caffè La Posta under the arcades in the Piazza della Repubblica, and talk it through, before he goes, before she goes. That broad pale face, her dark eyes smiling back at him over her tall glass of *latte macchiato*.

Loni Meadows had died in a car accident – something hard to set up without expertise, these days, given that most cars, if not Sandro's twenty-year-old Fiat, were complex, computer-controlled machines with liquid crystal displays and microchips. If you want to kill someone with certainty, there were other ways.

Luisa wouldn't want to see the preliminary photographs of the accident scene. The deep gouging in the frozen ground, the blood and hair on the car's door pillar, the skull dented like an eggshell. Nor would she demand to look at the initial police report on the determining factors – weather conditions, injuries, skid marks – all of which told Sandro no more than that the police were probably right: it had been an accident.

No, Luisa would ask him, what was she like, then? She'd want to see the photograph of the live woman first off, and only then would she spread all those pieces of paper in front of him, examining each photograph, each CV, each personal statement given by the Trust's guests.

This was what Sandro would have needed the time for, before heading off on his own down the potholed Siena highway. Time to set himself up with Luisa's angle on the case and time to tell her, after all that, I'm an idiot, darling. Forgive me. Have a wonderful time in New York, you deserve it.

Only that wasn't quite how it went.

Giuli hadn't let up. Patiently Sandro had stood in the office at their cheap little printer, copying the folderful of documents while she paced the floor and ranted at him.

'What do you mean, she was busy?'

'It's Saturday, Giuli,' he'd said quietly, slotting the papers into another file, handing it to her. She'd taken it, but hadn't even looked to see what it was. 'The shop was packed.'

'But this is important,' she'd pleaded.

'Giuli,' he'd said, with a calm he hadn't felt, 'you're getting hysterical. We've been married thirty years, and a week apart is not going to finish us off.' Even as he'd said it he'd felt sick.

And they *had* been busy, in Frollini; Saturday, and in sales season. He *had* gone in, he'd spoken to Giusy, the intermittently friendly, lip-lined till-girl (no longer a girl, as a matter of fact, but younger than him). He had asked her if Luisa was around. If she was available. She'd smiled and said, *Sure, I'll buzz upstairs. She's um, actually I think she's with Frollini.*

'So you just – what?' Giuli had said.

'I've written her a note,' Sandro had replied. 'Left it at home,' and at that Giuli had only shaken her head. Sat down, looked at the folder and sighed. 'And this?'

He'd shrugged. 'For the files.'

Giuli had dropped it on the desk bad-temperedly. Poor kid. Just when she thought she was part of the deal, a comrade in arms, he was off. The remote

189

possibility of another evening's surveillance of a girl smoking a bit of dope obviously hadn't seemed quite the new start Giuli had hoped for. He'd remembered something, scribbled CHECK LONI MEADOWS BLOG: LONESTAR on a luminous pink Post-it note, pasted it on the desk beside the computer. LOOK FOR NAMES.

She was pulling open the drawer where they kept the new laptop. Her mouth set in a line, resignedly she'd pushed it across the desk to him. 'All the cables are in there, and the wireless card, and the battery's got good charge.'

She'd shut up after that, and Sandro had been able to call the front desk at the police station in Pozzo Basso, in the province of Grosseto, and arrange an appointment with Commissario Grasso, whose case this routine incident had been. The desk officer had seemed entirely indifferent to Sandro's inquiry: Sandro could picture him, fat, complacent, with *brioche* crumbs on his uniform.

Sandro checked his watch, the potholes jolting his hands on the wheel. He'd hit the *superstrada* by two and should be in Pozzo Basso by 3.30, an hour or so at the police station then, with luck, find his way to the castle before dark.

He could have got going an hour earlier, if he hadn't spent at least that sitting at the kitchen table in the midday gloom of the apartment, trying to think what to write in the note he was leaving for Luisa.

Something's come up; off on a job for a while. See you when you get back.

Love.

Curt, peevish, petulant, childish. He could see her screw the paper up in a ball and throw it at the kitchen wall, thinking all those things. But every time he'd written *darling*, even though that was the word he'd wanted to use and actually not bother with the rest, he'd just felt this resentment boil up inside him. Why should I be the one? The one to beg and compromise? He'd given her little packed suitcase if not a kick then a shove with the side of his foot as he left, then felt ashamed of himself.

Enough, he thought, and with an effort transferred his mind to the job, and the darkening horizon to the south.

By the time he saw the sign for Pozzo Basso, the sky was iron-grey with snow not yet crystallized, just waiting for that small shift in atmospheric conditions to begin to fall, softly, and the light was already failing. Within five minutes of leaving the *superstrada* Sandro was on the town's dismal outskirts: Gallo had been right about it being an ordinary little place. Curiously pancake-flat, considering the hills that rose up almost immediately beyond it; the flyblown station building and the open crossing over the railway line, the rows of aluminium *capannoni* housing light industry, the

191

ugly ersatz shopping-centre built up around a cheap supermarket chain. A one-horse town, with no aspirations to bettering itself.

Things improved slightly as he drove on; an avenue of dusty acacias led to what was left of a mediaeval centre, complete with fortifications. He'd been told to look for Pozzo Basso's only hotel, which turned out to be one of the town's few attractive buildings: the Hotel Liberty, with a dignified art deco frontage and a particularly elegant acacia shading its balconies, set back from the town gates. Follow the signs to Grosseto, second left after the hotel, the desk sergeant had told him in an unenthusiastic monotone.

Although Sandro had mentioned that he had the full authorization of the deceased's husband, Avvocato Mascarello, for his investigations into Loni Meadows's death, his guess was that the desk officer was too dumb to register the name's significance, because the man's phone manner had remained unchanged.

Skirting the old wall, turning between high gates with the insignia of the Polizia di Stato so familiar to Sandro – the crest, the motto, 'Freedom under the Law' – he reflected that he was not, in fact, prejudiced against the provincial outposts of the service that had once been his own employer. Genuinely he was not: there were plenty of intelligent officers outside the big cities, and some of the regional centres had challenges significantly tougher than those Sandro had faced in Florence:

immigration, people-smuggling, Mafia, terrorism. Poverty; there were some awful dead little towns down south, and poverty did terrible things. Pozzo Basso, though, was better off than that; Sandro had already put in a call to Pietro about the place even before he met with Luca Gallo. He'd been able to hear the bustle of the police office behind his old partner as he talked; had he also heard weariness, caution, pity? Poor old Sandro, out in the cold. No. His imagination: Pietro would be on Sandro's side. Always.

He pulled up in a space designated for a named officer; there were no others. A silver Audi was parked in another officer's space, so he wasn't the only civilian breaking the carefully calibrated rules of the car park.

No, the biggest challenge Pozzo Basso faced on the whole would be teenagers smoking pot and pickpockets in the holiday season, when the little towns filled up with seaside trippers, even this far back from the coast. Pietro had snorted. 'It's a dump,' he'd said. 'And they're all country in-breds. Wouldn't trust them to find their own backsides with both hands.' But his old partner hadn't heard of Commissario Grasso, so as he locked the car Sandro was none the wiser.

Passing behind the Audi, Sandro glanced through the driver window with an instinct honed over three decades for registering detail. The laminated green card of a Florentine parking permit, Zone E, leaned against the windscreen. A sign at the main entrance to the squat, ugly one-storey police building indicated that the entrance to the morgue and coroner's office was around the back. Sandro went inside.

The man kept him waiting for twenty minutes; reasonable enough, as Sandro was himself five minutes early. Not a matter for offence; and in any case Sandro spent the time examining the preliminary material the police had seen fit to share with Luca Gallo and Giuliano Mascarello. Mascarello, he noted, had identified the body; he must have come down yesterday. Had he given them hell? Or had he held back, waiting for evidence?

There were photographs of the rear end of a big SUV, nose down in a river, though not submerged. A wide shot, taking in the steep, frosted hillside in the grey dawn, a few scrubby trees, the sharp bend and the patch of black ice. Flytipped detritus on the roadside, even in that lovely spot; a tangle of reeds and brambles at the edge of the river. And in that shot the body hardly visible, just a gleam of white that was the woman's bare leg.

She had died at around midnight, and it was clear that she was heading in the direction of the town, away from the castle; she had never got to Pozzo Basso, or wherever she was going. For some reason Sandro thought of that hotel, with its art deco frontage.

He was still absorbed when Grasso's door opened. He caught the whiff of expensive aftershave but by the time he looked up whoever had been in with Commissario Grasso before him was disappearing through the door, broad shoulders in a dark cashmere overcoat.

If he was impressed or intimidated by Giuliano Mascarello's name, the senior policeman, a small, stocky man with black, close-set and unintelligent eyes, was determined not to show it. He was also, Sandro grasped in under a minute, not going to change the position he had taken on Loni Meadows's death.

Grasso had dismissed the anonymous email with a contemptuous wave. 'Conspiracy theory nonsense. Everyone has enemies; even people with enemies drive dangerously.' His small hooded eyes drooped lazily, as if he could barely be bothered to keep awake.

Sandro kept his temper; just gave the man a courteously inquiring glance. Grasso clicked his tongue impatiently and went on. 'Preliminary toxicology reports indicate that she had drunk a moderate amount of alcohol.'

'She was over the limit?' said Sandro, knowing that she had not been.

The man looked at him levelly, and went on as though he hadn't spoken. 'She was not wearing her seatbelt; on the evidence of the skid marks she had been driving very fast, on a dangerous stretch of road. Two weeks ago, the last time there was such a hard frost, there was a similar incident. There were also traces of cocaine in her blood sample.' He shrugged. 'If Avvocato Mascarello wishes to waste his money on a – a –' words seemed to fail him briefly '– on a private investigator, then it is his right.'

Sandro pulled out the photographs. 'And the car? It has been examined for – any defects, anything that might have contributed to the incident?'

Grasso inclined his head slowly. 'So far it seems only that the tread on the front tyres was very close to being illegally worn. She drove that car hard.'

'But not actually illegal. And the brakes?'

The policeman smiled sardonically. 'No one had cut her brakes,' he said. 'If you drive too fast on a narrow, icy road late at night, seatbelt or no seatbelt, then the brakes hardly come into it. You read too many cheap paperbacks, Mr Cellini.'

Sandro ignored the insult; wild horses would not have dragged from him at that moment the information that, not so long ago, he would have been Grasso's superior in the Polizia di Stato. 'Do you know where she was going?' he asked quietly.

Grasso was taken aback, as if the question had not occurred to him. 'There is some suggestion,' he said, eyeing Sandro with hostility, 'that she may have been going to meet someone with whom she was having a – relationship. A casual relationship. In Pozzo Basso.' Sandro got the picture: Grasso and his locals, his gossips and cronies, had this sewn up between them. A nudge and a wink.

'Have you managed to trace this person? This – casual relationship?' Sandro didn't see any reason to pull his punches.

'No,' said Grasso shortly, his jaw set. 'We haven't.'

'And that doesn't bother you?'

The small, dark, animal eyes hardened. 'I have no doubt that that aspect of the incident will be resolved,' he said. 'To pursue it actively at this stage would be a waste of public funds: it is *my* duty to consider that. The woman died because she was driving at dangerous speeds under the influence of drugs; we should – Avvocato Mascarello certainly should – consider it a stroke of fortune that she only managed to kill herself. Otherwise he would not simply be wasting money on a private detective, but on a rather expensive lawsuit.'

The two men stared at each other a moment, and the queer thing was, the more obdurate Grasso became, the more certain Sandro was that there was something to investigate. Why? Stubbornness? The fact that he felt an implacable dislike for the man? Not only that, nor the missing lover, nor even the email, no. It was to do with Loni Meadows. It was something to do with the picture Sandro now had of her last moments, something to do with the fact that the woman with the light blue eyes that had gazed at him so directly out of that photograph, had regained consciousness for long enough to climb out of the car, and die there, where she lay, in the cold.

Perhaps waiting for help, perhaps knowing no help would come. It wouldn't have taken long, but those were the minutes that drew him in, those cracks between which her life had fallen, those unfathomable, precious last minutes between life and death, when help might have come, and her life might have been saved.

Sandro got to his feet. 'I will need to collect her personal effects,' he said.

'Ask at the front desk,' said Grasso. 'Close the door on your way out.'

At the front desk Sandro was given directions to the morgue: a simple matter of telling him to go round the back. No one offered to accompany him. He handed over the release form Mascarello had signed and authorized to a young woman in an overall manning a reception desk so cheap-looking it might once have belonged to a fly-by-night tyre shop. She had a tattoo up one side of her neck, a lip-piercing and her hair was dyed jet black. Sandro wondered what kind of careers advice she had received at school.

The girl led him through some double doors fitted with wired glass, and into an office lined with filing cabinets. Another set of doors led to the morgue itself; through more wired glass he could see the familiar sets of long drawers, and the cashmere-coated back of the man who'd emerged from Grasso's office and was now in conversation with a technician. He weighed the plastic bag she handed him in his hand, not looking at it.

'Clothes in here?' he inquired mildly. She shook her head. Destroyed already, then; Sandro sighed. Would it have killed them to hang on to the stuff for a day or two?

'The car?'

'In the pound. There's a backlog for the crusher. D'you want to see the body?' she asked indifferently, following his gaze.

Sandro studied her; was she even interested in who he was, before letting him in there? He shook his head: he had the photographs; he would have the post-mortem details. They'd taken plenty of photos. But really – he'd seen enough dead bodies.

The man in the cashmere coat behind the glass had half-turned, presenting his profile to them: high, thick hair swept off his forehead, strong Roman nose, luxuriant moustache. It was the man Sandro had seen yesterday morning saying goodbye to his son outside the Liceo Classico Marzocco, which happened to be in Florence's Parking Zone E, before driving a silver Audi away down the hill. It also happened to be the man whose photograph he'd seen in the brochure for the Castello Orfeo, and half-recognized: Niccoló Orfeo, heir to the Orfeo estates, landlord and servant to the Trust.

His phone bleeped; a message. Under the indifferent gaze of the lip-pierced orderly, he got it out and looked at it.

It was from Giuli: *Bellagamba called, Carlotta announces she's going out, won't be back till morning. I'm to follow.* He snapped the phone shut.

And something clicked into place.

'Maybe I will view the body,' he said.

*   *   *

199

The pots sat in a row on a high shelf in the airy, white studio, and they freaked Cate out.

'I'll make some coffee,' said Michelle, unscrewing the little Moka machine, filling it from a tap.

In six weeks Michelle had only ever been wound up and angry; but as she moved between patting Tina's shoulder and the small electric ring in the corner of the studio, talking half to herself, even her harsh accent sounded mellow, likeable.

The pots were still freaking Cate out: it was as though they were looking down at her. Each one was slightly misshapen, and yet they were ranked so lovingly, so carefully, as though they were on display in the therapy unit of some hospital ward, testament to distress or breakdown. The wisps and scraps of things stuck to them made her think of bodily growths, hair coming out of a nostril, bulges, scar tissue. The more she stared, the more they seemed to assume features, looking back at her, grimacing or scowling. They were – good, Cate had to admit. She didn't know what they stood for – or maybe she didn't want to know – but they got to her.

Just tell me, she had wanted to shout, when first they'd come into the room. Tell me what you meant. She made herself wait; she looked at the pots to begin with, to give herself patience.

'Do you like them?' asked Michelle, arms folded across her solid front.

'Don't ask her that,' said Tina quickly.

200

'I – I don't like them, exactly,' said Cate, knowing there was no way to say the right thing. 'They're frightening me.'

'That's good,' said Tina. 'That's what I want them to do.'

And she sounded suddenly at ease. It came to Cate that this was their space, these two. This was where they were happy. Outside – in the library, the dining room, the castle's spaces – that was a different matter.

'That was what she didn't understand,' said Michelle to Tina. 'All that stuff about it being crude psychodrama – she didn't understand.'

'Who didn't understand?' asked Cate, although she knew the answer.

'Loni didn't understand,' said Tina, and her voice had deadened.

'Baby,' said Michelle warningly.

'I thought she liked your work,' said Cate. She paused. 'I remember her coming to see your stuff. Was it the first week?'

The atmosphere changed subtly; the bright room seemed suddenly cooler.

'That was before she knew. Knew I knew what she'd said about me. Liked my work?' Testing the words. She shook her head. 'No. She hated my work. She pretended to like me, so I wouldn't guess.'

'Little Loni,' said Michelle in a nasty, baby voice. 'Everyone had to love her. Never around to take the fall, if she did something bad.'

201

'Wouldn't guess what?' Cate asked, holding Tina's gaze.

Tina just shook her head, frozen suddenly.

'You can say it,' said Michelle softly. 'She's gone now.'

When Tina remained silent Michelle turned to Cate patiently. 'There was an anonymous hatchet job, of Tina's last show, in New York. A blogger. Rubbished it. Said Tina was – what was it?' Tina shook her head, her mouth set and bloodless. 'A suburban Goth.'

Cate had no idea what that meant. 'Anonymous?'

'It was Loni: the blogger was called Lonestar. Plenty of people knew it was her, and one of 'em told Tina.' She shrugged. 'People are like that. They like to pass that kind of stuff along.'

'I shouldn't've read it,' said Tina, her face in her hands, sounding like a kid. Michelle nudged a cup of green tea into her hands; gave Cate a tiny cup of coffee. Reached up to a small cupboard and took down a bottle of brandy and a shot glass.

Cate realized she had no idea what time it was. She hoped Ginevra and Nicky had got the lunch hampers out; she couldn't hurry this.

'But she did read it,' said Michelle.

Tina stared into her tea. 'It was really stupid.' And looked up.

For what felt like the first time since her arrival in the castle, Tina's pale, washed-out face under the hoodie seemed to come sharply into focus. A scattering of light brown freckles all over her white skin, her eyes not indeterminate at all but hazel, green and gold and black together. Her stiff, unbrushed hair like hay. A kid.

She looked back down. 'Should never read critics. Never; just get on with your work, get back in the studio. I guess I thought it would make me feel better about it. Mine wasn't the only life she trashed.'

Michelle put out a calming hand. 'Come on,' she said in a low voice. 'Don't beat yourself up about it. I know it feels bad – but she didn't wreck your life, baby. It's nothing.'

Cate found herself wondering whose idea it had been to light the fire, to destroy the stuff? Tina's? She doubted it.

'And then?' she prompted gently. And Tina raised her blotchy, unhappy face to hers. 'So I did it,' she said.

'Did what?' Tina's head went down again and she mumbled.

'I made her. Made a – made a Loni doll.' And lifting her head to Cate's mystified face, she said, 'You know what obeah is? Vudou? I made a poppet. A voodoo doll.'

'Voodoo,' repeated Cate, and her eyes went to the row of pots ranked above her, with their malignant little misplaced features. On the Caribbean cruises, the kindly, overweight American women came back with those rag-dolls, of sticks and cloth, and fake scrolls. Disney witchcraft.

'I didn't think it would work,' said Tina tonelessly.

'It didn't work,' said Michelle roughly, interrupting her. 'Just stop it, kid. Now.'

Cate's mother believed in exorcism, and evil spirits, and faith healing; Cate had always groaned and held her head at the mention of this or that creepy priest, and now it seemed downright dangerous lunacy.

'She's right,' she said, taking hold of Tina's arms at the elbow and looking into her face. 'You mustn't talk about this. Are you crazy?' No one should know about this: they'd lock the girl up.

It was this place. If Cate was anywhere else, down in Pozzo, hanging out with Vincenzo, at home with her mother or eating ice-cream in her home town with the girls she'd grown up with – this would just be laughable. Stupid. Kids' stuff; a girl with a grudge makes a voodoo doll of a mean teacher. In this place, with the high grey walls of the castle always at her back, the cold, dark corridors, the wide, empty, frozen countryside that stretched for miles, with only taciturn farmers between her and civilization – here, Cate was frightened. And Cate was not easily frightened.

She took a deep breath. 'You did something stupid, but you didn't kill her.' She turned to Michelle. 'What did she put on that – thing? The doll?'

'I made it out of clay,' said Tina. 'I – got hold of some of her hair.' She looked to Michelle, as if asking permission, but Michelle's face was just set grimly. 'From out of her hairbrush. And that cloth – it was a headscarf of hers.'

Cate looked from one of them to the other, barely able to believe the madness of it.

'The scarf got mixed up in my laundry,' said Michelle defiantly. 'It's what gave Tina the idea.'

The pots stared down at her, Tina and Michelle's faces each distinctly and separately crazy, in the open door the smell of burnt hair and cloth still hung, and all at once Cate found she couldn't stay in there any more.

Outside the sky seemed lower than ever, and darker; the wind had whipped up and it felt bitterly cold, and damp with impending snow. Far off in the woods came the crack of hunters' guns, followed by the dogs' baying.

Cate looked inside the oil drum: the blackened and incinerated mess looked disgusting. Tina and Michelle came up behind her. Cate leaned in, extended an arm, hesitated.

'What should we do with it?' said Tina.

From above them, where the cypresses ended and the grey bulk of the castle rose dark in the feeble afternoon light, came a shout. Cate turned at the sound: it was Tiziano, muffled up in his wheelchair. He raised a hand, and Cate waved back. He shouldn't try to come down; the gravel path was tricky. Unwillingly she looked back into the drum, and saw a longish piece of crumbling, blackened clay that might have been a bone.

'I don't know,' she said, averting her eyes.

She looked back up; Nicki was up there now, a hamper in her arms, walking awkwardly down towards them on the uneven path, tottering as she turned back to wave to Tiziano. Ridiculously, Cate didn't want Nicki to look inside the drum; Nicki was just a kid.

'I'll get rid of it for you,' she said quickly. 'Just put it round the back.' Tina smiled, with timid gratitude.

And Cate almost ran, up over the stones, towards Tiziano, in time to see his wide smile turn wary. 'Are you OK?' he asked with concern as she reached him. Kneeling next to him, getting her breath back, Cate managed a smile. 'I'm fine,' she said. Over Tiziano's shoulder she saw someone else emerge from around the side of the castle, walking fast under the trees.

'I thought you might take me for a walk,' said Tiziano, and Cate smiled more broadly, because Tiziano didn't need someone to push his chair. She stopped herself, not wanting him to think she was laughing at him.

She sat back on her haunches. 'Sure,' she said, her eyes on the thin, tense figure skirting the walls in a long overcoat. It was Alec Fairhead. Seeing them, he came to a halt. Getting to her feet, Cate waved, then looked back down at Tiziano. He caught her hand. 'So you will?'

'Yes, *caro*.' Cate frowned. 'Did you get something to eat? Things are a bit – chaotic at the moment. In the kitchen; I don't know if I'm supposed to be in there, or out here, or what.'

'Nicky brought me something earlier,' he said.

206

'I'm well taken care of. And I'm sure it would count as part of your duties, helping the disabled.'

'Don't be stupid,' she said sharply, then immediately regretted it. She was no good at this; was she these people's equal or not? Was she Tiziano's friend, or his servant? The odd thing was, before Loni Meadows's death and her own abrupt promotion, Cate would have said, friend, one hundred per cent.

'I'll just get a coat,' she said. Tiziano had several layers on as well as a woollen hat and gloves, whereas she'd come out in no more than a sweater. It was freezing now, the wind whipping round her legs; a stupid idea to go for a walk in this weather, and with snow on the way, but anyway. Alec Fairhead was coming over.

Cate waved at the Englishman again as she set off to her room; Tiziano would explain. But what she heard as she hurried across the stones was the Englishman's soft, hurried inquiry, 'Mind if I tag along? Could do with some fresh air,' and Tiziano, in whose voice she thought she detected resignation although it might have been wishful thinking on her part, answering, 'Sure, yeah. The more the merrier.'

Damn, she thought, damn.

CHAPTER 13

Stationed at the big old computer in the office in the Via del Leone, Giuli was wondering what she was doing there on a Saturday afternoon, when no doubt Sandro wouldn't be paying her, not that she was doing it for the money, God knew. But then the phone rang and startled Giuli out of her bad temper. And it was a good job too, because it turned out she was answering the phone to her own first client, thanks to Sandro, and sounding like a truculent school kid wouldn't have been a good move. Fabrizio Bellagamba even asked for her by name.

The man was in a state because his daughter wanted to go out on a Saturday night. Giuli had to bite her tongue so as not to say, just chill out. That wouldn't be appreciated.

'You did the right thing, calling us,' she said. 'Absolutely. Getting into a fight with her will not improve matters; she needs to feel that you trust her.' Even though you don't; even though you can only trust her if you've got a private detective tracking her, but clearly it wasn't Giuli's place to question that.

'I'll look after her,' Giuli said. 'Don't worry.'

The words escaped her before she could think; it wasn't something Sandro would have said to the man. Now she corrected herself. 'I'll stay close to her. I'll be out there by 5.30?'

And there was a brief pause before Fabrizio Bellagamba said, 'Thank you.'

Texting Sandro practically the minute she'd put the phone down Giuli was full of her triumph, then after the message had been sent, full of nerves.

Come on, call me back, she thought. Tell me I've done great, then tell me what I do next. She got up, paced the room, checked her phone had charge and that her clothes would do, not too noticeable, not too shabby. She'd do fine: her best dark jeans, white shirt, fake cashmere sweater, the warm padded jacket Luisa had given her for Christmas.

That stopped her short: Luisa, who would be still at work, wearing herself out all day on foreigners, and wouldn't know until she got home that Sandro had done a bunk.

Was that what he'd done? No, of course not: he was on a job, it was the truth. But Giuli hoped he'd written a proper note, straightening things out. Fat chance. And then she started pacing the room again; she couldn't actually be thinking about Luisa now. Come on, she said to her mobile.

As it turned out, he didn't call her back for a good hour, and when he did, he didn't say anything she expected.

★   ★   ★

209

'You're a popular lady, today,' the morgue assistant had said, pulling out the drawer and addressing the comment to the dead body it contained. He was a fat, inappropriately jovial man, with a habit of muttering to himself; Sandro wondered what Niccolò Orfeo would have made of him. He knew it was Orfeo because as he waited for the man to be done, eyeballed stonily all the while by the girl with the pierced lip, he had gone back to the brochure Gallo had given him and looked him up. Niccolò Orfeo, father of Carlotta's hero Alberto, whose surname he had never asked.

Niccolò Orfeo, sixty-nine years old and looking good on it, photographed in the castle's old library standing at the grand piano, then photographed in patriarchal mode with his wife and son at their villa in Florence, on a wide terrace with expensive garden furniture and a striped canopy and the Duomo floating serene in the background. The house was up behind the Porta Romana somewhere, judging from the view: Poggio Imperiale or Arcetri, both in Zone E. Open house, the janitor at the Liceo Classico Marzocco had said, when he's off with one of his women.

The wife looked like a bolter, too thin, with a deep tan of the sort acquired in the southern hemisphere, a distracted smile on her face as she stood between son and husband, and no wonder. To Sandro's experienced eye Niccolò Orfeo didn't look much of a man for the marriage vows. Too aristocratic, perhaps. And other evidence, too, was accumulating.

210

And then he was coming through the swing doors and Sandro stepped back, hoping to make himself as close to invisible as could be managed in the space. A gust of carbolic mixed incongruously with the man's aftershave and his face pale, his eyes staring fixedly ahead, Niccolò Orfeo marched straight past and out of the morgue.

A popular lady: so Orfeo had come to look at her too. Sandro knew very well that not just anyone could walk in off the street and be shown the recently deceased, on state premises, but Orfeo was a name in these parts. The question was, what was he doing here?

As to that, Sandro was beginning to formulate his own reasons. Either he'd been fond of her, or he wanted to make sure she was dead. Or both.

As the morgue orderly, a good ten centimetres shorter than Sandro and a broad, questioning smile on his round, shiny face, stood holding the handle of the long steel drawer that contained Loni Meadows, Sandro found himself wanting to tell the man, no, he'd changed his mind. He'd asked to see the dead body to be sure that Orfeo had been here for the same reason he was, and now he knew that, it was the last thing he wanted to do. Instead he inclined his head, took a deep breath and said, 'Yes.'

Niccolò Orfeo would be climbing into that big silver Audi now, slipping on to the ringroad of the dirty little town, his polished, powerful car a superior beast amid the shabby provincial traffic.

But Sandro couldn't use that as an excuse to run out of the morgue and after him, because he had a pretty fair idea where he'd be going. And Luca Gallo had given Sandro a good set of directions to the Castello Orfeo from Pozzo.

The drawer slid out with ease; Loni Meadows had not been a big woman, and under the crisp white sheet she hardly took up any space at all now. The orderly folded the sheet down to reveal her face and neck, and Sandro nodded briskly, holding up a hand to stop him there. The eyes were closed, of course. The light blue, sky blue eyes, and without them she was almost ordinary. Almost; there was nothing ordinary about the dead. Her skin, had she been alive, would have been remarkable for a woman of her age, hardly a wrinkle or a blemish, although it was dull as mud now, and one cheekbone had been smashed. The consequent bruising and swelling had made her face lopsided, brutalized.

Her lips were bluish grey; Sandro couldn't see more than a wisp or two of the hair, because like the injury that killed her, it was hidden under the white linen folded into a sort of cap to protect the viewer from the pathologist's incisions. He could ask the man to expose the injury, to fold back the cap, but he didn't. Even from what Sandro could see, from the extent of the collapse in the skull at the eggshell-thin temple, a dent the extent of perhaps a large grapefruit, she could not have survived this one injury. It was an injury common in car crashes, where the head met the door pillar, and commonly fatal, and there would have been others. Sandro leaned down closer; there were photographs in his briefcase, he knew he did not have to do this, but now he was in so far – he stopped short, his downturned face over hers, like a lover's; he did not want to breathe. He wanted to close his eyes, but he kept them open.

From this close he could see a diagonal mark on her neck, a small, reddish abrasion like a rope burn, which might possibly have been the mark of a seatbelt as it tried to brake her body against the force of the crash. Grasso, though, had said she had not been wearing one, and for a moment Sandro pondered the inconsistency. It might, or might not, prove significant; at this stage, he simply couldn't know.

Sandro breathed in, against his will, and smelled it, the smell of the morgue, of the body that has been through all the invasive processes that follow death, filled with the alien fluids and coagulants of the laboratory. What would Loni Meadows have smelled of, in life? Of soap, face cream, one of those heavy, expensive scents, the musk of her own skin. He jerked his head back.

As he stared into the orderly's pasty, knowing face, Sandro wished silently for Luisa, for the soft white neck in which he could press his face and inhale until she was all he could smell.

'Thank you,' he said. 'That'll do.'

The swing doors, the front desk, the pale, pierced face and black hair of the receptionist, all passed in a blur as he retraced his steps through the ugly little building and its equally ugly surroundings until he was back at his car, opening the unlocked door and inside. Taking deep breaths.

Don't be ridiculous, he told himself. You've seen dead bodies before. Not for a long time, though. Five years, even. With his last two big cases, one as a policeman, one as a private investigator, he'd expected a dead body but had managed to get there first. A matter of dogged persistence and luck, he'd told himself. But you couldn't rely on luck. With Loni Meadows, though, he'd been too late, although it couldn't be said to be Sandro's fault.

Or could it? Of course not. But what if he'd summoned up enough curiosity to ask why the Orfeo Trust wanted to check the references of such a woman? And what if he had managed to extract from Luca Gallo, then no more than a person-able, likeable voice on the end of a phone asking him to carry out a perfectly routine control, the information that a nasty anonymous email had been sent about her? Would that email have told him that its sender was dangerous and might, in time, have tracked Loni Meadows down and brought about her death?

He – if it was a he – certainly would have known where to find her.

One, two: he breathed in the friendly, musty smell

214

of his car's interior: fake leather, old carpet, stale something or other he'd snatched for breakfast a week ago and was still in the glove compartment.

Around Sandro, things normalized; beyond his car window the world carried on, traffic moved on the ring road. He got out his phone, and thinking once again with longing of the city – the light, quiet office in San Frediano, the wide green river, the sound of *motorini* audible inside the familiar, gloomy flat that smelled of Luisa's scent – he called Giuli.

'Yes,' he said. 'Yes, well done. Good girl. Now listen.'

When he'd given her his instructions, Sandro folded the phone and put it in his pocket, sitting for a long moment as he considered what he had to do next. Then he started the car and drove away.

If they'd wanted fresh air they could have walked down behind the castle, past the *villino* and the laundry and the studio and the plain new house where Mauro lived to where there was a small hill and a ruined tower; that was the little constitutional guests sometimes took to walk off a heavy lunch. They could have walked into the winter fields, although they'd been warned of the hazards presented by trigger-happy hunters; they could have taken the path that led off the back entrance, down to a pretty little stream. They did none of these things.

As Cate came back out of the door to the stable block wearing hat, scarf, gloves and a long padded coat buttoned up to her ears against the bitter wind, she saw the car. The little black car with the hire logo, parked up against the office entrance; looking up, she saw light behind the shuttered windows. So Luca was back; she should go and bring him up to date, Cate knew that. But the light was going, and Tiziano and Fairhead were waiting for her – and it was all too complicated. Wives were not allowed – and most particularly, she suspected, noisy, emotional, betrayed wives – and it was quite possible Luca would take the position that she, Cate, should have sent Yolanda Hansen packing. She didn't want to see that disappointed look in his eyes, and so she hurried past.

By the time she reached them Alec Fairhead had pushed Tiziano's wheelchair across the rougher ground behind the castle and round to the front, to the smooth tarmac of the road that led down between the grand avenue of old cypresses, where they were waiting for her. The two-hundred-year-old trees between which Yolanda Hansen had approached the Castello Orfeo at speed, as if she wanted to ram the great gate; the avenue by which Loni Meadows liked to come and go, seeing herself as the castle's mistress. Not for her the tradesman's entrance.

With Cate alongside they set off without a word, only Alec Fairhead giving her a shy, apologetic

216

smile. She smiled back, forgiving him; feeling exhilarated at the thought of leaving the bounds of the castle keep for the first time in what seemed like weeks, not just twenty-four hours. And given the pace at which they set off, Tiziano in the lead and turning his wheels with furious energy, she wasn't the only one.

No one spoke for a while. They knew where they were going.

The wide winter landscape stretched in front of them, the sun no more than a feeble glare not far above the western horizon, behind a sky low and heavy with layers of snow cloud. When they reached the end of the old cypress avenue Tiziano stopped, and they turned and looked back.

The great squat bulk of the castle sat there, more forbidding than ever and entirely uninterested in them. All of it, sky, trees and stone, in shades of grey, except the flash of red that was the car Yolanda Hansen had arrived in, no longer on the grass, now parked askew on the drive.

'Poor old Per,' said Alec Fairhead abruptly. 'What a mess.' Tiziano barked a laugh, rubbing his hands in leather gloves in his lap. Cate looked down at the pianist's hands and found herself instead gazing at his legs, lifeless and thin in padded trousers, his booted, useless feet on their foot-rest.

'You can say that again,' he said. 'A mess.'

'Do you know what's going on?' said Cate, looking at Fairhead. They were neighbours, after all, the

Norwegian and the Englishman. She thought of him typing away there this morning; thought of all those other mornings when he would have done nothing but stare down to where they stood now, down between the tall, dark trees to the distant hills and the silver strip of river winding between their spurs. Surely if Per talked to anyone, it would be to him?

'He's got himself into a mess,' Fairhead repeated. 'That's what's happened.' There was something resigned about the way he said it, as though it was a situation he knew all about, had seen before.

'His wife said he'd written to her asking for a divorce,' said Cate tentatively. This was gossip. It made her uncomfortable. 'Said he'd fallen in love with another woman, and he wanted a divorce.' She shook her head. 'I can't believe it. I always thought –'

'Thought he was a nice family man?' said Tiziano, twisting his wheels and turning back downhill. 'Me too. Someone certainly turned his head.'

Cate had to hurry to catch up, but Fairhead's long stride enabled him to keep pace easily with the two of them.

'Do you know who?' she asked. Tiziano shrugged; she turned to Fairhead.

'Yes,' he said. 'I know.' He looked uncomfortable. 'I don't think – I think he'll tell you himself, if – when – it becomes appropriate.'

'Oh, for God's sake,' said Tiziano, echoing Ginevra with savage cheerfulness, his face red in the wind as he looked curiously at Alec Fairhead. 'Who else could it be? The only other good-looking woman in the place was Cate, and I think she would have said, don't you? If she and Per were planning to ride off into the sunset together?'

Cate blushed furiously; Tiziano kept going regardless. 'Do you think he bumped her off, as well? How would you go about it, though? Cut the brakes? Surely it can't be that easy, these days, and if she'd had no brakes, she'd never have made it to the end of the drive.'

As Cate stared at Tiziano in disbelief, Alec Fairhead spoke. He was quite white. 'I don't think – I wish you wouldn't talk like that,' he said, sounding very English.

'So it *was* Dottoressa Meadows? He was leaving his wife for Dottoressa Meadows?' asked Cate.

'Yes,' said Fairhead, so quietly she could hardly hear him. 'Yes. That was what he thought.'

They had come out of the small cluster of low trees that marked the end of the drive, and they were on the road, a D-road, curved, narrow and, if it had been busier, far too dangerous to go walking on at the approach of a snowstorm in bad light. None of them asked which way they would turn; they all turned downhill together, each of them silently pondering what had just been said. It occurred to Cate that without Tiziano and the wheelchair, there would probably have been an alternative to this road, a path cross-country to their destination. The hills were scored with such paths, rabbit runs and sheep tracks and riding trails; one of the weird aspects to the landscape, considering, was how empty it always seemed. All the time, there must be secret movement, in the scrub, between the willows and juniper and myrtle bushes, skirting the trees.

'So kitchen gossip had it right, then?' asked Tiziano. 'Might have known Ginevra would have her finger on the pulse. Don't tell me you didn't notice anything, Caterina? You're a clever girl.'

'Notice anything?' said Cate, 'I didn't notice anything, actually. I don't look for –' She wanted to say, I don't look for that kind of thing. Was that true? Not on the cruises, no; on the cruises she'd been very good at spotting those romances that sprang up and died down among the elderly passengers.

'Think we're above all that?' said Tiziano, reading her mind, not for the first time. Cate wished Alec Fairhead, a metre ahead of them with his arms wrapped around himself, would say something.

'Mr Fairhead?' she asked gently. 'Alec? What do you think of all this?' And he turned towards her, and she saw his eyes bleary with the wind.

'Stop,' he said. 'Stop.'

And though that wasn't what he'd meant, they all literally did stop, in the middle of the road. In the sudden silence Cate could hear, from far away, the sound of a car that came and went, baffled and bounced by the hills. A powerful car.

Alec Fairhead was rubbing a fist in his eye, facing

up to the brow of the hill from which they would be able to see down into the next valley, where the road curved sharply, and then Cate remembered how he'd looked that evening when he'd arrived, as though he'd wanted to run away, the moment he saw them all standing there waiting for him.

'I'm sorry,' she said, and she meant it. 'You knew her. I'd forgotten that. I'm sorry.'

'That's not it,' said Fairhead, his face drawn and haunted. There was a long pause, then he spoke hesitantly. 'It's Per. I just feel sorry for Per, to be honest. He – fell for her. He's a man who doesn't do things by halves – he's a man who can't pretend, either. He fell for her.' The distant car was louder now, and closer.

'You mean, fell in love with her?' Cate hugged herself, rubbing her arms; in the lee of the hill it was even colder, if that was possible, than it had been at the castle. No sun got down here in these valleys, not between November and March.

'Fell in love with her, yes,' said Alec Fairhead, and Cate saw that he was shivering. He was not warmly dressed; a dark corduroy jacket, thin gloves, an insubstantial scarf – but that wasn't it. 'I also mean, that he was taken in by her. Deceived.' He spoke, Cate saw, with grim understanding. 'She was – a flirt, is the kind word for it.'

'Never flirted with me,' said Tiziano, ruddy-faced and healthy in contrast to Fairhead, but his smile was cool.

The sound of the approaching car was suddenly

much closer and Cate became aware at once that they were standing in the middle of the road. It had to be coming this way; there was nowhere else. She edged towards the verge. 'Come on,' she said, but they weren't listening to her. She came around behind the wheelchair and leaned to push and at last the two men responded.

'Would you have wanted her to flirt with you?' said Alec Fairhead quickly, tensed as he tried to stop the shivering. 'She was good at that, knowing who it was worth bothering with.'

'You knew her very well, didn't you?' said Tiziano.

It wasn't really a question, but if Alec Fairhead had wanted to answer no one would have been able to hear him because at that moment the big, powerful silver car leapt the brow of the hill above them, its engine a deafening roar as it passed without a swerve or a touch on the brakes, within centimetres of the little group. The driver didn't turn his head to acknowledge they were there – it was possible, thought Cate with a sick feeling, that he had not seen them at all – but they all knew who it was. They knew Niccolò Orfeo's car, and the way he drove it; like Loni Meadows, as though he was immortal, untouchable.

'Well,' said Alec Fairhead stiffly. 'Our lord and patron.' They turned to watch, but they knew where he was going; up through the cypress avenue behind them, carelessly fast because, of course, unlike poor Yolanda Hansen, if he wanted to ram his own gates, no one could stop him. The car was obscured by a puff of white dust as it hit the dirt road, and they turned away.

'Is there any sun over there, d'you think?' said Tiziano, nodding up towards the brow of the hill. Cate made an apologetic gesture. There was no sun anywhere; at the horizon the cloud was blue-grey with unshed snow.

'Should we go back?' she suggested hopefully. The men both looked from the castle to Cate and back.

'No,' said Tiziano, just as Fairhead shook his head.

But when they set off again it was slowly, reluctantly. What were they going for, anyway? To inspect the scene of the crime? Ghoulishly to look for blood or scraps of clothing, or tyre treads? Or was it just that having escaped the castle they were in no hurry to go back, particularly not now Niccolò Orfeo had arrived?

'She led him on,' said Cate.

Fairhead nodded, head bowed as he walked. 'She told him she would divorce her husband – at least, that's what he says.'

'You don't believe him?'

'I think he convinced himself; it's possible she led him to believe she would, but if I know Loni –' Fairhead broke off, and Cate could see he was shivering uncontrollably now.

She pulled off her hat and held it out; he took it, puzzling over it a second before pulling it on.

He tried to smile his thanks, but his face was grim. 'If I know Loni, she'd have covered herself. *Only a joke, darling, only in the heat of the moment, darling.* But of course Per would have taken it seriously, being Per.' He twisted his mouth. 'Per can't conceive of anyone saying such a thing lightly. So he wrote to Yolanda, in Oslo, a week ago. When she got the letter she dropped everything, and came out, only by then – it was all what you might call academic.'

'He told you this – when?' said Tiziano. 'Last week?'

'No,' said Fairhead, shaking his head energetically, 'they were arguing, this afternoon – I couldn't help overhearing. I even understood some of it. I tried to help. I'd never have let him send the letter, if he'd told me. I'd have told him she'd never leave her husband.'

Tiziano sat very still in the wheelchair, arms rigid by his sides. 'The husband,' he said; 'the famous human rights lawyer.' He sounded uncharacteristically sharp. 'You think not? He's old, though, isn't he? Old and ugly.'

'Old and ugly and rich,' said Fairhead, gazing away from them and towards the grey line of the horizon. 'But it's not just that. They're two of a kind, Loni and Giuliano Mascarello. Were. Ruthless, charming, clever, and the rest.'

So Fairhead didn't just have a passing acquaintance with Loni Meadows and her husband before he came here. It had been more than that; it had been something that had stopped him writing; something had happened.

And then they heard another car. Far off, slower, quieter than the first, but getting closer. Silently, as if by mutual agreement, they hurried now to get to the brow of the hill, to see and be seen. And then they stopped, and looked down into the narrow valley, the sharp bend at the foot of the steep hill, the spidery willows, the churned earth. The last ragged flicker of the tape, caught on a bramble.

They stood, getting their breath, and then Cate decided. 'You knew her,' she began, and before she could ask it, ask Alec Fairhead what Loni Meadows had done to him however long ago it was, he turned on her fiercely.

'We were the last ones to see her,' he said, 'Per and I. I couldn't see it. I can't believe I couldn't see what was going on. We were the last ones to see her before she died.'

'What happened?' asked Tiziano quietly.

'The women left,' Fairhead said, his voice stilted, formal. 'Tina left the table early because Loni had said something that upset her. Talking about one of the galleries in New York.'

Cate nodded. 'It was to do with a show she'd had in New York,' she said reluctantly. 'Loni had posted a bad review of Tina's work at the same gallery, and I suppose just mentioning the name . . .' She tailed off, not wanting to tell Tina's secret.

'Michelle and Tiziano went after her.' Fairhead stared down the slope at the red and white tape.

'She was running,' Tiziano said, and sighed. 'I could hear her crying. I let Michelle follow her; I couldn't keep up. I went to bed.' Cate looked down at him, feeling a tiny pulse of adrenaline as things slotted into place. Tina first, yes, then Michelle, then Tiziano.

Fairhead went on in a distant monotone. 'And we sat there, just the three of us; she said something about poor Tina, talking to Per. She was saying Tina needed to toughen up if she was going to survive, that art wasn't just about the studio, that you had to engage with the world. Per was just gazing at her, she might have been saying anything.' His voice was strained, dull with resignation. 'Then her phone went. She got a text message on her phone.'

'No phones at dinner, I thought,' said Tiziano drily. 'Isn't that the rule?'

Alec Fairhead shrugged, the ghost of a smile on his thin face. 'One rule for Loni Meadows,' he said, 'another for the rest of us. You must have learned that by now.'

Tiziano was sitting upright in his wheelchair, and Cate knew he wanted to ask Alec Fairhead outright what she'd done to him to set him off wandering the world like he did. She put a hand on his arm to stop him.

'Did she read the message?' she asked gently.

He nodded unhappily. 'We might as well have not existed. She read it and just gave us a vague

226

sort of smile, pleased with herself, oblivious. Then she got up and went out.'

There was a silence, save for the sound of the second car. It was slower, quieter than Orfeo's, but it was getting closer.

'Did Per leave with her?' Cate asked softly. She found herself thinking of Loni Meadows's bedroom, still smelling of her, clothes flung around as though she'd just left. The green silk of the blouse she'd worn at dinner, left carelessly on the floor; she'd changed in order to leave again. She wouldn't have done that with Per in the room? Unless she was a bigger whore than they thought. 'Did he leave with her in the car that night? Did he have something to do with – the accident?'

'After she'd gone, Per just sat there a moment, looking – I don't know. Like he'd been slapped. I should have understood.' Fairhead looked haunted. 'But I had enough trouble myself, getting through those dinners. Then he got up without saying anything and left too; and I went after them.'

'You mean they were together?' Tiziano's voice was probing, insistent. Alec looked at him as if he didn't recognize him. 'Together? No. She was going upstairs to her room, holding her phone. She was in a hurry. Of course, our rooms are on the floor above, so we had to pass her – but Per stopped. I went on. When I looked back, she was at the door, talking to him. Impatient. I don't know if he went in. I went to bed. I heard him come up about five minutes later.'

227

'You heard him? You didn't see him?'

But Alec Fairhead didn't answer; he was looking away from her, and Cate followed his gaze. His eyes were fixed on the far hill, where another car had appeared, only this one was small and brown, humble as a forest creature by comparison with Orfeo's great sleek roaring machine, and moving slowly, as though it was looking for something. Looking for them.

CHAPTER 14

The three figures on the brow of the next hill and perhaps eight hundred metres away from Sandro didn't move; they were watching him. A tall man, coatless; a woman with long black hair that blew about in the wind and whom, even at this distance, as he climbed out of the car, Sandro could tell was beautiful; and a man in a wheelchair. Broad-shouldered; strong. Three people not necessarily friends, but allies.

It was a professional habit; in the police or out of it, the ability to evaluate people and the dynamic between them from a distance was useful. To know whether they would coagulate, group and turn on you, or scatter. In either case you would have to know which of them would move the fastest; Sandro thought the guy in the wheelchair might have the edge, disabled or not.

Standing a moment, leaning on the roof of the car, Sandro watched them. They had to be from the castle; in fact from his examination of the guests' CVs, the one in the wheelchair would be Tiziano Scarpa. Pianist? Composer and pianist. Sandro had imagined him a twisted, angry figure;

no joke, paralysed from the waist down since the age of twenty-two, in a Red Brigade bomb blast that had killed his father. He didn't look stunted from this angle.

The three figures watched him back, and they didn't move, and it came to Sandro that they had been coming here too. Relaxed, Sandro held his ground; let them come back tomorrow. In half an hour, forty-five minutes at most, it would be dark, and they had a walk ahead of them. And as if they had read his mind the man in the wheelchair turned his head so Sandro could see a profile, tilted it up to speak to the girl, whose head then turned to the skinny man, he nodded, and they were gone.

Forty-five minutes was not long, for Sandro's purposes. He got started straight away, walking up the slope opposite him almost as far as where the three had stood and watched him. Then back down. The ice had melted somewhat, although it could hardly have got above zero today, and most of it was still visible. Black, glassy, fanning across the tarmac from halfway down the hill. He looked along the verges, in the pale winter grasses on either side, carefully criss-crossing the site. He wasn't used to traffic accident investigation beyond the city, and anyway, although there were country lanes enough close in to Florence, ice was never much of a factor. The city held the temperature a degree or two too high for the most part. He couldn't see where this ice came from; in the fading light, he gave up.

At the skid marks Sandro paused, kneeling in his old quilted jacket, nothing like warm enough. He looked down the steep gradient of the hill. She had braked, hard, then had come across the patch of ice on to drier tarmac, but even that would have been frosted and it hadn't given her enough purchase, the tyres had lost grip again. The big car would have thumped and teetered on to one side, still moving too fast – you could see from the skid marks. That alone might have been enough to knock her out, side of the head on the door frame as the car tilted.

Those blue eyes, wide in the darkness. Is this happening, she'd have asked herself, in the split second before she hit her head, as her feet pumped uselessly on the pedals. Sandro thought that he should have gone to the pound to have a look at the car, after all. Though he had the photographs: blood and hair on the front pillar, some on the car door, a smear on the window.

In car accidents, people always had that look of disbelief as they stepped out of the wreckage, stunned not just by the impact but by the real-ization that they were mortal, that their fate could slip out of their own hands so easily. The moment at which they lost control of the situation – until then as comfortable as their own living room – still mirrored in their startled, dilated pupils; the realization that the car wasn't simply the benign and obedient carriage they were used to, warm and padded and computerized and safe.

It was a cage and a weapon; a blowtorch and a blunt instrument.

At the foot of the hill, on the bend, Sandro straightened, looking at the churned and frozen earth. It was bitterly cold, and the sun hadn't even gone down. Some of it was wind chill – in the city, one was largely protected from the wind too, but out here there seemed to be nothing between Sandro and Russia. It was hard to believe that in the summer people flooded down here from the city, to swim in the rivers, lie on the beaches, bask in swimming pools on these baked and barren slopes. Far off, he heard some dogs begin to bay, and the sound echoed mournfully around the hills.

The bend was indeed very sharp; in the dark, if you didn't know the road, it could be lethal. Although Loni Meadows *had* known the road; she would have known the curve was coming. There'd been a sign too, a kilometre back, warning of bends – not of ice, however, whatever Grasso might have said. The accident scene – or whatever it was – had been contaminated considerably. The tow-truck had churned up the verge, although because the earth had been so hard-frozen there were no footprints at all. Sandro returned to the car and took out the envelope of photographs and looked through them with fingers stiffening with the cold until he found the one he wanted. His back to the road, he held it up in what light was left, comparing the image with the reality.

There in front of him was the crushed long grass,

frosted over again in the shape of Loni Meadows's outstretched body. He looked at the photograph: one stockinged foot turned inwards, one shoe off, her head down the bank and in the water. Her skirt – heavy dark silk by the look of it – had ridden up, and the stocking top was visible. She would have staggered in the dark, the car's headlights shining pointlessly into the river. The car door open behind her.

In some of the photographs they'd used the flash; it had still been very early. There was a lot of disturbance to the grass where the body lay. She might have wandered about, dazed, before the bleeding in her brain sent her irreversibly into a coma. He would have assumed she would have fallen to her knees, then forwards, although in the photograph it looked more as though she'd fallen headlong.

The car hadn't been that badly damaged; still driveable, according to the report. If it hadn't been nose down in the riverbank. Sandro studied the photographs again, then the turned earth in front of him. She'd tried, hadn't she? Perhaps bleeding, perhaps concussed, she'd revved the engine, assuming she was still in control, the rear wheels turning uselessly in the air, the front pair churning themselves deeper into the frozen mud of the riverbank. Stuck.

That didn't help.

Or did it? At least, it ruled one or two things out; if there'd been someone else in the car, someone who'd wished her harm, would that person, having somehow caused the accident, allow her to assume control again and try to get the car out of the mud? It seemed unlikely. But that scenario had a number of flaws, in any case; anyone planning to cause an accident while in the car themselves would risk death or injury too. It might only feasibly have happened on impulse, a row, an attempt to grab the wheel. But where would that putative passenger be now, supposing no one had seen him, or her, get into the car with Loni Meadows? Bloodied, injured, traumatized, frozen, in shock? Certainly such a person might not expect to escape notice. Then again, anyone who had somehow managed to disguise all these after-effects was unlikely to be the impulsive sort.

It didn't make any sense. She would have been alone, revving the engine, in the dark, swearing to herself. Yes.

Carefully Sandro slid the photographs back into their envelope and replaced them in the car's crowded glove compartment.

Stockinged leg. She dressed the part; she didn't think she was going out into the dark, the cold, she wasn't dressed for a winter expedition, she wasn't prepared for this. She was going to meet her lover, in a warm hotel room. Sandro picked up the little plastic pouch containing Loni Meadows's personal effects, and studied them. Not prepared, careless, focused only on her destination; a bit like Sandro, who was now reproaching himself for not taking a closer look at the bag's contents earlier in the day. And if he was going to find for certain what was missing from the pouch, he had to get on with it.

It was possible that the police had missed it, yes. Sandro began at the river, working back, fingertip-searching, checking possible trajectories. When after twenty-five minutes it was simply too dark to go on, and he still hadn't found anything, Sandro began to persuade himself out of it, another wild goose chase. It could be in her car, it could be in her room at the Castello Orfeo; odds were, surely, that even Grasso and his boneheads would have found it, if it was there to be found.

Surely.

He crossed the road, walked back a hundred metres, then a little way forwards up the hill from whose crest the threesome had watched him, then back down. A sheep track led off to the left, circumventing the hill the way to wherever the three had come from – as if he didn't know – a track that might also have been a shortcut, only they would not have taken it with a wheelchair.

The light had almost completely leached from the lonely valley, the ridge of distant hills was black against a rapidly darkening sky, and now, whether he wanted to or not, Sandro had to go and meet the residents of the Castello Orfeo.

The little digital clock in the corner of the old computer told Giuli that it was 17.10 as she carefully attached the document to an email addressed to Sandro, pressed send, then closed the computer down. The document contained the dates and places and times she'd managed to glean from the internet and the sheaf of papers Sandro had filed, under Orfeo/Meadows, in the old filing cabinet. Giuli had tried to set up a kind of grid, cross-referencing the current guests at the Castello Orfeo as painstakingly as the time available and the limitations of her English would allow. The classes Giuli was taking were only for holidaying and conversation purposes, and weren't much help in deciphering the migrations and stop-overs of artists. Visiting Fellowship in Installation Art in Uppsala, Sweden? Poet in Residence at a prison in Holland? The lives of the residents of the Castello Orfeo didn't seem entirely enviable to Giuli, who had secret dreams of settling down in a more modest version of the Bellagamba villa in Galluzzo.

Teaching English at the Sorbonne in Paris sounded all right. But didn't any of this lot want to settle down? Perhaps they didn't have the choice.

Sandro's instructions had been very clear. 'I want you to find out which of them has crossed paths with Loni Meadows in the past, say over the last fifteen years. I know they will have, Mascarello and Gallo already intimated as much, it's a small world, if you're a struggling artistic type. Obviously I don't expect you to find out everything. But the public stuff: festivals, lectures, exhibitions, sabbaticals, book tours. As much as you can.'

Giuli had only had a couple of hours, and she

didn't think she'd made a comprehensive job of it. It had been uphill work; she wasn't sure what a sabbatical was in Italian, let alone the English word for it, but she used her initiative, and an online dictionary. She was fairly satisfied; it meant nothing much to her, but it would mean something to Sandro.

She hadn't asked him if he'd called Luisa, yet. There came a point, when you just had to take a back seat, she could see that. And surely they were rock solid; nothing could derail Sandro and Luisa, certainly not a little misunderstanding like this. Giuli remembered when Luisa had told her about the cancer, and how she'd had to swallow hard and pretend not to be scared out of her wits; this was a bit like that. But no one was dying, here. She had to remind herself of that.

As if as an afterthought, before he hung up Sandro had said, 'Carlotta Bellagamba will be going to Alberto's house tonight, I'd bet on it. I have a feeling Alberto's father's out of town, and it's going to be party time.'

'How d'you know that?' she'd asked curiously.

'Because I've just seen his father coming out of the police station in Pozzo Basso; because his father's Niccolò Orfeo and I'm betting Alberto's having a party tonight because he's told Alberto he's not coming home. He's staying over, at the family castle, and who knows, I might even be having dinner with him myself.'

And before Giuli had even begun to digest this

new information, he'd continued, 'D'you know what would be really useful, Giuli, would be, if you could get in there? Into the party; into the house. Get talking to those kids. Think of it as part of the surveillance of Carlotta, if you like. But what I want to know is, when the old guy usually plays away. Dates, if possible; in particular, if he was playing away, the night Loni Meadows died.' There'd been a pause. 'Oh, and if he did cocaine.'

After a stunned silence Giuli had said, 'All right.'

'You can do it, kid,' Sandro had said, and she'd softened. What the hell. She could try.

And if she wanted to get to Galluzzo by 5.30, she was going to have to get going.

On the way Giuli picked up about fifty grammes of dope from the dealer on the corner of the Piazza Santo Spirito, sitting on the wide stone bench that was spattered with pigeon shit, holding court looking like some Native American wise man. She'd known him since she was thirteen; he looked at her without surprise as he handed over the little foil package, even though she'd been clean for three years now.

'It's all right,' said Giuli uncomfortably. 'It's not for me.'

'Sure,' he said, 'whatever.'

Not even going back to her room to take off her coat, once she was inside the castle's bounds Cate went straight to the office.

Tiziano and Alec Fairhead had gone their

separate ways without much more than a muttered farewell; the three of them had hurried back under the darkening sky, an element of shame, of anxiety in their shared silence. Had it been the sight of the man climbing out of his car? A ghoul, like them, a sightseer? Cate wasn't so sure about that; the slow, considered way he looked up at them made her think the bareheaded man in his shabby coat had an agenda that was more serious.

As Fairhead raised his hand to say goodbye under the great arch Cate suddenly felt rather anxious for him; he actually looked ill. And frightened. But he caught her eye and hurried away, before she could ask him if he was all right.

Outside the office door Cate hesitated at the sound of voices. Luca's, and another, deeper – lower, angrier – voice she recognized as Niccolò Orfeo's. 'Impossible,' he was saying. 'Out of the question.'

She knocked. There was an abrupt silence, then Luca said warily, 'Who is it?'

He sounded tired, and when she tentatively pushed the door in response to his reluctant, 'Quickly, then,' she saw that he looked it too. He was at his desk, shirtsleeves pushed up, jacket crumpled over the back of his chair. He seemed to have grown a week's stubble since this morning. Niccolò Orfeo was standing by the window, his broad shoulders blocking what remained of the light; he looked at Cate over his shoulder, eyeing her up and down, then looked back outside. There was a strong smell of cigar smoke, in defiance of every rule of the castle.

Cate remained standing, in her coat, as she hadn't been invited to sit.

'Count Orfeo – will be staying,' said Sandro wearily. 'For dinner, at least.'

'I see,' said Cate, waiting for further instruction, but none came. Orfeo would be keeping them all dangling, she saw; it was his house, and if he decided a bed needed making up at two minutes' notice, in whichever room he chose, then they'd have to jump.

'I wondered if you'd called Beth yet,' she said hurriedly.

'Beth?' Luca looked blank for a moment. 'Oh, Beth. Right, yes. I mean, no. No, I haven't called her.'

'Well, she should know,' said Cate. 'Before she reads it in a newspaper. Don't you think? I mean, they were close.' From the window Orfeo looked back at her a moment down his aristocratic nose, but this time it wasn't with quite the same casual lecherousness.

'Yes, yes, I suppose so,' said Luca distractedly.

Cate looked at her watch. 'If it isn't done tonight,' she said, 'the time difference and everything – it won't be for another whole day.'

'What is your suggestion?' said Luca impatiently. She saw him glance back over at Orfeo; did the man have power over Luca's job? Cate had always assumed that the Trust was a quite separate entity,

240

but she supposed the castle was still his. She thought about what Ginevra had said about Loni Meadows causing trouble for everyone who worked under her: Mauro, Nicki, Luca.

'I'll call her,' said Cate. 'You give me the number and I'll explain it to her. Gently, you know.'

'All right,' said Luca, sounding uncharacteristically uncertain. He began poking through the chaos on his desk in search of something, then stopped, seemed to forget what he was looking for. Was it the presence of Niccolò Orfeo that was throwing him, or was he playing for time? Why would he be worried about Beth?

'The number?' she prompted. He resumed his poking, found his mobile, scrolled down a list of numbers, read the number out to her. Beth lived on the East Coast: Westport, Connecticut. It would be late morning there. Cate looked up from entering the number in her own *telefonino* and found them both looking at her, their meaning quite plain.

'I'll call her, then. I'll do that now.' And she left hurriedly, her coat still on, not having relaxed for one second of the exchange.

Outside the door Cate hesitated a full minute, listening, but she heard nothing. Perhaps they were listening, too, for the sound of her departing footsteps, before they resumed their conversation. She went.

Stopping off in the kitchen, Cate meant to promise Ginevra she'd be there in a moment, once she'd made that call to Beth, only another row was brewing. Of course it was: it was Ginevra's night off, she remembered belatedly, the cook was supposed to go home at five on Saturdays. Cate had simply lost track of time, of her usual routines. And there was no escaping the row.

'What does he think I am?' Ginevra was fulminating. Mauro was standing in a corner, a coffee cup in his hand and an unpleasant gleam in his eye. He never drank coffee without a little something in it; Cate found herself wanting to ask him, what happens if you come off that tractor, break your neck?

The kitchen's surfaces were already spread with the dishes for the evening's buffet, each covered with its separate clean ironed cloth. 'He thinks I'm housekeeper, maid, cleaner? He sends Anna-Maria home, he takes you off kitchen duties –' at which the full force of her glare turned on Cate '– then he decides we need beds making up, and I'm supposed to send Nicki off to clean the intern's bathroom.'

'Intern?'

'The little bedroom,' said Ginevra impatiently. She tugged off her apron. 'Well, you can do it. Nicki's done enough. You can do it, and you can help her clear after their dinners, too. Saturday night and Sunday morning, my time off. I hope someone remembers that.'

'The intern's room needs making up? I thought –' and Cate broke off, confused.

'Two extras for dinner,' Ginevra grumbled on. 'And no warning. Well, they'll have to make do with rice.'

'Two? Who's the other one?'

'Don't ask me,' snapped Ginevra.

'A snooper,' said Mauro, speaking for the first time from the corner. 'Someone coming to ask us questions.' His voice was dangerously ragged; he was properly drunk, Cate realized. 'That husband of hers is behind it, if you ask me.' His laugh was phlegmy and slurred. 'And then there's Orfeo too, that's a bit of a turn-up. Overcome with grief, no doubt.'

Cate wanted to get out of there; she didn't like this.

'Where's Nicki?'

'She'll be up on the *piano nobile*,' Ginevra said, relenting. 'Doing the intern's room.' Then she scowled. 'You'll have to walk her back to the farm, you know.'

'I'll sort things with her,' said Cate. 'You get off home.'

Ginevra stared at her, then pulled off her apron without a word. Passed her hand over the gas taps on the stove, straightened a tea towel on the rail. 'You coming?' she said to Mauro brusquely. He shrugged, his eyes red-rimmed. He was definitely worse, Cate thought, since the *Dottoressa* had died: drunker, angrier; perhaps that was why Ginevra was protecting him. Protecting him from himself.

'All right,' he said. 'Watch a bit of television.'

'And a bite to eat.' Ginevra had her coat on, and wearily she steered Mauro ahead of her out of the door. An icy wind swirled in out of the darkness. 'Bite to eat,' he repeated, as if unsure what the words meant, as the door closed behind them. Cate hoped Ginevra was driving.

At the kitchen door she paused and listened; heard the dogs begin to bay on the other side of the hill as the cook's Punto hove into view. Ginevra knew something was wrong, that was why she was keeping Mauro on a tight rein. Cate looked down the hill the other way, towards the *villino*. There was a light at one of the squat building's upper windows, and as she stood there more light blazed out, closer, off to the right from beyond the laundry. The modern apartment with its glass wall: Michelle must be turning on every light in the place. Soon the guests would be turning up one by one like kept beasts sniffing around for the next meal, no matter what.

As she crossed the courtyard towards the stone steps and the great door, two things happened more or less at once. Snowflakes started gusting down from the black sky and inside the castle someone – it could only be one person – began to play the piano. Though that seemed too tame a description for the sound that reached Cate, stopping her where she stood. Like liquid, the music flowed out through every crack in the shutters, between door and doorframe, climbing and spilling, soft and melancholy, into the courtyard,

244

filling the space enclosed by the grey walls and the black sky overhead as if Cate was in her own private concert hall. For just a moment, as she stood there and forgot what was fretting at her or where she was going, she understood the point of it all. The big, forbidding castle with its metre-thick walls, the closeted rooms, the seclusion, the feeding and watering of the unhappy guests, the torment. For this.

She saw him as she tiptoed past in the hall, like a minotaur, his big head between those great shoulders bent over the gleaming black piano, oblivious, and climbing the wide curve of the stone stairs she held her breath.

Nicki was in the doorway of the intern's little room, leaning against the cut stone of its corner, damp cloth in one hand. She was transfixed, listening. Cate put a finger to her lips, and Nicki nodded. Her eyes were round; they'd heard Tiziano play before, but he had never sounded like this. The music swelled and rolled, now flooding every corner of the ancient building; her eye caught by a movement higher on the stairs, Cate looked up and saw Alec Fairhead on the upper landing, his eyes glittering in the light from below. It seemed to her that the music was calling them all out of their hiding places – a celebration and a warning and a funeral march, all rolled into one.

Fairhead's focus shifted and he looked at her and then, quite unexpectedly, she saw an expression she'd never seen before, a smile of pure happiness and release spread across his face, as if he had been taken by surprise by something that delighted him. Cate bobbed her head back down and at that moment she felt Nicki take her hand and hold it tight.

Turning, she smiled into the girl's face. 'It's OK,' she mouthed, because Nicki's look of dazzlement had turned into consternation as the notes thundered, and she smiled reassuringly. As if Tiziano realized, below them, that the music was passing beyond his control, it changed, or he tamed it, and beside Cate, Nicki let out a long breath. Feeling the tension ebb, Cate looked over her shoulder into the small, neat room that had been Beth's: one long, shuttered window, a narrow bed with faded, soft red velvet cover, a corner turned back in the circle of light shed by the bedside lamp. A desk had been set out, with paper and a telephone. Seeing her questioning look, Nicki just shrugged.

'It's you and me,' Cate whispered. 'I've sent Ginevra home.' Nicki nodded obediently.

Still looking into the room Cate saw no trace of Beth's occupancy, not a discarded paperback on the shelves, not a mark on the walls. 'Do you miss her?' she said softly, and Nicki moved her head, see-sawing, ambivalent. Then nodded.

'She didn't like it here,' she whispered. 'She told me, it scared her. Something scared her.' Cate examined her expression a moment. Remembered that Nicki believed in ghosts too; gently took the damp cloth from her hand and pulled the door of the intern's room to behind them.

'Come on,' she said. 'They'll all be turning up soon, and there's no booze out.' The music seemed to bear them down the stairs, measuring their steps as though they couldn't help but walk in time to it, as though they were dancing. When Cate reached the bottom, she stopped.

On the doorstep stood a middle-aged man with a broad, tired face, in his hand a small holdall, his head tilted as he listened. He wore a hat, with a light dusting of snow just melting on its brim. As if on cue, the music lifted to a perfect point, and came to rest.

'Sandro Cellini,' said the man in the new silence, and he held out his hand.

CHAPTER 15

The two girls – women, he should say, he knew – stared back at him, one small and mousy and sharp-nosed, one tall and strong-shouldered and black-haired and clever. He'd seen the tall girl already, with the two men on the rise looking down at him, and he hadn't been wrong to think her beautiful. She had the full, downturned mouth of a Piero della Francesca: the face of the Queen of Sheba and the strong shoulders of a girl soldier. Sandro could imagine her striding into battle without a second thought.

'Caterina Giottone,' she said, and held out a hand. 'I'm the manager's assistant. Luca's assistant.'

She had an accent close to the Sienese, so not from around here. Her grip was warm and firm; her black hair parted in the middle, and she looked at him with curiosity, not unfriendly, as though she had a feeling about him. As though he might be bringing good news, but she wasn't quite sure yet; as though she trusted him. It made Sandro feel creaking and ancient to remember it, but she looked like every girl he had ever wished he might ask out, had he not been too shy and lonely, since the age of thirteen. She looked like Luisa.

The piano playing had stopped. It had been quite remarkable: Sandro didn't think of himself as having an ear, nor of being susceptible to atmospheres, or superstition, but while the music had been playing he had felt as though none of this was quite real. Not the slit windows of the big, dark, unforgiving building that had loomed over him in the dusk, not the tall, silent cypresses enclosing him on the approach, not the snow whirling in the empty courtyard. The only real thing had been left behind him on that sharp bend: the rutted mud and the flash of police tape clinging to a willow.

'You're the – um – investigator,' said the thin girl with the sharp nose and the scarecrow hair, and reality returned. Something about her reminded him of Giuli. 'I've just made up your bed. Next door to the *Dottoressa*'s rooms.' She gave him a beady-eyed look. Next door; Sandro wondered who would have occupied such a room under normal circumstances.

'Shall I show you up?' said Caterina Giottone. She hadn't known he was coming, but the other girl had. Caterina was an outsider here, like him, and she was thinking on her feet. Good. 'Or do you need to see Luca first?'

'I'll just leave these – things,' Sandro said, lifting his little case.

The room was small, but that was fine in a big draughty place like this; it seemed warm and well lit. There was a table he could use as a desk, and a long window. 'You're very kind.'

'I'll tell Luca you're here, shall I?' said Caterina Giottone. Behind her on the landing the other girl shifted from foot to foot, eavesdropping.

'That would be great,' said Sandro. 'Thank you, Miss Giottone. You've been very helpful.'

'Caterina,' she said, inclining her head. 'It's a pleasure.' She frowned. 'There'll be – dinner, or sort of, a little later. We're a bit – upside down. And Saturday is Ginevra's night off; she's the cook. There'll be something laid out, in the dining room, from eight. But I'm sure Luca – Mr Gallo – will show you.'

As Sandro gently closed the door he heard them on the stairs, Caterina Giottone's low voice and the other one's excitable chattering. He didn't know what Gallo had told them; the minimum was what he imagined, but it didn't take people long to work things out. He didn't need to worry about that.

The computer took forever to start up. Sandro knew that computers saved any amount of time; all the same, the effect they had on him was only to increase his impatience. The blue screen asking for his password, the icons appearing, one by one, the whirs and clicks. The screensaver came up: it was of the view from a little house they'd rented on the Ligurian coast a long time ago, he and Luisa; Giuli had downloaded it for him. A strip of scalloped, green and white awning and the sun going down in the sea, a couple of moored boats black on the silver water.

To the left of the computer on the desk, Sandro set out the green card folder containing the information he had on the castle's guests. He decided, thinking about Caterina and the mousy girl, the absent cook, whoever drove the tractor and the pick-up he'd seen parked up at the back of the castle, that it wouldn't do any harm to have a note or two on the place's staff too.

Would a cook or a gardener or a girl with long black hair and the soft accent of the Valdichiana send an anonymous email through a proxy server about a woman they were very unlikely ever to have met? No, they wouldn't. But Sandro didn't believe in putting all his eggs in one basket; closing off his options this early on in an investigation would be rash. And now he was here in these bleak and empty hills, now he breathed the air of the castle keep, heard its creaks and whispers and felt its thick walls close around him, the puzzle of Loni Meadows's death had turned into something different, something subject to change, something still living, its consequences yet to unravel. All of a sudden the darkness of this castle and its grounds were teeming with possibilities.

It would come. It always did.

Almost never easily, but it came; you had to stand at the still centre of a place like this, and listen, and watch. This was a closed circle, like many murders; you just had to map the edges, then look at those gathered inside. Like the Roma site Sandro and Pietro had once been called to because the body of a young man lay just beyond the light cast by the trailers and abandoned container lorries, stabbed more than twenty times and left to bleed out in the dust on a sweet-smelling April evening.

Some of the travellers had stayed in their trailers, others had gathered on the edge of the policemen's vision as they shone their lights on the body, then inspected it minutely with their gloved hands. One or two had come to offer information, of a sort, not to be trusted. The young man – not much more than a boy – had been one of theirs, and they knew they would be suspected.

It had taken time, that was for sure. There had been physical evidence to be retrieved, pollen and dust analysed, the shape and pecularities of the murder weapon identified – but for the most part it had been a question of waiting. Waiting to be trusted, for the suspicion to abate, for people to begin talking – not even to Sandro and Pietro, but between themselves. And then at last a small and angry Roma boy ran to Sandro, his face streaked with dirt and crying, who told him his big brother had been in love with a girl from outside.

The seal breaks, and the world rushes in. Sandro still remembered the feel of that small boy's head against his ribcage, hot and damp, the feel of unwashed hair under his palm.

He stood and went to the window.

There were internal shutters, first, then the

window; he opened it to push back the outside louvres. The cold took his breath away, but he stood there a moment at the open window, looking. The snow was still falling, but softly now, quietly; the wind had dropped, and he could sense the change that came over a landscape as snow covered and muffled it, could smell the clean coldness of it in the air. Below him the drive and lawns were uplit but even the dark, distant hills gleamed white as they reflected some mysterious source of light: the moon, perhaps, shining briefly through a break in the canopy of snow cloud. Had there been a moon, two nights ago? Sandro tried to remember; it had been the night, hadn't it, that Luisa had told him she was going away.

He'd got up to use the bathroom in the middle of the night. As he always did, his age and all that. Sandro closed his eyes, trying to think back, and for a moment all he could remember was the despair that had come over him in the chilly bathroom, its frosted window unshuttered. Not that he would be alone for a few days, but that he was being left behind, somehow. He opened his eyes again. It had been dark, or almost; no more than a sliver of crescent moon visible overhead.

For some reason the thought depressed him; would it have been better if a full moon had shone that night, when Loni Meadows died? Because he wouldn't like to die in the dark, himself. And for other reasons he couldn't quite put his finger on now, but which would come to him.

Sandro closed the shutters carefully, and returned to the desk.

Find the lover. Find the sender of the email.

He stopped there, frowning. Would those two be the same? It was possible, yes. He could imagine a scenario in which a man might send hate mail then become the victim's lover. But it was a stretch. With a woman like Loni Meadows, sharp, pushy, inquisitive? A stretch. He stood very still, thinking.

It occurred to Sandro that he couldn't even be sure if the sender of the email would have also been her murderer. If it had been murder. Speculation made his head hurt: he needed to start looking at facts.

If you wanted to send someone off to crash their car, alone, how would you do it? Sandro could think of at least one way, but of none that would be guaranteed to succeed. She might, after all, have been badly injured, crippled or paralysed rather than killed. So your handiwork would need to be invisible, in case she came back to tell the tale. Although perhaps injury would have been enough; perhaps someone had only wanted to bring Loni Meadows face to face with a reality she could not charm away – with the fact that she, like everyone else, was mortal.

He set his mobile phone on top of the green folder, and it blinked patiently back at him, indicating that it had a strong signal. There must be a transmitter somewhere around here, though he couldn't remember seeing it. He should have checked for a signal in the valley, shouldn't he? Would she have been able to call for help? If she had a phone with her. Would she have been able to get a signal?

Everyone always had a phone, these days; if Sandro could remember to keep his on him and charged, then anyone could.

Moving his finger tentatively across the laptop's touch pad, Sandro logged on to the Castello Orfeo's broadband network, which was unsecured. No one for miles around to freeload off it, so why bother?

The clock in the corner of the screen said 18.45. Giuli would be watching Carlotta Bellagamba, and waiting for her moment. She'd manage it, Sandro was certain. For a second he felt a twinge of guilt; this wasn't really about the girl and her drug-taking boyfriend, was it? He was using her – using them. But Giuli was another matter. Giuli had her own agenda; she saw Carlotta as her case now. On screen Sandro opened the mailbox, pressed send and receive, astonished at how quickly these things had become second nature to him.

Messages pinged into his mailbox, a flurry of rubbish, spam that Giuli had programmed the thing to delete, then one from Giuli.

Downstairs the music began again, softer this time, quiet and pretty. Chopin? Sandro liked Chopin, even if he couldn't claim to know much about music; Luisa enjoyed a concert now and again at the Teatro Communale or the Goldoni, a bit of Verdi, a bit of

Mozart, and Sandro would go along if he wasn't working, happily ignorant. This music calmed him now, rills of notes like water, as if it had been expressly composed to ease troubled thoughts. What thoughts could have troubled Chopin's patrons though? Rich men and women, in castles and palaces.

Leaning back in his chair, Sandro breathed in the scent of old money, of stone and wood and polish, thinking. He opened the email from Giuli: a list, then a kind of table setting out dates and times and ages. Per Hansen, born Trondheim, Norway, 1953; Alexander Fairhead, born London, 1954; Tiziano Scarpa, born Mestre, 1966; Michelle Connor, born Williamsburg, Brooklyn, 1956; Tina Kreutz, born Orlando, Florida, 1977. Sandro tilted his head, trying to make sense of the graph. Did these people have no homes to go to? London, Paris, Caracas, Yarra; they hardly seemed to settle. No: one of them did, the Norwegian, the one whose home country sounded the least hospitable had spent the most time there: a visiting fellowship in creative writing to Barcelona in 1985, then Oslo ever since. The family man. Difficult to see how he, at least, would have come across Loni Meadows before coming to Orfeo, unless she'd visited Oslo. Which he couldn't picture.

Alec Fairhead and Loni Meadows had both been in London between 1981 and 1982.

Then he heard something. Over the seductive variations of the music, Sandro heard someone on the stairs outside his room, not loud but unmistakable. Out of instinct he closed the screen of the computer and got to his feet, quickly, quietly, holding the chair back to stop it scraping. There was a knock.

On the threshold, careful not to enter, Luca Gallo looked anxiously apologetic. Did apologize, in fact, several times over, for the fact that Sandro had had to be admitted and welcomed to the Castello Orfeo by someone other than himself.

'But she was very personable,' said Sandro, feeling the need to defend Caterina Giottone. 'I couldn't have been treated more – ah, correctly.'

'Yes,' said Gallo, taken aback, 'yes, well – of course. Caterina has only recently – she has had to step into the breach, if you understand me. But she's doing a good job, yes, an excellent job.'

And again Sandro had the feeling that he and Caterina were in some way in the same boat: outsiders, and not much expected of them.

Then Luca Gallo was fretting over arrangements. There would be supper, of a kind, laid in the dining room, and Gallo would show Sandro, if he would like, where to find it, close to where he'd parked the car in fact, an informal arrangement, people could come and go as they wished on Saturdays, but today was slightly unusual.

Gallo grimaced a little. 'Niccolò Orfeo – Count Orfeo, although he doesn't really use the title, you understand – he's dining with us tonight. So if you'd like to join us?'

'Of course,' said Sandro. 'If I could have, perhaps, half an hour?'

Gallo was looking into the room, and the things laid out on the desk. 'Of course,' he said absently, 'yes, you'll have things to do, first. I – ah – I've, um, mentioned your presence here to the guests. A – condensed version.' He moved inside the room, half closing the door behind him; the little space seemed suddenly smaller.

'Yes,' said Sandro. 'I can imagine.'

'I gave them the impression it was – a kind of formality. Mascarello, in his grief – you know.'

'And the staff? Some of them seem to have a good idea of why I am here. Not all.'

'Ah,' said Gallo distractedly. 'Yes. I only said – well. I mentioned you in passing, to Ginevra. News seems to travel, somehow.'

'And Orfeo?' He spoke casually, watching Gallo out of the corner of his eye.

'Orfeo? What about him?' There was something there. Gallo knew something.

'Does he know?' Sandro smiled encouragingly. 'Why I'm here?'

'Ah, yes. Although clearly – well. He lives in Florence, even if this is his family seat. You won't need to talk to him?' Bluff, and panic.

The man Sandro had seen cut an imperious swathe through Pozzo's dismal little police station would have shouted at Luca Gallo without a second thought, Sandro could see that; as though he was a mediaeval peasant. And the mere suggestion that

the Count might co-operate with a private investigator's inquiries on any subject would certainly have
been perceived as an offence to his dignity.

'But he knew Loni Meadows?'

Luca Gallo shrugged, his nonchalance not
convincing. 'Of course.'

'And when – ah – when was he last here? On
the night of the accident?'

'Oh, no,' said Gallo quickly. 'He didn't usually
come in the evenings, not often, it's a long drive,
you understand. No, I think he was last here
on – let me think – on Sunday. There's really
no need – no need at all. To talk to him.'

'Well, perhaps just a word or two,' said Sandro
mildly.

Gallo shot him a glance. Sandro saw that the
man's nails were bitten down to the quick. He
leaned past Luca Gallo and pushed the door to,
then sat down on the corner of the bed.

'Mr Gallo,' said Sandro, looking up at him. 'Luca.'
Alarm flickered in Luca Gallo's soft, monkey-brown
eyes. Could he really suspect this man, this twitching
bundle of anxieties? A walking breakdown.

'Luca, is there –' he hesitated, gently probing. 'Is
there anything else I should know? About – you and
Dottoressa Meadows, for example? Any – animosity?
Any upset? Because if there is, it will come out, you
know. These things always do.'

'I've told you,' said Gallo, his face pale under
the stubble. 'We were a good team.'

Sandro said nothing, just looked at him.

'We were not friends,' said Luca with resignation. 'All right? But we worked together.'

'Fine,' Sandro said quietly, getting to his feet, sidestepping Gallo, who stood as though rooted to the spot, and opening the door again. 'So, I'll find my own way down.' He gestured with a hand, and Gallo preceded him out of the door on to the wide landing.

'And I'm happy to make my own introductions.' Gallo nodded, eyeing him warily, as though he knew he'd been let off the hook, for now. Sandro went on cheerfully. 'In the meantime do you think I might – ah – make a quick examination of Dottoressa Meadows's apartments?' He used the word as if she'd been a princess. This place was getting to him.

'Of course.' Fishing in the sagging pockets of his jacket Gallo looked anxious all over again, nervously overeager. He pulled out a bunch of keys, detached one. 'They're right next door; she was the first of our Directors to occupy those rooms.' There was something sharper in his tone when he said this.

Sandro eyed the key, still in Gallo's hand. 'When the police – when they came to notify you of her accident, did they ask to see the rooms?' he asked casually.

Gallo shrugged. 'They looked in. That was it. I – I didn't think anything of it. I mean, as far as they knew, she died in a car accident.'

'Yes,' said Sandro, and their eyes met. 'I suppose

so.' Grasso certainly had seemed arrogant enough to consider it a waste of his time, or perhaps they had a little too much respect for Orfeo's property.

'Would you like me to show you?' Gallo's hand closed around the key; it occurred to Sandro that he would not have been exactly encouraging to policemen tramping through his precious castle.

'I can probably find my own way around,' said Sandro again, easily. 'And the dining room too, close to where I parked the car, you said? I'll follow my nose, shall I?' Gallo didn't move. 'Thank you,' said Sandro, 'I'll be fine.' And held out his hand.

With reluctance Gallo dropped the key into it. 'Oh,' said Sandro, looking at it thoughtfully. 'Just one more thing. Do you have her number? The *Dottoressa*'s mobile number?'

Gallo blinked back at him, alarmed. 'Her number?' As though he'd asked if he had the dead woman's underwear.

'Her mobile number,' said Sandro patiently.

Fishing in his pocket again, Gallo got out a small, battered phone and prodded at it until the tiny glowing screen yielded up what he was looking for.

Sandro offered no explanation beyond a smile. 'Thank you,' he said. Gallo went on standing there until eventually Sandro put a hand to the door and took a step forwards, and only then did the man finally turn to leave.

As he turned the key in the heavy panelled double doors, Sandro thought about Niccolò

Orfeo. Too arrogant, would be his first thought, to bother with murder. Too stupid, his second.

The apartments were dark, a warm, velvety, scented darkness: even without turning on the lights Sandro would have known a woman inhabited them. Would have known, perhaps, what kind of woman too. A woman who liked to make her presence felt, who liked to trail her distinctive fragrance through other people's lives; a woman who liked her comforts, and her pleasures. He reached around the door for a light switch; he expected a blaze of overhead brilliance from some great monstrosity of a chandelier but the switch turned on a series of lamps, peach and gold, casting a soft glow through the large, untidy room. He closed the door behind him.

The room wasn't just large, it was palatial. Opposite a panelled wall it had three long windows to match the one in Sandro's little room, and was dominated by a huge bed, with an ornately carved wooden headboard, a dark velvet cover, and scattered with at least half a dozen items of discarded clothing, some laid out as if to suggest entire outfits. She'd taken some time choosing what to wear. On the floor an emerald green shirt of some fine material lay crumpled; it had clearly been worn. A pair of trousers; silk underwear. Also worn. Sandro stepped over them, wondering what Luisa would have said. Getting the picture.

A door in one corner stood ajar: the bathroom. Leaning in, Sandro flicked on another light; this one was lit like a star's dressing room, soft light glowing round an antique mirror. A big marble bath like a Roman emperor's, soft mottled green tiles that looked very subtly expensive. It seemed only recently fitted out and decorated, and Sandro remembered what Gallo had said, that previous Directors had not occupied these rooms. So she had appropriated the most beautiful rooms, and had them done out in her colours. Sparing no expense.

Set into the tiles in one discreet corner, Sandro eventually discerned what he was looking for: a bathroom cabinet. It yielded nothing that interested him very much: some painkillers with codeine, heavy-duty, but only one had been taken. A woman who didn't fuss about with herbal remedies but went for the nuclear option, only sparingly. Had he been looking for contraceptive pills? Well, he found some. Fifty-five, but not yet menopausal then. And something he thought was HRT medication, so belt and braces, this was a woman still powered on her own hormones, but she wasn't taking any chances. The last thing this woman wanted was a baby.

Stacks of expensive creams and lotions. What would she have done when the signs of getting older couldn't be ignored or moisturized away any more? Plastic surgery, probably. Sandro compelled himself not to judge. Why shouldn't she want to hang on to her looks? Feeling the woman's presence around him like a warm, suffocating fog, he closed the cabinet door thoughtfully, and returned to the big bedroom. The dressing table held cosmetics and a small leather case of jewellery; it looked like the real deal, or most of it. Some pearls with a diamond clasp, a star-shaped diamond brooch, a ring with big sapphires, opals, garnets. A dark red lipstick lay unsheathed, worn down to a nub; her favourite shade. Luisa would enjoy this, wouldn't she? Or perhaps it would upset her; perhaps one then the other. Sandro got out his mobile, and dialled the number Luca Gallo had given him.

There had been no mobile phone in the plastic bag the orderly had handed him at the morgue. He had not found it at the river, on his hands and knees in the frosted grass as the light ebbed. Was it here, buried under the discarded clothes, in a drawer or a purse?

Would it still have charge, two days on? Plenty of phones would, these days. He raised it to his ear. It was ringing, somewhere. He lowered it again, covered it with his hand, and listened. Ringing somewhere, but not here.

If it was locked, overlooked, in a drawer at police headquarters in Pozzo Basso, would it be heard? Probably. Would they have turned it off? Probably; and yet this phone had not been turned off. Just as Sandro raised his own mobile to his ear again, the answerphone message came on, and he felt the hairs rise on the back of his neck and the sound of that voice, speaking softly to

264

him out of the past, completed the picture he had of the dead woman to perfection. He knew her scent, the precise colour of her eyes, even the shape of her neat body imprinted on those clothes left lying on the floor and the big gilded bed, and now her voice. No mechanical default message for Loni Meadows, no: she had to record her own, in two languages, breathy and sweet, her English perky, direct and intimate, the Italian lazily, seductively American. She would never have bothered to get it right, Loni Meadows would never have felt the need to camouflage herself among the locals.

She couldn't get to the phone right now. As if she was talking to him, and only to him.

You're falling in love with her, Sandro jeered at himself, in love with a dead woman, and not a nice one. Perhaps it was because the thought of Luisa smiling into another man's eyes had not been out of his thoughts for forty-eight hours, but he had a sudden and startling image of one of those rooms full of old coats and broken crockery and dusty pictures that the unloved dead leave behind them, his hoard of forgotten and embarrassing emotions, among them, hopeless infatuation. He quickly clicked his mobile shut, terminating the call.

The bedside tables, matching walnut cabinets with delicate legs and each with a tiny drawer. Which side did she sleep on? Both, by the look of it. Capricious, prone to self-love, sprawling across

265

the bed. A book on one side, its spine cracked, a half-full water glass on the other. Sandro went to the cabinet with the water glass and pulled open the drawer and took out the silver blister pack of triangular pills he saw there, had expected to see there. Not always blue but all colours, these days, although these happened to be a light grey-blue, four gone, one of which he had glimpsed through the plastic of the evidence bag containing Loni Meadows's possessions. Viagra.

There was a desk in a corner, and on it a small white machine he barely recognized as a laptop computer, so small and slender was it. Of course, she'd have a computer. It was open. Sandro stood there, contemplating it. Would she have left it open? He pressed the on button with a fingernail: the screen turned blue-green; he waited. Nothing, just the silent, blind glow. No request for a password. The feeling grew in Sandro that someone had tampered with this machine. If he had been in the force, with a whole department devoted to extracting information from computers – well, he wasn't. Did this compact little assembly of plastic and circuits and silicon hold all her secrets? Probably not: machines had their limitations. Sandro knew he could put it in his bag and take it back to Florence for one of Mascarello's technical contacts to take apart – but for the moment Sandro would have to go on without it. It was only a machine, after all, a modern shortcut to someone's private life. There were other routes.

Footsteps were coming downstairs, from above him. Turning towards the sound Sandro saw that he had not quite closed the door behind him, which was stupid. Swiftly he crossed the room and gently eased it shut, hearing the person pass on down without pausing. He took one last look around the room, for now.

She had changed in a hurry. She had taken Viagra with her, and her mobile, because it wasn't here. She had been going to meet her older lover.

In his own cramped maid's quarters, Sandro checked his mail one last time, but there was nothing.

19.45; Luisa would have left work, surely? If they'd sent her home early, as they should have done after a long Saturday with a busy few days ahead of her, she might be turning her key in the apartment's lock right now. She might have been there for half an hour, sitting at the kitchen table, even supposing she didn't see the note straight away – Sandro found himself grinding his teeth. Forget it. Below him the music was rising steadily, building to a point of no return.

Luisa didn't do email; he didn't know why he'd felt that surge of mingled hope and dread as he'd pressed send and receive. Downstairs the last notes thundered out, there was a brief silence then a spattering of applause.

Time to meet the locals, thought Sandro.

'Private investigator? Into the *Dottoressa*'s – accident? You knew that?' Nicki wouldn't show Cate her face, letting her hair hang down, but she nodded almost imperceptibly.

They were in the kitchen, hurriedly polishing glasses and cutlery and setting them on trays, because everything was behind schedule now.

Even as she said it, though, Cate realized that somehow it wasn't as much of a surprise as it should have been. Even when they'd first seen him, from the brow of that hill, climbing out of his modest little car, there'd been something about Sandro Cellini. Something careful and meticulous. Tiziano and Alec Fairhead had seen it too, she'd known that by the way they fell silent in the dusk beside her.

'Who told you?'

Nicki shrugged, looking truculent.

'Ginevra?'

'Actually, Mauro. Luca Gallo told him an investigator was coming, to put the wind up him, maybe.'

Cate took a step back and eyed Nicki more closely. 'Because?'

'Oh, I don't know,' said Nicki dully. 'Mauro says Gallo wants to get him sacked, just like the *Dottoressa* did. Thinks it's a big conspiracy, the whole thing.'

'Really?' She didn't believe it.

'Maybe he's being paranoid about Luca,' Nicki said, fiddling. She looked listless and uncomfortable, her skin even blotchier than usual in the heat of the kitchen.

'Nicki,' said Cate, 'don't take this the wrong way,

but you need to get out of this place. I don't mean just move to Pozzo, I mean, far away. Living down there, your mum, Ginevra, Mauro –'

'You think so?' said Nicki, frowning, as if the possibility hadn't occurred to her. She eyed Cate. 'Well,' she said, in a burst of confidentiality, looking around as if she might be overheard, 'the *Dottoressa* certainly didn't like Mauro, even before – that morning. She gave him a written warning. She said if she caught him drunk again he'd be out; she even said she was going to get some kind of breathalyser.'

Cate recalled her recent trip into Pozzo to collect her things, Mauro sloping back from the bar with a flush and brandy on his breath. 'Well,' she said slowly, 'she had a point, didn't she?'

'It's his home,' said Nicki simply. She came and stood beside Cate at the door. 'This place is his life.'

Dangerous to turn a man out of his home. They stared at each other, both sensing that this was serious; the presence of Sandro Cellini in the castle confirmed that. Had she always wondered whether it had been an accident? Cate realized that she had; also that she, for one, was actually glad Cellini was here.

'It's snowing again,' said Nicki, looking past her. Cate pulled the door open a little more and together they looked out. The snow was falling steadily under the arc of the wall light, thick and soft and silent. The bumpy surface of the back road was already carpeted with white, and the night seemed muffled.

'Snowed in, are we?' said Cate. 'Does that ever happen?'

Nicki gave her a scornful look. 'Once or twice a year. Mauro should be out there clearing the drive.' Cate nodded, thinking. 'He works hard,' said Nicki, and she looked troubled.

'I know,' said Cate, and sighed.

They both took a step out; the air was clean and sharp and Cate felt the flakes falling soft as down on her upturned face, then cold and wet. She shook her head, feeling it in her hair, seeing it beginning to settle on the trees, on the hire car parked under them, the saddle of her own *motorino*. In the wider, deeper dark beyond the castle Cate even thought she could see the glimmer of white on the hills around them. It suddenly seemed extraordinarily quiet.

'The music's stopped,' said Nicki, but as they listened to the silence a distant shout went up from the other side of the castle, a kind of football cheer. 'Are they coming for food?' said Nicki, alarmed.

'Quick,' said Cate. 'Come on.' It must be eight, at least; how could she have lost track of time? The kitchen clock said half past.

But when they hurried in, loaded with dishes, the dining room was empty. Cate took off the cloths: *zucchini* filled with minced meat, cold rolled stuffed veal in slices, grilled aubergines with parsley and slippery red and yellow stewed peppers.

The *crostini* she'd helped prepare herself, what seemed like a lifetime ago.

'Where is everyone?' said Nicki, but Cate could hear them in the corridor, coming across from the library down the awkward passageways. She met Tiziano in the doorway.

'*Boicotta*,' he said, triumphantly.

Behind him stood Per, his wife Yolanda clinging fiercely to his arm. Per looked determined, like a man whose only hope was to get as drunk as he could. Alec Fairhead brought up the rear; his face behind Yolanda's shoulder was pinker, healthier, and he still had that look she'd seen on the stairs, of being surprised by happiness. Freed; or perhaps he was just drunk too.

Cate set her hands on her hips. 'What do you mean, boycott?' There was a gleam in Tiziano's eye she didn't recognize; of malice, of wildness, or rebellion. 'What would you be boycotting?'

'This place,' said Tiziano.

She knelt, and still in Italian, so the others wouldn't understand, she said, 'You know, don't you? About the detective.'

Tiziano nodded. 'Luca told us,' he said warily. 'We were in the music room, before I played. Captive audience.' She thought of the music that had poured out, after.

'What – how did they take it?'

Tiziano put his head on one side. 'Are you asking me to snitch?' he said softly, using the word they'd have used in school. She smiled.

Tiziano pursed his lips thoughtfully. 'Well, Per just said, what? What? Like he'd lost his marbles. Tina looked petrified. Michelle started shouting at him that it was an outrage.' He shot a glance over his shoulder at Alec Fairhead. 'The Englishman – well. I thought he was going to burst into tears at first but then he seemed – you know. All English. Stoical: resigned, like he was facing a firing squad.' They both looked now at Per Hansen and Alec Fairhead behind them, the former beginning to frown.

'*Tuttavia*,' said Tiziano loudly, and again, in English. 'Anyway. We've come to tell you, we're not eating. Or at least, not in here.' He reached out for a tray of stuffed *zucchini* and set it on his knee.

'I'm sorry,' said Alec Fairhead, his voice slurring. 'We're sorry, Miss Giottone, Cate. We don't mean it personally.' He was still being polite, but his hair was untidy, and Cate could see the tie he always wore stuffed into his jacket pocket. 'The girls are having a party.'

'Girls?' Cate couldn't imagine who he meant.

'Michelle and Tina,' said Tiziano. 'Michelle's place.'

'Is there any booze left in the library?' Cate asked crossly. 'Have you drunk it all?'

'The music did it,' said Per, his face comically solemn as he gazed down at Tiziano. 'All his fault, the fault of the musical genius. A Bacchanal, I think it is called. A breakout from prison.'

Tiziano set his muscled forearms on the wheel-chair's armrests; he looked like a warrior; he was certainly the ringleader and perhaps the only one sober. 'We don't like this private investigator business,' he said. 'I don't think it was part of the deal. Not conducive to artistry.'

'No,' said Fairhead, his face wilder. 'Not in the contract, being suspected of murder.'

'We do not co-operate,' added Per. At his side Yolanda looked up at him, her eyes shining.

It was funny, thought Cate, looking at them, that having spent six weeks avoiding each other like nervous cats, these artists were now united. By Loni's death. She took a step back, hands up. 'Look, that's nothing to do with me,' she said. 'I'm just the kitchen slave.'

'We know,' said Tiziano impatiently, and Cate bit her lip. He gave her a sharp look and for a moment she thought he was going to say something to soften it, but instead he put his broad hands down and spun the wheels, turning away in a tight circle.

Obediently the others followed, Alec Fairhead only pausing, hovering a moment on the way back out into the corridor. 'Sorry, Caterina,' he murmured again, and she heard the slight slurring in his voice. 'You see how it is.' He frowned, seemed to brighten. 'You could come too, you know. We'd like you to – at least –' Cate was aware of Nicki listening avidly at her shoulder. 'At least, I would.' Only then he clamped his mouth shut as if regretting what he'd said, and hurried off after the others.

'I'm going to call Beth now,' Cate heard herself say to Nicki. And perhaps they heard that too, only she closed the dining room door on them.

CHAPTER 16

Giulietta Sarto had never been in a house like this. She had to make herself move coolly through the wide white corridors, from one big pale, glass-walled room to another, making herself invisible as she passed among them, as if she'd been doing this all her life, but inside she was rooted to the spot, eyes on stalks.

It had been easy. Or if not exactly easy, then a hell of a lot less of a nightmare than she'd expected. In fact Giuli was resentful, almost angry, that it had been so easy, and found herself wondering why she'd spent her life expecting to be refused entrance to almost anywhere. She knew it was only the dope that had made the boy she attached herself to turn and give her a smile as he preceded her through the gate and inside the Orfeo villa's magic circle. They were all stoned on one thing or another, and full of the milk of human kindness; she hadn't even needed to hand her own stash around. The little fraternity of dope heads; dope the great leveller – well, up to a point. Giuli wasn't the only older person present – she spotted a guy with long white hair and earrings who ran a club in a *fondo* behind

Santo Spirito, holding court on a big leather sofa –
but she wasn't under any illusions that if she didn't
watch herself, she'd be out on her ear. Because after
brotherly love came paranoia, in the big warm
wonderful world of drugs.

Carlotta had left the house at seven. At a discreet
distance Giuli had followed, knowing roughly
from Sandro where Carlotta would be headed. It
didn't occur to her to doubt Sandro, and of course
he'd been right.

High on the southern hills of Arcetri overlooking
the glittering city, on a silent, narrow street whose
long, clean-plastered walls indicated a garden
bigger than most parks, the high flank of a villa
built on a grand scale had loomed, and up ahead
of Giuli, Carlotta had slowed. Giuli had promptly
killed the engine of her own *motorino*, then placed
the machine carefully against the wall and lit a
cigarette. There was a bend in the road here, and
if she leaned forward a fraction she could see what
was going on, keeping herself in the shadow of a
big evergreen overhanging the wall. It was very
very cold, and still, the pavement glinting with
frost; snow, she'd have said, only it never snowed
in the city.

Carlotta had stopped by a gate further along the
wall and had soon wheeled her little pink Vespa
through it, leaving Giuli on the outside, with the
night sky and the sparkling carpet of the city
spread out below them.

Every ten minutes or so for the hour Giuli had

stood there, feeling her toes turn numb, more visitors had turned up, singly, now and again, but more often in groups of five or more, chattering, laughing, oblivious to Giuli leaning in the drive opposite, on her third cigarette. Biding her time, watching what happened when Alberto Orfeo's dad was away. She'd found herself thinking of Sandro, down there in the Maremma in that big ugly castle in the dark. Leafing through the pages he'd given her, it had seemed to her a funny sort of set-up for the 'guests'. No TV, no boyfriends, no one you knew, stuck in the middle of nowhere without a car; sounded an awful lot like rehab to Giuli.

At least Sandro would have a car.

Giuli's phone had rung; glancing around, grateful that for the moment she was alone in the street, she'd wrestled it out of her buttoned pocket: it would be Sandro. 'Yes?' she'd hissed, not bothering to look at the caller's identity.

'Giuli?'

It hadn't been Sandro. Giuli's heart had lurched; shit. Why had she felt guilty? Like being back in school, called out as the dunce.

'Luisa,' she'd said, faltering, straightening instinctively out of the half-crouch she'd adopted. 'How are you?' Stupidly formal; she'd given the game away already.

'So you know about this – idiotic game, do you?' As usual, Luisa had cut straight to the chase.

'Game? What game?'

'Giuli,' Luisa had said, warning her. 'Don't bother. You know where Sandro's gone, don't you?'

'Yes, of course.'

'And why are you whispering?'

'I'm working,' Giuli had said, raising her whisper to a mutter. 'Following the girl. Carlotta Bellagamba.'

'Oh, yes,' Luisa had said, her voice steely with scorn. 'That girl he was getting all fatherly over. And where's he? In some hotel somewhere while you do the legwork, trying to teach me some kind of lesson? Staying with Pietro?'

'What? No, no,' Giuli had replied urgently, forgetting herself, looking round to see if anyone would have heard. The street was empty for the moment. 'He's gone down to the Maremma, on a new job. Really.' She'd paused, listening to the silence. 'Luisa?'

'All right,' Luisa had said wearily, and Giuli had felt a prickle of anxiety at the defeat in her voice when she'd continued. 'So you're not going to tell me.'

'OK,' Giuli had said, 'I've told you the truth, he's down in the Maremma.' No response from Luisa. 'Look, he said, he was – upset, yes. About you going away, not telling him till it was too late. He's worried he's going to lose you.' Should she even mention Frollini, the old lizard? She'd decided not to.

'He's an idiot. Lose me? I should think he *is* worried, behaving like this.'

Her voice had been ragged with anger; Giuli had tried to work out what it meant. Even though she'd

278

steered clear of men since rehab, she knew well enough what it was like when a relationship ended. Things you might have accepted for years suddenly you couldn't tolerate any more, and there was no going back. You let yourself hate someone, and it's finished.

She'd taken a step into the street, looking out over the frosted city, the black skeletons of trees in the villa's garden motionless in the icy, windless night. Luisa was down there, alone in the cold flat with her suitcases and her plane ticket.

'When do you leave?' she'd asked, cautiously. 'Monday morning, is it?'

'He's told you all about it, has he? It's a business trip; someone dropped out. It's a big opportunity.'

Had there been a splinter of defensiveness there?

'I'll come over tomorrow,' Giuli had said. Silence again. 'Please?'

'I'll be busy. Packing.'

'I'll help.' And this time she had to take Luisa's silence as agreement. 'I'll come at eleven. I'll bring *pasticcini*.'

Pasticcini, the little cakes you brought when you visited your loved ones on a Sunday. Giuli had spent a few months in a halfway house after she'd been let out of psychiatric hospital. And every Sunday morning she'd call in on Luisa and Sandro – this odd couple who were better parents to her than her real ones had ever been – but only after stopping at the *pasticceria* in the Viale Europa.

It had been a shameless, sentimental appeal on

Giuli's part, but it might have won her a chance to talk over this stupid business. Luisa's response had been to let out a sound of exasperation, one Giuli had had no choice but to take as assent.

'Luisa?' But she'd hung up.

Now, after close to an hour inside, Giuli still hadn't spotted Carlotta, and she was starving. There was a dining room with a long table laid out with stacks of takeaway pizza boxes, and she pulled herself off a couple of slices. There were two crates of beer and some half-full bottles of champagne warming on the table; a couple was lying under it, kissing. She moved back into the room with the leather sofas where the man who ran the nightclub now had a girl thirty years younger than him nestling under his arm. Who cleared all this stuff up, in time for the old man's return?

When a burst of laughter followed her as she passed a little group sitting cross-legged and rolling joints behind a sofa, Giuli decided it was time to lower her profile. She went outside, into the garden.

Behind her someone put some music on, loud R&B, and the lights went out; for a paranoid moment Giuli wondered if they'd been waiting for her to leave. She moved away from the noise to the end of one wing of the big house and stood there and let her eyes adjust. It was dark, but the garden was not quite empty – she could hear murmured voices, some way off. There was a sloping lawn, with flowerbeds and a big, closely trimmed hedge beyond it. Giuli listened. Got out the dope, some

280

papers, broke up one of her cheap state cigarettes into dry tobacco and began to roll a joint. Not for her; this was camouflage, or perhaps a lure. It felt strange, though, going through the motions after all this time. Not good.

Someone appeared beside her, and she handed the joint to him; it was the boy who'd let her in.

'Do I know you?' he said with mild interest as he lit up. She weighed him up in the dark.

'No,' she said kindly.

'Didn't think so,' he said, dragging deeply, and despite herself Giuli sighed. 'What?' the boy asked sleepily.

'You ever tell yourself you're going to give it up?' she asked.

He shrugged. 'Sure.'

'Good,' she said. 'That's good.' He straightened up, uncertain as to whether she was going to call his parents, or something. 'It's OK,' she said. 'Don't mind me.' He'd think he dreamt her, in the morning. She hesitated. 'You seen Alberto or Carlotta anywhere?' By the glow of the cigarette's tip, she saw his lazy eyes examining her without curiosity, nose wrinkling at the taste of the cheap tobacco; perhaps he wasn't one of her kind, after all. He nodded across the sloping lawn, then turned away, back towards the music.

For a while, Giuli didn't move, then she walked calmly in a diagonal across the grass, between flowerbeds, to an arched gap in the hedge. There was a light source somewhere, discreet, bluish, low down among the greenery; she heard people talking somewhere off to her left, in murmured voices. She edged closer. 'Berto,' she heard a voice whisper. Was that Carlotta? When the boy spoke she thought it was him, for sure.

'Come here,' he said hoarsely.

The conversation wasn't exactly a conversation. Pet names, laughter, mumbled kissing. Then the girl said petulantly, 'What about next week?'

Then they were making an arrangement to meet. 'Not this week, don't think so,' he said. 'It's too much. Look at this lot; no chance of being alone.' He sounded sulky, eager, tender. Perhaps he was serious about her, after all. 'And besides, the old man – I don't know what his plans are now. Something's happened down there, that's why he's away tonight. He said there'd been an accident.'

'An accident?' She sounded querulous, haughty. 'What kind of accident?'

Her voice wasn't right, thought Giuli as Alberto mumbled a response, 'Dunno, *cara*. Nothing to do with him, anyway,' and then they moved and the girl was in view, and it wasn't Carlotta. Alberto had his face in her neck and she was pulling away, looking down her long nose between wings of straight blonde hair.

An accident.

Giuli took a step back, trying to think, suddenly not wanting to be a witness, looking back through the arch towards the bright windows of the villa and thinking, Carlotta mustn't see this. Then there was Carlotta, walking towards her. Towards them.

Giuli's first impulse was to deflect the girl, moving towards her with hands outstretched and a smile fixed on her face, although what she thought she was going to say she didn't know. Then she took in Carlotta's stiff-legged walk, her clenched fists, and, as she came closer and Giuli saw the gleam of tears as the other girl brushed past without even registering her, she thought, *Well, she knows.* Too late. Giuli stood aside, and behind her all hell broke loose.

Didn't she have to find out at some point that Alberto wasn't her sort? Wasn't it better this way? But Giuli knew it never felt better at the time, and she could hear the tears in Carlotta's voice as she raged. She backed into the shadows, turned and ran inside. As she did so, someone flung open a window at all the noise – they really were like cats squalling – and hooted derisively.

It wasn't heaven in the house, after all. As Giuli slipped unnoticed past the leather sofas and the champagne and the handsome young people watching themselves in every reflective surface, she could only see the pieces of congealing pizza stuck to their boxes and a cigarette burn in the cream carpet. She picked her way back through the rooms, out of the side door to the gate where she'd got in, and waited.

It took forty minutes, but Carlotta came, in the end, hair flying, eyes streaked, jacket ripped, banging the gate behind her. She looked as if she'd given as good as she got.

Giuli set off after the pink Vespa at a discreet distance, although perhaps not discreet enough; waiting at a light apparently stuck at red on the Via Senese, Carlotta turned and looked at Giuli over her shoulder, as if in acknowledgement, and something like recognition dawned in her eyes. For a long moment they held each other's gaze. They were level with a shabby all-night bar Giuli knew, its original, silvered sign from the thirties still in place. Old men were standing at the counter, talking sociably, and the glow from the place suddenly looked welcoming.

The light stayed red. Carlotta's head turned to follow Giuli's gaze. Giuli set down her feet and pulled off her helmet.

'Who are you?' asked Carlotta.

'Fancy a coffee?' asked Giuli.

They sat drinking warm milk, Carlotta fiddling with a damp tissue and blurting out her misery. Giuli set her mission aside to start with, patting the girl gingerly on the shoulder, telling her she was better off out of it, which was true. Carlotta was happy enough to tell her what she knew about Alberto's father, although she did give Giuli a faintly puzzled glance when she got out a notebook.

'You investigating him, or something?' She sniffed, blew her nose, looked better. Looked curious.

'Something,' said Giuli. And they both smiled.

By the time they got back to Galluzzo and Giuli

284

saw the girl safely inside, a few flakes of snow were beginning to fall, almost invisibly. Giuli sat a while outside the house texting Sandro, rubbing her fingers inside her leather gauntlets as they stiffened and turned numb. She saw a light go on inside the house and another, then the sound of voices. You'll survive, she thought.

If he'd known how little time he'd have to size up his suspects at their first meeting, Sandro might have taken notes. But things didn't always go to plan, notes could be misleading, and sometimes that initial glimpse was all you needed. That, at least, was what he told himself.

Sandro's phone had chirruped at him as he stepped off the broad stone staircase and into the great cavernous hall. There had been a murmur of voices through the archway where the piano had been played, congratulations being offered; Sandro thought he could distinguish Luca Gallo's voice among them, strained and hearty.

He stopped, thinking how cold it was in this great monster of a building. Opposite the wide-arched entrance to the music room, the vast studded door was closed tight; at the far end of the hall was another, smaller door, and it annoyed him that he didn't know where it led, yet.

Already Sandro hated this place; it was a labyrinth, uncomfortably huge, with its secret doors and mysterious, icy currents of air, and lightless as a dungeon, full of ghosts. But it wasn't just the building – it was everything. He was uncomfortable, out of place; too far from home. From the wide green river, the basin of the city filled with red roofs and narrow streets full of people and suspended above it all the big marble and terracotta ship of the Duomo. Dome-sickness, the Florentines called it, or someone had called it anyway. Ghirlandaio? He'd been right, whoever he was; nowhere else was civilized, least of all the barren hills and once-malarial swamps and brutish castles of the Maremma.

Loni Meadows had tried to fit out her boudoir up there, with silk and cushions, but it was a great stone prison still, and it had got her in the end.

Staring down at his phone Sandro had felt as grumpy as a teenager. *New message, read now?* But as he clicked to open it he heard the sounds of group movement and looked up. Hastily he put the phone away.

'Hold on, hold on,' Luca Gallo was saying, his hands held up. His back was to Sandro, standing in the wide doorway to the music room as if attempting to block it. Over his shoulder Sandro could see faces. A stocky woman had her mouth open ready to talk back; her blonde hair was loose and greying, and her big, ravaged features might once have been handsome. Michelle Connor: he ticked her off mentally. Standing some way off on the far side of the room, one hand on the piano, with a haughty look of discomfort on his face, was Niccolò Orfeo. Distancing himself from the mob.

286

They did indeed seem a bit like a mob; the only question was, who was to be strung up?

'Sorry, sorry,' said Michelle Connor sarcastically, and even though she was talking to Luca, she was looking straight at Sandro; 'but we don't buy this, no way.'

Gallo moved his head a fraction in Sandro's direction, pleading out of a corner of his eye, and Sandro took his cue, stepping forward.

'Hello,' he said, shoulder to shoulder with Luca Gallo in the doorway; he heard Luca breathe out quietly. 'I'm Sandro Cellini.' He held out a hand to the woman, who ignored it.

'We know what you are,' she said disdainfully.

'You do?' He spoke mildly, head on one side, and felt an uneasy shifting among the others. He reminded himself that these northerners had a different attitude to courtesy; they didn't understand it. Their rudeness didn't always mean hostility – although in this woman's case, he thought probably it did. All the same, nothing was going to provoke him. 'And?' He lowered his hand with an air of disappointment.

'Come on,' said an English voice – very English, apologetic and uncomfortable – and as the owner of the voice made to move past him, Sandro took in a thin face, deep-set eyes, close-cropped hair: this was the one, the one he had been looking for. You, he thought, you were in London with Loni Meadows twenty-five years ago. How beautiful she would have been then, those cold bright blue eyes. Had Alec Fairhead been handsome too?

He looked like a monk now; he held out a hand, and when Sandro took it it felt to be all bones, and cold to the touch. 'I'm Alexander Fairhead,' he said. I know who you are, thought Sandro, but now he had the man in front of him, he wasn't so sure. Behind Fairhead the little crowd fell back a fraction, loosening as it did so.

Sandro nodded, matching the face to the name he'd glanced at on the screen, on Giuli's chart plotting this handful of people's lives.

'I think I saw you earlier,' he said. 'Out for a walk.' And he thought the man flushed.

Whose idea had it been, that walk? Had they been looking for something too? And now the snow had come, covering the scene.

'Will you all come *on*,' said the fierce, stocky woman, pushing past Sandro; he felt the warm, powerful bulk of her displace him, and involuntarily ceded ground to her. 'I'm going to get the place ready.' She peered aggressively back inside. 'Tina?'

'This is Michelle Connor,' said Luca valiantly, as she ignored him. 'A wonderful poet. And Tina Kreutz, our sculptor.'

Tina Kreutz was a thin woman, girl he'd have said from a distance, who now threaded her way out from the music room, bobbing her head.

'Pleased to meet you,' he said kindly and Tina pulled her head back.

'Are you really here about the accident?' she

288

said, her voice not much more than a frightened whisper. 'About Loni?'

'Please don't worry,' he said, as gently as he could. 'I plan to talk to everyone. Just a chat.'

As if that would reassure her. She was scared of something all right, but then she looked like it wouldn't take much. An abused child? A battered wife? That was what Tina Kreutz looked like to him, one of those girls in a shelter, afraid of their own shadow, who would put a chair against the door every night and hide kitchen knives to defend themselves, only to end up cutting their own throats with them. Connor put out a protective arm and the girl leaned into her, and Sandro wondered which of them needed the other more.

'Well, I'll hope to catch up with you tomorrow then,' said Sandro, conceding defeat; the pair of them made him feel like an abuser. Michelle Connor made a sound of derision, and the women disappeared out through the heavy door, letting in that unmistakable new smell, a gust of cold, wet air and a brief glimpse of flakes whirling under a light.

Their disappearance seemed to signal a kind of surge, and others pushed out through the arched doorway, Luca stepping back wearily to let them past. 'There's food in the dining room, as usual,' he threw out as a last-ditch attempt to maintain control, or a semblance of normality at least. Sandro saw that the man was close to despair, and put a hand on his arm.

'I'm sure we can all talk tomorrow,' he said, addressing the little group but keeping his hand on Luca Gallo. He felt the man's arm stiffen in rejection.

They looked back at him. The Englishman, seeming on the edge of a kind of hysteria; a strongly built Scandinavian type who had to be Per Hansen, swaying slightly with drink, bushy fair eyebrows and a pretty, dark woman sticking like glue to his side. His wife? And from waist-height the clearly intelligent, penetrating gaze of the man in his wheelchair, demanded that he look down: Tiziano Scarpa, the producer of the extraordinary sound that had ushered Sandro across the threshold of the Castello Orfeo.

It came to Sandro that a man who could make that music would have no need of any other outlet. All anger, all fear, all love could be rolled up in that sound; could such a man commit murder?

'That was you, playing?' he said humbly. Scarpa gave a faint smile, and inclined his head in a parody of modest acknowledgement.

'Me,' he said lightly.

'I'm sure you're just doing your job,' said Fairhead awkwardly. 'We don't mean –'

But Tiziano Scarpa interrupted him. 'Come on,' he said, spinning the chair with ease. 'Let's make our apologies to La Giottone. Michelle will have our balls if we keep her waiting.'

As he spun away Sandro saw the muscles in his back move under his shirt, saw the powerful

290

forearms flex and extend, saw the callouses on the balls of his thumbs, the worn patches on the strap arrangement over his wrists. Even without the use of his legs, there wouldn't be much Tiziano Scarpa would allow to defeat him. And they moved off, not out through the main door but through the smaller exit Sandro had wondered about earlier and which, to judge from the cooking smells that issued distantly through it, led to the dining room.

Luca Gallo made a distracted movement to follow but Sandro shook his head. 'Let them go,' he said, speaking with relief in his own language. 'It's late.'

'You wouldn't think it was my house, would you?' The bullying, aristocratic voice of Niccoló Orfeo broke in on them and Sandro felt his jaw clench; bullying, but also rather too insistent. 'Might I be introduced, do you think?'

His eyes dull with tiredness, Gallo straightened. 'Sandro Cellini, this is Count Orfeo. Count –'

'Yes, yes,' said the man rudely, raising a large, ringed hand to wave him away. No wonder the son was a spoilt little pig.

'*Un piacere*', said Sandro, his hand out.

Orfeo ignored it. 'Shall we go into the library? I need a drink, after that display.' And the man was already walking away from them into the next room. It was colder in here, and an elaborate heavy chandelier shed a gloomier light; a small fire had been laid in the vast stone fireplace but it wasn't doing much more than smouldering.

Without offering Sandro or Luca Gallo anything, Orfeo poured himself a drink from a selection of bottles on a tray. Campari, sweet vermouth, whisky. As he watched him, the only thing that prevented Sandro from being openly rude was that the Count might in fact be quite close to getting the arrogant smile wiped off his face. Did he need to wait for his suspicions to be confirmed by Giuli? Eventually Orfeo turned to face him.

'I imagine that you understand why I am here?' Sandro kept his voice respectful.

'Oh, yes,' said Orfeo with an airiness that wasn't entirely convincing, and Sandro felt a stir of satisfaction. 'That ghastly husband of hers, Luca tells me. I suppose he wants to have the last word. Perhaps he would like to sue me, because his wife drove dangerously. A very unpleasant little man, you know.' He tipped the glass back and half-emptied it.

Sandro regarded him levelly. 'Avvocato Mascarello, you mean? Well, I suppose one doesn't get to be so powerful without making some enemies.'

'Powerful?' Niccolò Orfeo wrinkled his nose in theatrical dismissal. 'Well, I don't know about that. He has some rather unsavoury connections, I know that.'

Sandro, who felt a sudden surge of admiration for Giuliano Mascarello, just smiled.

'And where is the damned food?' said Orfeo disagreeably. 'Everything seems to have gone to ruin.' He drained his glass and Luca Gallo quickly refilled it.

'Will you be – returning to Florence tonight?' asked Sandro mildly, eyeing the dark oily liquid.

'You mean, am I intending to drive? Well, it would be none of your business if I were.' He looked at Gallo. 'I'll be sleeping on the *piano nobile*.'

Loni Meadows's room. Luca Gallo looked from Orfeo to Sandro and back, panic in his eyes. 'Well – I – I'm not sure –'

'I don't mind a little untidiness,' said Orfeo dismissively. 'Just have the bed made up.'

Luca Gallo closed his mouth. 'Yes,' he said.

I know your game, thought Sandro. Orfeo was looking at him as if defying him to argue, to say something about evidence or investigations, and Sandro was looking straight back, as if to say, you might have Commissario Grasso bowing and scraping and not dreaming of trespassing on your privacy by taking a step into Loni Meadows's bedroom, but I'm not Grasso. But before a word was spoken Sandro's phone chirruped again and Orfeo's look of contempt hardened.

'Do you mind?' said Sandro, taking the phone out. Knowing how rude Orfeo would consider it. He looked down.

Two new messages. The first from Mascarello, short and to the point. *Call me before 8.30.* The phone said 8.38. He looked up, calculating, to see Orfeo watching him. A quick smile to acknowledge that he knew how disrespectful he was being and did not care, then Sandro looked back down again. The second message was from Giuli, and

293

equally typical of its sender. All over the place, gabby, eager.

Dad has girlfriend somewhere down that way. Carlotta says party tonight because he was called away suddenly tonight accident, better call later maybe. All fine Carlotta fine, home safe.

OK. Sandro looked up and saw the wariness in Orfeo's face, returned it with a broad smile.

'Look, I'm so sorry,' he said with elaborately false courtesy, 'but I have a message to call the *Avvocato*. And as he is my employer, to me at least he is powerful.'

Orfeo frowned down at the mobile Sandro held up, as though it reminded him now of something faintly disturbing. Sandro put it away. 'So,' he went on, 'if you will excuse me?'

As though galvanized by the lawyer's name, Luca was suddenly at Orfeo's side. 'Yes, that would be fine,' he said, and Sandro heard the relief in his voice. 'We'll – ah –', he looked at the door through which the guests had disappeared, then went on nervously, 'we'll just let the guests – we'll let them –', he took a breath, '– In a moment or so we shall make our way to the dining room.' And to Sandro, with a look that pleaded for understanding, 'In your own time, then?'

In the music room Sandro paused, reached again for his mobile, checking for a signal, then looked back over his shoulder into the dim cold cavernous library.

'Another *aperitivo?*' Gallo was saying, as Orfeo

pulled his arm rudely away to look back over his shoulder at Sandro, standing there by the piano with his phone poised in his hand.

'And that's another thing,' he heard Orfeo mutter, 'the blasted phone. Didn't I tell you? You were supposed to –' and turned abruptly back, so that whatever else he said was swallowed up.

Sandro stood a moment, thinking; staring at the blinking mobile screen that told him no signal. Thinking about what Orfeo had just said.

He took the stairs three at a bound. Closed the door behind him and crossed to the long window, knitting his brow as he stared at his own phone, still thinking. He heard a tiny sound from outside and looked up from the phone and out of the still unshuttered window to where a figure below him paced up and down on the half-circle of drive.

Here there was a signal. He dialled Mascarello's number; it rang. And rang. Damn, he thought, nearly nine. Giuliano Mascarello, he guessed, had a thing about time-keeping. Just as he was about to give up, a woman's voice answered brusquely, 'Yes?'

He asked for Mascarello. In the background he thought he could hear something, a mechanical hissing, hushed voices. 'Avvocato Mascarello is undergoing his dialysis treatment,' said the woman's voice coldly.

'Ah – he called me,' said Sandro humbly. 'Sandro Cellini.'

Muffled voices, and when she came back on the

line the woman's tone was fractionally less chilly. 'Call again at ten,' she said, and hung up.

All right, thought Sandro, looking down at the lit semicircle of snowy gravel below him. Get things straight. There's the sender of the email, and there's Orfeo. Orfeo her lover, whom she was going to meet. Only he was in Florence.

The figure below stopped, tilted her face and he saw her profile. It was Caterina, shoulders hunched in the cold as she traced and retraced her steps across the ground, and for some reason the sight of her made him feel better. Putting his face to the glass Sandro could hear the crunch of her feet in the snow and the sound of her voice, speaking urgently into her own *telefonino*. And then she looked up, and Sandro stepped away from the window.

Orfeo. Is he guilty of something? Yes.

He took a moment, before going down again.

CHAPTER 17

The phone had rung long and hollow on the other side of the world, Westport, Connecticut. Cate, leaning against the stove in the hot kitchen with Nicki eyeing her nervously from the door into the dining room, imagined a great white clapboard house like the ones on TV, with a lawn, gleaming boards in a spacious hall, but the longer it rang the more she quailed at the thought of breaking the news to Beth, and when the voice answered, breezy and confident, for a moment she thought with relief, wrong number. Because it sounded nothing like querulous, unhappy Beth who had moped around the corridors and had a constant migraine.

But it was her. 'Speaking,' Beth sang, when Cate asked for her by name, apologetically, ready to hang up.

'It's Caterina? From the Castello Orfeo? From the Trust.' The snow had eased, only a few dusty flakes whirling down now, but the cold almost took her breath away, and the beautiful, silent whiteness of it all. The trees seemed closer, denser, layered with snow and motionless. Over her head

297

the white was beginning to settle in the crevices of the massive façade.

'Oh.' Bemused, and a little flat now, Beth was wary. 'Caterina. Hey. How're you guys doing?'

'Beth, um, OK – listen.' And now Cate found she didn't know quite how to say it; thought of how she would sound over there, in the bright American day, in the great white house she imagined, with its green sloping lawn. 'There's um – there's some bad news.'

As she went on, Cate heard Beth swallow, then heard a ragged, incoherent sob and she imagined all that American bright peace fractured. 'Loni. Who – how did –' Beth stopped, seemed to collect herself. 'You said it was an accident?' Now she sounded disbelieving. 'You're sure?'

'Yes,' said Cate slowly. 'In her car. Why do you ask that? Beth?'

'She always drove too fast,' said Beth uncertainly, and Cate blinked, hearing the words she'd repeated to herself when Luca had told them, hearing the tears in the girl's voice.

'She did, you're right. That's just what I said.' But even as she spoke Cate thought with dull fear that she didn't believe it.

And as if to confirm her thought Beth said, 'They're sure, are they?' Sounding just like the timid, nervous Beth the castle had made of her.

Cate spoke carefully. 'Listen to me, Beth. Do you think anyone might have wanted to – hurt her?'

'Hurt her?' And Beth let out a small, sad, bitter

298

little laugh. 'She wasn't afraid of making people angry, was she? Even the ones who loved her. Especially them.'

Cate was silent a moment. 'The ones that loved her. Like – um – like who?'

'I know what you're trying to get at,' Beth burst out. 'Like who? OK, like me. She knew I was – she knew I was gay. She messed me around. That's why I left, OK? That's why. She let me fall in love with her. She had me up in her room, on her bed, sitting in her bed, gossiping while she got dressed, telling me stuff. Intimate stuff. Letting me think –'

'No, Beth,' said Cate urgently, 'I didn't want to – to pry, that's not what I meant. I know this is nothing to do with you.'

There was a hoarse sob and then silence, and Cate heard the mother's voice, whispering, anxious. Cate heard Beth collect herself. 'Five minutes, Mom, OK?'

Cate waited a full minute before beginning again.

'There's a private investigator here,' she said, trying to sound reasonable and logical and comforting this time. 'Seems like a good guy.' It was her turn to hesitate, then she spoke slowly. 'Loni's husband doesn't want to believe it was an accident.'

She didn't die immediately, you know. For a perverse moment Cate wanted to share this awful fact with Beth, to tell her how bitter the cold had been that night, tell her about the green silk blouse on the floor of Loni's bedroom, but she stopped herself.

Instead she asked again, calmly, gently, 'Is there anything – or anyone – you know about that might help him? In the investigation?'

'Anyone,' repeated Beth, sounding traumatized.

'Beth,' said Cate, 'Per had written to his wife telling her he wanted a divorce, because he'd fallen in love with another woman. What other woman could it be? You? Me? Tina Kreutz?'

'Per?' Beth was blankly incredulous. 'No way. I mean, she did her thing with him. Flirted –' She broke off, and when she spoke again it was with dull understanding. 'Well, I guess she might have done the same job on him as she did on me. Kind of – led him on.'

'Only Per wouldn't take no for an answer?'

A sharp intake of breath. 'You think he – you seriously think Per would hurt her?'

'No,' said Cate without stopping to think. 'Yes. Well, in the heat of the moment, maybe. But this wasn't –'

Unless he was in the car with her? Cate didn't believe that. Even if Fairhead hadn't heard him come up to bed, if Per had left the castle with her, if he'd struck her, wrestled with her, driven them into a tree – the whole scenario unspooled itself, horribly vivid. But he wouldn't have left her to die there, in the dark. He would have wept, tried to resuscitate her. Called an ambulance, given himself up to the police. He wouldn't have let her die.

'No,' she said. 'I don't think he would.' There was

a silence. 'So he wasn't actually her lover, as far as you know?' Another silence. 'Those nights when she left the castle late at night, that wasn't with Per? When she took the car and went into Pozzo?'

'Oh.' Beth spoke warily now. 'So you knew about that.'

'Everyone knew,' said Cate apologetically. 'Even Mauro knew. Though, I don't think he knew who she was going to.'

Beth spoke. 'She told me I was the only one. I mustn't tell a soul.' A pause, then thoughtfully. 'She told me about all her lovers. Bet Mauro didn't know about the English guy, either, did he?'

Cate stopped stock still. 'English guy? Alec Fairhead?'

'Loni said when he turned up with Mauro at the beginning of the retreat, last to arrive, she could see it all over his face. That he hadn't forgotten her, whatever he might say.'

'Forgotten her?'

'It was a long time ago,' said Beth. 'Years. She was – triumphant about it. He wrote that book about her, so she said, his only book was about her. About them. And when he turned up she said he hadn't seen her in years, but he still wanted her.'

Did he? Had he? Cate tried to process this, tried to stop herself actually hating Loni Meadows. 'He did say he'd known her, way back,' she said slowly. 'When – when we got the news. When we heard she was dead.'

Alec Fairhead's haunted face, in the library. Cate

took an involuntary step back from the great stone wall of the castle and paced across to the trees, arms wrapped tight around herself against the cold, to the beginning of the rough road that sloped past the laundry to Michelle's. 'Yeah,' said Beth, 'well, at least he admitted it.'

'Yes.' Cate realized that she didn't want Alec Fairhead to be a bad guy. 'You don't think she – started it up again?'

Through the trees she could see the light shed from Michelle's apartment through the big wall of glass, an elongated reactangle of dazzling white cast across the snow; she could feel the icy wet seep up from the hem of her jeans. Felt the impulse to go down there and spy on them, only poor Nicki trembling in the kitchen stopped her. She turned around and walked without thinking back towards the castle, skirting the grass to the front, where she stopped.

Over there, in the dark. She looked down the straight avenue of cypresses, swallowed up in the night, weighted with snow, behind her the great looming bulk of the castle's front elevation.

'Start something up with Fairhead? No way.' Beth was speaking. She sounded pretty sure; almost cheerful. 'She thought he was a loser. No way. She even said it. Like a dog returning to its own vomit.'

'Right.' What a horrible expression, thought Cate. And for some reason Vincenzo came into her head. What, she asked herself in a brief moment of distracted clarity, am I doing with him? Poor Vincenz.

It came to her that these were delaying tactics. 'So you're not going to tell me?' A light came on in the façade, and for a wild moment Cate thought it was in Loni's room and that she had come back to stop her secrets being spilled. The stocky outline of a man stood in the window, looking down: Sandro Cellini. Not in Loni's room but in Beth's, the room next door.

'I don't know.' Beth sounded frightened. 'She was so – obsessive, about people not knowing. She liked it that no one could ever guess, from how they were with each other. It was a – kind of a game, for her. Her secret life. That's why they met somewhere else, out of the castle. Sure, he was old, that didn't seem to bother her, though. She wasn't in it for love. And she got such a kick out of it. He'd come up for lunches, give his spiel and she'd wave him off back to Florence.'

'Back to Florence?' *Him?* 'Hey, listen,' Cate said with alarm, knowing that the man was right there, lording it in the music room, that she'd be serving him his dinner the minute this call was over. The growing realization that Beth was right; of course it would be him. Loni Meadows had simply gone to the top. 'You're sure?'

'Totally I'm sure.' Now it was Beth's turn to be patient. 'It was him, the lord and master. Niccolò Orfeo, of course. She wanted to be queen of the castle, didn't she?'

Queen of the castle. And Cate stared up at the window where Sandro Cellini had stood, until

303

eventually Beth's voice came back at her. *Caterina? Are you still there?*

The dining room in which they sat, like a parody of an old titled family, was nothing like as grand as the library: housed in some kind of extension, low-ceilinged, ill-lit, with dull, institutional furnishings. Sandro caught Orfeo looking around himself with disdain, as if disowning the modern addition and all it represented; Sandro supposed it had been part of the deal to accommodate the guests. Health and hygiene regulations, perhaps, and Orfeo didn't like to be reminded that this was no longer entirely his home.

Sandro bided his time for a bit; they ate in silence. He could see Luca Gallo eyeing him nervously from the far side of the oval table. They were waited upon by the sallow, shy girl; Nicki, Gallo said, introducing them. He'd hoped for Caterina but she spent most of the time in the kitchen, only appearing at the door with clean dishes for Nicki, darting him a glance. At one point he heard her phone ring in there, heard her talk in muttered tones. He supposed that wouldn't usually have been allowed, but there was altogether something ersatz about the formality of the set-up, the table hastily laid at Orfeo's imperious insistence even though it was the cook's night off. Eventually, aware that he had to call Mascarello back at ten, Sandro addressed Orfeo.

'You were in Florence?' he said. 'That night?'

And the old man looked at him from under heavy brows, his tanned face threatening outrage.

It seemed as good a way as any to broach the subject. Of course, he knew Orfeo had been in Florence on Thursday night because he had seen him drop his son off at school at eight o'clock that morning. Or did he? Under two hours to the castle, in a fast car. But it was the flaw, the thing that held Sandro back from making an outright accusation; it was the thing that didn't make sense.

She died on her way to meet her lover. Orfeo was her lover, ergo he must have set out to meet her. But he had been in Florence at around eight the morning after she died and fresh as a daisy. Sandro didn't know how they made their arrangements to meet, but he assumed it would be by phone. And where was her phone?

'What do you mean?' said Orfeo menacingly, knife and fork poised. Luca Gallo made a sound of protest, but no one looked at him.

Take it slowly, Sandro told himself: make sure you're sure. 'Just asking,' he said blithely, taking a bite of the rolled veal. Cold, but good. He pushed away the thought of Luisa, and her dishes in the freezer. 'The weather was bitter, wasn't it? Not a night to be on the road.'

'Oh, no,' said Gallo, 'Count Orfeo never comes up at night; anyway, certainly not during the winter.' He looked across at the man hopefully, trying to please. Orfeo eyed him narrowly but only grunted.

'Road's terrible,' he said dismissively. 'I suppose she was driving too fast.' He forked a mouthful of stuffed *zucchini* into his mouth and chewed.

Unable to detect even a trace of regret in the man's voice, Sandro felt himself seethe with frustration and dislike. How had it worked? Had they merely made use of each other? Was there not even affection? Or was this all in his mind?

Something sprang into Sandro's head. 'I – ah – encountered your son, the other week,' he said, on impulse, holding a smile as he willed Orfeo to look up from his plate. Not a nice impulse; a desire to upset. 'I'm based in Florence, you see.'

'Really?' Orfeo's voice was scornful, but he looked up sharply. Barked a laugh. 'Can't imagine that.' He turned to Luca Gallo and said, 'What about cheese?'

'A job,' said Sandro, knowing this was thin ice, where client confidentiality was concerned. 'Following a girl whose parents were worried she'd got in with the wrong crowd.' He'd phone Giuli, he decided. After Mascarello.

Orfeo was glaring at him with suspicion. 'Alberto's crowd? Who is this – girl?'

'A girl from a nice family,' said Sandro. 'Her father has a chain of shops.'

'Oh, I see,' said Orfeo, looking down his nose with something like amusement. 'One of those. Well, Alberto's a good-looking boy, he's entitled to have his fun. At his age – well.' He pushed his plate away. 'Clearly she won't be around for long, this shopkeeper's daughter.' Leaned forward. 'You can set your employers' minds at rest. Alberto might be putting it about a bit –' and his mouth twitched, unpleasantly '– but he's no fool.'

The shy girl set down a plate of cheese between them and Orfeo peered at it critically, as if Sandro had left the room.

Sandro reached for his glass of wine when what he would have liked to do was punch the man; it slopped in the glass. Good wine; the same Morellino that he and Luisa had drunk last night. Was it only last night? He felt overcome suddenly with disgust and weariness.

'Really,' he said flatly. 'Well, it would be nice to be able to reassure them.'

Nicki bobbed in between them, trying to clear. 'Should I bring coffee?' she asked Gallo nervously. Orfeo waved a hand at her, irritated, and she took fright, hurrying back into the kitchen.

Sandro turned to Luca Gallo, impatient suddenly with having to be discreet.

'Dottoressa Meadows left – immediately after the meal, on Thursday night,' he said, and Niccolò Orfeo made a grumbling sound of disdain. Sandro held Luca Gallo's gaze.

'She did,' Gallo replied, pale.

'Were you there – at that meal?' Sandro persisted. 'Did she say anything, to give a clue as to where she was going?'

'I stayed only for the *antipasto*,' said Luca Gallo, trying a smile. 'I – ah, I had work to do.' A grunt from Orfeo. 'And to be honest,' Gallo went on, 'it's not really my – ah – my area of expertise. Dinner party conversation. All a little too combative for me.'

'Under Dottoressa Meadows, you mean?' Nicki came back in with her tray of coffee and slid a cup and saucer in front of each of them before scurrying away.

Gallo looked alarmed, as though he'd given away more than he intended. 'Well – I –'

'Didn't suffer fools gladly,' interjected Orfeo from under his thick grey brows. 'That's what you mean.' Ruminatively, as if oblivious to how insulting it sounded, 'And she didn't understand the value of a good servant.'

Meaning Luca Gallo. Sandro had to look down at his plate, not wanting to see the humiliation in the man's eyes.

'She – well. She liked to engage in debate,' said Gallo bravely. 'She enjoyed a strong opponent. Some of the guests find that kind of – engagement uncomfortable. We should respect that.'

It was the first time Sandro had heard anything like criticism from him. 'Really,' he said, unable to conceal his interest, but Niccolò Orfeo had also registered the comment and under the stare he was now directing across the table at the man he clearly considered to be not much more than a butler, Luca Gallo was already backing down.

The girl was back again. '*Digestivi?*' she asked, and apparently grateful for the interruption, Luca turned to smile at her, shaking his head.

'It's all right, Nicki,' he said. 'We'll manage. You need to get home, don't you?'

'Not for me, anyway,' said Sandro abruptly, getting to his feet. 'I've had enough.' It sounded rude, and he made no effort to correct the impression.

Damn it, he thought, damn, damn; he was itching to challenge the man, but somehow, with Luca Gallo there, he couldn't bring himself to.

You were her lover. Where were you when she was dying?

'I need some fresh air,' he said, as Luca half stood, politely.

And as Sandro looked at it, the door to the kitchen opened a few centimetres, then wider. Caterina was looking at him intently through the space. She moved her head a fraction to the side, and her eyes, but unfamiliar as he was with the geography of this great stone prison he could have no idea what she meant. Hesitantly he tried to indicate cautious assent. The door closed, just as Gallo seemed to register that he was looking towards it.

'Tradesman's entrance,' said Orfeo, without looking at either of them. He reached for the Armagnac.

'Don't be too long,' said Gallo as he opened the big studded front door for Sandro. And turned to hurry back to the dining room, an expression of weary patience on his face.

'Hold on,' said Sandro, putting out a hand to detain him. 'About the phone?'

'Phone?' Gallo looked blank, then wary. 'What phone?'

'Orfeo said something about a phone,' said Sandro. 'Just after I left you in the – whatever that big cold room is. Library.' He could almost feel its chill from here, through the dark music room, colder than the air outside the front door. 'Whose phone? Loni's phone?'

'Look,' said Gallo hurriedly, 'please. Just drop it. Leave him – this is nothing to do with him.' He seemed desperate. 'You really don't understand, do you? He's a powerful man. For eight years the greater part of my job has been keeping Orfeo on an even keel, stopping him from upsetting the guests, dealing with his threats to raise the rent, his tantrums over the gallery extension, the studio. How could this be anything to do with him?'

Gallo looked anxiously towards the dining room, then back at Sandro. 'Listen,' he hissed. 'Do you really think – the man lives in the eighteenth century, for heaven's sake. I don't think he even has a computer. You're supposed to be looking for someone who sent an anonymous email, aren't you?'

Sandro looked at him. Sighed.

'All right,' he said, but there was a warning in his voice. 'We'll talk about it in the morning. I've – there are things I could have said tonight, you understand. But I didn't. But if you thought I'd be a tame detective, you and Mascarello – well. I believe in thoroughness. Even if people get upset.'

'All right, all right,' said Gallo, his face drained. He held the door open on the wintry night. 'Fine. In the morning.'

As the door closed behind him and Sandro stood in the snow and felt the cold around his ankles and tried to work out which way to go around the intimidating grey flank of the castle, his phone rang. It was Giuliano Mascarello.

CHAPTER 18

Ten minutes passed, twenty, while Cate hovered between the sink and the back door, watching for Sandro Cellini. Had he understood? Nicki ferried the few plates from the dining room to the dishwasher, giving Cate increasingly wary looks.

'Getting cold,' she said pointedly, nodding at the door to the outside, standing a crack ajar. Cate had positioned herself in front of it.

'Really?' Fanning herself. 'I think it's stuffy.'

Vincenzo had called just as things seemed to be getting heated next door, just as she would have liked to listen. From the little she'd seen through the door, Sandro Cellini didn't like Count Orfeo one bit; she was fairly sure, too, that he already suspected something. All Cate wanted was to get him alone and tell him what she knew; only the longer she had to wait, the more painful and complicated Beth's little story became in her head.

Her first impulse had been to get rid of Vincenzo as hurriedly as possible: if Loni had been there the sound of a staff mobile ringing during dinner – and being answered – would have been grounds for a serious bawling out as soon as the guests disappeared.

'Sorry, V'cenz, darling,' she had begun, feeling sick at herself. 'I can't talk right now –'

But he'd paid no attention; he'd been drinking, she'd quickly realized. His voice slurred; it seemed as though everyone was drunk tonight. Cellini wasn't: just one glass, he'd had. Could she trust him?

'Hi babe,' Vincenzo had said, drawling cheerfully; in the background Cate could hear the sounds of the biker bar beneath her old place.

'They told me you'd moved out,' he'd said, and she'd heard that the cheerfulness was masking something else. 'You never said. I thought it'd be a day or two. A week at most, then we could –' Querulousness had crept in.

'Not permanent,' Cate had said, pleading. 'Look, V'cenz, it's all just a bit crazy here at the moment. When things settle down –'

Coming back in at that point, Nicki had given her a curious glance, before setting down the half-cleared platter of *zucchini*.

'They want to know if there's cheese,' she'd whispered.

Cate had put a hand over the receiver and pointed wordlessly at the larder door. Nicki disappeared, emerging with a red-skinned *pecorino* and a nub of *grana*. It would have to do.

Vincenzo had been talking over her, his voice coming and going tipsily, and she had imagined him looking around the bar as he spoke. 'Yeah, you said that before. I bet it's crazy. It's big news in Pozzo, you know, your lady killing herself.'

'She didn't kill herself.' Cate had heard the sharpness in her voice.

'Well, whatever. You know what I mean, babe.'

Don't call me that, Cate had thought. 'Big news?' she'd said tonelessly. Had they nothing better to gossip about?

'Big Simone came in, full of it,' Vincenzo had said. It came to Cate that he'd decided to blame her for not being able to do this more often, hang out with his gang of lads, the boys he'd grown up with. Even though he was the one who wanted to settle down.

'Big Simone?'

'Works at the Liberty,' Vincenzo had said. 'Ha, now you're interested, aren't you?'

'V'cenz,' Cate had said wearily.

He didn't seem to have heard her. 'He's the night porter at the Liberty.'

'The hotel,' Cate had said slowly. The hotel where she'd seen the castle's car, the Monster, parked at seven one morning, out at the front.

'Yes, the hotel,' Vincenzo had answered with exaggerated patience. 'Where your lady – your dead lady – was a regular guest. She always came in late, on her own, her companion arriving a little later, in a car with Florence plates. Older guy, with a nice expensive tan and a moustache.' He'd mused for a moment. 'Funny thing is, he didn't book any room

314

that night, Simo says. The guy thought they didn't know him, but they did.'

'Or maybe he just didn't care,' Cate had said absently. 'He's not a man who cares about the little people, Mr Orfeo. I mean, *Count* Orfeo.'

There'd been a silence, only the din of raucous Saturday-night drinkers at the bar in the background. 'You knew about this?' and Vincenzo's voice had been petulant.

'Sort of,' Cate had said carefully. 'Well, we knew she – did you say, he didn't book a room that night?'

'Whatever,' Vincenzo had replied angrily. She could see how it looked; perhaps he thought they were having orgies out here. Little do you know, she'd thought.

'*Caro*,' she'd said, with a last attempt at conciliation, 'don't –' but he'd hung up.

The conversation seemed, all in all, like a nail in their coffin. Orfeo's, or hers and Vincenzo's.

In the dining room Nicki was dithering over the tray of *digestivi*. Looking from the door Cate tried to catch Sandro Cellini's eye; she thought he'd understood. But there was no way of knowing. She went out to the bins: no sign of him. There was music drifting up from Michelle's studio.

When she came back in, Nicki plonked herself in front of Cate, untying her apron.

'Luca said I could go,' she said, peering into Cate's face. Behind the firmly closed door quiet voices came from the dining room, but the investigator's wasn't one of them.

315

Cate frowned. 'Sure,' she said distractedly. 'Off you go.'

Nicki faltered. 'You were going to walk me home.'

Cate exhaled. 'Sure,' she said, only this time with resignation.

It was only at the back door, the kitchen dark behind them, floor mopped and every appliance switched off and unplugged, that they remembered the snow and had to spend another five minutes searching through the assortment of boots and coats in the cupboard for something that would stand up to a one-and-a-half-kilometre walk in these conditions. And back again, for Cate.

That thought only just seemed to have occurred to Nicki as she watched Cate struggle into a pair of damp rubber boots a half size too small. 'Is this OK?' she asked fearfully. Cate straightened on the doorstep, about to reassure the girl, and then a sound came from behind her, under the trees and they both stopped still, a whimper dying on Nicki's lips.

'Ladies?' The voice was gruff and apologetic, and even though she'd only heard it fleetingly before, Cate knew immediately it was Sandro Cellini. She grasped Nicki's hand reassuringly, and turned. He stepped out from under the trees.

'So this is where you were hiding,' he said. 'This place is a nightmare to find your way around. Or perhaps it's the snow. Everything looks different in the snow.'

'I was about to walk Nicki home,' said Cate,

willing him to understand. 'I'd – um, I'd like a word, though.'

'Walk her?' He frowned incredulously. 'In this? Is it far?'

Cate nodded down the hill. 'One and a half kilometres, maybe.'

'I'll give you a lift,' he said immediately.

Nicki's hand still in hers, with impatience Cate felt her tense. Frightened of her own shadow; what could be wrong with getting a lift?

'What about the snow?' said Nicki. 'Have you got chains?'

Sandro took a few steps away from them, looking down the slope with his hands in the pockets of his padded jacket. Old, worn, one cuff frayed, it reminded Cate of the one her stepfather wore. Why was she always so hard on her poor old step-father, Cate found herself thinking, remorseful. A better dad than her biological one ever was.

'We'll be fine,' Sandro pronounced. 'It's not as cold as it was; the snow won't have settled. And it's not far.'

Nicki said nothing, but Cate could feel her shivering a little. 'Come on,' she whispered. 'He's right.' The girl shrugged, and Cate turned to Sandro and said, 'Thanks.'

But when he walked away towards the little brown car Nicki said sullenly, 'I wanted it to be just you and me.'

Cate looked at her. 'It's been you and me all evening,' she said, not understanding.

317

'Oh, never mind,' said Nicki, and clamped her mouth shut. Cate still didn't understand. Sandro drew up beside them and, without asking, Nicki climbed in the back, the kid in this set-up. 'Cate's coming too,' she announced, without thinking to ask if she might.

Settling herself in the front seat, Cate realized that she'd never spent so little time in a car as she had these past six months. Suddenly the world was different, in the metal cage of the car, the cold white world reduced to what they could see through the windscreen. Insulated, safe, mobile. No wonder Loni Meadows had claimed the Monster as her own.

Sandro engaged the gears and the car crept forward on the snow-covered drive. The road began to slope and still the tyres held firm on the dark, unmade surface. Overhead the cloud shifted and separated and the slice of moon slid out, silver-bright, shedding its pale light on the smooth white hills. As they came to the foot of the hill, the dark shape of the farm's roof appeared over the curve of the slope.

'Someone's still up,' said Cate, turning to look at Nicki. She sat there, white-faced, like a rabbit frozen in the headlights. Nodded stiffly.

They reached the two squat pillars that marked the end of the drive and turned on to the snow-covered tarmac. Sandro Cellini was moving slowly but not quite slowly enough, and Cate felt the car's rear end slew as he turned, a queasy, sickening motion; it slid further. And just at the moment of panic Cate felt something soothe her, some steady emanation of calm and certainty; she saw Cellini's broad, weathered hands tighten on the wheel but he gave no other sign that there was any danger. With infinite slowness, infinite care, he changed down, only one hand on the wheel now, and then, at last, the car seemed to straighten and steady and they crept forward.

'Sorry about that,' said Sandro, not turning his head. 'Not far now, is it?'

And it wasn't, perhaps eight minutes to cover just over a kilometre, because they crawled along at a snail's pace, even if it felt like an hour. It wasn't till they got to the broken-down gate across the farmyard entrance and Cate climbed out to open it that she wondered how they were going to get back up.

But it turned out that Sandro Cellini had chains in the back all along. 'Should have put them on up there,' he said apologetically as he opened the boot. Nicki had climbed out too and they were standing in front of him; Cate's legs felt like jelly. 'It's just, I'm a city boy. And a lazy sod.' He pulled a rusting, clanking mass out of a plastic case, and at the sound a dog began to bark somewhere on the other side of the building, then another, and another. They barked in tireless volleys, taking over from each other in a kind of round; Cate looked up at the house, expecting lights to come on, but the blind windows stayed dark.

'They won't shut up for hours now,' said Nicki,

with grim pride, shoulders hunched. Cate put an arm through hers.

'Sorry,' said Sandro. 'Won't take a minute.' He knelt at a back wheel.

The farmyard was dark and untidy, nameless shapes under tarpaulins, a strong, ammoniac smell of cattle urine, and whatever light had been on upstairs was off. It was cold and wet, but Sandro had been right, not as cold as before, not much above freezing. Nothing like as cold as the night of Loni Meadows's death. An unprecedented low, it had said on the news on Thursday morning; she only just remembered that. They'd been listening on the kitchen radio.

The dogs barked on. 'They'd drive me crazy,' said Cate.

'Sometimes I think it's just me and them,' said Nicki. 'They're all right.'

Cate thought of something. 'Tiziano comes to visit them, doesn't he?'

'Does he?' said Nicki. 'Must be a hell of a slog across the gravel.'

It must be; Cate had watched him negotiate it that afternoon, jaw set, biceps flexing. 'He doesn't let things stand in his way,' she said. 'And he likes animals. I suppose dogs don't discriminate.' Nicki was silent, and something Per had said came back to Cate, something he'd said up there in his room as they watched Yolanda Hansen's red car approach the castle. *We don't know Tiziano.*

At the door Cate said in a reluctant whisper,

'Shall I come in with you?' She'd been down here a handful of times by daylight, when the place was scruffy but ordinary; she found that in the dark, what with the formless obstacles littering the barnyard, the brainless hostility of the dogs, the sharp stink of muck, it was a scene she wanted to escape from as soon as possible. Nicki shook her head stiffly, then flung her arms around Cate.

'Thanks,' she said, and Cate could feel Nicki's hot breath in her hair.

'What for?' said Cate, pulling back.

'Dunno,' said Nicki. 'Everything. Seeing me home. Telling me I should get out of here. It made me realize – it seems impossible, you feel like you're stuck forever. But there's always a way.'

Cate looked at her white, earnest face, then back at the car. Sandro Cellini was still on his knees somewhere in the dark, out of sight.

'How bad is it, Nicki?' She looked up at the crumbling frontage of the old farm, thought of its inhabitants, Ginevra, her widowed sister, Mauro, cooped up in this place for generations. Damp and dark in the winter, baking in the long dry summers, but it was home. Unthinkable to leave. Dangerous to turn a man out of his home.

And just as though she'd read Cate's mind, Nicki said hurriedly, craning her neck to try and see where Sandro was, 'Look, what we said – I don't think Mauro – did anything to her, though. To the *Dottoressa*? Do you? I mean – I know he's got the pick-up, and he knows the road, and all that.

321

And he was out that day.' She'd been thinking about this, Cate could tell. 'But I don't think he's clever enough. Even sober.'

'No,' said Cate slowly, marvelling at how daft Nicki could sometimes seem, and then say something like that. But she had to say it, unwillingly. 'But we don't know – it might not have required anyone to be clever.' She kept her voice low.

He might have just – run her off the road, was what she didn't say. Chased her in his pick-up. Per couldn't have watched her die – but Mauro? She could see Nicki shivering, arms folded tight across her body. Cate put out her own hands and rubbed the girl's shoulders vigorously. 'Don't worry,' she said. 'Now get inside, you'll die of cold out here.'

Nicki didn't move. 'Not Mauro,' she said, sounding like a stubborn child, knowing she was wrong but refusing to admit it. She took Cate by the sleeve, her thin fingers pinching through the fabric. 'You be careful,' she muttered, pulling her down and closer. Sounding frightened. 'You just be careful.'

Then she ducked away abruptly, the door banged sharply behind her and Cate turned to see Sandro Cellini standing in the moonlight no more than a metre away.

'Ready when you are,' he said in the gruffly apologetic tone Cate was getting used to. She climbed in.

'Now,' he said, engaging the gear and leaning to look back over his shoulder as he reversed carefully out of the farmyard. 'Was there something you wanted to tell me?'

Sandro watched Caterina go, as composed and calm when she got out of the car as when she got in. It had been a slow crawl back up the hill, the tyres grinding and crunching as the chains gripped, but an interesting one.

The twenty minutes the journey had taken had not in fact been enough; they'd sat side by side in the car after he'd turned off the engine and gone on talking.

Outside the snow had been beginning to drift down again; he had seen it settle on the roof of the stable block that housed the kitchen. A light on above it; Luca Gallo's office, she'd said, and his room and bathroom; her own little apartment was accommodated further round in the same block. Servants' quarters.

He'd listened to what she'd had to say, slotting it in alongside the information he already had.

Orfeo was what she'd wanted to tell him about first. That he had been Loni Meadows's lover; ever circumspect, Sandro didn't tell her he already knew, because there might be more. And there was. 'She used to go and meet him. At the Hotel Liberty.' Even in the dark he'd seen her blush. 'My boyfriend knows someone who works there.'

'So you'd have assumed that was where she was going?' Wide-eyed, she'd shrugged.

'Now? I guess. I didn't know before. I think the others did.'

'Guests, or staff?'

'Both,' she'd murmured. 'Except – not Per.'

And that was a new piece of information. Per Hansen, whom Loni Meadows had charmed and flirted with until he fell in love with her and wanted to leave his wife.

'And this man – was the last man to see her alive?' His meaning had been unmistakable. The man he'd seen clinging to his wife like a lifebuoy.

She'd stared at him. Nodded slowly. 'She got a message, Alec said. Just as they were leaving the table, and then she didn't have any time for either of them. Alec went to bed. But –'

'But what?'

'He couldn't have – Per couldn't have –' and she'd stopped. She was clever enough to know there were things she didn't know. 'He's a good man.'

'Do you think he knew her,' he'd asked gently. 'Before he came here? Per?'

She'd shaken her head, bemused. 'No. Why?'

'And what about the others?' he'd prompted. 'The women? Did they – show any sign of having known her?' Saving Fairhead until last.

'I don't know if they knew her, exactly,' she'd said slowly. 'I don't think so. Michelle couldn't stand her from the word go, though. Nor Tina. Tina, just because she was horrible about her work in her blog, some time last year.'

He'd interrupted. 'When was that, exactly?'

She doesn't create, she destroys, the email had said. Might an artist have written that? But Cate had scotched that one. 'Last summer some time? Not long ago.'

'And the other one.' Sandro had pursed his lips, remembering her: the most vivid and fierce of them, to him, with her wild hair, her aura of rage.

'Michelle,' Cate had said. 'I don't know why she hated Loni. Because they were so different, perhaps. Because she was a widow and Loni had all the men she wanted.' She'd frowned. 'It seemed more than that. She was protective of Tina too.' She'd opened her mouth, then closed it again, as if she'd been going to say something else.

'And Mr Fairhead?' Almost casually.

'Oh, yes,' she'd said, as if this was what she'd been waiting to say. 'Oh yes, he did.'

And another piece of the puzzle slotted into place. He wrote a book about her, said Caterina Giottone, with wonder. His book.

And then he had waited, letting her thoughts settle, before he asked, 'Now tell me. Now tell me what happened, that last day.'

Of course, he had told her nothing himself; that wasn't his job. Rather like being a shrink, if the TV dramas were to be believed; they talked, you listened. Although by the time she'd climbed out of the car and walked down the hill towards the bright square of light and the loud music, it had occurred to Sandro that he might take Caterina into his confidence, before too long. Too early, though, to tell her what Mascarello had said; he wasn't entirely sure what it meant himself.

Mascarello had not wasted any words. Standing in the dark lee of the great building, wondering if Luca Gallo was still in earshot and frustrated by the realization that he had no idea which direction would lead him back around to the kitchen entrance, Sandro had the sense to remain silent while the man spoke; he'd made an effort to focus on what he said. At his back the rough wall had held a deep chill that seemed to transmit itself into his bones through his faithful old coat, designed only for the city's mild chills.

'I hope you're busy,' the lawyer had said drily. 'I hope you've got down to work already, and that's why you didn't have time to call me back. I don't suppose I have to tell you how much my time is worth?'

Grudgingly Sandro had found himself almost smiling. Even when hooked up to a dialysis machine, or whatever it was that he could hear humming like a butcher's flytrap in the background, the man was unshakeably convinced of his own power to command. There were characters out there – and fleetingly, painfully Sandro thought that Luisa was one of them – immune to fear of their own mortality. And then there were the rest, like Sandro, pushing the fear like a stone uphill.

'Yes,' Sandro had said, as humbly as he could manage. 'I was busy.' There was a whistling exhalation and for a moment Sandro had thought it was the machine, before he'd understood that it was the air being expelled from Mascarello's lungs.

'All right,' Mascarello had said hoarsely. 'It's unfortunate, but it has to be me – I don't like delegating this matter. It's enough that you should know; I don't want the secretaries chewing it over, I don't want this turned into gossip.' And Mascarello probably knew more than most about how easily what one left on an answering machine or wrote in an email might be intercepted.

How did their marriage work, wondered Sandro, as he tried and failed to picture them side by side in the same bed, reading before turning out the light. But Mascarello had really loved her; he didn't want her sullied.

'No,' he'd said.

'Gallo's safe enough,' Mascarello had said, with a trace of contempt that extinguished the spark of fellow feeling Sandro had just begun to experience. 'He won't talk. A good servant, only promoted beyond his competence, as Loni would say. I expect he's at his wits' end.' There'd been a pause. 'And how are things, down there? That little nest of vipers, all squirming and wriggling, are they, with you in their midst?'

Sandro had wondered if the man was merely lonely and wanted to talk, improbable as it might seem. He could hardly ask him to get to the point.

'Well,' he'd said. 'I've only been here a couple of hours. But everyone does seem a bit on edge.'

'It's an ugly old place, isn't it?' Mascarello had

commented with rusty satisfaction. 'Orfeo might style himself the great nobleman, but it's hardly the Villa Borghese, is it?'

He knows, Sandro had thought with awe as he registered the contempt in the old lawyer's voice. *He's known all along.* 'You've been down here?' he'd said.

'Well, not since Loni took up residence, clearly. She likes –' and he'd stopped, cleared his throat. 'She liked. To spread her wings.'

'He's here,' Sandro had said carefully. 'The Count, I mean. Arrived just before me.'

'Yes, I thought he might be.' There'd been a pause. 'There's no need to spare my feelings, man. I can hear in your voice that you've managed to work it out. That that puffed up old fool Orfeo was her – her second string.' He'd cleared his throat wetly. 'Well done.'

'Was that why you were calling?' Sandro had asked. And Mascarello had let out a wheezing laugh that turned into another cough. Over the machine's monotone Sandro had heard someone say something to the old lawyer, remonstrating.

'I like your directness, Cellini,' he'd said when the coughing eased. 'Luca Gallo wasn't sure about you himself, when he brought you to me; I wondered about that. But it doesn't matter what he thought; what matters is that I'm sure.' A pause, heavy with meaning. 'Don't disappoint me, though, will you?'

Sandro had said nothing; foolishly he had not

considered what it would mean, working for a man like Giuliano Mascarello. If it went badly, well, he'd be pretty much finished. But even success wouldn't be uncomplicated. Mascarello had a great deal of influence, if he lived long enough to exercise it, but Sandro wasn't sure he wanted Mascarello as his patron. And almost as if Mascarello had read Sandro's thoughts about his employer, he'd decided to get to the point.

'All right,' he'd said flatly. 'Two pieces of information for you; that's what you were waiting for?'

Looking around him in the inky dark, listening to the faint rustlings and creakings from the woods, ghostly under snow, Sandro had murmured assent.

'The first, my team of technicians came up with. They got through the proxy server used to send the email and came up with an internet café in northern Paris, since closed down for failure adequately to monitor their clients.' He sighed. 'The anti-terrorism laws, you see. These days, anonymity is harder to come by.'

Sandro knew this; he had no doubt, however, that Paris, like Florence, had any number of un-regulated backstreet internet shops. He'd spoken without any expectation. 'So they don't have a – a log, of any kind? CCTV? A record of customers?'

'No. My technicians have the precise time, though, some cooked-up email address, invented on the spot.' A pause. 'Sent 4.15am, 23 April, the week after the announcement of Loni's appointment. The email address was Eduardog82@hotmail.com.'

'Just a moment,' Sandro had said desperately, and heard Mascarello sigh. He'd scrabbled in his pocket for his notebook and pencil. Moved away from the wall and hurried towards some light further around the great mass of the castle; saw two figures downlit by a lantern light, in the porch of what must be the kitchen entrance. Laboriously he'd written it down.

Eduardog82. Sandro had been on a course long ago about internet crime and bank fraud and remembered being told how those trying to disguise themselves almost never succeeded; passwords and addresses and ciphers always contained something, some clue. What it came down to quite often was, people wanted to be identified; wanted their stamp on things. Particularly the mentally unstable.

'Ready?' Mascarello had asked, impatience creeping into his voice. Time was the one thing Mascarello couldn't buy.

When he'd spoken again Mascarello's voice was changed. Evasive, bluff. 'And the other thing. Tiziano Scarpa.'

'Right,' Sandro had said warily, and the man had come into his mind with no effort at all, the bulky, energetic figure in his wheelchair, the bright, fierce eyes, the muscular shoulders. Ringleader of the artists' mutiny. Pianist from whose strong fingers the music had flowed out and up and filled the vast ugly castle. 'Scarpa. Yes. I've met him. In a wheelchair.'

'Paraplegic,' Mascarello had said brusquely. 'Spinal-cord injury in the bombing of a station in

Mestre in the late eighties, later attributed – wrongly – to the Red Brigade.'

'Right,' Sandro had replied, and the case sprang into his mind as fresh as it had been back then, when in Florence they'd all still been reeling from a bombing behind the Uffizi that had killed two *carabinieri*. He'd remembered how many deaths in Mestre – nine killed. The injured – well. There was less publicity surrounding the injured.

'His father was with him at the station,' Mascarello had said.

'On their way to a football match,' Sandro had finished as that painful detail fell into place.

'Yes,' Mascarello had said curtly. 'Well, that's not the point. The point is, that I was the defence counsel. The accused, a political activist, rounded up at random –'

'I remember,' Sandro had cut him off. The accused – the political activist – hadn't been some peacenik from the Christian Socialists; he'd been a fully paid-up terrorist, an extreme right-wing member of a splinter group of the northern separatists. Mascarello had got him off; there'd been a lot of publicity around it. Suggestions that witnesses had been paid off and false alibis provided. The man had gone into hiding. Two years later his prints were found all over a bomb factory in the suburbs of Verona, by which time the 'political activist' was long gone, last seen in Syria, of all places. Though not as long gone as Tiziano Scarpa's father.

331

Mascarello's wheezing breath, and the tinny hum of the machine that was keeping him alive, had been the only sounds. 'So you understand,' he'd said finally, gasping a little now.

Sandro had understood. They were a power couple; Mascarello's money funded his wife's glamorous bohemian lifestyle, they were photographed together, or certainly back then they had been. She might be as guilty as him, in some people's eyes.

Was it enough of a connection? It was certainly something.

'I'll have to see if Tiziano Scarpa was in Paris last April, won't I?' he'd said reluctantly.

There'd been nothing much more to say after that. Sandro had been polite; informed his client that he would update him in the morning. And set off in the freezing dark to find Caterina.

Later, after they had driven slowly back up the hill, Sandro and Caterina had stood together under the wall lights of the castle.

'I want to be of help,' Caterina had said with lonely determination. She seemed tired and deflated, after all the talking he'd made her do.

Someone shouted something from a little way down the hill in the trees, where the music was playing, and they turned. 'That's the studio, Michelle Connor's in there, and further down is Tina's place. The *villino*, where Mauro was born. That's got a studio too.'

The voice shouted again, and they both heard it this time. Caterina said, 'They're calling me.

Someone is calling my name.' There was the distant blur of motion, the figure of a man waved, then stopped, watching. Fairhead. Caterina didn't move, jammed her hands further down in her pockets, and the man went back inside.

'Go on,' said Sandro. 'Go. They like you.'

'They'll talk to you eventually,' she said apologetically. 'They're just – ganging up, for a bit. They'll come around.' She frowned.

'I know,' said Sandro. 'You don't need to worry about me.'

'Where will you go?' Caterina asked. 'You look tired.' He turned and looked up at the castle, where the window of Luca Gallo's office was dark now. Silhouetted against the moonlit clouds, the monstrous old place seemed to absorb light; Sandro found it hard to believe that the small comfortable bedroom was somewhere inside it, waiting for him.

'I'm always tired,' said Sandro, surprised at his own admission. 'But the older you get, the harder it is to sleep. And there's work to do.'

CHAPTER 19

Cate stood in the lee of Michelle's studio, a little way back up the hill, hidden from the light, and wondered if she should go in. Wondered if she had made a terrible mistake, talking to Sandro Cellini.

She'd sat there a full minute, struck dumb suddenly, as he reengaged the gears and turned in the farmyard. He didn't rush her, looking at the road ahead, waiting. Listening. Then nodding, patient, unsurprised. As if he already knew.

At school Cate had never been a goody-goody or a telltale; even now she hated to gossip. But sometimes you had to go to someone in authority, sometimes you had to take responsibility.

He'd taken in all she had to say, about Orfeo and Alec Fairhead and Per, about how they'd been the last to see her, about how Loni upset everybody, absolutely everybody. Sandro Cellini, quiet, attentive, patient, had interjected only once, when she had said Fairhead had known Loni Meadows before.

'Knew her well?' he had asked.

'Beth said Alec had a book about her. His book.' And Sandro had sat back in the driver seat.

'Now tell me,' he'd said. 'What happened, that day, the day she died?'

And that was when Caterina had known he had a theory. He knew something.

And it had been as if she was thinking about it clearly for the first time.

'It was an awful day,' she had said. 'I was dreading coming back in. Everyone seemed so – wound up. Every time you turned around, some kind of row seemed to have flared up.' Concentrating. 'It was mostly down to Loni, I guess.'

'When did it start?' Sandro spoke gently.

'First thing: about nine. She was having a go at Mauro about cutting back some of the trees down by the *villino*, and he was ignoring her. We could hear that from the kitchen; she was – giving him orders, outside.' Caterina had taken a deep breath, wanting to go on, now she'd started. Was this how detectives worked? It was like being hypnotized.

'And then at coffee time, it was Luca. I was serving the coffee in the library: all the guests were there, for once. It was about eleven. We could hear her shouting at him in the music room, because she'd seen Mauro heading off in the pick-up across the valley, disobeying her, and that was supposed to be Luca's fault.' She had felt his eyes on her. 'Some farmer across the valley needed help with his cows,' she had said, faltering. 'That's what Ginevra said.'

'When did he get back?' Sandro had asked quietly. She had swallowed. 'He didn't – um – I didn't see him come back.' She had looked down. 'I think he might have just got drunk, and stayed home.'

The detective had nodded.

'And she was shouting at Luca Gallo?'

'Luca was in charge of us, of the domestic staff,' she had said quietly. 'Mauro spoke to Luca before he went, he must have OK'ed it, and I suppose she blamed him.'

She had seen Sandro Cellini chew his cheek thoughtfully. His city face was pale under the yellow castle light.

'They didn't get on,' he had said, and it wasn't a question. 'Her and Gallo.'

Cate had shrugged helplessly. 'He's great,' she had said. 'Luca works so hard. It's getting him down, all this.'

'And after that?' Sandro had leaned forwards, arms draped on the steering wheel. 'I need to get an idea of – the timing, you see.'

'Well, there was supposed to be some kind of gallery trip, after lunch, to Siena. Only at coffee – Michelle wanted to go for her run and Tina said to Loni that she wasn't going to go because she had something in the kiln she needed to keep an eye on. They were backing each other up. I'm not even sure who started it.' She had looked at him. 'Then Loni blew up all over again, said well, in that case, she'd cancel the minibus. And marched out.' She had hesitated. 'I heard her shouting at Luca again after that, up in his office. When I was in the kitchen making the lunches; his office is just upstairs, pretty much.'

'So by lunchtime she'd had a go at pretty well everyone?'

Too right. 'In the afternoon everyone seemed to be lying low.' She had tried to think what she'd been doing herself. 'Loni asked me up to bring her herbal tea at around three. She was on her computer.'

'Ah,' he had said thoughtfully. 'Yes, the computer.'

'I guess you're going to look at it?'

Sandro had just smiled. 'I don't like computers,' he had said.

'And at dinner she upset Tina and Michelle all over again. Talking about the gallery in New York where Tina had had a show. Which reminded her of the blog, and she ran off crying.'

And suddenly Cate had felt close to tears. She hadn't wanted to be doing this, spilling people's secrets. She must have made some sound, because suddenly he had been looking into her face.

'Caterina,' he had said earnestly. 'Thirty years in the police doesn't teach you as much as you'd like. But I know when someone's telling the truth. It's all right.' He'd turned his head, cheek against the window, and looked up at the castle. 'What else?'

She'd stayed silent.

'It's just – there might be things you don't even know you saw. Something might come back to you,' he had said. 'You said, they were all in the castle, all day. Then you said, *pretty much*, as though you weren't absolutely sure. How could you be sure, you haven't got eyes in the back of your head, I understand that. But think back again. The afternoon, particularly; what did you see? Did anyone go for a walk, borrow the car for a drive?'

He had leaned forward then in the dark, peering at her intently.

Cate had felt suddenly anxious. 'I don't know,' she had said, stammering. 'I don't know.'

'I'm not asking you to take sides,' he had said as they sat in his car, feeling the small warmth they'd generated between them over the journey evaporate in the great cold of the outside. 'But you have already, haven't you?'

And she realized that she had.

She stepped out of the shadow of Michelle's studio and into the light, and saw that Alec Fairhead had been there all along, waiting for her.

There were two libraries in the castle, Caterina had said; one of which was a real library, as Sandro understood the word, containing books to be borrowed and read. The other was the great dark cold room where Orfeo had stood in chilly and hostile isolation, master of all he surveyed; a room Sandro would be happy if he never entered again. It had held a deeper, damper cold than any place he'd ever been; it represented everything that he found he hated about the Castello Orfeo.

Coming back inside he saw through the darkened music room that a light was still on in the old library, and Sandro passed the open door as quietly as he could, back towards the windowless corridor that led to the dining room and kitchen. He was still trying to work it out, the layout of the place: grand apartments at the front, staff quarters – the kitchen with Luca Gallo and Caterina's apartments above it – in the sober, modern extension of the stables at the back. The dining room was here too, and just beyond it a room where any books written by guests were kept; one knew it wouldn't be locked. He found himself hurrying.

It was a shabby little space, under-decorated and ill-lit, with a small, ancient television in one corner, and just like in the most underfunded of school libraries, the books had rudimentary stickers on the back. Sandro found Fairhead's book almost straight away; it was a short book, 150 pages, and there were English, German and Italian editions. In Italian it was called *Nascituro*. Unborn. He puzzled at that before turning it over. There were quotations from reviews on the back, all sombre and admiring; looking inside he saw that it had been first published fifteen years earlier. He slipped it into his pocket.

Coming back out of the room Sandro felt the corridor's oppressive airlessness even more; although he knew perfectly well how to find his way back to the great hall and the music room, for a moment he thought it might be a trick, a labyrinth made to trap him. He could not imagine how these artists, these guests, could profit from a stay in this place; already he was finding that the atmosphere was stifling his own ability to think clearly, the great weight of the old castle above him, the narrow windows and the thick walls. He heard sounds too; creaks and whispers from the centuries-old stone and wood; he needed to get back to his room.

The music room and the great gloomy space of the library beyond it were dark when he came back past them, but as he stood in the great hall Sandro could hear something, the faintest of movements. Was anyone else in the building except him and Orfeo? He and Caterina had seen Gallo turn out his light; Sandro felt a stab of pity for the man. Caught between Mascarello and Orfeo, trying to keep it together; at least he had Caterina, a good girl if ever Sandro had seen one.

Were all the guests down at their party? Sandro had assumed so. He came up the stairs to the first floor, and there was light from under the door, where Loni Meadows had slept. Like the lord he was, Niccolò Orfeo had taken it as his due; he thought he could get away with anything. And although Sandro had planned to tackle the man in the morning, although all he wanted to do next was to go into the small room where his own things were waiting for him so that he could clear his head, he stopped. And knocked on the door.

'What is it?'

The door was wrenched open: Orfeo stood, still

dressed, but with his shirt open at the neck. Sandro could see greying chest hair. 'Not now,' Orfeo said peremptorily. 'I'll speak to you in the morning.'

Sandro felt the man's eyes on him, looking him up and down, taking in the shabby jacket, the old trousers crumpled after the long drive. And for a second he felt as though without Luisa, without the certainty of Luisa brushing him down and straightening him out for the day, all the sense Sandro had of himself, all his pride, was so fragile that one sneering look from this man might turn it to dust. Then Orfeo made as if to shut the door again.

'No,' said Sandro, putting out a hand and staying the door. He felt the pressure as Orfeo struggled a moment, the man older but fit with summers of tennis, perhaps, or sailing. But Sandro had anger on his side. Orfeo might not have killed her. However much Sandro wanted it to be him, he had been in Florence that night. But Orfeo was hiding something, and he had got away with too much already.

'No,' he said again, hearing the policeman in his voice, and stepped through the door.

On the bed was a small overnight case; the clothes that had been there earlier – Loni Meadows's clothes – had been unceremoniously dumped inside the wardrobe.

'Don't you miss her?' he said, before Orfeo could say anything. 'Didn't you want some kind of keepsake?' Orfeo's mouth fell open, preparing some form of bluster, but nothing came out. His tanned, handsome face, his thick hair and moustache might all say, here is a powerful man, but his frightened eyes betrayed him, just as the loose skin at his neck gave away his age.

'You can bully that poor Luca Gallo,' said Sandro. 'You might have some kind of hold over that buffoon of a superintendent of police in Pozzo Basso. But you aren't paying me, you aren't my superior, social or otherwise. You were sleeping with her, weren't you? And now you've come back to make sure there isn't any evidence.' He paused. 'You won't find the Viagra,' he said, deliberately coarse, seeing the man flinch. 'I've already been in here. Did you come down that night? Did you send her a message?'

'I was in Florence,' said Orfeo faintly. Then, his voice strengthening, 'You can't talk to me in this way. I'll have your licence removed.'

'It's only two hours from Florence,' said Sandro. 'One and a half in that car of yours, if you break the speed limit all the way as I imagine you do. You could be here and back in time to take your kid to school.'

Orfeo blinked and stared at him. 'I have broken no laws,' he said. 'I was not here. I don't know where she was going.'

'What did you do?' asked Sandro in frustration. Thinking, I'll nail him. I'll nail him for something. 'Did you sit in the Hotel Liberty waiting for her? What did you do when she didn't turn up? Did you even try to contact her?'

At the mention of the hotel's name – for which Sandro thanked Caterina Giottone – Orfeo's eyes widened, bloodshot. 'I – I didn't – I was in Florence,' he said again, and this time he seemed bewildered. 'You can ask my son. I was there. We sat up until midnight, he was refusing to do his schoolwork and I said I'd stand over him until it was finished if I had to.'

Damn, thought Sandro, hearing a shred of truth in the desperate, faltering voice. Damn, damn, but it had been too late to stop. He had stood his ground. 'We know you were having an affair with her,' he said, forcing some certainty into his voice. 'You were seen at the Liberty on many occasions, even if you thought you were not. It seems that half the staff here, the guests, indeed, had a good idea of what was going on. Her husband knew, for Christ's sake. Mascarello knew.' Orfeo's lips tightened disdainfully. He didn't care about Mascarello; the cuckold. 'And she told the intern, Beth.'

'Beth,' said Orfeo coldly. 'That one.'

Sandro seized on the dislike in his voice, allowed it to spur him on. 'Perhaps you knew that. Perhaps they were too close for your liking, all that girlish giggling; perhaps you had Loni Meadows send her home to America?' And as Orfeo turned away Sandro saw he'd hit home there at least; he pursued the advantage. 'You can delete all those messages from your phone, can't you, the ones you sent her, the ones she sent you? Did you come back for hers? Was that why you paid a visit to the police station at Pozzo Basso?'

'Her phone?' And for a moment Sandro didn't understand what he saw in Orfeo's bloodshot eyes, heard in his strained voice.

'That phone could have evidence on it,' Sandro said. 'It would reveal who texted her that night. She might – she might,' and he cast about for what she might have done. Climbing out of the car, dazed. 'She might have tried to phone the emergency services. Stumbled about, looking for a signal.'

Orfeo's eyes widened. 'No,' he said blankly. 'No.' Did Orfeo really not know what he was talking about? 'I don't have her phone. I didn't come looking for her phone – I simply –' He stopped, and started again. 'I needed to know what had happened. I didn't understand – I know the *Soprintendente* I simply asked – as a friend –' He took a breath. 'It placed me in a difficult situation.'

At least he wasn't trying to fake emotion, to pretend he wanted to see her, one final time.

Sandro made a last-ditch attempt. 'You said to Luca Gallo. The phone, you said.'

Orfeo drew himself up, looked down his patrician nose, beaked like a Roman senator's. 'Not her phone,' he said with a hint of the old impatience. 'I don't know what you're talking about. No. Not hers. My *telefonino*. My phone.'

Sandro stared at him; he felt Orfeo gather strength from his silence.

344

'I left it behind here, in the library, or some-where – I don't know.' The man spoke with disdain. 'The last time I was in the house, Sunday? I – I – this is my house. I assumed I would pick it up on my return. I have another phone, in any case, I only used it for – to –'

He was lying; he had to be. A cover-up, an absurd, desperate attempt to escape the truth. The only problem was, Orfeo was telling the truth; Sandro could hear it, see it.

He only used the phone to contact Loni Meadows, and she was only his mistress, good in bed, a younger woman, his social inferior, whose clothes he had shoved into the bottom of the wardrobe now she was dead. What did it matter? Orfeo had some vague idea now that it might involve him in – unpleasantness, that was all he cared about. Everything about the look he turned on Sandro said to him, you will never understand our sort. We have different desires, we have different requirements, we live in a bigger, bolder world. Damn him, thought Sandro, damn him and Frollini, because the two of them were one and the same; damn them for taking what they wanted and escaping the consequences.

He didn't kill her: he was too stupid, too lazy, too self-absorbed; he had too many options. She might have grown troublesome, demanding, although Sandro couldn't see it; she might have wanted to become his *Contessa*. But Orfeo would merely have brushed her off, as he had to Sandro and Luca. And he had not been here on the Thursday night; he had been in Florence with his spoiled brat of a son.

Damn it. Sandro's head ached with the implications.

'You have no morals,' he said calmly. 'You have no conscience. The woman is dead.'

And Orfeo said nothing. Just slowly opened the door and waited until, eventually, Sandro couldn't stand the sight of him any longer, and went.

Sandro was not in the habit of taking his blood pressure, nor his pulse, but it took at least half an hour in the small room next door to Niccolò Orfeo's palatial apartments, painstakingly noting everything he knew and thought and had been told by Caterina Giottone and Luca Gallo into a new document, before he felt his body return to normal.

Might this be what killed him, one day? This unreasonable sensitivity to every slight, since he had left the force, his keen ear for an insult, his frustration. Had it always been there, this anger, boiling under the surface? Or had it built up, as the country filled up with fast-food restaurants and toxic garbage dumps, as its children were found overdosed on veterinary tranquillizers and its politicians slept with underage prostitutes? The rage that had come out of nowhere, just at the thought of Luisa sitting in a restaurant with another man. At this rate one day he might simply burst like a geyser, and no sooner had Sandro had that thought than it was followed by another, that he did not want to die without Luisa. That he simply would not be able to live without her.

He might not be able to live without Luisa, but he could not call her. Too late, he told himself. She'll be asleep, we'll have another row, it'll make things worse.

In his shirtsleeves, unshaven, Sandro sat at the desk prepared for him by Caterina. He put his notes beside the computer, pressed the button on the machine and booted it into life. He set a hand flat on either side as he contemplated the lists Giuli had made for him, the where and when, which eventually, if he looked hard enough, would tell him why. He made a note. Then another.

About forty minutes later he reopened the email programme and started a message to Giuli, thinking he'd just jot down a few things, paste in the document he'd already begun, only forty minutes later Sandro was still at it. Rambling now, he said to himself, signed off hurriedly and pressed send.

He took the slender book of Alec Fairhead's from his pocket, and began to read.

In the flat she'd shared with Sandro for more than thirty years with barely a night apart – but for one notable exception, even if it was three in the morning and he smelled of the morgue, cigarette smoke and disinfectant, he'd still come home and slide into that bed beside her – Luisa sat on her big bed and listened to the sounds of the city.

347

The Via dei Macci was never going to be peaceful; it lay on the most direct route between the crowds of Piazza Santa Croce and the hawkers and haggling women of the Mercato di Sant'Ambrogio. They'd talked about it when they'd first taken up the lease, as newlyweds, how it might be too noisy, but just around the corner was the market, the statue of Dante grim as death, the perpetually lovely church and its chapels. And over the years they'd absorbed the changes for the worse, the crowds of teenage drunks from other countries, the scrape and smash and stand-up rows of a street too narrow for motor traffic, the constant high-pitched mosquito sound of *motorini*. She heard one go whining past even as she remembered it, their first night here, half-unpacked, sitting on a second-hand bed in the moonlight, holding hands.

In the corner sat Luisa's little suitcase, packed, zipped, locked and labelled. It had been newly bought for the occasion; Sandro had not remarked on that, which was just as well. What would she have said? That she couldn't embarrass Frollini with the battered nylon overnight bag that had served her perfectly well for a decade or more. That she didn't want to look like an old lady from a Third World country as she stepped down that gangway, into that arrivals hall, all nervous and frightened coming into the New World, her possessions bulging out of a tatty holdall?

In her padded dressing-gown, slippers and

warmest nightdress, ready for bed but wide awake, Luisa went to the window. She could feel the cold through the glass, but she pressed her cheek against it, looking down the street. There was snow, she'd heard, in the Casentino, the Mugello, on Monte Aperto in the Appennines and Monte Amiata down south; even, it was said, in the inland portion of the Maremma. That was where Sandro was, if Giuli was to be believed, the guest of a castle and a count.

It rarely snowed in Florence. What would Sandro be thinking, wherever he was? Would he be marvelling at it, the hills covered with snow? He would, for a bit, then he'd start to grumble because he didn't like the countryside and he wouldn't have the right clothes, the right shoes.

There was a pair of snow boots they'd bought during a snowfall close to a decade ago, but they were sitting in the hall cupboard; Luisa knew because she'd seen them there when she got home and looked. Wanting to make sure that he'd taken a coat, at least, wanting to see, too, if he'd taken a bag. Wondering how long he was planning to be away.

It had gone beyond Luisa being angry with him. With such childish behaviour, storming off like that, in such a hurry – because he hadn't taken anything much with him at all, as far as Luisa could see. Leaving a note. *A note,* she'd said to Giuli, expecting an echo of her outrage, and she'd heard the unease in the girl's voice as she tried to excuse him. Giuli was close to being Daddy's little girl where Sandro was concerned, far too ready to give him the benefit of the doubt.

But her anger had always been tempered with something else, anyway. Something so unfamiliar to Luisa that she wasn't sure if she recognized it; something like guilt.

Would it have been different if they'd had children of their own? It would, there was no point denying that. Even leaving aside the painful thing, the love they might have given a child between them and received back. Whatever people might say nowadays a baby brought you together, it didn't split you up. And would it have been different if Luisa hadn't had a breast removed and three months of chemo? But Luisa's mother had told her thirty years ago that there was no point in imagining how things might have been different. You had to take what you were given, and make the best of it. It was advice Luisa had followed unquestioningly for almost all her life. Until now.

I am not having an affair with Enrico Frollini. Was that what she should have said? Her mother would certainly have said yes. What would she have had to lose from saying it? From telling him the plain, unvarnished truth? *Well,* she imagined herself saying to her long-dead mother's sceptical old face, *why should I even bother to answer such a stupid question? And besides, he wasn't in a mood to believe me.*

She could imagine what her mother would have said to that. What Giuli wanted to say, but didn't quite dare. *Are you sure it's the truth?*

Luisa looked at the neat, handsome little suitcase. She was an excellent packer; there was nothing she enjoyed more. A new suit was in there, grey cashmere and silk mix with a fine pinstripe, layered in tissue paper. Three shirts, a plain smart black dress, the two-string pearl necklace Sandro had bought her for her fiftieth; a pair of flat shoes, a pair of heels and a pair of evening shoes. The flight was at nine o'clock on Monday morning from the city airport; Frollini had said he'd collect her at six from the Via dei Macci. She could imagine the look on his face, comic horror, at the scruffy façades, the bulging dumpsters, the smell of cat in the ugly little street before dawn.

She could call Sandro, she knew that, she could email him, for heaven's sake; the phone was there by the bed, the big computer on the desk – everyone had them, said Sandro, when she'd complained about how ugly it was. She could talk to him, but she wouldn't.

It was not even late, but Luisa closed the shutters, climbed into the cold, clean sheets and turned off the light. And as she lay and stared at the ceiling, for the first time Luisa understood with dull certainty that she could get used to this, if she had to. A night apart turned into a week, separation turned into divorce, people grew apart. Was that what was happening to them? All Luisa knew was, she had changed, and Sandro had not.

Sleep, she commanded herself, and eventually she did.

CHAPTER 20

There was a strange new quality to the light that dazzled through the shutters as Cate surfaced in the room that itself was not yet familiar, and she lay there half-asleep for a while, eyes still closed, with the blue-white glare trying to pry them open.

Snow, she thought as she came awake, bit by bit; the snow was what had changed the light from yellow to blue-white. Lying still, Cate could detect no sound from the kitchen. Was it early? It was very quiet, but even with the snow it was too bright to be early. Reluctantly Cate squeezed open an eye, turned her head a painful fraction and looked at her battered old radio-alarm. 8.20. She groaned.

Pushing back the duvet, Cate swung her legs out and sat up, and the nagging pain behind her eyes worsened abruptly. Five hours' sleep, give or take. And quite a lot of wine. She scrabbled in the bedside table for some *tachipirina*, swallowed them with water straight from the bottle, and made for the bathroom.

The shower was not hot enough, but Cate stood under it anyway, letting the water run over her, flushing away the night before.

She shouldn't have gone, most definitely she should not have gone. But Sandro Cellini had wanted her to.

'Go,' he'd said. 'Go and have your party. See what you remember; see what they say.'

I won't be a spy, Cate had thought stubbornly, leaning a moment on a sharp stone corner of the building. But he'd started something going in her head.

Then the music from inside had changed and someone had yelled out something, drunken and jubilant: they were letting off steam, all right. But as the cheering was taken up by another voice, for a wild moment, she had thought what if they all did it between them, what if they've planned it all, some elaborate scheme to lure Loni Meadows out on the coldest night of the year and with hard frost forecast? And she'd remembered all over again that the *Dottoressa* had not died straight away; could they have stood around as she climbed out of the car and watched her stagger, dazed and dying? Cate had tightened her grip on her arms in the cold and told herself stoutly, no. Don't be ridiculous.

'She *was* a dangerous driver,' she'd said unwillingly to Sandro Cellini as they sat in the car. 'She threw that car around. Worse than Mauro. Never wore a seatbelt.'

At Michelle's studio someone had stepped out of the shadows.

Him; no more than a metre away from her. Cate

had felt as though she suddenly knew everything about the man: the whole picture. From the moment he arrived at the castle to complete the group, stepping out of the car beside Mauro, to his haunted face on the gallery of the library, the morning the police came to tell them she was dead. She should have finished that sad, dangerous little book he'd written about her.

'You came,' Alec Fairhead had said, his eyes happy and unfocused, looking ten, twenty years younger. Looking like the boy he must have been when he had his affair with Loni Meadows. He'd taken her hands in his; he was very drunk, Cate had seen. It wouldn't have been fair to ask him anything, in this state.

'You're a lovely girl,' he'd said earnestly. 'Don't know what you're doing stuck in this place. Come back to London with me, Cate, come to Paris.' She'd laughed, and he'd looked at her, crestfallen.

'Thank you,' she'd said seriously. 'I'll get my passport straight away.'

He'd looked at her again with sadness. 'Come inside,' he'd said, rubbing her hands clumsily between his, 'you're freezing.' Reluctantly she'd followed him through the wide glass door.

They'd all been there, in the big room. Sandro Cellini had asked her, what are they like? Could any of them have hated her enough? To hurt her.

No one had noticed their entrance for a moment or two; the lights had been dimmed and the music was playing loudly, a cheesy hit from last summer.

Michelle was pouring water into a glass on the edge of the kitchen corner's draining board, wearing a red dress; Cate had never seen her in a dress before. Rage, Tiziano had said, rage drives Michelle. But where did it come from?

There'd been a faint but distinct smell of dope in the air and in the centre of the room Tina was dancing, with complete abandon, an ecstatic expression on her face and arms swaying over her head. The space had seemed too big for one person to inhabit; Michelle's possessions seemed hardly to have made an impact. A handful of books sat lonely on a long shelf, a wheeled hanging rail for clothes held only Michelle's parka and a solitary pair of jeans, carefully folded over a hanger. It wouldn't take her long to pack up, when it was time to move on. Although when they'd had that conversation around the dining table about who was going where after their tenure at Orfeo was done, what would be the next gig, Cate remembered now that Michelle had been the one who'd said nothing. Her husband was dead.

The long table she worked at was pushed back against one wall. Tiziano was in his wheelchair at one end of it next to a computer on which graphics were moving with the music. One hand had rested on the computer touchpad and with the other he was quietly smoking. He leaned back in his wheelchair in an attitude of ease she hadn't seen him in before, not ever, the broad shoulders relaxed, his clever, watchful face calm. As Cate had studied him, feeling a sudden sadness she couldn't explain, Tiziano had leaned forward and tapped the touchpad, and another song came on. *Brown-eyed girl,* the voice sang; she'd known this one.

In the far corner a kitchenette was heaped with dishes. Per and his wife were standing over there, pressed into the quietest corner and entwined against a work surface. His wife was leaning back, a hand up and touching his cheek, and Cate had seen his face, pale and stunned and grateful, like a man climbing out of the ruins of his house after an earthquake.

Per and Alec had been for a walk together in the early afternoon. It had come to Cate, just like that; he'd said she would remember, and she had. She'd wished Sandro Cellini had told her why he wanted to know.

'Look who I've found,' Alec Fairhead had said in the end, lifting her hand in his. She'd wanted to ask him about Loni; if it was true what Loni had said to Beth, that he hadn't forgotten her. But now wasn't the moment.

They had all looked at her, Per nodding while wrapping his arms tighter around his wife, Tiziano smiling faintly through a blue spiral of smoke, Tina twisting her slight body on the space they had cleared for a dancefloor and lowering a hand to wave limply. Michelle, still filling a glass of water from a bottle, watched her. Cate had seen that she had make-up on too; the hostess. Quickly Cate had crossed the room to stand beside her, feeling Alec Fairhead's eyes on her as she went.

'Is this all right?' she'd said to Michelle quickly.

Michelle had taken a long drink of the water, eyeing her over the glass. They must all have known where she'd been, Alec Fairhead would have told them. Seen climbing out of the enemy's car: she had to explain to them that whoever the enemy was, it wasn't Sandro Cellini.

'All right with me, baby,' she'd said drily. Not drunk, thought Cate; interesting. The rest of them get wasted by way of celebration, but Michelle sobers up. Her face under the make-up – not much of it, red on her lips, her eyes outlined – was transformed; not younger so much, her skin still weathered, fine lines around the eyes, but more alert, defined, cared for. There was something faintly challenging about the look she'd given Cate, bright as a bird's, defying her to ask her questions. She'd poured a tumbler full of wine and handed it to Cate, who wondered where it had all come from, all this booze. Bottles of wine and vodka on the long table, at Tiziano's feet; pinched from the castle's cellars? She hadn't recognized the label.

'Our little act of subversion,' Michelle had said, seeing where she was looking. 'Those market trips? Turns out we were all stashing a private supply. It's not always nice, to be dependent, like a little kid. To have to ask for everything. And it turned out kind of useful, huh?'

Saying nothing – because to agree out loud would have been to betray the Trust – Cate had just raised the glass and taken a drink. Nice enough.

Michelle had shifted slightly and looked away, across at Tina on the dancefloor.

'Poor kid,' she'd said after a while. Then abruptly, 'That was kind of you. To tell her it wasn't her, with all that voodoo shit. She needed someone to tell her, and she didn't believe it when I said it.'

'No, well, maybe she wouldn't,' Cate had said. 'You're so close.'

'You think?' Michelle had taken Cate's wrist in her rough dry hand, holding it tight. 'She wouldn't hurt a fly, you know that? I mean, really.' Looking into Cate's eyes.

Cate had looked across at Tina twirling and singing to herself; seen Alec Fairhead look at her too. Realized Michelle wanted to know what she'd said to Sandro Cellini. 'I know,' she'd said. 'But he's a good guy, you know. Sandro Cellini; he's not one to misjudge her.' And she'd realized that she believed it. 'You don't need to worry.'

Michelle had looked at Cate a moment longer, then let go of her wrist abruptly. The music stopped and Tina let her arms drop, looking across at them.

'You never had kids,' Cate had said, without thinking, the wine making her careless. There was no answer and then she'd realized, and said, 'Oh, God. I'm sorry. I – Tiziano told me. You lost your husband.'

359

'Lost him?' Michelle had said wonderingly. 'Huh.' There was a long pause, in which Cate had wished she could be swallowed up. Then, with bitterness. 'Lost him. It didn't feel quite like that. It felt like – he was stolen. Hijacked, run over, thrown off a cliff, dismembered by gangsters. Murdered.' She took a deep breath. 'Yeah, I lost him. He's gone.'

'Murdered?' The word had seemed hard to ignore.

Michelle had looked at her a moment, weighing something up. When she spoke again her voice was level. 'I found him. Early in the morning on our bathroom floor in Queens, last August. It was so hot. He'd taken an overdose, after I went to bed; I slept through it, then I got up to go to the bathroom at around five and I found him.' She'd taken a breath, then let it out. 'He was on the floor, and his eyes were open.'

Cate had nodded, staring at her. 'Why did he – did you –'

Michelle had shaken her head violently, as if to stop Cate talking. 'Dying's a violent thing, always, however. That's all I meant.' She had folded her arms tight across herself, pulling the red dress around her, her face pale and her made-up eyes smudged dark.

Cate had nodded, saying nothing. How could you go on living in a place where someone had died? It was no wonder Michelle didn't want to talk about the next gig; maybe she was wondering if she'd ever go home again. Even in this place, which was no one's home, Loni's death was everywhere.

Tina had sidled up, nudging in next to Michelle. Wearily Michelle had dropped an arm on her shoulders, and setting her cheek on the older woman's forearm Tina gave Cate a timid look from under her colourless fringe, out of her faded eyes.

Cate had smiled at her, wanting to reassure her, feeling Michelle's watchful gaze on her.

And remembered that Michelle had gone for a run, as the light began to go, on the day Loni Meadows died. Mid-afternoon, perhaps two o'clock.

That was what had started it, the row over the minibus and the museum trip being cancelled; Michelle didn't want to go, she said, because she needed a run, really needed one. Then Tina said she wouldn't go, then there'd been no point hiring the minibus and Loni had gone all thin-lipped, in her coat with the fur trim. Per had been hovering around saying awkwardly that he'd like to go, though, and maybe Loni and he could go in the Monster, then Luca had made the mistake of arriving and Loni had grabbed him by the arm and stalked off with him. Frogmarched him up to his office.

Tiziano had appeared, and together they'd tried not to listen to Loni shouting at Luca. They'd seen Michelle emerge from the studio in her running kit, jogging up across the stones and looking around almost as if she wished Loni was still there to see her. All the gear: trainers, shorts, water pouch on her back.

Now Michelle was watching Cate. 'Have another drink,' she'd said, and Cate had let her fill the tumbler again. Across in the kitchenette Per was looking down into his wife's face, one hand on her shoulder, the other stroking her hair, while she spoke intently up at him.

Had Cellini believed her, when she'd said Per couldn't have done it? He'd reserved judgement; she supposed he had to do that. She knew, though. And she wasn't as green as Cellini thought.

Something had nudged against Cate's hip, and setting down the glass of wine she looked down and saw Tiziano.

'Dance?' he'd said, and as he said it she'd heard the music, an old plaintive Neapolitan song that everyone knew, that brought tears to the eyes of every old man in every village the length of the country, thinking of his first kiss.

Reaching up in a swift movement Tiziano had caught her arm and pulled her down so quickly she'd gasped, landing on his lap in the chair. He'd smelled of dope smoke; he'd whirled the chair away and Tina had clapped wildly. Cate's head had spun, with the wine and the movement and the dope smoke and the proximity of Tiziano's face to hers; she'd scrabbled for the wheelchair's arms. 'Stop,' she'd said, and he'd stopped. In the background the old ballad was still playing.

'Sorry,' Tiziano had said. 'Got carried away.'

Cate had extricated herself, knelt beside the wheelchair until her head stopped spinning, while he'd watched her.

'It's all right, you know,' he'd said. 'Nothing below the waist.' Cate had blushed furiously; he'd waited till the colour subsided.

'I wasn't worried,' she'd said. He was looking at her with perfect equanimity and she'd thought of Per saying Tiziano can't be what he seems. The bomb killed his father, on their way to a football match.

'So what's he like?' Tiziano had asked. 'Our friend from Florence?'

'He's nice,' Cate had said without thinking. 'He's like my dad. I mean my stepdad. He's just doing a job.'

'Not just here to stir up trouble?' He'd looked at her. 'The police don't think there's anything to investigate.' He'd looked around the room. 'He could ruin someone's life, you know.'

'You think, if someone – if it wasn't an accident, whoever did it shouldn't be punished?'

Tiziano had put his head on one side, as if considering it. 'She caused a lot of trouble herself,' he'd said eventually. 'A lot of pain.' He was looking at Alec Fairhead, then at Per in the corner with his wife. 'I talked to the wife. Per's wife. They've been married twenty-five years and not one moment's doubt, she said. Neither of them, until Loni Meadows came along. Is any of us as bad as she was?'

'So she deserved to die?' Cate had looked fiercely into Tiziano's face, making him look back. 'There's something bad here,' she'd said, meaning the castle. Their high prison, with its labyrinth of corridors and rooms, and all around the trees clustered close, penning them in, and the lonely, echoing hills.

She'd persisted. 'Can't you feel it? The way she died.' And as he looked back at her coolly she had blinked so as not to think about it, the dark and the cold, tried not to wonder how long it would have taken for Loni Meadows to die.

'I don't know,' he'd said. 'Perhaps you're right.' He'd passed a hand over his stubbled head. 'Well. Has he got any ideas?'

Cate had shrugged unwillingly. 'Come on, kid,' he'd said. 'You don't think it was me, do you?' And smiled sadly.

'He wants to know who went out that afternoon,' she had blurted.

Slowly Tiziano had nodded, frowning. 'That's interesting. Does he think someone – went and put something there? Like some kind of obstacle? Some kind of tripwire, some kind of trap?'

It had sounded crazy. Cate shrugged uncomfortably. 'I don't know. He just asked, did I see anyone go out?' She had looked at him. 'Did you?'

'See anyone?' She'd waited. 'Oh,' he'd said. 'Did I go out? Well, you know I did, Caterina. I went over to the farm to see the dogs, late afternoon.'

Cate had nodded. 'Yes, I did know that.'

'Do you think I need an alibi?' he'd added cheerfully. 'Someone to say that's where I went? Well, you saw me go, but I guess I could have turned and gone the other way out of the back gate. I could have gone towards the river instead of the farm.' Cate said nothing. 'Only actually, Mauro saw me. He was there when I arrived. Pissed, though, so he might not remember.' He'd set his elbows on the arms of his chair and watched her.

'He was at the farm, and he was drunk?' Cate had frowned. 'I thought he was – over on the other side of the valley.'

'That's where he was supposed to be?' Tiziano had shrugged. 'Well, I wouldn't want to get Mauro into trouble, but when I saw him, he looked like he hadn't been anywhere but the bottom of a glass for a good few hours.'

Cate had straightened, thinking furiously, and Tiziano had looked up at her. 'Are you going to tell him all this, then, our friend from Florence?' And she'd looked back down at him, unseeing. 'Whose side are you on, Cate?' he'd said softly. 'You've got to decide, haven't you? You've got to take a stand.'

And then she had looked into his face, wanting him to tell her what to do, as across the room Alec Fairhead had stepped up to Tina, on the dance floor, and held out his hand to her.

The water in Cate's shower was running cold. The paracetamol had dulled her headache. She turned off the water and heard voices from outside her window. Michelle and Tiziano were there on the snow; she was in her running gear again, and from the flush in her face Cate guessed she'd already been out. She hadn't been drinking last night, Cate remembered. In the wheelchair Tiziano was muffled up for once in a padded jacket as he talked to Michelle. From above, his legs looked as thin as sticks under the jogging pants. Cate pulled on her jeans and a sweater and opened the window.

They both looked up at the sound. 'Good morning, sleeping beauty.' Tiziano's good cheer sounded just a bit forced. Embarrassed: about last night. 'How's your head?'

'Hi,' she said, uncertainly; three days without Loni Meadows, and everything was different. It was as if the roles had all been reversed, the guests looking after her. And an eerie silence had descended with the snow; even Mauro's dogs were quiet. Sleeping beauty. 'I'm fine.'

But there was still a nagging ache, behind the buffer of painkillers; it was just waiting, compounded by guilt. Vincenzo. She hadn't given him a thought last night. Cate looked at the sky; to the east, it had cleared, and the sun was uncomfortably dazzling. But a new bank of cloud was building to the north.

'More snow coming, they say,' said Tiziano. Nodding towards Michelle. 'She had to get her run in before it kicked off again.' Michelle smiled down at him, serene, but the look she directed up at Cate was warier.

Since when, thought Cate with a trace of sullen childishness, did Michelle get so full of beans? 'Where is everyone?' she asked.

Michelle set her hands on her broad hips, head on one side. Her breath clouding in the cold air. 'Packing, I guess,' she said in her harsh accent. Watching Cate for a response.

'Packing?' Cate felt herself gawp.

'Well, we reached a joint decision.' After she'd gone, no doubt. 'We figured, we don't have to stay. We'll talk to your guy –'

'Not my guy,' said Cate uncomfortably.

'Whatever.' She eyed Cate warily. 'It's too much, Caterina. We decided, we'll talk to him, sure we will. But then, that's it, we're out of here. Per's already booked himself on a flight out with Yolanda tomorrow night.'

Cate stared back at her. Shit, she thought, Luca will be in meltdown. And stupidly, what about lunch? Maybe no one cared any more.

'Does he know?' she said falteringly. 'Does Luca know yet?'

'You want to tell him?' Michelle smiled. 'Go ahead, baby. Feel free.' She gestured at Luca's window, further down the façade, his shutters open.

Cate stuffed her feet into socks and the boots she'd dug out of the kitchen cupboard. Hair still damp, at least she was clean; but she didn't feel ready for whatever was coming. And something *was* coming, as sure as the snow.

Banging out of the door she was surprised to see

that Michelle and Tiziano were still there, looking down the hill. Close up, Tiziano looked pale.

Cate stopped. 'Where is he?' she asked. 'Has he started yet? Cellini? Has he started talking to people?'

Michelle stamped her feet. 'He got Alec this morning,' she said, eyes narrowed. 'Poor guy.'

'Mr Fairhead?' said Cate stupidly. As if she hadn't watched him dancing with Tina last night, watched him whisper and cry on her shoulder. Watching while he tried not to look at Per and his wife, kissing in the dark, and poured out his heart to her.

'What do you mean, poor guy? What did he say?'

'Don't ask me,' said Michelle toughly. 'None of my business. He was white as a sheet, though. I was just getting ready for my run and I heard him. Wandering about in the trees; I came out to see if he was OK, only he walked on down. Going to see Tina, he said.'

Tina. Cate tried to get her head around that one.

'Where is he?' she said. 'Where is he now?' She looked up at Luca's window. Shit, she thought; she had a job to do.

'Alec? He's with Tina. I just said.' Michelle frowned.

'Not him,' said Cate. 'I meant, where's Cellini?'

'Ah,' said Michelle. 'Him. Right. I saw him, on my run.'

'Your friend from Florence,' said Tiziano, and his teasing grated on her for the first time.

'He's a good man,' she said fiercely. 'You'd do well to remember that.'

'All right,' said Tiziano, surprised by her vehemence, holding up his hands in surrender. 'All right, whatever you say. Your good man – he's down at the river, throwing stones.'

CHAPTER 21

The cold and wet seeped up through Sandro's boots and as far as his ankles, but he didn't care. He was out of the Castello Orfeo, at least for the moment, standing in what he might before this weekend have avoided like the plague: open countryside, not a roof in sight, not a chimney.

He was at the foot of the hill where Loni Meadows had died. Around him the wide hills lay soft and white and silent and alien, merging with the pale sky at the horizon, the snow-laden trees on a nearby ridge motionless. After the deep damp chill and dark corridors of the Castello Orfeo, Sandro felt as though his lungs were expanding properly for the first time since his arrival, and even though he knew that the purple cloud was massing again at his back, overhead the sun shone out of a band of electric blue sky. The temperature must have risen just fractionally, because on the road down the tarmac had been beginning to show black through snow, and the noise of the chains had echoed round the hills until he thought they must all be at the windows of the castle, watching him. But where Sandro stood now, in the lee of the slope where the sun didn't reach, the cold was shocking.

The sound of the running woman had taken him by surprise. At first, it had even alarmed him; he had thought it must be an animal. Deer? Wild boar? In the crusted snow beside the road there had been tracks, delicate splayed bird feet, and the rounded depressions of a small cloven hoof. A tiny cluster of droppings, black on the pristine verge. Sandro's understanding of wild animals was restricted to the manner in which they might be cooked, and he didn't relish the prospect of coming face to face with one.

Since pulling up carefully in the car, he had spent the first five minutes just standing and orienting himself in the wide and barren landscape, and he judged that the furrowed track over the hill where she first came into view would have led around from the back of the castle, down to the left where the outbuildings stood among the trees. Michelle Connor, her skin flushed bright from the exercise and the cold. She didn't seem even faintly disturbed to see him, but nor did she pause. She approached through the snow, stepping high; it must, he thought, be a track that was used by humans, animals, or both, for the snow already to have been trodden down at all. She reached the road and expertly leapt a shallow ditch on to the dark strip of visible tarmac, turned and was gone. Away from him. He had watched as she moved away, steady, strong, the muscles in the backs of her legs pumping. She hadn't looked back.

Sandro knelt at the river's edge and felt for another stone, a smooth, rounded one, fitting in the palm of his hand. He threw it; tried to imagine it was dark. Or had the headlights still been on, casting their beam into the undergrowth? It landed with a splash, perhaps eight, ten metres away.

Talking to Alec Fairhead had not been like talking to Orfeo, although Sandro had felt himself to be in possession of even greater certainties as he climbed the stairs wearily, his head thick with lack of sleep, and his stomach sour with reluctance. From behind Orfeo's door as he passed, there had come the sounds of confident movement, brisk and assured. That would be typical; but Sandro no longer cared about Niccolò Orfeo. He would be glad never to see the man again; he would be delighted when he was out of his big brute of a house for good.

It had taken Alec Fairhead – Alexander Fairhead, born in London in 1954, educated at Harrow School, novelist and travel writer, veteran of such far-flung and dangerous places as Afghanistan and Colombia – a long five minutes to respond to Sandro's knock. Sandro had sat and waited on an oddly shaped wooden chair, so like something he'd seen in the Uffizi that he wasn't sure if sitting on it was allowed. He had knocked again, and sat back. Had thought of the Uffizi with yearning; of the long windows, the wedge of the long grey courtyard with the tower of the Palazzo Vecchio rising out of it, a symbol of civilization. Then, reluctantly, had thought of the awful little book he had struggled through before he could finally lay his head on the pillow and sleep; Alec Fairhead's first and only novel, *Unborn*.

Sandro read the newspaper religiously but he was not and had never been a reader of stories. Luisa was the one who sat and read novels, a stack of them beside the bed; she wanted words, she wanted characters, she wanted those structures with happy endings, or endings at least. Closure. But even Luisa would have hated this book; especially Luisa, she would have hated it. It would have made her cry. He had no idea whether this was a good book or not, whether the fact that it might have the power to make a thoughtful woman cry meant that it was good. It had won a prize, and from what was written on the back, it had many admirers.

It was about a man who fell in love with a woman who left him, and aborted his child. The man was called Edward Grant. Edward was Eduardo in Italian. It had been written in 1982. These were the things Sandro concentrated on; literary criticism was not called for, even if he had been capable of it. But there was something about the stiff, pained writing that he recognized.

The door had opened and Fairhead's face had stared down at him: gaunt, unshaven, but not surprised. Not frightened, either. Sandro had

373

thought he might be frightened, but then sometimes it came as a relief, to certain kinds of offender, to be found out. To stop having to pretend.

'Come in,' Fairhead had said. He had sounded tired; he was wearing a sweatshirt with nothing under it and loose trousers, and his feet were bare.

After finishing the book, just to make sure, Sandro had gone back to the little chart Giuli had made him. Between 1981 and 1982 Loni Meadows, married by then, had been on a visiting Fellowship at the Courtauld Institute in central London; a part of London University, very close, it appeared from the information he had subsequently obtained within seconds from the campus's official website, to University College, London, where Alec Fairhead had been registered as studying for a Doctorate in English Literature between 1979 and 1982.

Loni Meadows's Fellowship at the Courtauld had ended in June 1982; she took up another at Columbia University, New York, that September but she must have left London for America almost immediately.

There was a record of her winning an award for her reviewing for the *New York Times*. Her awards were listed on her website, and her journalism enthusiastically described, using terms like 'savage' and 'coruscating'. It had not occurred to Sandro, revisiting it, that no one would have bothered to update Loni Meadows's website: it was a shock. The bright blue eyes in the same photograph she had submitted to the Trust in her

374

application shone from the corner of the screen; *Loni Meadows is engaged in projects in southern Tuscany, but she continues to review widely.*

The room had been warm and gloomy and the air stale and sour. Fairhead had opened the shutters and the influx of damp cold had seemed to sharpen them both.

In the light, the room had been revealed as exceptionally neat. All doors firmly closed on wardrobe, cupboard, bedside table; a laptop, turned off, its screen folded flat, dead centre of a desk between the small windows. It would have been a maid's room once; Orfeo's forebears might have made their way up here to inflict their bullying needs on their social inferiors; not much change there, then. Even as Sandro had thought as much, from far below, at the front of the castle where Orfeo had parked, there had come the unmistakable roar of that powerful car. Good riddance.

Sandro had crossed to the window and looked down. The avenue of cypresses dipped straight down the hill below towards the road, each one twenty metres high at least, black spears topped with white. Not as carefully maintained as they might be; the weight of the snow was beginning to splay them. One factotum wasn't really enough, for a place like this; Luca Gallo had a lot on his plate.

You couldn't see the road or the river clearly from up here; you could see the horizon, hills one behind the other, but closer to, the river, like the strip of tarmac, wound and dipped behind the undulations of the landscape. You couldn't see the place where Loni Meadows had died.

Feeling Alec Fairhead hovering at his back, Sandro had turned to face him. He hadn't wanted to beat about the bush. 'You were in Paris last year,' he had said. 'April last year.' And abruptly Fairhead had sat, at his desk, set his hands flat on the leather surface.

'I was,' he had said, and his voice had been steady. He'd been waiting for this; he wanted to be found out. Start from the beginning, Sandro had thought.

'You had an affair with Loni Meadows, nearly thirty years ago,' he had said. 'Which ended – badly. You wrote a book about it.'

'I did,' Fairhead had said, his voice very quiet, but still firm.

'You never got over it, did you?' Sandro had said softly. And Fairhead had shaken his head quickly, just once. 'Until now,' he had said.

'You hadn't got over it last April, when you sent an email to the Orfeo Trust from an internet café at four in the morning. Edward Grant, whose girl-friend aborted his child in 1982, is Eduardog82. Is you.'

Fairhead had put his face in his hands.

'You wanted her to know, didn't you? You hid yourself behind a proxy server, but somewhere deep down you wanted her to know it was you.'

His face still in his hands, Fairhead had moved his

head from side to side before raising it to look at Sandro. 'I read about her appointment in the *THES*, would you believe it?' Sandro had had no idea what this publication was, so he just waited. Seeing his polite blankness, Fairhead had explained. 'For universities, a newspaper. *Times Higher Education Supplement*. I had given a lecture at the Sorbonne, and I was sitting in a brasserie in Montparnasse with a beer and I opened the paper and read about university appointments, that kind of thing. I read a review of one of Per's plays, actually.'

His hands had rested on the arms of the chair, searching Sandro's face for something as he spoke. Needing him to understand something.

'I was – at ease. I don't know if you – well, perhaps you will understand, but I don't relax all that often. It's rare for me to feel as I was feeling then; it was a warm spring evening, the beer was cold, there was even some kind of tree in flower on the boulevard.' He had taken a breath. 'I had been told not long before that I had been accepted for a stint here, and I have always loved Italy. Even though – well. When I met Loni, you see, there was nothing Italian about her; she was a clever girl from the Midwest. Sitting in that brasserie I knew she was married to an Italian but I didn't associate Italy with her. I thought it might be the thing – the experience that got me back on track.' His face had dropped. 'Even though that seemed to get less likely each year.'

'Back on track?'

377

'Writing,' he had said. 'Proper writing. I couldn't write after – the book. After *Unborn*. Only hack stuff.' Sandro had looked at him questioningly. 'Journalism. Travel. It was never what I wanted to write.'

'The work was what mattered to you? Not – other things?' Not a family, not – children? The man hadn't been even thirty: were there really people who put off those things, in favour of something like writing?

Alec Fairhead had looked away, pained. 'I thought they would follow on, you see. I thought, I had to get the work right first. Then I would do the living.'

'And then you read the announcement of Loni Meadows's appointment.'

Fairhead had nodded. 'I finished the beer, then I had another one. That didn't work. Then I went back to the hotel, and I couldn't sleep. It was hot and stuffy, and my head ached, and I tried to think about the lecture I'd given because it had gone well – but nothing worked. Everything had turned to – shit.'

The word had been deliberately ugly.

'So you went to an internet café.'

Fairhead's shoulders had dropped, and slowly he had nodded. 'Just one,' he had said. 'Just one email. I thought I could disguise it: I knew about proxy servers from a piece I wrote about Indian call centres.' He had breathed out slowly. 'I could feel myself losing it, the things I wrote, but I couldn't stop myself. I had to send it quickly before I changed my mind. And then of course I did change my mind, but it was too late.'

Sandro had pulled up a chair and sat at the corner of the desk.

'But you came, anyway,' he had said. 'You could have resigned your tenure here. Given your place to someone else.'

There had been a silence. 'I could,' Alec Fairhead had said. 'Perhaps I should have.' He had twisted his neck as if he was in pain, his few clothes suffocating him. 'I did write a letter,' he had said eventually. 'Asking to be excused, some family reasons, but when I looked at it it seemed – so pathetic. So cowardly. I tore it up; I told myself it might be – I don't know. Fate.'

'Do you know why I'm here?' Sandro had asked, after a silence.

'I – I think so,' Fairhead had said uncertainly.

'That email brought me here.' And Fairhead's face had grown paler, the shadows under his eyes darker. 'Loni Meadows's husband is a man called Giuliano Mascarello,' Sandro had said. 'And he thinks that whoever sent that email also brought about his wife's death.'

That hadn't been enough. 'He thinks whoever sent that email killed her.'

Fairhead had jerked back in his chair. 'What?' he had said, breathless. Then incredulously, 'What?'

Sandro had sat as still as he could and looked.

Had examined Fairhead for any hint that might betray his reaction as anything less than total, unfeigned shock, and found nothing. 'Did you?' he had asked softly. 'Did you kill her, Mr Fairhead?'

Fairhead had stared straight back at Sandro, not even shaking his head. 'Kill her? Kill *her*? No!' Still staring. 'No, no, no, never. I didn't even want to kill her when – not ever.'

Sandro had wondered if he was losing his touch. The man had seemed to him to be telling the truth. He had felt the cramped proportions of the little room around him, Alec Fairhead sitting up here at his computer day after day, struggling with his unhappiness. Then he had seen that that was all it was. Not violence, not madness. The same kind of banal daily unhappiness that Sandro and Luisa had dealt with themselves, their own small tragedies.

'After I'd written the email,' Alec Fairhead had said slowly, as if in confirmation of what Sandro was thinking, 'it was as though the sting had gone out of it. It was – less. Everything was greyer, but it was better. Funny thing was, I almost liked her, being back here. She's – good value; a kind of old-fashioned spectacle. If you're not in love with her.' So she'd been wrong, Sandro had thought, Loni Meadows had reckoned she still had him in her hand. Fairhead hadn't killed her: the certainty had settled in Sandro's mind. But he had had to be sure.

'I need to know something,' he had said. 'Did

you go out, that day, that afternoon? Before she died. Did you walk down to – the place? Did you go anywhere near the river? To where she – came off the road?'

Fairhead had looked at him as if he couldn't believe his eyes. 'So you really think she was – murdered?' He had swallowed. 'But how?'

Sandro had shaken his head briefly. 'That doesn't matter just now,' he had said. He would hold his theory in his head just a while longer; he needed to unpack it in front of someone he trusted; he wished for Luisa. 'Did you go down there?'

The answer had come slowly. 'We went for a walk –' Fairhead had said. 'I don't even know if we got that far. We walked that way, yes. After lunch: about two.'

'We?' An alibi, Sandro had reminded himself, was not everything. But it was unignorable. He had waited.

'Per and I,' Fairhead had said. 'We often walked together.' He had smiled unhappily. 'Perhaps it's a northern European trait. But we both like – to be with someone, but someone we don't have to talk to.' He had sounded confused, resigned.

'And that night?'

'I went to bed. I passed her on the stairs.' Fairhead had said precisely what he had told Caterina and she had recounted carefully to Sandro the previous night: Alec Fairhead had gone to bed after seeing Loni Meadows go into her

381

apartment. Per had come up soon after; neither of them had left their rooms.

'You're sure? About Mr Hansen?'

Fairhead had nodded. 'He put on some Grieg, quite loudly; he does that every night. He took a long time to go to sleep, which is also normal for Per. And for me.' He had frowned a little. 'Even through the wall, I knew it was him. You get to know people's – sounds, their habits, I suppose like a blind person does. Surprisingly quickly.'

Sandro had nodded. The man's lonely, he had thought. Just lonely.

'It's all right,' he had said, and Fairhead had looked up at him. 'You do believe me?' he had asked.

Sandro had looked at Alec Fairhead a long moment and realized that, for good or ill, he did. Hadn't been sure if it was wise to do so, but he had inclined his head, just a fraction. 'I'll talk to Mr Hansen,' he had said. Hesitated. 'Yes, I believe you.' He had hesitated again. 'But there's just one more thing. Niccolò Orfeo. Left his phone here, last Sunday.'

And now Fairhead had looked almost desperate with confusion, hands at either side of his head. 'Did he?'

'You haven't seen it?' Fairhead hadn't even shaken his head, but his expression was enough: complete lack of recognition. 'No one's mentioned finding it? Asked you about it?'

'Well, I – God.' He had frowned. 'Did Luca say

382

something about a phone? Perhaps he did. I don't know if I gave it a thought. Perhaps he did.'

'It's all right,' Sandro had said. 'It doesn't matter.' He had got to his feet. 'Let me give you some advice,' he had said. 'You need to put the life first, now. Before the art. Before it's too late.'

Alec Fairhead had looked at him wonderingly. 'That's what Per said.'

'Ah,' Sandro had said. 'Per.'

In the snow, in the dip that kept him out of the sun, the cold was really beginning to bite now. Sandro squatted down on his haunches. He could hear the river, gurgling and whispering as it slid over the stones, not deep, here, after a winter drought. When the thaw came it would be different; the snow would have changed everything, melting into the water table, washing things down and away.

In the dark, Loni Meadows would have been able to hear the water, staggering out of the car, falling. Lying in the dark. It was an accident; he rehearsed the words to himself. Yes, there was a nasty email, but this was a car crash, coincidence, a woman with many enemies can also die, mundanely, in an accident; the statistics proved it. She died as thousands do every year, even those who don't drive like madwomen.

Go back to Giuliano Mascarello, Sandro told himself, deliver him Alec Fairhead if necessary; the old man wasn't stupid. He'd know the truth when he heard it. It would be so easy. The temptation was great. The only trouble was, there was something stubborn and resistant in Sandro that would not believe it.

In part it was this place – this great thug of a prison-castle – and the people confined in it; in part it was superstition. An uneasy, half-defined feeling of something unhealthy breeding quietly in the small rooms, in the spindly trees pressed up against the walls, in the rundown farmhouse. And then there were the scraps and tatters of a story, of evidence, that he could not entirely ignore.

It had not been necessary to spend long with Per Hansen to know that the man was completely incapable of dissimulation. Sudden violence, possibly, if pushed to an extreme. Followed by abject remorse.

Sandro had seen signs of neither; in addition he had told the same story as Alec Fairhead. They had walked together in the early afternoon, perhaps as far as the river, he couldn't remember. He had said good night to Loni Meadows, gone to his room and not emerged until the following morning; he had played Grieg.

'You were perhaps the last person to see Loni Meadows,' Sandro had then said abruptly.

The man's wife had left early on: Yolanda Hansen had opened the door to his knock, wearing a long nightdress and a dressing-gown, sensibly brought from home, no doubt. She'd understood straight away, and hurried downstairs, saying something about bread.

The room could not have been less like Fairhead's; it had been a tip. There had been signs that the wife had tried to make inroads, clearing a space for a cup on the table. Hansen himself had looked only bewildered, as if Loni Meadows had happened to someone else, in a different lifetime.

But eventually he had responded. 'I – yes,' he had said, and he had begun to flush, darkly. 'I went to her room. I – she had been very attentive to me.' He had passed a hand over his forehead. 'I don't mean that it was – her entirely. I –' and he had cast about, as if looking for his wife. 'I have always liked women,' he had said finally. 'But I'm not experienced with them. Only my wife. I thought this was a great – emotion. A great love; it was like madness. I don't – I didn't understand what I was feeling.'

'I know,' Sandro had said, and he had sighed.

Hansen had gone on. 'I didn't understand anything – until that night. I was standing at her door and she was looking at her telephone, reading something there, and she simply wished I would go away. I suddenly realized that she wanted me to disappear, I was inconvenient.' He had put his hands to his head. 'And now it seems that everyone else knew, all along, that she was having this – affair. This other affair, going to hotels.' He had sounded sick.

'But you have your wife, now,' Sandro had said, intending to comfort him. We have our wives.

His head resting against the window, Per Hansen had straightened, looking at him gratefully. 'You're an odd sort of detective,' he had said.

Sandro had laughed abruptly. 'I suppose I am,' he had said. Hansen had been looking down out of the high window, and there had been something about the way he was looking that had drawn Sandro to him.

'You didn't hear her leave?' he had said quietly, following his gaze. Down between those cypyresses. Sandro had seen that from this room slightly more was visible to the castle's right – or left if you were facing it from below, from the river. Down where the women lived, the *villino* and the studio. 'You didn't hear – anything?'

'I was listening to my music,' Per Hansen had said, stiffening, chastened to the point of anguish by Sandro's implication. Might the sound of the accident have echoed across the hills, might it have come up this far? 'I didn't hear anything.'

And if he had, Sandro had thought as he'd examined the man's hollow-eyed look, he would have gone to help. And then a shadow had passed across Hansen's face in the thin morning light. 'Later,' he had begun hesitantly, then stopped. 'Later, though. I did see something. Thought I saw something.'

And so another little shred of evidence had joined the rest; a threadbare little collection, but stubborn. It would not go away.

Sandro straightened, the whisper of the water in

his ears, and threw one last pebble, heard it splash, saw it enter the black water between the mounded snow overhanging the banks. There, he thought, following the stone's trajectory, and as he thought it someone called his name.

When Cate came in, Luca was sitting at his desk reading a letter. Handwritten, on the heavy-gauge paper the castle provided to the guests, a small representation of the castle's silhouette in one corner. He didn't look up for a good minute after she entered the room, staring at the page as Cate stood awkwardly wondering if she'd misinterpreted his distracted answer to her tentative knock, wondering if he had not in fact wanted her to come in at all.

It was different, Cate thought as she stood there; the room that had on her last visit seemed full of life and purpose, busy with Luca Gallo's energy, stuck about with itineraries and Post-it notes, now seemed dusty, chaotic and neglected. The photograph of Luca's lover, Salvatore, had gone from its place in the corner of the computer screen.

At last he looked up from the piece of paper, and Cate saw that Luca's face was quite pale under the cheerful beard, and the look he turned on her in that moment was completely desolate.

'What is it?' she said, taken aback.

'Oh,' he said, blinking back down at the paper. 'Oh,' then sighed. 'It's nothing,' he said, but Cate just stared back. 'It's Orfeo,' he said briefly, when she said nothing, and let the piece of paper fall to the desk. 'Sounding off.'

'Orfeo?' Cate looked towards the window. 'But he – he's –'

'He's gone back to Florence,' said Luca. 'First thing this morning, and left this,' he flipped the piece of paper with a forefinger. 'We know where to find him, he says, if he is required.'

'Know where to find him?' Cate didn't understand.

'He means Sandro Cellini,' said Luca, following her gaze towards the window. 'Apparently Cellini did something to offend him last night. Spoke to him about the *Dottoressa*'s death. About his – relations with the *Dottoressa*. He's very angry.'

Cate felt herself grow warm with the knowledge of her own guilt. 'I – ah – I see,' she said. Luca looked at her consideringly, but when he spoke it was not on the subject of who might or might not have known about Loni Meadows's affair; anyone might have told him, pleaded Cate silently, suddenly sure that she had been the last to know.

'He says he intends to dissolve the Trust,' said Luca briefly, and Cate stared at him. 'Take back the castle.'

We'll all be out of a job, was Cate's first thought, and it came with something surprisingly like jubilation. But her second was for Luca Gallo, for whom leaving the Castello Orfeo would be the end of the world. 'Can he do that?' she said.

Luca took the piece of paper with a sudden

movement and crushed it into a ball. 'Maybe,' he said. 'Probably.' And made an impatient gesture, waving something aside. 'Lunch,' he said, and the old Luca seemed to be back, albeit in a faded version. 'With this snow – I'm worried Ginevra will be running out of provisions. We can't let the guests go hungry. Care will need to be taken, things may have to be rationed.'

Cate looked at him warily, a number of questions presenting themselves, not least whether Luca knew of the guests' plans to go their separate ways as soon as Sandro Cellini had talked to them. And certainly when she had come past it on her way to Luca's office, the kitchen had been dark, no sign of Nicki or Ginevra; one of the questions she had come to pose to him was whether they were snowed in down there. Had Luca simply been holed up here for too long to know what was happening?

'I – um –' she began, but then Luca's mobile began to vibrate on the desk, jiggling among the papers. He answered it, giving Cate a quick look that told her to stay where she was.

'Ginevra,' he said, frowning. Cate heard a gabble, weary, anxious, pleading.

'He's what?' More gabble. 'All right, all right.' Luca's tiredness sounded extreme, as if he had reached breaking point. 'Look, just leave him where he is. No, leave him. You stay there, I'll be down, the snow's melting. I'll be down.' He hung up and let a long breath out, his face between his hands.

'What's happened?' said Cate.

'Mauro,' said Luca, with resignation. 'He's – it looks like he's pushed it too far this time. Some kind of crisis.'

For God's sake, thought Cate, as if we didn't all know. 'Is he drunk?'

Luca looked at her sharply, then gave up. 'Not exactly,' he said wearily. 'More like – withdrawal. He's hallucinating, got the shakes, she says. Can't stand up. She's worried.' He looked up at Cate, his brown eyes wondering whether she might conceivably be able to help him out of this. 'Looks like lunch might have to be late today.'

She should have gone straight to the kitchen to get started, she knew that. But the roads had begun to thaw, Luca had been right, and as she watched his hire car creep down the hill towards the farmhouse, Cate found her gaze shifting across to her little *motorino*, forlorn under the trees, its saddle freighted with snow. Found herself wondering what Sandro Cellini was doing down there, throwing stones in the river. And before she knew it she was back in her room, collecting her helmet.

She left by the front drive, on impulse: the quicker route to the river, swooping down between the cypresses, slowly at first then faster as she reached the main road and more clear tarmac, holding her breath and feeling a ridiculous euphoria to be out of there, under her own steam. Tempted for a second just to keep going, until she wondered, where, though? Home? To Pozzo Basso, and Vincenzo? The thought gave her a queasy feeling, of guilt and aversion. She came to the brow of the hill and stopped. Sandro Cellini was bent over, up to his knees in a snowdrift by the river and looking at something. She called his name.

Looking up briefly, he hardly seemed to register she was there; just a hand over his eyes to shield him from the snow glare, and the slightest of nods. By the time Cate was down there, Sandro was practically in the river itself, one foot on the bank, another on a stone in the shallow flow, hanging on to a branch.

She came down slowly, because it was steep, this last bit; on a *motorino* you had to stick to the middle of the road even when it wasn't half-covered with snow. Not the first to die down there, was that what Mauro had said? Poor Mauro. Shaking with the DTs in a dark room, in another sunless dip between the hills. Everyone knew it was dangerous; but Loni had thought she'd live forever.

The rear wheel of the Vespa slid a little on the snow, but Cate held steady. What was he doing down there? She came to a stop, breathless, at the foot of the hill and set her feet down on either side just as Sandro's head jerked up. A dripping arm held over his head in triumph, something small and silver in his hand; the hand bone-white from cold.

'Got it.' He spoke to no one in particular, in a

fierce mutter. Cate dismounted, pulling off her helmet.

'Got what?'

He looked at her a moment then held it out, a smoothed silver pebble, a piece of dead technology. Loni Meadows's phone.

State of the art cameraphone on this model, Cate had heard Loni say that – to whom? To Tina, the artist. *You mustn't reject the new*, Loni had said. *Embrace the technology.* Aiming the phone around the dining table and pretending to snap them each one in turn. Per looking bashful, Michelle scowling.

'It's not art, though,' Michelle had said. 'It's like blogging. Incontinent photography. The world's full enough of shit as it is.' Michelle was always back at her, from the moment she'd arrived at the castle. Was she happy, now Loni was dead? That question gave Cate pause.

Sandro Cellini was sticking his hands under his armpits to warm them, grimacing in pain. 'It's hers, isn't it?' he said, teeth chattering.

Cate turned it over in her gloved hand. 'You found it,' she said wonderingly. 'Will it do you any good, after all that time, under the water?'

Cellini had now folded his arms across his chest and was rocking to keep warm, his weathered, face, his kind brown eyes fixed on the strip of dark water between snowy banks.

'We'll see,' he said, and she heard the chatter in his teeth, saw his blue-knuckled hands.

'Haven't you got any gloves?'

The detective nodded at the verge and she saw a pair of woollen gloves on the snow; not warm enough to start with, and now soaked into the bargain. And his coat, she noticed, wasn't thick enough, either. Sandro Cellini looked sheepish, but happier than he'd seemed since he arrived at the castle, as if enjoying her exasperation. Cate stuck the phone in her pocket and pulled off the leather gauntlets she wore on the *motorino;* two sizes too big for her. An old boyfriend's. The thought depressed her; too many old boyfriends. As she handed the gauntlets to Sandro, Cate realized that she'd already consigned Vincenzo to the same status.

'How come you found it,' she said, 'and the police didn't?'

'Who knows?' he said. 'Maybe they don't think like I think; maybe they don't look anywhere but the obvious places, maybe they think anything but the obvious things.' He sighed. 'Look, I don't want to badmouth them: and often enough the obvious is the answer. Maybe they're just lazy, or maybe they turn up at an accident scene, and they see what they want to see. And when the local big man comes along and flatters them a bit, when they know the deal at the Castello Orfeo, they don't think, let's have a closer look. They smile like a girl receiving a compliment, and they forget all about what job it is they're supposed to be doing.'

'You think it was Orfeo?' Cate thought of him heading back to Florence in the big car. 'He's gone.'

'I heard him,' said Sandro. 'No, it wasn't him, he was at home in Florence with his delinquent son. He's too vain and self-centred and stupid, anyway. But I think he wanted to make sure he didn't get in the papers over it, that's all.'

Cate took her hands out of her pockets and folded them across her body in the biker jacket, thinking.

Slowly Sandro took off the gloves and handed them back to her, and they both looked to the road, in shadow still, and the crest behind which stood the castle.

'Are you going to tell me what you think happened now, or not?' said Cate, pulling the gloves back on. He looked at her for a long moment, then said, 'Come with me.'

They walked up, Cate pushing her *motorino*; fifty metres. Overhead the thin band of blue had narrowed and the sun was dimming, edging back behind the cloud. The air was cold and damp, and a wet wind had got up. They stood at the top of the short hill and looked together at the castle, black against the snow. The flag, Cate noticed, was still at half-mast. To the left of the castle's dark, symmetrical bulk, through the spindly trees, she could see the shapes of the outbuildings; the laundry, the *villino* lower down. To the right, Cate noticed, the roof of the farm was just visible, and when her eyes adjusted to the snow glare, a criss-crossing of animal tracks in the soft white contours.

'You think it wasn't an accident,' said Cate.

He nodded. 'There was nothing wrong with the vehicle,' he said, as if he knew what she was going to say next. 'The police report was categorical: no failure, only slight wear on the brake pads. No one tampered with the car.'

Cate felt colder, all of a sudden. 'So do you think – there was someone in the car with her, after all?' Someone like Per?

Sandro turned back, looking down the hill to the black ribbon of river winding behind the sharp bend, and the bare clumped willows that had obscured Cate's view of the car and the tow-truck as she had come into work on that icy morning. All around them the empty landscape stood silent, waiting. Slowly he shook his head. 'It's possible,' he said. 'Barely, though. The passenger side of the car was completely caved in. You'd have had to be in the back, and wearing a seatbelt, to have escaped alive, and even then you would almost certainly have sustained some kind of injury. And I think it happened another way. I think it was worked out in advance.'

'But you can't,' said Cate stubbornly. 'You can't cause a crash by – by remote control.'

Sandro turned towards Cate, looking at her thoughtfully. 'There was a patch of ice,' he said, 'running down the side of the road. Down the slope. It's the patch she hit that sent her off on to the verge.'

'Yes,' said Cate, waiting.

'You all knew she drove dangerously, and that she didn't wear a seatbelt: all of you. From Luca Gallo down; anyone who'd been in a car with her or even seen her climb into one and drive away. You all knew that this was a tricky bend. Did you all know how cold it was going to be that night?'

Cate eyed him. 'I guess. When you're stuck in this place, the weather's pretty important.'

Sandro nodded, took a deep breath. 'I saw the ice,' he said. 'Yesterday evening. I saw the skid marks. A thick sheet of black ice a metre wide, down the side of the road for maybe four metres. That's quite a lot of ice; quite a lot of water.' He kicked at the snow on the side of the road: some ice still showed dark beneath it.

'Only thing is,' he said, 'I can't work out where that water came from, to turn to ice. There's no culvert, there's no spring up here. Because if there had been, it would have made the road so dangerous every time there was a hard frost, it would have had to be diverted long ago.'

Cate stared at the dark patch beneath the snow, glassy and dangerous. 'You think someone – made the ice?'

'I'm not a scientist,' said Sandro. 'The police have forensics teams for that kind of thing, only in this case it didn't seem to occur to them.'

Thinking of the policeman, cosy in the kitchen of the castle with Mauro and Ginevra, Cate could see how he might have overlooked all sorts of things.

Sandro was still talking. 'But even I can see that it could be done. You'd need water, and you'd need to know how cold it was going to get. It would have to be done while it was still light, but starting to chill right down.'

'Someone came down here,' she murmured, feeling the hairs on her neck prickle and rise.

'I think,' Sandro said softly, at her shoulder, 'that this was a murder by degrees. At each stage, she might not have died. The crash might not have killed her; if she had been wearing her seatbelt she might even have walked away from it.'

Cate nodded, chilled to the bone.

Overhead the sky had thickened, turned grey as the last shard of sun died. It wasn't human, to live in a place like this, Cate thought, without neighbours, with no one to hear you if you called. Did someone hear Loni Meadows?

He went on. 'If she hadn't answered the call.' He held up the mobile. 'It'll be on here; they'll find it eventually, they'll resuscitate it. Even the police at Pozzo Basso.'

'The call? What call?'

'The text, saying, at a guess, *Meet me at the Liberty, the usual room.* Something like that.'

Cate stared at him blankly. 'I don't understand.'

'Only the text wasn't sent by the person she thought had sent it: Niccolò Orfeo wasn't waiting for her at the Liberty, no room had been booked there.' He looked at her and she remembered Vincenzo saying just that. 'Did you know Niccolò

Orfeo had left his phone behind here, last week?' said Sandro.

She gazed back at him, starting to shake her head, then stopping. Remembering Luca coming to the kitchen door one night, Monday night? 'Luca – yes. Luca asked if anyone had seen it.'

'And had anyone? A cleaner?'

'Anna-Maria? No. No one, as far as I know,' she said falteringly.

'But someone did find that phone,' Sandro said. 'Someone found that phone; perhaps that someone already had a shrewd idea that she was having an affair, or perhaps they looked – he or she looked at the messages and worked it out from there.'

Cate stared at him. 'Hold on,' she said. 'Hold on. Wouldn't he have told Loni he'd lost his phone?'

Cellini looked at her contemplatively. 'Do you think he would, really? No direct communication, all this secrecy; Orfeo's not a man who bothers to keep anyone informed about his business, about these minor irritations. Not even his lover; she could just wait for his next call, as she'd always done. He'd instructed Gallo to find it, and he expected it to be returned to him.'

'Maybe,' said Cate; she saw that he was right.

Sandro Cellini pressed on. 'Perhaps finding that phone was what started it all off: perhaps if Niccolò Orfeo hadn't been a careless, lazy man who always had other people to clean up after

398

him, to pick up what he left behind – then perhaps Loni Meadows would still be alive.'

There was a silence. 'It's getting dark,' said Cate, feeling the low grey sky pressing down on them. 'It's not even midday, and it's getting dark.' She swallowed. 'Alec Fairhead said she got a text, after dinner.'

Cellini looked down at the phone, still in his hand.

'That someone laid the ice. An outlandish idea; crazy. But crazy ideas sometimes work. Maybe they thought, it's an experiment; not my fault if she drives like a madwoman.'

'But then you'd have to make sure she went out.' She spoke dully and at last she understood.

'Poetic justice, isn't it? Using her own – weaknesses. Her recklessness. Her adulterous relationship.' The words were heavy and unforgiving, and Cate looked up at the detective sharply.

'So,' said Sandro Cellini. 'Was there enjoyment in the planning? Possibly. Was it someone obsessed, or someone clever, someone precise?'

'They're all clever,' said Cate numbly. 'All the guests are clever.'

'And what about the others? The workers. Luca Gallo's a smart guy too, isn't he?'

'Luca?' Cate took a step back.

'If you pushed him hard enough, could he do something like this? Because she did push him, didn't she? Bawling him out for everyone to hear.'

'That was over Mauro, though,' said Cate. 'That wasn't Luca; Luca was just sticking up for him.'

'Ah yes,' said Sandro, 'Mauro,' and he sighed, a long breath out. 'He knows the roads, does he, this Mauro? Has his own vehicle. I need to talk to him, don't I?'

'He's not well today,' said Cate, wondering why she felt the need to defend Mauro, just for Nicki's pleading look. 'Luca's gone down to check on him. Look, Luca's a good guy, a decent man, and Mauro's not clever, he's not calculating. He couldn't stand her, but – but – it's just not him.' And she stopped, defeated.

Sandro Cellini was looking at her, oddly intent. 'Well,' he said. 'Yes. Well, you know him, I suppose, and I don't. That's the thing, you see,' and he was almost talking to himself. 'He said I was a funny sort of detective, your Per Hansen. Maybe I am. All I can do is add things up, get facts and add things up. And hope I still know when I'm being lied to.'

He looked lost for a second, his eyes on something far away. 'My wife,' he said. 'Now, she can tell so many things about someone. Just from one look. It strikes me you're a bit like that, Miss Giottone. Do you know if you can trust someone, from one look?'

'I suppose,' said Cate. But she thought of Tiziano, and felt as though a stone had lodged in her chest. 'It depends.' She hesitated. 'So, what?' she blurted, feeling desperate. 'What reason did Tiziano Scarpa have to hate her?' It was very quiet suddenly, in the lee of the hill; nothing but the tiny sounds of the snow settling in the hollows of the wide landscape around them.

Sandro Cellini seemed to be weighing something up; Cate noticed that his lips were losing their colour, and he was shivering steadily, but eventually he spoke. 'You like him, don't you?' he said. Cate wrapped her arms tight around herself, frowning. He sighed. 'Well,' he said. 'Her husband – Giuliano Mascarello, *human rights lawyer,*' the words spoken with great contempt, 'he defended the human rights of the man who was eventually proven to have set the bomb that killed Tiziano Scarpa's father and left him in a wheelchair.'

She looked at him a long moment, absorbing this. Saying nothing, only feeling the cold, wet wind around her legs.

'Tiziano was out that afternoon,' she said, her mouth dry. 'He can get down the road if it's dry. He went down to the farm to see Mauro's dogs and he says he saw Mauro, but Mauro was very drunk.'

'Well,' said Sandro, 'that's almost an alibi, I suppose. Almost an alibi for both of them. Shame this Mauro was drunk. Has he got the shakes this morning, then? I wonder if he'll remember.'

Cate felt as though her brain had slowed in the cold, as though nothing made sense any more. Tiziano? Sandro Cellini stood there, very still it seemed, his arms thrown around himself, and then she saw it was to stop himself shivering. His eyes seemed to burn dark.

'You're freezing to death,' she said. 'Have you had anything to eat today?' He shook his head just barely.

'Come back to the castle,' she said. 'Come to the kitchen.'

He stared at her a long moment, unfocused, and she couldn't tell if it was the cold deadening his brain or if in fact his mind was somewhere far off, adding it all up.

Then he nodded. 'Thank you,' he said. 'Thank you, Caterina Giottone.'

CHAPTER 22

Giuli had watched the television weather report after the morning news and she knew that it had snowed right across the country, down as far as Rome. There'd been footage of beaches down the Tyrrhenian coast, with snow on the fallen umbrella pines. Freak weather conditions, it said. More snow this afternoon.

It never snowed in Florence, was the theory. The reality was worse; a wet kind of sleet had fallen heavily in the night, and the gutters were soaked and slushy as she splashed through them on her *motorino* to the Pasticceria San Giorgio, out among the modern apartment blocks of the Viale Europa.

It was Sunday, and the San Giorgio was Luisa's favourite pastry shop. But as the pouty girl at the counter loaded her little cardboard tray with raspberry tarts, miniature rum babas and tiny *sfogliatelle* stuffed with ricotta and candied peel, Giuli felt only anxiety – and some childish resentment – at the prospect of Luisa's face at the door of the apartment. This argumentative, loving, childless couple might be about to split up after a lifetime together. But it wasn't going to happen, not if Giuli had anything to do with it.

'Enough,' she said belatedly to the girl still heaping up profiteroles; there was enough cake for a starving family, and she had a shrewd idea neither she nor Luisa was going to have much of an appetite this chilly Sunday morning. Somewhere over towards the Isolotto, where the big villas backed on to the green river, she heard church bells beginning to ring.

As the girl curled ribbon round the package, Giuli pondered her strategy; she was still pondering it on the street outside the apartment, as she listened for Luisa to answer her ring.

The face that greeted Giuli at the door to the flat – Luisa's handsome, dark-browed, lively face whose new thinness Giuli, like Sandro, could not adjust to – was set and defensive. Wordlessly, Luisa stepped aside to allow her inside the hall; the place was cold and underlit. Typical, thought Giuli; she's off first thing in the morning, Sandro's not around, so she turns the heating down, never mind if there's snow on the hills. And then, as she followed Luisa towards the familiar kitchen – chequered laminate on the surfaces, ancient fridge, Tyrolean-style carved wooden cupboard all framed in the doorway – Giuli thought of a plan.

The place was scoured cleaner even than usual, and Giuli, sharp-eyed, detected signs of a fretful night. Luisa was prone to emptying cupboards and scrubbing when in a state over anything. Well, she thought, that was all to the good.

She waited until the small cups of coffee were on the table and the package carefully unwrapped – with a sigh from Luisa – to display the cakes like little jewels.

'Well, I suppose you're a good child,' Luisa conceded. 'Thank you for coming over.'

'You're off in the morning then?' Giuli kept her voice bright, as if it was only cause for celebration. 'Wow. What an opportunity!' Luisa gave her a sharp look, and Giuli picked up her coffee cup. 'Have one of these *sfogliatelle*,' she wheedled, 'I know they're your favourite.' Luisa sat down with another sigh, and placed the little cake, ruffled as a party frock and dusted with icing sugar, on her plate, and looked at it. Giuli could tell she was building up to tackling the subject of her stubborn, childish, jealous husband, and got in first.

'Look, Luisa,' she said. 'This is more of a – a bribe than anything else. The cakes.'

'Bribe?' Luisa gave her a sceptical look.

'I need your help,' Giuli said. 'Well, if I'm honest, Sandro needs your help.'

'Oh, yes?' She didn't believe a word of it; Giuli persisted.

'It's this case, down in the Maremma. In the castle keep, or whatever the word is; the American woman dead in her car. He –' and she improvised, 'he's out of his depth, he says. These weird artistic types, and he's got enough on his plate trying to untangle the how and the why down there. He says he needs my woman's eye on it.' She rolled her woman's eyes at that. 'He needs a judge of character, he says. To look over it all again, just to look at their resumés and their photographs, see what my instinct tells me. But I – I just don't think I'm good enough.'

Giuli didn't know if that was true. But it was true that she'd be better with Luisa on her side, and she spoke with conviction.

Luisa looked at her levelly, her eyes saying, *I know what you're doing.* But she couldn't resist. She picked up the *sfogliatella* and took a bite, and downed her *espresso*. 'Well,' she said, 'I'm already packed, and I suppose I'm not doing anything else this morning.'

'Just one thing,' said Giuli, suppressing a smile at the dusting of sugar on Luisa's upper lip. 'We'll have to get over to the office. If you don't mind.' And helped herself to a rum baba. Her favourite.

Giuli gave her a lift on the *motorino*, Luisa helmetless and risking prosecution. She'd started to laugh outside on the pavement, looking at the decrepit machine, at the snow, at herself in a neat, smart woollen coat and polished leather shoes. 'We could walk,' said Giuli, eager to say the right thing. But Luisa was in a reckless mood, for once.

'What would Sandro say?' she muttered, and that seemed to decide her. 'Oh, well, no *vigile* would dare fine an old lady like me, would he? Let's get going.'

The narrow streets of the winter city were gloomy in the sleet, unusually empty on this bitter

February Sunday; empty without Sandro too. Giuli took a roundabout route to avoid the *vigili*, down the high-sided, shadowy curve of the Via delle Terme, out in front of the rose-pink scalloped windows of the Palazzo Salimbeni, a quick dash across the Tornabuoni and into the gloom of the Via dell'Parione. Zipping carefree across the river on the Ponte alla Carraia, a brisk wind blowing and her spirits lifting, Giuli felt the warm pressure of Luisa's hands on her waist, like a blessing.

Luisa had found Sandro's offices for him, but had hardly been back since, Giuli knew that. She'd had a lot on her plate, with the operation and the chemo and the funny moods it had brought with it, but it did occur to Giuli that it wouldn't do any harm for her to see the place. So she could see Sandro a bit more clearly too, somehow.

Of course, before she was through the door Luisa was tutting at the state of the windows. Peering down into the builders' yard full of plastic piping, registering, with her sharp eye, the little sliver of the back of the church of the Carmine that compensated for it.

'We do clean,' said Giuli, standing guiltily at the doorway with hands behind her back like a school-girl in the *Direttore*'s office. 'It's just – maybe not often enough.'

'Maybe not,' said Luisa, running a finger along the chair set for visitors at Sandro's desk. She plumped herself down. 'So,' she said. 'What does he want us to look at?'

Files spread on the desk, Giuli pulled up a chair beside Luisa, leaned across her and turned on the computer. The ancient machine always took an age – and a lot of humming and whirring – to present her with a request for the password. 'Sorry,' she said to Luisa.

'Have you got one of these at home?' Luisa asked, out of the blue.

'No,' said Giuli, 'I wish.'

'Maybe I should get into it,' Luisa mused.

'Maybe you should,' said Giuli bravely. 'Email's a great thing. Free, you see. And sometimes – now say, if you wanted to say anything to Sandro, you could put it in an email. That sort of thing.' Luisa compressed her lips.

'Don't you know the password?' she said. 'Go on.'

Giuli typed it in.

Luisa watched her fingers on the keyboard. 'LUISA66?' she said gruffly. 'Is that it?'

'Uh huh,' said Giuli. Hesitated. 'What's the 66 mean?'

Luisa's eyes were closed, and when they flickered open Giuli thought there was something softer there, something more forgiving. 'That's the year we met,' Luisa said. 'Come on, I haven't got all day.'

Giuli checked the mail. There was one from Sandro: she could hardly believe it: it was as though he'd been party to her plan all along. *These are just notes*, it said, *just in case.* (In case of what? thought Giuli). *But I want you to go back over the*

408

stuff you've got: concentrate on the characters. Do some more checking on the internet.

'Told you,' said Giuli. Idly skimming the notes. 'Right,' she said to herself, 'so Orfeo *was* the man. The secret lover, right.'

Luisa snorted. 'Not Niccolò Orfeo?' she said with scorn. 'I could have told him all about Orfeo. Lecherous old bastard.'

Giuli drew her head back to take in Luisa's expression. 'You *see*,' she said. 'You see? You could have saved him a fair bit of time. With both those cases, as a matter of fact: your woman's eye.'

And then, without allowing herself to think, Giuli asked the question.

'You're not – um – having a – a – an affair with Frollini, are you?'

Luisa gave her a long, blazing look, and said nothing.

'I have to ask,' said Giuli, clinging to what courage she had.

And then suddenly the anger went out of Luisa. She let out a long sigh of resignation. 'Giuli,' she said gently, 'you're young. You've seen a lot – but there are things. Things you don't know about.'

'Like love?' Giuli heard the tremor in her voice.

'Like getting old. Like seeing the end of your life take a jump closer.' Luisa hardly seemed to take a breath before going on, her voice getting quieter, her eyes dark in her paper-white face. 'There were things I saw – people I saw. In the ward at Careggi. Women younger than me. I saw their children, I saw

409

them come in with bandannas, bright scarves around their heads, I saw them being brave for their husbands. And they died all the same.'

There was a long silence: *and you're still alive*, Giuli thought with gratitude, but did not say.

'I'm not having an affair with Frollini,' said Luisa into the silence, brisk as a teacher. 'I'm fond of him, but he's a vain old fool, and not my type, besides.'

Giuli laughed, despite herself.

'Do you think I'm going to go down on my knees and tell Sandro he is the only man I have ever loved, ever in my life, or ever will love? Even if it happens to be true. But I'm going to New York. I've never seen New York.'

Giuli sat dumbly, eyes round with unshed tears.

'Now let's get on with it.'

When she came back with another cup of coffee for each of them from the bar along the street, Giuli found Luisa in front of a patchwork of papers and photographs, laid out on the side table, a list of names in alphabetical order. She unpacked another little sugar-dusted cake from the package Luisa had insisted she take away with her – 'Ridiculous waste,' she'd said, not unkindly, 'they'll only make me fat' – and slid it on to the saucer with the *caffè macchiato* that was Luisa's favourite, setting everything in front of her at the table. *You need feeding up.*

'He says, take a look at that Gallo too,' Luisa spoke without turning round. 'The manager of the place.' She tapped a brochure for the Castello Orfeo, where there was a photograph of a round-faced, smiling man with a beard. Giuli stood at Luisa's shoulder, looking down at the picture.

'He looks nice, doesn't he?' said Luisa. 'A nice man, who enjoys his food. A kind man.' She studied the face. 'Sandro thinks someone set ice on a dangerous road, and called her out on some – pretext in the middle of the night, knowing she was a reckless driver. Would that man do that? A kind hardworking man who's worked in that place for eight years without a moment's trouble?' She closed the brochure. 'I don't want it to be him.'

Giuli laughed nervously. 'I know he said instinct,' she said. 'But –'

Luisa turned her head and looked at Giuli. 'And he's gay, Giuli. Gay men don't murder people.'

'You can't say that,' said Giuli, shocked.

Luisa shrugged. 'I can say what I want,' she said, then relented. 'I don't think it's likely, is that all right? I think it is –' she reached for a phrase, 'statistically improbable.'

Giuli took the brochure off the table, and put it under her arm. 'And what about paraplegics?' she said, now looking down at the shaven-headed, humorous face of Tiziano Scarpa. 'Is that likely, either?'

'I don't know,' said Luisa thoughtfully. 'It would make you angry enough, wouldn't it?'

Something occurred to Giuli. 'How would you know, though,' she said, 'setting up a car

411

accident – you couldn't guarantee the person would die, could you? Not unless you were there in the car with them or something. What if they were just –'

'Left crippled?' said Luisa, picking up the photograph of Tiziano Scarpa. 'Maybe that would be enough, for some people.' And she set the photograph down.

'Sandro said to me once, it's not the strong who murder, it's the weak,' she said distantly. 'Those who have no option.' Giuli waited for her to say something else but she fell silent then, gazing at her patchwork quilt of faces and names; she seemed suddenly absorbed, and oblivious to Giuli hovering at her elbow.

Outside the sky had darkened, the computer screen glowing bright on the desk. Giuli had an idea; picking the list of names from the desk, she went to the computer and sat in front of it.

Alec Fairhead, Michelle Connor, Luca Gallo, Per Hansen, Tina Kreutz, Tiziano Scarpa.

About ten minutes later Luisa, emerging abruptly from her absorption, was saying something. 'This one,' she said, though Giuli's attention was elsewhere by now and it only filtered belatedly into her consciousness. 'Do you know, I'd swear that if any of this lot had a screw loose, it'd be this one.' And Giuli heard the tap of her nail on the table, but she wasn't really paying attention to the face that had caught Luisa's attention.

'And what's this mean?' Luisa was at her shoulder

now, leaning down and pulling the neon-pink Post-it from the desk. 'Lonestar blog? What does it mean?'

Giuli leaned back, distracted. 'Her blog, you know, kind of internet diary. I was supposed to – but look at this. What d'you think of this?' She tapped at the cursor, scrolling down. 'Come and look at this.'

And Luisa leaned down past her, peering at the screen, and together they read a news report filed in the *New York Post*, six months earlier. Soon after, Giuli had already registered, Loni Meadows had taken up her responsibilities at the Orfeo Trust. The report was about a woman called Michelle Connor, and there was a photograph.

'*Merda*,' groaned Cate as she flicked the switch inside the kitchen door, on, off, on again, in vain. 'Damn it.' She heard footsteps and there was Sandro Cellini's face, still unshaven, peering in.

'What?' he asked.

'The power's gone.' It had happened before, a high wind back in October had brought some lines down. Cate reached in a drawer for a candle and matches, groped by memory for the coffee pot. 'Come in,' she said impatiently. The room was cooling, but not yet cold. 'Shut the door.'

By the feeble glimmer of the candle she filled the coffee pot, assembled it, set it on the stove – thank God for gas. Instinctively they both moved closer to the flame as the small burner sputtered into life.

'Where is everyone?' asked Sandro, his pale stubbled chin illuminated by the tiny flicker of flame.

'God knows,' said Cate, laying a place on the big table, reaching for a bag of sweet biscuits from a shelf in a larder, just visible in the gloom. 'I'm not sure what to do. It's all falling apart. I'd better call Luca.'

'Falling apart?'

'Since she died. It's as if it's all crumbling bit by bit. The guests are packing to leave.'

'They are?' said Sandro. 'We'll see about that.' But Cate turned to look at him and added, 'And Orfeo wants to close the place down now. Something you said to him last night.'

They were going: now in the cold dark kitchen it hit her; it was over. And Tiziano would be going, too: in an hour, roads permitting, the specially equipped taxi that had brought him from Pozzo Basso six weeks earlier could be here, loading him in.

Sandro sighed. 'He'll get over it,' he said. 'Don't you worry. Just a little tantrum.'

'Poor Luca,' said Cate, almost to herself. 'They all treat him like a dog.' She took out her phone and dialled, holding it to her ear with her shoulder as she opened a vast refrigerator, dark inside: she caught an unpleasant stale whiff, things beginning to sour. She brought out milk and set it on the stove.

Watching her, Sandro seated himself at the table; with the phone jammed under her ear, waiting for

Luca to pick up, she brought his coffee to the table, then a jug of warm milk, before moving away to stand by the half-glazed kitchen door, looking out.

'Yes?' Luca sounded beyond the point of exhaustion. Cate watched distractedly as Sandro gulped the coffee as soon as it was cool enough; he poured another. Saw the pallor begin to leave his cheeks. Luca was talking.

'It's what?' she said, 'Oh, I see. Power lines, OK. How long – he's what?'

'Mauro,' whispered Luca, 'he's had to go to hospital.'

'What?' Cate thought of the dark farmhouse, last night. 'He's all right, is he? He'll be all right?'

'I don't know. They seem to think so. Just the – the alcohol. Stress.'

'I don't know what to do about lunches,' she said dully, grasping at what once had been her purpose here.

'It doesn't matter,' said Luca, and she thought, Oh God, it really is all over. 'They can go hungry for a bit,' he said wearily. 'It won't kill them.'

Turning off the phone, Cate sat down and mechanically poured herself a cup of coffee, filled it to the brim with milk, two sugars. Crumbled a biscuit between her fingers.

'I didn't ask him about Orfeo's phone,' she said, startled by panic. 'Should I have done?' She felt stupidly on the verge of tears.

'You're doing very well,' said Sandro wanting to put an arm around her shoulders. 'Drink your

415

coffee.' And for a crystalline second she saw them both, suspended in the moment, in the fragile peace of the cooling kitchen, with their life-giving coffee, in the eye of a storm about to break.

She took a sip of her coffee. 'He's coming back up, anyway,' she said. 'An ambulance has come for Mauro. And then her eyes, looking down, fixed on something and there it was on the table: she didn't remember Sandro putting it there. Loni Meadows's little phone.

Cate frowned, then raising her head, she tilted it, like a gundog catching a scent. 'So how did it get into the river?' she said, with a curiosity that faltered as she went on. 'The *telefonino*.'

'Ah,' said Sandro. 'Yes.'

'It didn't just slip out of her pocket, did it?' she said slowly, challenging him with her eyes.

'No,' Sandro said brusquely. 'It didn't fall out of her pocket. It didn't fly out, either, on impact.'

'Can you be sure of that?' Cate felt as though she could hardly take a breath.

He shrugged. 'You mean, have I worked out the angle of descent, her position in the car, simulated the trajectories? No. But I know, all the same.'

'Someone threw it,' said Cate slowly. 'That's why you were throwing stones. Someone chucked it as far as they could. Someone –'

'Yes,' said Sandro. Cate clasped her hands around the cup that, now empty, held no more heat. 'Someone. Someone else was down there, and that person threw the phone.' He got to his feet abruptly,

416

the chair moving back on the stone floor with a loud scrape, followed by silence. 'Getting rid of the evidence.' He laid his palms flat on the table and leaned down, looking into her face.

'Someone was down there,' she repeated carefully, meeting his gaze. 'Went down there.'

'Let's go to the library,' said Sandro. 'There's something I want to show you.'

The windowless corridor that led back to the old part of the castle, which had been gloomy the previous night, was now close to pitch dark, and like the interior of the fridge it too smelled of things turning sour. As though without electricity it was reverting to some primitive state: the thought unnerved Cate. Coming into the great shadowy space of the library, dark even though it was still the middle of the day, only intensified the feeling.

Both of them moved straight to the long windows: the sky was steel-grey with more cloud. Cate shivered, looking back inside the room at the huge and dusty chandelier, barely visible in the thin light, the spindly balustrade of the gallery. 'Supposed to be a ghost in here,' she said. 'What was it you wanted to tell me?'

And then something began to chime, as she looked up at the gallery, a tiny, insistent nudge of memory. Loni and Orfeo up there, on his last visit, looking down.

But Sandro had begun to talk.

'Per Hansen saw a light, that night,' he said. 'Or thought he did. He was in his room, looking out.'

'A light?'

'When I went to see him he told me. He said something to me about ghosts, or fireflies, or souls; I didn't really understand it. That the next morning he thought he might have dreamt it, and that when he found out – about the accident, he had some wild idea that it had been her soul escaping.'

'What time?' asked Cate with a kind of faltering horror as she grasped what he was saying, as she looked out to where Per Hansen might have looked, that night.

'About midnight,' he said. 'Coming across country, from his right, as he looked down. Perhaps not wanting to be seen.'

And they looked down, to the right: into the thin trees that shielded the outbuildings, the studio, the *villino*. Even in the low grey light, they could see what looked like tracks, leading away from the castle; something had certainly left a darker, rusty trail across the white ground. But on Thursday night, there had been no snow, and the ground had frozen hard; no chance, they both knew, of leaving tracks then.

'It could have been –' Cate said, suddenly not wanting to continue.

'Yes,' said Sandro. 'It could have been. A real live human being, going to find out what had happened to Loni Meadows.'

'Wait –' there were so many questions. Cate strained to be methodical, not to jump straight to the terrifying fact he was presenting to her. 'You believed him?'

'Per Hansen?' Sandro laughed shortly. 'I believed him. Of course – they might be backing each other up, those two. Hansen and Fairhead, it might be a conspiracy, they might be giving each other alibis. But I don't think so, do you?'

'No.' Cate could hardly hear her own whisper. Above her the balustraded gallery waited, full of shadows, and around her the castle waited, breathing along its nooks and passageways.

Sandro was continuing. 'Their interests, you see, would not coincide; the betrayed lovers, each betrayed separately, one a lover only in his own imagination?'

Cate nodded; she didn't want to look up, but she didn't want to look out of the window either. She felt the deep dark cold of the room close around her.

'So someone went down there,' she said. 'Someone knew exactly what had happened. Exactly when.'

'Because they had called her down there.' Sandro was intent, sure and focused as he spoke. 'That person poured water across the road, then returned. Waited. Gave the ice time to form. Waited until dinner was over then sent a message. The usual message: no doubt the last one Orfeo sent would be there on the phone. Easy to imitate.'

Cate said slowly, 'She dropped everything and went. I saw her clothes on the bedroom floor.' She took a breath, surprised by her relief. 'After dinner

419

Fairhead saw her receive a text, so did Per. So they can't have sent it.' Sandro inclined his head and then looked out of the window again; the oppressive grey sky and the bleak, empty white of the landscape set up a nagging headache behind Cate's eyes.

'So that leaves – who?' Sandro asked. 'The light came from down there.'

'Michelle. Tina.'

'Luca Gallo? Your Mauro?'

'Luca didn't leave the castle that day, I'd swear it, not while I was there. And Mauro was dead drunk in bed that night, on the other side of the hill.'

'So the one was accounted for all day, the other all night,' Sandro said. 'And your Tiziano?'

'Across country? In his wheelchair?' Cate felt a sudden rage. 'Are you crazy?'

Sandro only shrugged.

'Someone went down there,' he said. 'You don't know what drives people.'

And there was a silence, one in which the small, insistent sound of an engine became audible: a car, although it could not be seen from the library's window. Sandro took Cate by the upper arms and looked into her face. 'She wasn't dead yet, you see.' He put two fingers to Cate's neck and pressed, very lightly. His hand was so cold.

'There was a mark on her neck,' he said quietly, 'a mark that might have been caused by a seatbelt, only she never wore a seatbelt.' He paused to let the meaning of his words sink in.

'Someone came across the fields, quickly in the dark, carrying a light. Someone found her, dazed, concussed.'

His other hand came up to her neck and the pressure increased just a fraction but for that second Cate felt her eyes widen in panic: both cold hands stayed where they were. 'She might already have sustained some kind of head trauma,' he said. 'I think she had. I think she would have had to be confused, weakened.'

'She was so strong,' said Cate.

'Yes,' said Sandro, and Cate heard it in his voice, sadness for the life ebbing from a headstrong woman. He took his hands away. 'Two people in the dark, one full of adrenaline, the other dazed and groggy. She might have thought it was help coming.'

He removed his hands quickly and Cate squeezed her eyes shut, so as not to see the picture he made of Loni Meadows, blue eyes turned gratefully towards her murderer. Something bleeped, unexpectedly, as if she had prompted it herself.

Sandro made an impatient sound, *tcha*, and from behind closed eyelids Cate heard the tiny blip of mobile phone keys, an intake of breath. 'Hospitalized?' she thought she heard him say.

She opened her eyes again, leaning back against the frame of the long window, feeling the cold leak through, and she was looking up at the gallery. The thin light from the window shone along the banister and there it was, whole and perfect, the image of whenever it had been. Last Sunday, in fact, and Orfeo up there, looking down his long nose, Loni hanging on to his arm. And further along the gallery, in a corner: Michelle, leaning against the shelving, stretching her bad back, eyeing them both.

Loni and Orfeo's talk over, Per nodding shyly below, bowing, Loni coming down the narrow wooden staircase and giving him one of those featherlight, breathy kisses, just a fraction too close to the mouth. Orfeo impatient to be off, huffing at the doorway, about to drive back to Florence.

And as Cate had cleared the glasses from the table, the guests had filtered off, one by one. And then Cate had seen her, down the staircase now, the last to leave, looking at something in her hand. Michelle, staring at a tiny glassy screen. Michelle, with Orfeo's mobile phone, and her face alight, and slipping it into her pocket so that Cate wouldn't see.

But Cate *had* seen, even if the memory of it had eluded her until this moment, as she stood looking up at the gallery.

'Michelle,' she whispered, and Sandro turned sharply, his own phone in his hand.

'Michelle Connor.'

'What about her?'

'She was always so angry,' said Cate, hardly hearing what he said. 'Her husband died, you know. He was supposed to be coming here, only he died.'

'Yes,' said Sandro, holding up the screen to her. A text message, it said. From someone called Luisa.

Michelle Connor hospitalized following the suicide of her husband, Joseph, composer, August 2007.

'Hospitalized,' he said and cleared his throat. 'That means she was put in a psychiatric institution.' She could hear the reluctance in his voice. 'August. He died in August. But Per Hanson's appointment was made in July.'

Cate heard the words but she didn't know what he meant by them: she had her own train of thought and she had to pursue it. 'She went running with that thing,' she said, 'that thing on her back, filled with water. Would that have been enough water?' She felt Sandro turn towards her then, through the enfilade of doors and walls that held them trapped in here, she heard the distant muffled sounds of tyres on gravel and a door slamming and a familiar voice and finally she got the words out.

'She got the phone. He must have left it up there in the gallery and Michelle was up there too and when she came down it was in her hand.'

And then Ginevra was in the doorway, Nicki bobbing behind her, half-hidden. 'Well, this is a fine bloody mess,' she said, with grim satisfaction.

CHAPTER 23

'Her husband committed suicide,' said Luisa, gazing at the screen. She had sat down abruptly, edging Giuli to one side on the office chair. Giuli felt the nudge of her hip bone, hard and sharp. 'He was supposed to go out to this castle place with her, only he committed suicide.'

The news picture on the screen was of a hospital trolley in a New York street, one of modest brownstone buildings and trees in full, dusty summer leaf, and the bulky shape of a woman on the stretcher under a white cotton blanket. People in summer clothes were hovering, staring, but the woman's strong, hawklike profile only gazed blindly up from the pillow at a cloudless sky, oblivious.

'She doesn't look the type. Not the weak type.' Luisa turned to Giuli, angrily. 'And why would that mean anything, why would she kill this – this Dottoressa Meadows, because her husband killed himself 3,000 kilometres away?'

'I don't know,' said Giuli, staying calm: anger was Luisa's way. If something upset her, if she felt guilty, if she found out she was wrong about

424

anything – anger was her first response. With herself, although other people didn't always see that.

'We don't know why he killed himself. But she was in a psychiatric unit for a week, it says here.' Giuli could feel the tension through Luisa's shoulder: she could feel it subside, just fractionally.

'What should I do now?' said Luisa eventually, still staring at the screen.

'Do?' said Giuli.

'About Sandro.' Luisa's voice admitted defeat. 'I can't leave it like this. I'm going away tomorrow morning, whatever.'

'Give me your mobile,' said Giuli. Luisa handed it over, frowning. Giuli typed in the message: *Michelle Connor hospitalized*, she began.

Luisa was still looking perplexed. 'He'll see it came from you,' explained Giuli patiently. 'It's a start: he'll know you're trying to help.'

Luisa had a piece of paper still in her hand, the information sheet on one of the other inmates – guests they called them, didn't they? – of the Castello Orfeo: she'd stuck the Post-it note to it. She set the paper down but pulled off the pink sticky scrap, transferring it from one finger to another distractedly, twisting at her wedding ring with a thumb.

'Talk to him,' said Giuli. Impatiently Luisa jabbed the Post-it note back on to the computer screen, obscuring the face of one of the gawpers on the New York street.

'And say what?' Her voice was stifled, as if something was hurting her. 'He's busy. He's on a job, you said it yourself. He might be too busy to talk to me.' She leaned across and plucked her mobile back out of Giuli's hands.

'D'you think he'll call back?'

Giuli tugged the little pink square from the screen, minimized the page, opened the internet browser. Typed in *Lonestar*.

'Not if he's busy,' she said. 'So why don't we get on and do some more digging for him? And if – when – we find out anything else, then you call him.'

The screen filled with text: in the corner a cameo of a beautiful woman's profile, *Lonestar* across it, and a long column, the most recent, posted a couple of months back. A review of some New Zealander's paintings. Not particularly anonymous, thought Giuli. And text: the word 'atrocious' jumped out at her, next to an inset illustration of an abstract painting. 'Puerile', 'imbecilic', 'idiotic'. She was surprised by how instantly recognizable insults seemed to be, in any language.

'So how does this work, then,' said Luisa, frowning at the screen, 'this blog thing?'

'Blogs are where you go to express your opinions, you can be anonymous, or not, or a bit of both. You can tell lies about people, insult them; the internet loves that,' said Giuli. 'But hold on.'

Luisa waited, attentive.

'Hold on. We need to be clever about this.'

'Clever?'

'We do a search,' said Giuli, her curiosity quickening as she scanned the screen. 'Put in the names. A word search. Her name – Lonestar – and the names of Sandro's suspects. Yes?'

Luisa nodded slowly. 'Here?' she said, moving the cursor to the box. Giuli nodded. And with two fingers Luisa began to type.

The small, fierce woman with hands on hips stared at Sandro pugnaciously, like a guard dog. 'Ginevra,' said Cate faintly. 'This is –' but Ginevra didn't let her finish.

'I know who he is,' said Ginevra, her hostile stare unwavering. 'The private detective from Florence. Because of him, my Mauro's in hospital.'

'I'm sorry?' said Sandro warily. 'Because of me?'

'Is he all right?' asked Cate, sounding genuinely anxious.

The little woman grunted, unmoving. 'No thanks to anyone here,' she said. 'It's too much. Where is the Trust? Mauro's given his life to this place. His life. And since that damned woman turned up –'

'All right, all right,' said Sandro, his palms up and conciliatory. 'He's in good hands, I expect. At the hospital?' Ginevra's eyes were small, black and contemptuous. She said nothing. I wouldn't have put it past the pair of them, thought Sandro, to get rid of her. But they didn't have Orfeo's mobile.

427

'You can go to the hospital,' Cate was saying to Ginevra, earnestly. 'I can manage here.'

'No way,' said Ginevra. 'They'll get rid of *me* next, if I give them the chance. And Mauro'll live.' Folded her arms across her bolstered chest. Sandro looked at her with grudging admiration.

At Sandro's side and in an urgent undertone, Cate said to him, 'We'd better get down to Michelle.'

Sandro looked at her sidelong: he wasn't sure about this. She was a good girl but he felt the need, suddenly, to be the one in that confined space with the suspect, asking the questions, just like the old days; no other voices whispering in his ear. Face to face.

'Michelle?' Nicki piped up. 'We just saw her. Waiting outside Luca's office. She's talking to him.'

'All right,' said Sandro. Wondering what she would be doing there. 'Look,' he started, turning to Cate, only the old cook got there first.

'And you, my lady,' said Ginevra, 'haven't you got a job to do?' He saw Cate stiffen at the cook's tone.

'I've been here all morning,' she said quietly.

Ginevra gave her a long considering look. 'So you have,' she said. 'Looking after your precious guests.' Paused, maliciously. 'And did you happen to see your Tiziano Scarpa?'

Sandro felt the change in Caterina even without looking at her.

'What do you mean?' she asked stiffly. 'Yes, I saw him. He was out early. I saw him talking to

Michelle, they told me –' and then she stopped. 'Why?' she asked. Ginevra shrugged.

'There was some funny noise coming from his room,' Nicki confided, whispering.

'Funny noise?' Cate was pale.

'Heard it when we parked the car, only when we knocked, there was no answer. I think he –'

But Cate was gone without waiting for her to finish, running out through the great door, tearing off her apron as she went, and the door banged behind her with a sonorous, echoing crash. And with Nicki gazing after Cate, Ginevra turned to look at Sandro with silent satisfaction.

He stared back, refusing to be intimidated. 'I expect you're busy,' he said. 'Don't let me keep you.'

Sandro gave it a couple of minutes before leaving the room; between them these women were a Greek chorus he could live without. He was curious about Tiziano Scarpa, but Caterina knew how to handle herself. And Michelle Connor was in his sights now: he knew he couldn't afford to look away.

Coming around the great flank of the castle, Sandro could see his breath cloud in the air; the sky seemed even lower, even darker, and the tangle of trees even closer. There was movement at the window of Luca Gallo's office: Sandro stood a moment on the gravel and looked up.

The door at the foot of the stairs to the office was not locked, and Sandro went up slowly: he could hear voices. On the small landing he stopped and listened. 'There are contracts,' he heard Gallo say, pleading. 'This is not – this is irregular, Ms Connor. You cannot simply –' and then he stopped, and Sandro held still, but it was too late. The door jerked open, and Gallo looked out.

'You,' he said, with grim resignation.

'Me,' said Sandro sadly. 'I'm sorry.'

Michelle Connor was inside the room, in a shapeless grey sweatshirt, uncombed hair and tracksuit pants, standing by the window and watching him with an air of calm determination.

'I need to talk to Signora Connor,' Sandro said humbly. 'I didn't mean to interrupt.'

'Couldn't it wait?' said Luca wearily. 'Did you have to come here? We – we are talking.'

'I am afraid that it can't wait,' said Sandro, standing his ground. He felt a sweat bead on his forehead despite the cold and realized even the couple of glasses he'd drunk last night had been too many, and he'd gone to bed too late.

'It's all right,' said Michelle. 'We'd finished.'

Gallo looked at his feet, but she didn't move.

'We can talk here as well as anywhere,' she said, holding Sandro's gaze boldly. 'Can't we?'

Between them, ignored, Luca Gallo said, 'I'll just – I'll get my – of course, do feel free to talk in here.' He hurried to the desk, reaching for a small leather satchel. Sandro felt a spasm of pity for the man. 'No,' said Michelle Connor swiftly, 'I'd like you to stay, Luca.'

Both men looked at her, Gallo blinking in surprise. 'I don't have anything to hide,' she said, her chin up. 'Let's hear it.'

Sometimes it went like this, remembered Sandro: sometimes. Nothing to hide, nothing left to lose; Michelle Connor had no children, and her husband was dead. Was that it?

'If you're sure,' said Sandro, stepping inside, pulling the door to behind him and standing in such a way as to block the exit. But from his position behind the desk it was Luca Gallo who looked trapped in the cluttered office, not Michelle Connor.

In the window she remained standing, ready for a fight. 'Say what you have to say,' she said, and as she spoke Sandro was struck again by the ghost of Michelle Connor's beauty in the worn face. It came into his head that somehow these were the traces of having been loved. Was that sentimental?

'Because I'm leaving when you're done,' Michelle went on defiantly. 'I'm packed and gone.' Gallo's shoulders dropped at the desk and Sandro guessed her leaving was what they had been talking about.

'Signora Connor,' Sandro said. 'When did your husband die?'

And he didn't know what it was she had been expecting him to say, but he guessed not this. She paled abruptly, her eyes suddenly dark in her wide, lined face.

'I'm sorry,' he said. 'I have to ask.'

431

'Joe died August 18, last year,' Michelle said quietly. At the desk Luca Gallo made a small sound, a clearing of the throat.

'Mr Gallo told me that Per Hansen was appointed to replace your husband after his death,' said Sandro, without turning his head to include Luca. Holding her gaze, one that was full of pain. 'That wasn't strictly true, was it?'

Slowly she shook her head. 'No,' she said, and her gaze flickered across to Gallo, then back. 'I guess Mr Gallo wanted to avoid – embarrassment. Or something.'

Sandro sighed. 'He'd already been told he couldn't come here, hadn't he? Shortly after Loni Meadows was appointed: I'm guessing she made that decision.' She turned her head away, and Sandro saw something gleam in her eyes, in the thin grey light from the window. He saw that he was right, and then Luca Gallo spoke.

'The *Dottoressa* was adamant. No spouses.' His voice faltered. 'We had to respect her decision; it was her first decision as Director.'

'Although she herself was conducting an affair?' Sandro couldn't conceal his distaste.

Gallo bowed his head. 'I think perhaps his work was also not to her taste. She could be very – scathing.'

'Did she put anything on that blog of hers about him?' asked Sandro softly.

Michelle shrugged, barely perceptibly.

'Did she do one of her –' and he searched for

432

the words, 'character assassinations? Or was it only his rejection from a position here that did it? That led your husband to take his life?'

'It came at a bad time,' she said, and he could hear only grief in her rough voice. 'He didn't have it easy, my Joe. He was fighting it every day of his life.'

He supposed she was talking about depression: to Sandro it appeared as a low grey sky, pressing down. Like the sky beyond the window, like the thick grey walls of the castle closing in. What a place, he thought. Enough to drive anyone crazy.

'And so you must have hated her,' he said as gently as he could. 'Blamed her; how could you not? And then you came here anyway, because at the very least you'd get the chance to tell her what you thought of her?'

Michelle Connor remained silent, but the look she turned on him said enough. All the same, he had to go on. 'And to have to observe her, flirting with guests and visitors. Her evenings away from the castle.' She shook her head, just minutely.

'Really,' pleaded Luca Gallo, sounding frightened, turning to look at the door, the window, as if he might escape through them. 'What are you saying?' They ignored him.

'You found Niccolò Orfeo's mobile phone,' said Sandro carefully, and Michelle's wide eyes told him Caterina had been right. 'He left it behind, and you picked it up. Why didn't you return it to him immediately? Did you know already that they were having an affair? By all accounts, it was fairly obvious. Or did you discover it only from the messages he sent her? I imagine it occurred to you quite quickly that it might be – interesting. At least. To have that telephone. What you might do with it.'

There was a silence, and then at last she spoke.

'I didn't care about her damn love life, I'm too old to find that stuff rewarding.' She closed her eyes and her ashen, weary face, briefly shadowed with shame, might for an instant have been a death mask.

Then she opened her eyes. 'Yes, I got the phone,' she said flatly. 'Yes, we even laughed, looking at his messages. What an old fool he is, and what a whore she was. Yes, for a second or two.' She twisted her mouth. 'I shouldn't even have looked.'

Sandro stared at her, trying to make her out in the dim room. And as he stared it felt smaller; all around him the stacked shelves, the pinboard covered with photographs and brochures, pressed in on him. The bitterness rose in the back of his throat and Sandro felt a sudden reluctance to go on with it. But he had to. He took a breath, wanting to express himself as precisely as he was able.

'You are an angry woman, Mrs Connor. And you are intelligent, educated at college. You are certainly intelligent enough to devise a way to send Loni Meadows to her death.' He took a breath, remembering what Cate had told him. 'You could have gone out running with water in your backpack.

434

You could have observed how that water froze when you poured it across the road. And then, on the coldest night of the year so far, you could have used that phone to send a message from her lover. Perhaps you had found that each day here made you hate her more, not less: perhaps you were so angry you could not stop yourself.'

At his desk Luca Gallo was on his feet and stuttering but it was the look in Michelle Connor's eye that stopped Sandro.

'Are you making this up?' she said slowly, as if something was only just occurring to her. 'Ice? Do you think I'm crazy? Crazy enough to cook up this – this plan?'

'You were hospitalized,' said Sandro in a low voice. Not wanting to say it. 'In a psychiatric unit.' But Michelle didn't even seem to hear.

'Angry?' she said. 'Sure, I was angry. I'm still angry, but with her?' She made a small explosive sound of contempt. 'She was not even worth a minute of my time. You want to know who I'm angry with? I'm angry with him. With Joe.'

She leaned down and struck the table. 'With Joe. For giving in, after all this time, because of some shitty little position here. I told him, I won't go without you. Told him, jeez, we can go and have fun in Italy if that's what we want, we don't need those guys.' And then her voice cracked, and was gone. 'But he went and did it, didn't he? He went and did it, and I found him on the bathroom floor.'

Luca Gallo was still trying to say something, but Sandro was struggling with the sensation of dizziness her words induced in him, the unmistakable sound of truth in the claustrophobic room.

'But what about the *telefonino?*' he said, in despair, grappling even for that word, his English suddenly exhausted. 'His mobile. His cell phone.'

And Michelle took a step towards him, the thin light behind her.

'The *telefonino?*' she said, and she swung her arm out to include Luca Gallo at last, something like jubilation in the gesture. She laughed bitterly. 'I don't have the *telefonino*. Tell the man, Luca.' Then, gazing straight at Sandro now, she went on. 'All right, I will. "Has anyone seen Count Orfeo's cellphone?" Luca asked us, just the next day. If we found it, we were to give it to him, so that's what we did. Not straight away, maybe, but he's had it since that Wednesday, the day before she died.'

And then, finally, they both turned to look at Luca Gallo.

CHAPTER 24

Her face pressed to the window of Tiziano's ground floor apartment, with its hoist and specially adapted bathroom facilities, Cate called his name, then again, then banged on the glass through the security bars. And as she began to lose her breath through panic and fright, Cate thought about the fact that Tiziano never let anyone in there: he came to the door to take his lunches, or they left them on the step. A private person.

A funny noise, Nicki had said. What funny noise? Was he in pain? Was he in trouble? Cate thought about the expression on his face the night before, when he'd swung her into his lap in Michelle's apartment. Had he had anything to do with Loni Meadows's death? Had he done something – stupid?

Cate found she couldn't think about Michelle; she couldn't get her head around it. The abrupt realization that it actually hadn't been an accident; those theories Sandro Cellini had been constructing with careful determination suddenly standing up on their own: it was surreal, but it was true. That ice should not have been there;

Loni Meadows had been called out to a lovers' meeting that did not exist.

'Tiziano,' she whispered, trying to keep panic from her voice, '*Caro*, what are you doing in there?' Swallowed. 'Are you all right?'

And then the door opened. He sat there. Not blocking the door as he usually did, beaming but implacable, hands out for his packed lunch, but staying back with his face in the door's shadow, allowing Cate entry. She came inside, and the door closed behind her.

It was dark, even darker than it had been in the kitchen. 'Do you have any candles?' she asked. Not waiting for an answer, she crossed the square dim space like a blind person, bumping then skirting the great veneered bulk of the grand piano that was the sister to the one in the library and which dominated this smaller room. She knew where the candles would be as she was in charge of replenishing their stock for this eventuality: in a drawer in the room's kitchen corner. She lit one and set it in a saucer: it didn't give much light, but it was better than nothing. Tiziano shrugged, turning his face towards her and as her eyes adjusted she saw the change in him.

'Nicki and Ginevra were worried about you,' she said. 'You didn't answer.'

'I'd forgotten what it was like,' he said, his voice rough. 'That's all. I'd forgotten what leaving was like. Saying goodbye. And we should have had another four weeks together.'

438

Could that be all? That he would miss them, this strange family of misfits and loners? It couldn't be all. Cate came back to his wheelchair and squatted beside him on her haunches. She could feel her feet still wet from the snow, her body feverish with tiredness and cold and wondered how long it would be before life returned to normal. If ever.

What if it wasn't Michelle? What if she'd given that phone to someone else? She and Tiziano had always been close.

'Tiziano,' she said, and she couldn't keep the fear out of her voice. 'Darling.' Cate used the endearment as her mother might have used it to her, as she might have used it to the brother she had never had. 'He told me. Cellini told me, about your accident. About the bomb that killed your father. About Loni's husband the lawyer, who defended the bomber.'

'Did he?' said Tiziano, and his voice came from somewhere buried deep.

'Why were you – upset?' She didn't want to say, crying. 'Just for leaving this bunch behind?'

'Does he think I did it?' asked Tiziano, not answering her question. 'Does Cellini think I fixed her car, or drugged her, or – or – parked my wheelchair on the bend in the middle of the night to scare her off the road?'

Cate found she couldn't speak.

Eventually she found some words. 'I told him no way,' she said.

439

'You don't think I could do it?' And Tiziano took her hand quickly and raised it to his mouth and held it tight against his face; against her skin she felt the softness of his mouth and the prick of his stubble and the strength of his hands.

'Physically?' she said, and felt something like adrenaline surge through her, as it might have surged through him. 'I think you could do it. Yes.' Then bravely, 'Do you know how to get there, across the fields?'

And he made a sound, in his throat, like a growl of pain. 'Let me tell you,' he said, 'I could have done it. There's nothing I can't do, in or out of this chair.' And abruptly he let go of Cate's hand. 'Nothing,' he repeated, though they both knew that wasn't true.

'Do you know,' he said in a voice so close to normal it was bizarre, 'that bomber killed at least three other people because of her husband? Her husband the human rights lawyer: where were their human rights, those dead people? Where were mine? One of them a woman just married and four months' pregnant.'

With awful inappropriateness, Cate wondered if Tiziano wanted children. And for the first time in what seemed like days Vincenzo came into her mind, V'cenz who'd said cheerfully when she'd turned in the street one time to look into a buggy, 'You don't want kids, do you, Cate? No way.'

'I remember that,' she said, and she did. A bomb in a station in Mestre.

'You think I'd kill anyone? Leave anyone crippled, like me? D'you think I'd want that revenge?'

And Cate didn't know what to say because that was exactly what they had contemplated silently, her and Sandro Cellini. The rich dull sheen of the piano gleamed in the thin light from the window; on the side the candle flickered. The room was bare, apart from the great instrument and a narrow bed. A monk's cell; but he'd cried at the thought of leaving.

'Revenge on a woman simply for being married to that old crook? Kill her to get at him? Who thought that? Did you? Did Cellini?' His voice was ragged with emotion.

'He doesn't know you,' said Cate. 'It's not his fault. And besides – he doesn't think it was you, not any more.'

'I could have done it,' said Tiziano, sitting up straight in the chair beside her, taller than her as she crouched beside him, her hand now on his thin, hard knee, though of course he couldn't feel it. 'I could have done it, but I didn't. She didn't even figure, with me.'

Then he turned to her as though he'd only just heard what she said. 'So who?' he asked. 'Who does he think did it?'

'He thinks it was Michelle,' Cate said, and there was a long silence. She had thought he would defend her, but he did not.

'Because of her husband,' he said, and she wondered how he knew. 'Meadows vetoed him,

441

did you know that? Said she wasn't having married couples here. And he topped himself. No wonder she was angry.'

'You'd never do that,' she said, without being able to stop herself. 'Would you?' He took her hands and clasped them in his.

'Never say never,' said Tiziano, as though he was murmuring an endearment. *Mai dire mai.*

'No.' Feeling the dark creep closer to them, feeling the cold rise up through the stone floor, the walls, Cate whispered, 'Don't say that.'

'You don't know, sweetheart,' Tiziano said softly. 'You don't know what it's like. There are things that regenerate, you see, and there are things that don't. Spinal cord, that's one of the things that doesn't.'

There were words that Cate wanted to say at that moment, about how little it mattered to her that his legs didn't work, only she didn't know how you could say that. It mattered to him, that was the thing.

Besides, he was still talking. 'Look at Alec Fairhead, he's regenerated all right,' he said, with bitterness.

'What d'you mean?' she said, unsettled.

'After, what is it, more than twenty years of mourning, no relationships, no decent work to speak of, now Loni's dead and he's trying it on with everyone in sight.'

'Did you know about that? About Alec and Loni?' She stared at him.

'He told me. The morning after she died, he

told me. She aborted his child, did you know that?' Cate shook her head slowly. 'A new man now,' said Tiziano. 'Asking you to run away with him last night, haring off after little Tina. He's down there now, getting her to comfort him.'

'What?' she said. She hadn't known Tiziano had heard that last night. 'I don't know if that's a good idea, though, with Tina,' she said, feeling alarm rise in her. 'She's – she's vulnerable.'

'Or d'you want him for yourself?' She stared at Tiziano in the flickering half-light, startled by the anger in his voice.

He looked away, but not before she saw something burn in his eyes. 'Did you see that coming, then? Michelle?' And his voice now contained only casual curiosity, as if he simply didn't care any more.

Had she? And then Cate thought of Michelle standing by that burning oil drum, saw again the expression in Mauro's face as he ran up to stop them. He'd thought they were up to no good, hadn't he? Why had she swallowed Michelle's story whole?

She should have emptied that stuff all over the grass and picked through it until she knew what was in there. But she'd been afraid.

She should have told Sandro Cellini about it, but she'd wanted to protect them.

And Cate felt abruptly and completely alone, the burden of her failure falling squarely on her own shoulders, and no one else's. Her mother's voice rang again in her ears: *When are you going to take responsibility, Caterina?*

'I'm going down there,' Cate said, hearing her own voice as though from far away. 'I'm going down to the *villino*.'

'As you wish,' said Tiziano stiffly.

And it was only when she was out of the door in the cold and running in the snow, down into the trees, that she realized he thought that Alec Fairhead was the reason for her going.

Luca Gallo's face collapsed as they stared at him, and he sat, suddenly limp, in the chair behind his desk. He stared around at his surroundings as though he barely recognized them, and had no idea what was going on.

Sandro stood and watched, and waited; at his side Michelle Connor seemed entirely relaxed, and curious.

Gallo had pushed his chair back and was staring at the drawers. His desk was a total mess, an overflowing inbox, a small photo of a man's face fallen under the computer screen, loose papers slipping to the floor. Was this the sign of a man who was losing his mind?

'Is this true?' Sandro said quietly.

Luca Gallo was shaking his head slowly, from side to side, then eventually he looked up. 'Sorry?' he said.

'Did she give you the phone last Wednesday, the day before Loni Meadows died?'

444

'The day before?' said Luca slowly. 'I couldn't be sure of the day.'

'But before she died?' Sandro was patient. Luca nodded. 'Before,' he said, 'yes.'

It was like getting blood out of a stone: the man looked traumatized. 'I'm trying to think,' he said. 'Where I put it.'

'Are you playing for time?' asked Sandro as gently as he could. 'Because all you are doing is allowing me the time to realize that if anyone here could have set up Loni Meadows's car accident, you could have.' As they returned his gaze, Gallo's eyes came into focus, slowly: he seemed hypnotized into silence. Sandro went on. 'You could have sent Mauro down there, couldn't you? To do the dirty work, to work on the road surface. He'd be good at that; and now rather conveniently he seems to be unavailable for comment. You weren't at dinner: you could have waited until they'd left the dining room, and sent that message. Only you, in fact, could have sent that message, isn't that right?'

'How do you know?' Luca seemed to be grappling for a rationale. 'How can you be so sure that the message was from his phone?'

Sandro shrugged. 'Of course, I can't.' He pulled the little silver pebble of a phone that had belonged to Loni Meadows from his pocket and looked at it thoughtfully. 'Of course, even if Orfeo's mobile never turns up, this will tell me, in the end.' He flicked it open, passed a thoughtful thumb across its small, dead screen.

'It could tell you now,' interjected Michelle, and Sandro turned to look at her. 'What do you mean?' he asked, and she gestured to him impatiently. He handed the phone to her and watched, frowning, as she fished her own mobile out of her pocket, flicked off its back with a blunt nail.

Gallo was pulling open drawers now, in a panic. 'Hold on,' said Sandro, 'calm down.'

'It's here somewhere,' said Gallo. The drawers spilled out of the desk; he looked up, wild-eyed.

'It must have been tough,' said Sandro, arms folded across his chest. 'Working for a woman like that. And when she bawled you out in front of everyone –' Sandro saw something fierce come into Gallo's eyes.

'So,' said Sandro. 'Per Hansen said he saw a light, from around the side of the castle, heading cross-country at about midnight.' He leaned on the desktop with the tips of his fingers, eyeball to eyeball with Gallo. 'The police will know, you know. They'll find the shoes, or the trousers, they'll find her traces on you.' He paused. 'What did you do with the phone? Did you destroy it? Hope no one bothered to ask after it? Or were you just going to give it back and rely on Orfeo being too stupid and arrogant to ask any questions?'

Gallo stared down, pale-faced, into the chaos of paper, old telephone directories and files. Then he focused, and pounced. 'Here,' he said. 'Here, here it is.' And he brandished an envelope marked 'Count Orfeo' in a neat script totally at odds with the disarray in the room.

Sandro stopped.

'Right,' he said, and slowly he held out his hand. Gallo hesitated, then dropped the envelope into his palm, and at that moment Michelle looked up from whatever she was doing, held up her scratched and ancient *telefonino*, its screen illuminated.

'See,' she said. 'Gotcha. Her sim card in my phone. Her phone records, her messages, right here.'

'And here,' said Sandro, weighing the envelope in his hand, strangely reluctant to open it. 'So why didn't you give it back to him, Luca?' he asked, all of a sudden not feeling remotely triumphant. 'He asked you about it, last night.'

'He did, yes, he did,' said Luca eagerly. 'I told him it had been found. He was going to come and get it this morning.' His face fell. 'Only he left very early.'

Sandro ripped the envelope and pulled the phone out. Thumb hard down on the on button. Nothing happened.

'No battery, I suppose,' said Luca nervously. Sandro grunted, staring down at it, thinking. Pressed the button again, threw the thing down on the desk where it landed in a slew of museum brochures. Michelle came closer to him.

'Here,' she said quietly. 'Look at this.'

Messages. Last message received, from someone Loni Meadows's address book recognized as Nic.

447

Seem to find myself free this evening, it read, in English. Perhaps whoever sent the message thought that made it more aristocratic. *At the Liberty. You know I don't like to be kept waiting.*

'You were right,' said Michelle, wonderingly.

Slowly Sandro took the phone from her. Clicked back to get to the call history. The last number she called.

Nic, 00.09 22 February. Call out, at nine minutes past midnight on the Friday morning.

'She called,' said Sandro. 'She was down there in the dark, concussed, frightened, certainly in shock, probably hypothermic.' They were both staring at him now. 'She called her lover,' he went on. 'Of course. She thought he'd come to help her.' Turned to Luca Gallo. 'More fool her.'

Gallo was staring, shaking his head, but Sandro wouldn't wait.

'Did you even answer? Did you listen to her sobbing, or was she incoherent?' He stared into Gallo's face, refused to let him look away. 'You weren't even content to leave her to die, were you? You had to go down there to make sure. And then you went through her pockets to find her phone and throw it in the river.'

Sandro looked at the shambles of the office and wondered that this man could have the presence of mind to do that. He must have hated her.

'Did she threaten you, did she write about you on her blog? Did she write to the American office, perhaps? Did she make allegations? Was it you, sabotaged her computer, thinking you might destroy evidence?'

There was a silence, and in the dim, stuffy room Sandro felt something, almost as palpable as a change in temperature, coming from Michelle Connor at his shoulder.

'Luca?' she said, with horror. 'No.'

'Did you get Mauro to lay down the ice for you?' Sandro went on. 'He'd have done it, wouldn't he, no questions asked? And then later. You came up here, you left the dinner table. You said you were coming up here – but no one saw you, did they? You might have been – anywhere.'

And Gallo said softly, 'No.'

'No?' Damn it, thought Sandro, damn it. Just admit it.

'I was on the phone to my lover Salvatore, in Sicily,' said Gallo simply, and all his anxiety, all his fear was gone. 'He'll tell you. The phone records will tell you. We talked until very late.' He shrugged. 'I don't know when exactly. It doesn't matter. He'll tell you.'

On the desk between them Niccolò Orfeo's discarded mobile glowed into life.

NO SIM, it read.

Sandro frowned at it. 'What does that mean?' he said impatiently. His own phone might be invaluable to him but he regularly found himself infuriated by its intricacies, its gnomic utterances.

'It means the sim card isn't in there,' said Michelle slowly. She sounded sick.

'But it was in there when you found it. And when you handed it over –'

'I didn't – it wasn't –' and Michelle froze.

'Hold on –' said Sandro because something occurred to him, something that should have sounded an alarm an hour earlier. 'You said,' and he spoke carefully, 'didn't you say, *we laughed*? You said, *we thought, what an old fool. What a whore*. We.'

He looked from Gallo to Michelle. 'It wasn't Michelle gave you the phone, was it?' he said to Gallo. And to Michelle, 'Who were you looking at those messages with? Who did you trust to give it back to Luca?'

But he already knew.

'Is it really snowing down there?' said Luisa distractedly, the phone in her hand as she paced the floor. 'And it's possible there's no signal, either.' She pressed her face against the glass as though a glimpse of the Carmine church might come to her rescue. 'What if he's had some kind of accident?'

'It's pretty remote,' said Giuli, hardly listening. She was scrolling through a post on Loni Meadows's blog from six months previously, covering an exhibition in New York. It was slow work, trying to understand the English. The text wasn't so much about the art, which was just as well, as when she clicked on the small photographs of the exhibits inset in the text Giuli found them

450

at best incomprehensible, at worst downright disturbing. It seemed to be more of an attack on the artist.

'Come here,' she said to Luisa. 'Your English is better than mine.' Luisa crossed the room in two strides, impatient as always, and sat beside Giuli on the seat. 'Shift,' she said, peering at the screen, and Giuli got another chair.

'Cheap exhibitionism,' Luisa translated roughly. 'No canvas but her own abusive childhood. This is not art, it is indecent exposure. Trailer-trash –' she didn't know what that meant '– picking the lint out of her navel and sticking it on a pot.' She peered at the picture, clicking to enlarge it, the slender-necked, elegant shape of an Etruscan amphora. Close up a small, ugly creature had been fashioned on the vase's smooth bell, a thing horned and toothed and clotted with clumps of hair and nail, possessed of a horrible energy. Luisa recoiled.

'Abusive childhood?' said Giuli. Luisa's eyes refocused, looking into hers. 'Yes,' she said, and reached across the desk for the piece of paper she had plucked from the array they had set out earlier.

'I said, didn't I?' she murmured, looking from the page to the screen. 'I said, if I had to pick any of them out of a line-up as – what? Mentally unstable? I'd have picked her. And Sandro said, *Look for the weak, not the strong.* That's her.'

And Luisa took up her mobile. 'I'm going to

call him,' she said. 'He has to know about this. Because if I was this girl, this abused girl grown up to make monsters of her own life, and if I read this – if I thought millions of people were going to read this about me –' And she broke off to dial, her head shaking, back and forth.

'Her, then,' said Giuli. 'Tina Kreutz.'

CHAPTER 25

And Cate ran, around the back of the castle, past the kitchen, past the stairs to Luca's office, the door to her own apartment. She couldn't even have said why she was running or how she knew that she must be quick: she couldn't have said if she was running towards something or away from it. The snow clung to her soaked trouser legs and clogged on her boots, her feet as heavy and numb as lead. She passed the laundry and slid, landing heavily on her side, something hard and sharp catching her on the hip bone. She blinked with the pain, but it occupied only a part of her brain, she scrabbled and was upright and looking into the wide glass frontage of Michelle's bungalow.

There was the detritus of the night before, or some of it; there was a black plastic rubbish sack open to reveal crumpled cans and newspaper. As her eyes adjusted she noticed two suitcases, tagged, neatly upright and side by side, and scanning the room she saw that half the shelves had been emptied. It looked abandoned, a place where vagrants might have slept and from which they had moved on. But even as she strained to see behind the glass Cate knew, this wasn't it. This wasn't the place, this wasn't what she'd come to find.

The blue-white glare off the snow was deceptive: the light was failing, and behind the grey lid of the sky the day was closing. Cate realized she had no idea what time it was, only the cramping of her empty belly told her it was later than she thought. She floundered away from the bungalow to find herself up to her knees in a drift, waded on to the path and looked down through the trees.

The *villino* stood, perhaps half a kilometre away; over her left shoulder the bulk of the castle. Somewhere down here Michelle had set off on her run, somewhere down here Per had seen a light moving across the dark landscape. Cate could see fresh footprints in the snow, and she followed them.

Big prints, wide apart, wider than she could stride. Alec Fairhead, going down to see Tina; no prints coming back. Cate stopped a moment. They would be there together, of course. She would be – intruding. Uneasy, she shaded her eyes, trying to see; on the corner of the *villino* the black shape of the oil drum, at hip height and half hidden, was still there, where they had left it. Uncertainly Cate set off again stumbling and slipping on the track: unstable hardcore overlaid with snow. If they were there, she would just have to explain. She pushed away the image of Alec and Tina together – not because she had any interest in Alec Fairhead, she defended herself silently to Tiziano. But because it was somehow – wrong. Vulnerable was the word that she had used. Tina was vulnerable.

And just short of the *villino*, Cate stopped. A couple of metres away, it was as though her legs wouldn't take her any further. Her cheeks were icy, her fingers frozen, and quite suddenly she was very, very frightened.

Behind the *villino*, the little house where Mauro had been born, the trees clustered dark, ivy smothering their spindly trunks, almost as high as the house. Go on, she urged her legs, but they felt as useless as rubber. One step, then another.

The windows were dark in the rough stone walls, the door closed. Cate leaned against its peeling wood, and rapped, the sound feeble. And again, with as much force as she could muster, feeling no pain as the wood grazed her frozen knuckles. Then she leaned heavily on the bell push. It sounded inside, shrill and lonely. Cate waded through the snow to the window and, on tiptoe, peered in.

There was the long brick island supporting the work surface in the centre of the studio space, the potter's wheel and assorted shapeless things barely lit in the grey gloom. The high shelf with its row of watching pots, the faces on them obscure now: Michelle had packed to leave, but Tina had not. Why not? Did she not mean to leave with the rest of them? Something was different, all the same.

Something had been moved, or taken, but Cate didn't know what.

Cate heard herself swallow. Nothing moved, not a flicker, but it was not quite silent. There were the tiny, obscure sounds of the crusted snow as it shifted and settled; there were soft patterings and drippings from gutters and branches, not all close, falling from the eaves, but further off too, down the hill, among the trees. A sense of something breathing that Cate had heard before, as if the wooded hillside had its own system of lungs and veins and its own pulse, the castle its beating heart.

The wind. It would be the wind. Feeling her lungs burn in the cold, her breath short, Cate turned with awful reluctance away from the window. Where were they all? What had she come here for, when she might have just climbed on her *motorino* and escaped, once and for all?

The oil drum: that was what she'd come here for. It was on the far corner of the *villino*, carelessly shoved half out of view, abandoned, but just the sight of its steel edge furred with black gave Cate a sudden sick sensation. Just the memory of those soaked and charred fragments in the blackened interior, a bad smell of burnt leather and hair and things not quite discernible. What might Michelle have disposed of in here?

Cate knew now she should have told Sandro Cellini about it, this nasty little secret of feminine hysteria and illogic, but she had been ashamed,

456

hadn't she? For Michelle and Tina, or for herself, for half-believing in it too? Too superstitious even to begin to describe it; how would you begin? But she should have told him. Cate took a step, then another, cold hands set on either side of its charred and rusted edge, and she was looking inside.

The smell of old ashes and worse, something sodden and organic and stinking fused to other, chemical odours, rose to Cate's nostrils. Turn it out, she thought with a quick, violent revulsion, and she tipped the drum, heard it scrape harshly on the stone underfoot but not before she had heard another sound, down below the house and deep in the trees, a variation of that breathing again but this time more of a quick gasp or even a choking. And the drum was on its side only Cate was not looking at what had spilled out of it but listening, it seemed, harder than she had ever listened in her life.

'Who – who is it?' She tried to call and it came out as a whisper. But there was only that silence that was not quite silence but a hundred thousand tiny sounds and all of them mocking her. Her back against the stone of the house, she knelt, the knees of her trousers soaking instantly, and made herself look at the blackened rubbish now dirtying the snow in front of her.

The brittle remains of a burnt plastic bag. A strip of disintegrating printed fabric that had once been Loni's. Out of the corner of her eye the doll was discernible, a crudely stuffed limb flung out and something like hair, but Cate didn't want to look at it directly. Michelle had had nothing to do with this, she knew quite suddenly: this was horror-story schlock. But there was other stuff here: this was more than a doll and a few scraps of cloth.

With trembling hands, unable to look up for fear of the sounds from the trees, nor to the side, Cate forced herself to reach into the sodden heap of ash. And immediately she felt something solid, rubbery. Grateful for the numbness in her fingers, she flipped it out of the pile. It was – a shoe. A half-burnt little flat oriental cloth shoe, not much more than child-size. She stared: what else? Feeling her chest burn, Cate pulled at a dark piece of cloth that turned into a trouser leg, charred from the bottom, loose cotton trousers. And as she raised and opened them and saw whose hollow-bellied, thin-shanked shape they would have fitted, a scatter of smaller fragments fell. She didn't see the stamp-sized sim card or follow its trajectory into the snow because she was looking at something else. The grotesque melted remains of what might have been a condom but was in fact, as Cate saw when she forced herself to go on looking, one latex glove, of the kind a doctor might use, or an artisan working with glazes or chemicals or –

She thought of Tina, sitting, leaning forward in the little library, watching the old TV set. Watching the weather report, the night before Loni died.

Rocking, just slightly, hugging herself and rocking as she stared at the screen.

And then into the quiet she heard the gasp again only this time there was a finality to it, a sigh as if of love satisfied or sleep attained, and although all Cate wanted to do was run the other way and never turn around, she was up and stumbling through the trees towards the sound.

In her mind's eye Cate had thought the tree trunks stood there in ranks like soldiers that she might easily dodge, but she had not bargained for the brambles and the ivy that clogged and snared the space, ripping at her trousers, strangling the branches. Or for the cobwebs and nameless trailing things that touched her face so that she had to fight not to scream and bat at it all, to fight just to run. Or even for the horrible idea that each tree, those on the periphery of her vision as well as those blocking her path, might not be an inanimate thing but someone. Someone come to seize her from behind and pin her arms and bring her down and press her face into the dead things on the forest floor.

And then she saw it, white among the dark trunks, and she had to stop and lean against something and feel the bark against her cheek and listen to her heart pounding desperately and know that there was nothing she could do any more. Someone was coming, she could hear them, but there was nothing she could do.

⋆　　⋆　　⋆

459

Pale-faced, Michelle was at the door and pleading: Sandro didn't know at first if she was urging him to hurry or trying to block his path. She had either hand on the frame, cruciform in the doorway.

'I didn't know,' she said, over and over again, 'Jesus Christ, I didn't know.'

'Michelle,' said Luca Gallo gently, suddenly at her side with a firm hand on her shoulder; he seemed to Sandro quite transformed. She looked at him as if she didn't recognize him. 'It's all right,' he said. 'She's not your responsibility. Tina is not your responsibility.' Michelle held his gaze questioningly, the faintest colour returning to her cheeks, and Gallo turned to Sandro.

'The girl fetching water from the river,' he said slowly. Sandro looked at him, uncomprehending. 'Mauro said it,' Gallo went on. 'This morning; I thought he was hallucinating, or thinking about another time, maybe. He said he was out on the tractor, and he saw the girl from his house, he said, fetching water.'

'The *villino* was his house,' said Michelle. 'Once upon a time.'

In his pocket Sandro felt the throb of his mobile, an urgent summons, and before he realized that she didn't even know his number, for some reason his thoughts turned to Caterina. Was this like parenthood, he wondered for an instant, this constant grappling with where they were, were they safe? He pulled out the phone, its screen blinking at him. Jesus God, he thought, as the

460

pulse of elation combined with the need to get out through that door and find Tina Kreutz, why now? Why does she call me now? But he had to answer.

'Darling,' he said with impatient longing, and he saw both of them, Luca and Michelle, turn towards him at the sound of his voice. Luisa, though, didn't seem to hear what they heard; she was talking urgently about something he couldn't understand, something about the weak and the strong, as bossy and insistent and constant as she had always been. She the strong and he the weak.

'You told me once,' she was saying on the crackling line, 'it's not the strong who murder, it's the powerless,' and although he didn't know what exactly she was talking about, Sandro marvelled at it, as though she was inside his head. 'It's her, isn't it? Abusive childhood, it said on the blog.'

'Darling,' he said again, whispering with tenderness, 'I can't talk now,' and he hung up.

'I didn't know,' Michelle was saying still.

'But you know now?' Sandro asked her quietly. She turned her head and stared back at him and then, finally, she nodded.

'I knew she hated Loni,' she said. 'I always knew she hated her enough, deep down I guess I knew that.' She looked at her hand on the door frame as if it held some kind of answer. 'I gave her the phone to give back. I guess – I even thought, when I saw her burning her stuff, I guess deep down I knew there was something wrong with it.'

461

Then she looked at Luca. 'It's the work, with her, you see. That's all she ever had, after the family she got, goddamned Lutheran bastard dad.' And she turned to look at Sandro. 'You know what it's like when someone takes something you feel like you spent your life creating, and laughs at it?'

Sandro glanced into her honest, angry eyes, and slowly he nodded. She went on. 'Holds your baby up in public and says, what d'you call this? Says, is this all you have? Is this all you are? You imagine that. You got nothing but your work, then things get out of proportion. Love didn't interest her, see. Love, sex, no way.'

Eyes far away, Michelle took a hand from the door frame and passed it over her forehead and Sandro knew she was thinking about her husband.

Quietly, not wanting to interrupt her thoughts but knowing he had to, he asked, 'Where is she now?'

'She?' Michelle said, then something dawned and a hand came up to her mouth. 'He went down to her. Didn't he? We saw him go down to her, Alec went down. Oh, shit.'

The light was going, outside, and Sandro felt a rise of panicked unpreparedness as they emerged at the foot of the staircase, one after the other like rabbits from a tunnel, out into an uncertain gloom. He barely registered Tiziano Scarpa in his wheelchair heading towards them, hardly heard him call, 'Where is she? Have you seen Cate?' Not until he was halfway down the path, trying to keep up.

Michelle was faster than him: he observed her

strong back, the knotted muscle in her calves as she overtook him easily. Behind them Luca had eased up and was leaning down to talk to Tiziano in the chair, but Sandro couldn't look back any more. He saw her below him at the window of the *villino*, banging, heard her shout, saw her desperate face as she turned it to him. Michelle. He felt old and useless, but he had to keep going.

The weak, not the strong: of course. Luisa had remembered that, and Tina Kreutz had been weak, until suddenly she wasn't.

Michelle was on her knees at the door of the *villino*, doing something with the mat. 'She keeps a key under here,' she was saying, and as Sandro drew up at the door, his heart banging, out of the corner of his eye he saw rubbish scattered across the snow, as though a fox had got at the bins.

'Where is he?' he said, breathless, of poor, deluded Alec Fairhead: haven't we all been there, too dumb to know what's going on in a woman's head? Thinking it's all about us.

'Oh, Jesus,' he heard from inside the *villino*, 'Oh, Jesus.' And as he came in through the door, he saw that in the middle of the room there was a long workstation like the altar in a church and on the floor protruding from behind it a shoe, a foot in the shoe, a leg, and bending over it Michelle.

'Come on,' she was saying, panting, 'come on.' He saw the pieces of pottery across the floor, where something big had smashed. Something heavy. And coming around it again saw the whole

463

length of Alec Fairhead's body. Michelle raised her face to him, and beneath her Sandro saw Fairhead's head roll to one side on the stone floor under its own weight.

No.

Then roll back, eyelids fluttering.

'He's alive,' said Michelle. 'He's breathing.' And Sandro thrust his mobile at her.

'And her?' Sandro said desperately. 'And her?' Michelle looked at him, not understanding, but he found he couldn't explain: explaining would take too long. 'Ambulance,' was all he managed. 'Call 118, ambulance.'

And he ran out; above him, up at the top of the long, long path, the black shape of the castle behind them, he saw Luca and Tiziano, and even at this distance he knew from Scarpa's face that he wouldn't find Caterina up there, safe in the kitchen.

Sandro had heard the sound before he'd seen the two men. He followed it down, and then he saw footprints in the snow, scuffed and hasty, so he couldn't tell how many sets there were. He kept looking down, following the footprints instead of the sound, wishing he couldn't hear it, wishing he never would have to look up. But then he did.

There was no wind to move her, but she twisted, all in white, a long white gown, a nightdress. The branch bowed under her small weight but the belt she'd slipped over her neck had held, and her bare feet pointed downwards. Tiny feet, the size of a child's, barely into adolescence, small, perfect toes, perfectly white, perfectly lifeless.

The sound came from Caterina, crumpled on the ground below Tina Kreutz's small bare feet; a raw, half-swallowed sound of despair. She raised her face to his, her eyes huge and dark.

'I tried to hold her up,' she said with horror. 'I couldn't do it.'

'I know,' said Sandro.

The hand he took was black with something, her face was dirty and streaked as though she had been playing a game of Cowboys and Indians, her clothing when he pulled her up and put his arms around her to stop her shivering was so wet he felt it soak into his own. But he felt her strong heart beat through the layers of clothing, he felt the answering warmth of her shoulders under his, all telling him, this one's alive, all right.

CHAPTER 26

It was close to midnight when Sandro Cellini left. And as she watched the tail-lights of the little car dip behind the far hill from the position she had taken up at the head of the great cypress avenue, the grand, forbidding front elevation of the Castello Orfeo at her back, Caterina Giottone contemplated the strange truth that she would probably never see him again.

But as she turned away from the lonely vista, something miraculous happened. All across the Castello Orfeo, all at once, the electricity came back on, and this grim, isolated prison of a place was transformed. For a wonderful second, it resembled a funfair or even a great ocean liner sailing across the dark, snow-covered hills, its decks and ballrooms blazing with light.

'Finally,' a voice said brusquely at her elbow, appearing out of the dark and smelling of woodsmoke, sweat and cooking. 'Perhaps we can get back to work now. Or are you leaving us too?'

Ginevra.

Not everyone was gone. Per and his wife had packed up and left first in the jaunty little red car,

Per enveloping Cate in a brief, tobacco-scented bear-hug. Telling her to visit Oslo, as his wife fussed and protested around them, ferrying bags.

Cate didn't know what Sandro Cellini and Luca Gallo between them had said to the policeman who eventually arrived out from Pozzo Basso at close to seven in the evening, but it seemed he was convinced by it. The coroner's office had removed Tina's body to the morgue, where a post-mortem would be carried out. Posturing and pompous, the policeman had said that he would need to talk to Alec Fairhead, when he was considered fit enough by the doctors in Pozzo, where the helicopter had taken him.

Conscious now, although almost certainly with his skull fractured, Fairhead had looked ten, fifteen years younger as they carried him gingerly on a stretcher up to the helicopter whose blades whirred on the front lawn. Washed clean; born again. He'd looked up at Cate, who had been holding his hand, and somehow managed to say, with an odd delight, 'It's like they say when you have a stroke, and you wake up speaking a foreign language. It's like that.' She had nodded, not knowing what on earth he meant, but believing him all the same.

He'd tried to say more: to say that before he put his arm around her and tried to kiss her to calm her down, Tina had been talking about all sorts of things he didn't understand. Voodoo and burning and fetching water from the river: almost biblical, Fairhead had said, growing agitated and

467

bewildered at the memory. Cate had hushed him. 'Someone will talk to you about that later,' she'd said. 'Don't think about it now.' And she'd just smiled as calmly as she could and he had subsided back down on to the stretcher and allowed Cate to extract her hand from his.

'Nicki's going, you know,' said Ginevra accusingly. 'Going to live in Rome, she says; there's a girl there she was at school with.' And sighed. 'Now she tells me, with Mauro in hospital and all hell breaking loose.'

'Yeah, well,' said Cate, hearing a grudging resignation in Ginevra's voice. 'It was time, you know.'

The lights were back on in the bungalow: Michelle wasn't leaving yet after all. She wanted to talk to the police herself, she said. She wanted to make sure they knew everything. *I've done this before*, Cate heard her say to Luca earlier. *This suicide shit, it's not straightforward.* She had sounded tired, like a mother at the end of a hard day, hands in the sink and the floor still to wash. *It's OK*, she said to Luca. *I'm fine.*

And she'd gone to Tiziano's room, and they'd shut the door.

'Actually,' Cate said now to Ginevra, 'I'm not going. Sorry about that.'

'I don't know what I can offer you, Cate,' Luca had said as they watched Sandro Cellini pacing the front lawns once the helicopter had risen and gone. The detective had been on his mobile, an hour or more, the tracks of his boots criss-crossing the snow as he paced and talked. His wife, Nicki had said.

Luca had shrugged, tired but not unhappy, the burden of trying to love this terrible, draughty old place lifted from him. 'I don't know what Orfeo plans to do now.'

'I'll stick around until it's sorted,' Cate had said to him. 'No problem.'

Ginevra made a sound that only the privileged few would interpret as approval, and stamped away in the snow under the light cast from the library windows.

Tiziano had not told anyone his plans.

All Michelle had said, when she came out of his darkened room at last, was, 'He wants to see you.' And then she'd grabbed Cate's elbow, so hard it hurt, and pulled her down to listen. 'But you be sure you know what you're doing first,' she said levelly in the dark, 'because if you hurt him you'll have me to answer to.'

And inside the castle, Tiziano began to play.

Commissario Grasso had not been even faintly apologetic, but then Sandro had not expected that he would be. 'She was overcome with remorse?' the policeman had said, his lip curling. 'Ah, yes.' Refusing to believe a word of it. 'Well, let's wait and see, shall we? Post-mortem tomorrow or the day after. We'll expect your attendance at the coroner's court, in due course.'

At which Sandro had simply nodded, giving up

469

the fight. Why should he care what such a man thought of him?

Then he'd called Mascarello. Who had also refused to believe it. *It was Fairhead, wasn't it?* he had kept saying. *I knew it was him.*

old faces rested on the other's shoulder or pressed

which in their youth he and Luisa had countless times watched elderly couples turn slowly in each other's arms in one summer festival or another. And as they had looked at the expressions on the old faces rested on the other's shoulder or pressed soft against the other's cheek – absent, dreaming, resigned, content – each had secretly wondered what it would be like, in forty years' time. Fifty.

Had they both thought that they would still be together? That they might however have traded the hungry, speechless thing they felt for each other as twenty-two year olds for something more easeful and certain and dull? That they might have come to know and understand each other more like brother and sister than lovers?

Sandro drew up under the dark, dripping eaves of the tall, shabby *palazzo* on whose second floor he and Luisa had slept side by side for more than thirty years, and let himself in. Brother and sister? He felt a smile spread across his face for the first time in months. Easeful?

He slipped beneath the covers and felt the warmth she had made there, smelled her skin. Lovers. She turned over in her sleep, murmuring something indistinct, and her hand felt for his and held it.

Sandro lay awake until the clock that had always stood on his side of the bed told him that it was 5.30. He slipped his hand out of Luisa's.

'Wake up, sweetheart,' he said. 'Time to go.'